Not the Life Imagined

by

Anne Pettigrew

Copyright

SPARSILE
BOOKS

*This book is dedicated to the 130 million girls world-wide
denied any formal education – never mind a
university degree.
This book recognises the work of
Plan International UK,
which is dedicated to correcting this.*

Find out more by visiting: plan-uk.org

Contents

'*Go confidently in the direction of your dreams: live the life you imagined*'~

Henry David Thoreau

Prologue

Newsreel

October 1989, Oncology Clinic, St Mungo's Hospital, Glasgow

You don't see your life flash in front of your eyes when you are about to die. I know. When I fell in at the deep end of a swimming pool as a child, all I saw was water closing over my head and all I thought was 'Help – I can't swim!' Luckily my brilliant father was there to yank me out and give me a hug. He also gave me a lecture on stupidity, though to be honest, I'd have preferred a towel: the outdoor pool at Stonehaven is a Baltic place to stand around dripping when you're a skinny six-year-old. After my near-death fiasco, Dad insisted I take swimming lessons, which I did. I've always tried to learn from my mistakes.

But it is when you are told you might die *sometime soon* that your past life comes into focus and the newsreel runs. In my shortening days I try to dwell on happy memories, but the lengthening nights aren't so easy. The sleeping brain throws up shards of forgotten nightmares which wake me and shake me and leave me resolved to tell my story before I go. A story urging patients to beware of dark recesses in the medical world. When did you last see a physician or surgeon? Were they charming, knowledgeable, reassuring and trustworthy? Are you sure? I've known some who are not as they seemed, who had other agendas. Now one is dead. The other awaits his fate, just like me.

Medicine was a fun course, on the whole. We arrived at Gilmorehill in 1967 as teenagers and left in 1973 as pillars of society: well, most of us did. It was the Summer of Love. Though apparently a time of sexual revolution, in that direction we were mostly naïve and prone to stupid choices. Ill-judged sex had horrendous consequences for some of our number: suicide, insanity or needing to dispose of an incriminating body in a hospital incinerator, to name but a few. This isn't a tale for the faint-hearted. There were casualties and dark days, albeit tempered by triumphs and flashes of black humour. Overall, camaraderie got us through. Intense friendships were formed as we battled side by side. I suppose it was a bit like being in the army, though our main enemy was fatigue, intense numbing fatigue, during our six years of relentless study and long crippling hours as junior doctors watching one another's backs. Responsible for life and death. I suspect nothing bonds like it. Unless you have another agenda, crave advancement at any cost and by any means, are willing to trample over others who might be hampered by being of the wrong gender, sexual orientation, colour or school pedigree. The fittest survive – as everywhere, I suppose. Though my complacency in that direction has been shaken by my recent rare and nasty diagnosis. Dangerous beasties, are X-ray machines. Marie Curie has a lot to answer for. It is no consolation that radiation got her too.

None the less, no time for regrets, only for championing truth and justice. My truth is that I've done my best and can go with a clear conscience (a few white lies notwithstanding). And having finally identified the person responsible for the suicide of a great friend, I feel some sense of personal justice. I'm hoping more may come from exposing those few who prized fame and fortune over service, and sexual gratification over love. Trusty Ruth has supplemented my narrative using 'testimony and triangulation'. As an investigative reporter, she's well qualified to write our saga. And she was there- she knows all our secrets. Not being blessed by complete recall nor omniscience, we may have taken a few flights of literary licence, but our intentions are worthy: to highlight the discrimination and arrogance we encountered and to lift the age-old 'conspiracy of silence' that perpetuates abuse. It is present in all walks of life, even medicine. We want to show abuse can be survived. All that is needed is courage. And friends. Important, are friends. As much, if not more so, than family.

My girls are my life now. I'm desperate to survive for them and have great difficulty understanding anyone who wants to end their own life. For nineteen years I've had guilty nightmares about a friend who did. This story's for her.

Down the gloomy corridor, I recognise my destiny approaching in a bulky dog-eared case sheet clasped to the ample bosom of a smiling nurse whom I've never met. Is it a false smile? I know them well. They're often seen on cancer clinic staff when times are dire and all they have to offer is sympathy. Oh well, if it's to be curtains for me now, Ruth will have to finish this. Drat, this pen's running out. I hope my time isn't running out too. How I hate being a patient. I think it's a not-being-in-control-of-your-own-fate thing. The Bosom's smile is widening.

'That's us ready for you now, Dr Semple. Sorry to keep you waiting, but we had to chase your scan result. I hear you've been having a hard time.'

She has no idea.

One

Baling out

She longs for it to be over. It's been difficult trying to reach the highest point before daylight. Darkness is essential, though it's unlikely anyone will see her at this hour. A stone falls. Ripples weave outwards in the silver light. Concentric circles weaken as they disperse. The water stills. Her splash will be larger. Waves, not ripples, will reach higher, deeper, further until they also still and the water calms. A vision of her father weeping checks her progress but she dismisses it. If only he'd allowed her to study music this wouldn't have happened. She sighs. He'll get over it. Life will go on. Extending to her full height, she arches her back and breathes deeply. Hopefully her shame will be safe. The harbour is deep, and sharks have been reported. Anyway, bodies should drift out to the ocean.

She shivers. Might she black out falling from this height? The physiology escapes her. The resolve is almost there. No more the lonely anger and weeping of the last weeks. But it isn't easy. She closes her eyes. Her life hasn't been hers to live, but it is hers to end. Maybe if she hadn't tried to be so good she wouldn't care. What was the point of having morals? Other people had none, just exulted in deceiving you and rejoiced in taking whatever they thought they were entitled to. Why should she have been condemned to this situation? But she has. And there is only one solution.

The soft high clouds drift away. The full moon illuminates her arms, pale and freckle-flecked, ghostly already. Her hair blows freely in the breeze as she blinks at the stars in the assuredly empty heavens. There is no God, no such thing as a soul. Her father's religious fervour? Pointless. The Bible offers no recipe for happiness.

How would it have helped to love her neighbour? How could she have claimed an eye for an eye? From whom? She's forever spoiled, tainted. Life is futile: the future bears only shame. A strange calmness descends. They'll be better off without her. She means every word of her last diary entry. 'I can't go on. Sorry.' She jumps.

The water stills. Quivering stars reform on its inky surface. The moon is shrouded in mist as the sun slowly rises on another day.

Two

First Parade

October 3rd, 1967, three years earlier. Glasgow

Day One I was Daniel facing the lions. Panic seized my throat, constricted my chest and rooted me to the spot. Several hundred pairs of eyes were converging on me from the amphitheatre seating where rows of students sat with pens drawn, notepads on alert, staring down. The door behind me squeaked, creaked and rocked, back and forth, back and forth on un-oiled hinges, thoughtlessly discarded by the boy who'd held it open to let me pass. The squeaking subsided, and low-level chatter resumed. Gazes re-focussed. I sped up the nearest aisle to slide along a bench and fumble with my bag strap and wind-wrecked umbrella before disgorging hankies, pens, Kit-Kats, female unmentionables and a well-thumbed 'Information for New Glasgow Medical Students 1967.' Finally, I found my notebook and pen. Sighing, I patted down my wild hair. My knees were blue and blotchy: miniskirts were incompatible with West of Scotland autumn weather. Dad's pre-grant sub would have to go on a warm maxi-coat, pronto.

Sadly, it would have to be a C&A cheapie, not one like the opulent Queen of Coats currently hanging outside beside my thin anorak: an embroidered shaggy-lined, suede Afghan, the snug, confident coat of someone well-prepared for what lay ahead. Unlike me, sitting on the bus from Govan on the way here, twirling my new matriculation card, 'Civis Universitatis Glasguensis a Kal. October MCMLXVII,' trying to convince myself anxiety was normal starting medicine at a prestigious ancient university. But by nine-thirty fear was gripping me. The silence didn't help. Nor the scarcity of girls and the noticeable eagerness of my confident-looking fellow students. Despite there being fifteen minutes to go, the room was almost full apart from the front two rows. I stole a glance at my neighbour, a sandy-haired, blue-eyed boy in open-necked shirt and half-mast, knitted, red tie. He smiled. No earth moved.

'Hi,' said the Red Tie. 'I'm Daniel Sheehan.'

'Oh, hello, I'm Bethany Slater.'

He grinned. 'Bethany? That's pretty posh, isn't it?'

Just then my pen rolled off the ledge. I ducked to retrieve it and banged my head coming back up. He laughed. I didn't. Instead I turned to a girl who'd materialised on my other side, a pale, striking girl with large dark eyes, translucent skin and china-fine features dwarfed by a cloud of frizzy red-blonde hair just like Ophelia floating in that painting by Millais. At that moment I regretted not choosing Art over science at school. What made me think I could be a doctor?

Ophelia smiled. 'Hello, I'm Maia.'

Deciding to avoid any more comments on my unusual name, I replied 'I'm Beth. Say, aren't you surprised how few girls there are?'

A voice from behind cut in. 'I'm not! Any intelligent person knows few of you will work full-time, if even at all, once you're married. Why should they waste money gambling on the paltry work they'll get back in return for the fifty grand it costs to train a doctor?'

The scoffer was a boy with long dark hair and fashionable sideburns who was squinting down through hooded lids while puffing acrid tobacco smoke. I pointed to the prominent No Smoking sign but he shrugged and smirked, flicking ash from a purple velvet sleeve.

'Sod that! I'm Conor Towmey.'

As Maia shrank back, I turned to face this plonker. 'So how come you know so much about it? Your Dad the Dean? Anyway, we must be brainier than the boys if there are fewer places for us!'

He sniggered. 'I doubt that's true in my case. I was Dux at St Kentigern's.'

I'd never heard of it and couldn't have cared less but was incensed by the 'Feminist dyke!' comment I heard him mutter as I turned back to see the lecture room door open. Two men entered: a chubby chap in a flapping black gown and a thin beanpole in horn-rimmed specs and green tweed. One of the first things I noticed about academics: clothes are not a priority.

The Gown stepped forward. 'I'm Dr Bill Simpson, Assistant Dean. Good morning students.' The chatter ceased. 'The first thing I want to emphasise is that the career you've chosen is no sinecure – you're in for hard graft and lifelong learning. But be confident, you are the chosen few from the many who applied, the ones we think have the character and application to make it, though inevitably we may lose a few of you along the way ...' I felt sick – how could he joke about failure already? 'All you have to do is work hard to get 40% in Term Exams so you can get a Class Ticket for the Professional ones in June – and to enjoy yourself as much as you can, for trust me, these really are the best days of your life.'

I joined in the nervous laughter but felt then as I do now: people who say that have short memories for teenage angst and insecurity.

'You need to matriculate at the office soon as you can to collect your grants, and pick up timetables on the way out so you know where you're meant to be when.' He waved at a booklet-laden table by the door. 'Finally, check the notice board for your lab groupings.'

He grinned, stuffing his notes into his pocket. I hoped all the tutors were as nice as he. 'Any questions? No?' He nodded towards the Beanpole. 'Right, then I'll leave you to Dr Archie Young and the mysteries of mechanics.'

The lecture started. Maia scribbled furiously though Young was only listing term topics. I strained to listen but was distracted by movement behind as Towmey edged along to settle in my field of vision at an angle, slouched back, arms folded, nudging his handsome neighbour.

'Shan't be coming to more Physics lectures, Yousef. I've done all this before in sixth form. And I've bought a last year's results book for cribbing for lab report write-ups. Sorted!'

The neighbour frowned: a dark, dishy frown. I recall a passing curiosity about kissing moustaches before reining myself in. 'Shut up! This lecturer's hard enough to hear already!'

Conor smirked and blew me a kiss.

Dan whispered, 'Ignore him.'

I seethed while straining to read the illegible blackboard equations. My second observation on lecturers: they're not picked for communication skills. But we'd been picked for our *character and application* abilities. So how come Towmey got in? His character was smug and opinionated. What had they looked for apart from exam grades? And more to the point, what did this Mechanics lecture with all its pulleys, wheels and the Laws of Friction have to do with healing the sick?

After the lecture, perseverance and sharp elbows proved helpful at the noticeboard lists. Medicine thrives on endless tabulations of everything. Classifying and ordering disease might be necessary to enable transference of medical knowledge, but we students were also tabulated and classified from day one and allocated into small alphabetical groups which would define us for ever. Maia and I, being Szakolczai and Slater, were put with a 'Shaw' from Dundee (bespectacled redhead Jean) and a 'Scott' from Lanarkshire (bubbly, petite blonde Rosie.) Somehow, we met up, had lunch at the Refectory with Dan's noisy new foursome and returned back across University Avenue for a lab. Which was educational. And not just about Physics.

Our first experiment involved a small wooden-wheeled cart on a slope attached to a wire leading up to a pulley and down to a weight. Adding more weights dragged the wire down over the pulley and pulled the cart up the slope after overcoming 'inertia and friction.' Practical application? Pulleys straighten broken limbs. No mention was made of other possible uses, recreational but potentially fatal uses, which were not revealed until our Ten-Year Reunion, sixteen dark years away.

Grasping the lab manual, I read out the instructions to our group and handed weights to Maia to add. But missing her outstretched hand meant they clattered down, rolled along the floor and banged off a radiator before flipping over to reverberate noisily and finally clang to rest. One clouted Conor Towmey in the ankle. I didn't mind. He did.

'Ouch! Watch it, you butter-fingered bitch!' He glared. Maia cowered.

'Sod off, asshole!' snapped Jean, eyes narrowing behind big glasses, long red hair flashing as she tossed it back. Well, hadn't my first impression of Jean been wrong? She wasn't quiet, prim and studious. I later learned she'd captained mixed hockey. She was fearless in challenging boys. Conor paled. Rosie hooted. A big lad, Henry Thompson, ambled over from Dan's group to return a stray weight and give Maia a brotherly hug. She shrank down over her lab book, blushes shrouded by hair, fingers gripping a silver Parker pen. (I had a chewed biro).

The lads, apart from Dan who was travelling in from Clydeside, knew one another from halls of residence. Big Henry, dark Yousef, and a tall, blonde Somerset lad, Ralph, were in the same corridor in Kelvinside Halls which harboured Plonker Towmey. Jean was there too, but like 70% of Glasgow students in the sixties, Maia,

Rosie and I were staying at home. To meet so many people for the first time that day was overwhelming: I was struggling to grasp anyone's names or home origins. The last thing on my mind was who might be a potential date. However, on the way out I was confronted by Dan.

'Hey, Beth, would you like to come with me to the disco a week on Saturday and help set up our Year Club?'

'What's a Year Club?'

'Gordon Tindall told me about it- that's him, his Dad's a surgeon.'

He indicated a tall, skinny lad with shaggy hair and very prominent ears, ambling ahead. I wondered, if his Dad was a surgeon, why he hadn't had them... Anyway, poor thing, I thought.

'Nice guy, Gordon. He's told me year clubs do social things, like reunions. And stuff.'

Stuff obviously impressed Dan. 'Och, well, I'm not sure, Dan...'

'Come on! Yousef says I can kip on his floor since my last train goes at eleven.'

Unbelievable- we'd been here only five minutes and this guy already had his social life sewn up! But he had a nice smile, what was there to lose? 'OK. I'll have to check my late buses though. Now I'm off to get my grant cheque before the office shuts.'

'I'll come too. So, it's a date then for the Men's Union? It'll be good to meet more people.'

'Help! I've met enough already! And we're not going to have much time for socialising – have you looked at the timetable? Labs and lectures every day, all day, never mind studying time.'

'Och, well, Wednesday's a half-day. And students have managed it for years so expect we will too.' Standing back with a bow, he opened the exit door.

Dan says he fell for my green eyes (thanks Dad) and feistiness (my elbows had met his ribs at the notice board). We had a common bond of shipyard-worker dads and being the first of our families to attend University. My first impression of Dan was of kind eyes and courtesy, but I went home intending the date would be a 'one off.' I didn't plan involvement with him or anyone else. I'm good at plans.

His combed-back hair was damp from his post-work wash and he smelled of Imperial Leather. My father pushed away his empty plate and lit a Capstan. 'So how was the first day, Beth?'

I was still eating my stew, having not yet acquired the medic's knack of speedy eating in case your bleep goes off. 'It was OK. We're in alphabetical groups. Mine has a really clever Jean, all sassy and spunky, aims to be a professor like her Dad and a shy Polish girl, Maia. Then there's a posh boarding school girl, Rosie. Gorgeous. Wants to work in Africa. They all seem dead brainy.'

'I'm sure you can hold your own!' Dad smiled.

Mum turned from the oven with her speciality rice pudding. The aroma of hot cream and nutmeg replaced Imperial Leather.

'And what are the guys like?' Young sister Alice had an interest in the male of the species I'd never possessed at twelve.

'As it happens I've agreed to go out with one already. He's called Dan.'

'That's nice dear.' My mother heaped pudding and tinned mandarin oranges into little Pyrex dishes. 'What does his father do?' My mother always asked this (and her a socialist!).

'Oh, for goodness sake, mum. He seems very steady and reliable. If you must know, his father was a riveter at Ferguson's.' I didn't add *but I already know he buggered off years ago.* 'Anyway, apart from one, they're all nice.'

As I wolfed my pudding, Alice spoke. 'I got full marks in an Arithmetic test today.'

'Well, done – that's my girl! Numbers are the basis of everything, Alice. Do you know the Chinese even use them for fortune telling?' My Dad loved weird facts. Our house groaned with books. Criminal he'd had to leave school at 14. 'They think four is especially unlucky as it sounds like "death" in Cantonese.'

Alice looked baffled.

I laughed. 'So, what's number 44 then, double death?'

'No, it's a double-decker Corporation bus from here to Knights-wood, ha, ha!'

Funny old Dad, saw humour in everything. I'm glad he didn't live to see the mess I got into. The sixties were happy times. Before our fates were sealed by that typist assigning us into those wee alphabetical groups. If you ask me, letters are as inauspicious as numbers: S and T especially. H is ominous too. But I'm hopeless at predictions. The ones I made for my new friends were widely off beam. And as to my father's faith I could 'hold my own?' I'm not sure I did.

Three

First Manoeuvres

In the Union bar Conor Towmey lights a Marlboro and slowly exhales while assessing his classmates. Ralph Semple? Too English, too pukka and taller than him by four or five inches. Gordon Tindall? Gormless, but with his Dad a consultant surgeon, worth cultivating. Dan Sheehan? A boyo, but can't afford Halls, poor bugger. Lives on a poxy Clydeside housing scheme. Henry Thompson? Boring. English. A chubby PG Tips chimp. Malcolm Taylor? Ugly bastard, Malky, but laugh a minute. Ex-Gordonstoun boarder. Barrister Dad. Yep, given a punt it'll be him or Yousef for a good time. Yousef Shamoun's father sounds seriously minted, owning hotels and Nile riverboats. He's coughed up an Alfa Romeo Spider, Casino membership and an American Express card for Yousef. Best Towmey Senior's managed is a bloody toy-town Hillman Imp.

Still, it's wheels. Great that Yousef's next door in Halls, though the boy needs help – never had a blonde, never been to rugby and puts ice in malt whisky! As Conor stares at the sacrilegious bobbing cubes, Yousef nudges him, pointing into the hall.

'Conor, have you met her, Rosie Scott?'

'She's a looker, isn't she?' Conor takes a drag, trying to catch petite, curvy Rosie's eye.

'Her father owns the Casino here in Glasgow and a club in Edinburgh. Is that far away?'

'Well, we could stay over. She's cute. A ringer for Patti Boyd.'

'A ringer? Patti Boyd?' Yousef wrinkles his brow.

'George Harrison, from the Beatles, his girlfriend? Long blonde hair, big smoky eyes.' Yousef shrugs. Conor downs his pint. 'Never mind. Be back in a minute.'

He saunters over to Rosie. Claim staked, and drink order taken, he sweeps back to the bar via a blonde classmate in the corner who is unhappy to be told she's on her own. Tough. He couldn't think why he'd asked her out, what with that awful giggle and those definitely-suspect, probably padded 36Ds. Conor has a pint and a whisky chaser. Yousef pays. He gets another round in then takes one from Ralph before ordering Rosie's drink. Week two and life is sweet.

◆

Discos were an integral part of our university life. The first stands out. With ear-destroying decibels of Sergeant Pepper and Waterloo Sunset blaring, multi-coloured lights pulsing and clouds of cigarette smoke gathering in the gloom of the Men's Union, we elected our Theta Year Club Committee. A second year Hank Marvin in a yellow cord suit and purple-flowered tie urged us to nominate candidates. Each had to make a pitch before we voted by show of hands. First elected were blonde Rosie, boasting party expertise and surgeon's son Gordon offering 'insider' knowledge. Then in were Dan, promising distillery visits (a cousin worked at Glengoyne) and Conor, offering to buy a pint for anyone voting for him. Though I never accepted Dan and Rosie's nomination, I too was voted in. Jean became organising secretary and Henry, treasurer. We were now the Theta Club Committee of '73 (our hopeful graduation date) bound together forever. Short of failing. Or dying. Unimaginable to us then. Hank returned to the Beer Bar. The boys followed and the DJ played on to an all-female audience.

My school friend Ruth had come, lured by the thought of the plentiful males in my year, unlike in her Arts Faculty classes. She sat with Jean, Rosie, Maia and I chatting and occasionally dancing, but by eleven we'd all had it. Running the gauntlet into the male-dominated bar wasn't an option. My 'date' Dan was absent and Rosie moaned that Con had never returned with a promised drink. But as we rose to leave, a trickle of males sauntered in. Conor came bearing a pint, Rosie's Martini with lemonade and effusive apologies. After an 'About time – I'd given you up!' accompanied by a brief huff and a hair flounce, Rosie followed him to a table.

I watched Conor sit leaning forward, legs akimbo, hands clasped grazing his genitals. Rosie thought him the "Year's Best Looker," but to me he was a right plonker. Over Rosie's shoulder his eyes roved the room in that 'looking-over-your-shoulder-never-in-your-eye-when-talking-to-you' way, in case someone more useful or important might appear. She chatted on, oblivious.

The rest of the pack prowled in. The cattle market commenced. The jovial (if unfortunate-looking) Malky Taylor lured Ruth off with a nod of 'Are ye dancin'?' before Ralph swept me up. His height was a novelty for a five-foot-ten beanpole like me. I always had to stoop when dancing with West of Scotland boys whose pubertal growth spurts never matched mine. Dan ambled by to dance with Jean, stunning that night with her contacts in and her long red hair tumbling free. But a few numbers later I saw him double up as Jean stomped off. A gut punch or a knee in the groin? Not sure, but Dan slowly straightened up and ambled to the bar without a glance at me. Some date. But I wasn't bothered.

Entanglements were a nuisance. My past boyfriend of two years, fellow school prefect Findlay, had gone to Oxford and sent one card: 'Workload enormous. Tutor insane bully. Oxford girls all snooty dogs.' I hadn't replied. Out of sight...

Maia sat alone at the side. After the trouble I'd had getting her there, I wasn't happy. Her father didn't approve of discos. In fact, he didn't approve of much, keeping her on a ridiculously tight leash of study and cello practice. I appreciated he'd done wonders smuggling them out of Hungary (not Poland as I'd assumed) during the '56 uprising, but this was Scotland, 1967. Teenagers went to discos! While Ralph was fetching me a drink, I scooped up Henry and presented him to Maia, whispering 'She fancies you!' in his ear- my second white lie of the day. The first was my insistence to Maia's dad, Mr Szakolczai, that this was a compulsory course function. I'd even engineered that she'd stay over with me to share a taxi home thus circumventing his demand she be home by eleven. He sounded so different from my supportive Dad, who was often to be found patiently snoozing in his old Anglia outside school dances.

A laughing Ralph returned aping Henry's flailing dance moves. 'He's never been to a disco before, has he? Don't think Maia has either – our two class virgins together!'

'That's not funny. There's more than two. Not everyone's obsessed with sex!'

Ralph snorted, 'He's as shy as she is – told me he's never "done it."'

'I can't believe you discussed that!'

'Maia's not a good bet for him. Goes to the Chaplaincy. She's got religion.'

'For God's sake, Ralph, religion isn't something you "get" like measles! So what if Maia goes to mass? Give her a break.'

Ralph took his huff to the bar. Dan ambled back in and I danced with him, probably because I'd had a few drinks by then. I wasn't used to alcohol, being underage and Presbyterian. You couldn't see for the fug, or hear for the din, but we danced, laughed and drank from Dan's stash of Tennant's cans (courtesy of an accommodating barmaid before the bar closed). Late on, we sat cosily in a corner. Nearby, Conor sat snogging Rosie, intermittently downing beer and pouring her drinks from a flask. In the Ladies I found her reeking of brandy and slurred. I'd have been unconscious. As they left entwined, Dan started dozing on my shoulder. When I prised him off he woke to clasp me tightly.

'Gonna come back to Halls, then?' His wink, raised eyebrow and sideways head jerk reminded me of the onset of one of my poor cousin Billy's seizures. I removed his arms.

'You must be kidding? When you're sharing a room with Yousef?' I pointed over at him, pulling out a chair for our slight, pretty classmate, Patricia Bonham. 'Now, he's a gentleman!'

Dan slurred, 'Nonsensh! Conor says Pat's well up for it – she's a convent girl.'

'How can Conor say that? Yousef is only being kind. She told us yesterday she was struggling as she didn't do a Biology Higher. He's promised to help her.'

'He should help himself to her – I reckon she's a cinch!'

Ralph appeared and just caught a swaying Dan, now teetering on his feet, shirt-tail loose, hair dishevelled. Dan winked at him.

'We know what Pat needs, aye, Ralph? She's not experienced like Beth…'

'What d'you mean, "experienced?"'

Ralph patted my hand and leaned over. Whisky breath engulfed me. 'He doesn't mean anything, Beth. He's a wee bit drunk.'

'Really? And you're one to talk?' I recoiled from peaty fumes.

'Actually, you're higher in the pecking order of girls in the year than Pat is.'

'Pecking order? We're not bloody chickens grubbing for farmyard seeds. We're serious women trying to get a degree, not cannon fodder for immature boys!' The references to farms and battlefields met with baffled stares. They were now beyond any sensible conversation-with or without mixed metaphors. I reached for my bag. 'I've had it! I'm going home.'

'Please yourself!' Dan shrugged, lids drooping. 'Ah'll go an' chat up Wendy then. Ye see her? She's a cracker – that wee shortie dress, thae white boots – a real Barbarella! And those boobies... aye Ralphie – ye could get lost in thae boobies, eh?'

I followed his gaze towards Wendy. She was a tall, graceful slim girl with, none the less, an hour glass figure, waist-length hair and high cheek bones like a model: arguably our most striking female classmate. And she was the owner of the Afghan coat I'd coveted on first day, lucky thing.

Ralph slapped Dan's back. 'No chance, boy! Well out of your league! Wendy Tuffnall-Brown's from a big country estate. Grandpa's an earl. You couldn't keep her in lipstick!'

As I rose, Ralph clutched my arm. 'Don't go yet, Beth! The pecking order's just a bit of fun. Surely you girls have discussed the men?'

I removed his hand. 'Well, not like cattle or chickens. And there's few *men* about to judge. It's mostly immature schoolboys like you two. Good night!'

I fetched my coat then met Maia and an indignant Ruth in the lobby. She'd escaped from a groping Malky, now ensconced at the bar. Dan stood in its doorway gesticulating and sloshing beer towards Wendy, who was laughing coquettishly, fingertips on lips. Heavens! She was welcome. I couldn't see him as a doctor. In fact, I couldn't see *any* of these drunk lads as doctors. Mind you, I wasn't entirely sober myself. Linking arms with Maia and Ruth, I went out into University Avenue and hailed a taxi. On the way to the south side, Maia prattled about Henry. but Ruth and I sat mute, ruing our drink intake as much as our unsatisfactory encounters with the opposite sex.

Drink is as inexplicably bound up in this story as sex. Alcohol has perennially acted as students' main social lubricant. Perhaps facing a lifetime of propriety makes medical students particularly

24

reckless indulgers. Apart from Wendy, we all drank. In mitigation, we didn't appreciate its dangers then. Apart from causing post-alcohol amnesia (occasionally a blessing), it impairs the 'civilised behaviour' control afforded by the frontal lobe of the cortex, thus allowing disinhibited acts and the revelation of secrets best left undisclosed. From student days to our Ten-Year Reunion this pattern repeated itself. Sex and drink brought death and downfall in their wake. Going home that night I vowed to avoid all relationships with men till after finals. They seemed more trouble than they were worth. Next morning, my two-Askit-powder hangover resulted in another vow: abstinence from alcohol. As I said, I'm good at plans.

◆

Week four I was sipping a shandy in the Curler's Bar. With Dan. Two vows broken. I'd been worn down by Dan's pleas and excuses, though in truth I doubted his disco behaviour was solely due to him being 'an anxious poor boy out of his depth and unused to liquor…' It's hard to explain, but Dan can get around me. He's the most persuasive man I've ever met. It served me right. That date was a disastrous, relentless evening of depressing monologues. On his sister, Elaine, whose boorish boyfriend, a black sailor from a nearby US Naval base, had got her 'up the duff' (sic), agreed to a shotgun wedding and hustled her off to North Carolina where she was desperately unhappy. On his brother Robert, who'd escaped into the Army leaving him with his depressed mum. On his father, who left when Dan was six to work in a Belfast shipyard and never returned. My conversational contributions were restricted to a 'No, really?' and a 'What a shame…' The drama continued at the bus stop. Moving in for a goodnight kiss, Dan veered off to throw up in the gutter. I boarded my Govan bus, the 44: a lucky number for me.

His later explanation for his 'stomach upset' was 'a bad pub pie.' Mine was eight pints. Dan was history.

Four

Casino Royale, Cleopatra's Maiden & Dogfish

Week four found me at the cinema. With Dan. Something about the boy I couldn't resist. This time, minus soliloquies and booze, the evening went well. Spoof Bond film Casino Royale was hilarious and I got an interval choc ice. We laughed a lot. I'd had worse dates. But if studying medicine was hard, socialising at University was proving harder. On our next date I met Cleopatra's Handmaiden and Handcuff Frank: life wasn't dull.

The week after Casino Royale, a new bar opened in Byres road near the University. The Safari had a big game theme- all tiger heads and Masai shields. It was noisy and busy. We were on our first drink when Conor arrived, trailing Frank Hutton, his new Science Faculty chum and a girl with a perma-smile and bottle-blonde hair. She wore heavy Pan-stick make-up and the briefest dress I'd ever seen. Conor introduced her with a flourish.

'This is Ingrid. She's a waitress, sorry, 'a Cleopatra's Handmaiden,' at the Casino. You should see her in her fanny-grazing-toga!'

Ingrid laughed and fluttered furry lashes. They sat with us. With no other seats available, I felt I couldn't be churlish and refuse, or glare, or move away, though all three options appealed. By this stage of term, Conor and I were on polite speaking terms, but that night I was tired and not up to his gung-ho chauvinism. Nor his Maiden's simpering vacuity. Actually, I felt Ingrid's status as a maiden was pretty questionable as her hand nestled in Conor's crotch all evening. I suspected she'd had more than two brandy and Babychams as she veered between slurred comments, raucous laughter and somnolence. The chat turned to porn. There were several genres, I learned. Dan sat hypnotised by Ingrid's cavernous cleavage struggling to escape from her crocheted lime-green mini-dress. Conor and Frank continued winding one another

26

up, so I upped and left. Dan didn't murmur as I pulled my new maxi coat from under him. He'd moved over to accommodate Ingrid who was as capacious of bottom as she was of boob. Still, I was grateful my coat was warmed though. It was cold outside. The final straw for me had been the conversation on breast size, pubic hair and bondage.

'You can't have them too big,' waxed Conor. 'You should see the boobs in Dad's Dutch stuff – phew! You know, we should have a boy's blue movie night...'

Frank shook his head. 'Big isn't always best. Those oriental girls with neat tits, smooth bodies like schoolgirls ... did you know they all have less body hair than western women? You know, I think if Scots girls waxed more...'

My only waxing experience then involved dog-walking jackets. No one I knew got waxed. Body hair to me isn't an acceptable date topic, ever, even disguised as scientific fact. (Which it is. Japanese women do have less sexual hair). Then for some reason they got on to the Profumo and Christine Keeler scandal, whether the call-girl had given secrets to the Russians and whether, as rumoured, whips, rubber and handcuffs were involved. Frank's eyes sparkled brightly. My school sex education was scant on nitty gritty and entirely lacking on bondage. I rose and left for an early double-death: my 44 bus.

Next morning Conor collared me. 'You missed yourself last night, Beth. We went back to Halls. What a night! She's some girl, Ingrid. And isn't Frank a laugh?' He left without waiting for my opinion. I don't know whom Ingrid pleasured that night, perhaps all three. She was a generous girl keen to spread light and love. In the bar prior to insensibility, she'd thrust on me a phone number for a private doc dispensing the Pill without question to single girls. (Scots NHS GPs didn't in 1967). 'It's great now, isn't it, being able to have s-s-sex whenever you like?' she'd hiccupped. I was appalled and hoped her doc dispensed VD advice too.

Dan appeared next afternoon with little recollection of the

night. Our 'romance' I declared finally dead in the water. Along with sex, which now looked too much of a minefield to contemplate. Medicine was proving a bit of a battle in many ways. I wasn't sure I was up to it, on or off the field. On field was already littered with the dead bodies of animals killed for our benefit. The human casualties came later. Some of us found dead bodies a source of amusement, a means to show off. Not an especially good trait in a prospective doctor.

◆

It's Biology lab, fourth week Friday. Conor looks across the room clutching his dissection specimen and trying to catch her eye. She's two benches away. He's never met anyone like her: classy, stunning, sophisticated. A virginal challenge. Gazing aloft at his specimen's rheumy unseeing eyes, he delivers lines with a gravitas that would have pleased his old drama teacher.

'Alas poor Yorick! I knew him, Horatio: a fellow of infinite jest, of most excellent fancy…' He nods towards Malky across his bench. 'I've played Hamlet, you know.'

He sees she is now watching him from afar. So is Malky, but with a curling lip.

'Bloody hell, Con, what's with the Richard Burton act? Shakespeare's a load of long-winded pish!' Malky blows his nose while flicking his lab manual. 'Come on, let's finish and get out of this bloody stinking place.'

As Conor drops his fish on his specimen board he sees Wendy drop her eyes to her bench. The show is over. But he's had a smile. Progress. They all succumb in the end.

◆

Our corpses had scaly bodies, glassy eyes and whiskers. I'm not sure my *Squalus acanthias* was a 'he' and even in rubber gloves, I wasn't flipping it over to check. My eyes and nose burned. I'd have preferred rotting dogfish to these formalin-pickled horrors, but at least the fish was immobile. The scampering live cockroaches and wriggling worms of previous biology labs had freaked out

Maia. My damp, curling manual on the bench instructed 'Dissect, identify and flag the Cranial Nerves I to XII on one side.' Bloody slippery wee things, cranial nerves. I'd managed to expose the brain intact, but the Accessory (XI) and Hypoglossal (XII) nerves retracted into tiny coils when I sliced through then by mistake.

'Oh God, to think I fancied neurosurgery!' I sneezed, trying not to breathe in.

A laughing Jean sat back, finished despite having written out labels for us all. 'Neurosurgery's not like this, Beth! Dad says human brains smell sweet, if anything. You could come and assist him in theatre; he'd be happy to show you what it's like. My brother wanted to be a neurosurgeon like him, but it's not for me.'

'Your brother?'

'I had a wee brother, Josh, who died when he was ten from an inoperable brain tumour. Ironic really, dad being a neurosurgery professor. Sshh!' She nodded over my shoulder, red hair flaming in the overhead strip-light, before hissing 'Creep alert!'

'Did I hear you say you wanted to be a surgeon, Miss Slater? I don't think so – what a right dog's breakfast, or should I say dogfish breakfast, you've made of that!'

Eddy, our lab supervisor. A creep who'd propositioned Rosie and goaded us girls while completely ignoring the boy's carry-on. We'd dubbed him 'Snot.' His bulbous nose was constantly in a handkerchief.

'Women simply don't have the temperament for surgery, do they, boys?'

Nearby Conor nodded sagely. I glared angrily. A voice on my right chimed in.

'I say, steady on, Eddy! Surely it's better to have a careful woman dissecting your innards than some careless gung-ho. macho guy?'

Ralph towered pleasingly over Snot, who stood caressing his ridiculously slicked comb-over. Tortoiseshell glasses sliding down his nose bulged a yellow spot. I toyed with the joy of inflicting pain with a labelling pin but shuddering at the potential oozing consequences.

'Come off it, Semple. We all know women are irrational creatures, slaves to their hormones – crazy half the month with PMT! The Faculty shouldn't admit any.'

'Nonsense!' Ralph turned away from him, making a face at me.

'Watch it, boy! Don't expect alphas from me this term.' Snot swaggered off to berate a timid lab girl who'd dropped a tray of instruments.

Ralph came over beside me. 'Bloody idiot, what does he know about PMT?'

'Och, he probably saw last week's Horizon on TV. It was all about hormones. Started with a historical bit about Edwardian Harley Street surgeons whipping out ovaries to make 'hysterical' women docile. Didn't realise 'hysteria' was Greek for womb, did you?'

'No, not something my camp old classics master ever mentioned! That ovary op sounds pretty dangerous, though. Anaesthetics were crappy then.'

'Yes, but worst of all, only a husband's consent was necessary!'

'Truly?' Ralph grimaced, but still looked attractive. Weird thing, attraction, but then I suspect it's caused by hormones. But Ralph's 'truly' was quaint. Scots don't really use 'truly.'

Jean chipped in. 'Oh, the good old days! Though at least if those Edwardian guys had their wives 'seen to' like cats, they could stop using prostitutes for family planning.'

Rosie wrinkled her nose and tucked some disobedient long blonde hair back into its bun.

'What on earth do prostitutes have to do with family planning?'

'Come on, Rosie – if hubbies used prostitutes for their 'needs' then wives didn't get pregnant every year. Mind you, if they *did* have sex, they risked getting the clap or syphilis off him.'

Rosie looked appalled. I thought about wives getting syphilis, but then her mind worked differently from mine. 'Poor thing, can't have been much fun for her, not having sex...'

How she could think of sex while sitting surrounded by stinking dead fish beside me sporting tissues stuck up each nostril? I shook my head. 'Well, Rosie, if the choice was no sex or dying from childbirth and syphilis, I know what I'd choose! Oh well, maybe we are better off today, but we're still in the minority here and second-class citizens. For example, Ralph, can you name me a woman professor?'

Ralph pushed back his floppy fringe. 'Well, no.' He was an apologetic, mannerly boy with a mellifluous soft-spoken English accent surprisingly like Wendy Tuffnall-Brown's Scottish-high-society one. I saw her across the room twisting her hair over a shoulder while gazing at him. He was oblivious.

'Do you really want to do neurosurgery, Beth?'

'Och, I don't know, Ralph. What about you?'

'GP, probably. Though I said 'research' at my interview as the school suggested.'

'Mine didn't suggest anything. And the profs didn't ask me about specialities, only if my family was medical and if I understood medicine was a "long haul for a woman."'

'Really? Och, I suspect it's a lottery where we'll all end up. Let's leave the competitive bollocks to Prof Sheehan and Mr Consultant-to-the-Stars Towmey over there.' He nodded at Dan and Conor jousting with scalpels. 'Conor thinks that while VD medicine appeals, it being the quickest route to consultancy, surgery with all its private practice offers higher earning potential. Puts vocation in a new light!'

Ralph returned to his bench. I resumed chopping, labelling and pinning my severed nerves together with Jean's wee flags before copying a rough diagram of it into my lab book to fix later. As I wiped and wrapped my dissecting kit, Maia was blowing on her painstakingly perfect illustration. Her fountain pen took ages to dry, but as it was a present from her father, she felt obliged to use it. Like Jean, Maia was doing medicine to please him. My Dad didn't mind what I did, but I knew he was proud I'd chosen medicine and hoped it would be a passport to travelling the world to all the places we'd poured over in his National Geographic Mags. Maybe I'd even set sail on one of the liners he'd built? I was so lucky with my family.

Stuffing away my lab book, I saw Ralph hold up his. 'Seen next week, girls?'

'What?'

'Dissecting a pregnant rat!'

I felt sick. Maia made a face. Rosie shrieked out hairgrips. Jean just shrugged.

Ralph gathered up his duffle bag. 'All good character-building stuff!'

I looked out of the window at the trees wavering in the horizontal lashing rain: a typical blustery Scottish November day. Covering my corpse, I donned my new maxi-coat. 'Hope it isn't fish and chips today at the Ref, couldn't face it.'

'There's always macaroni. Why not go veggie, like me?' Ralph did wavy minstrel hands.

Dan dug him in the ribs. 'Vegetarians are wimps!'

The usual schoolboy scuffle ensued. Ralph though, overall, behaved more maturely than the others despite occasional moans about repeating work he'd done in A-level at Stow where he'd been a boarder. Like all privately-schooled students, he was confident of graduating. While I worried constantly I wouldn't make it, they took it as a given. I marvelled.

That day Ralph detached himself from Dan and his unruly group to take my arm down the stairs. In the Ref we had chips with fried-egg rolls and decided to meet for a couple of Wednesday afternoons in the new girls' Queen Margaret Union (boys only pm and by invitation), so he could help me with the huge daunting book of physics problems we'd been set. I found them pretty baffling, but using his templates for each type of problem, and despite remaining clueless about a lot of theory, I completed them all and was very grateful.

It was six weeks before my diary logs our first proper date. Refreshingly, his family sounded normal, he didn't vomit or discuss handcuffs. We became an 'item', going out every week, workload permitting. Weeknights he studied in Halls, alone. I preferred the Reading Room with Maia. Turned out she, like Jean, had hidden depths.

◆

As Conor lays the Chemistry book on top of his messy study pile, he regrets his third pint. He'd only intended one with Malky in the Curler's after chemistry lab, but Frank had turned, up so it was only fair to let them both buy a round. They'd buggered off for a Wimpy, but he's decided on a quick re-write of Chemistry lectures plus a bash at the week's lab reports using Vince's old books. He doesn't sit but, realising he can't ignore the pressure of that last pint any longer, he sets off down the corridor to the Gents. By habit, he scans the room. Nothing of interest. The Reading Room's never a good hunting ground: mostly swots like the 3B and the Dyke opposite.

◆

Maia and I studied together in the Reading Room three or four nights a week. I liked going home well after rush hour: traffic jams wasted valuable study time. Maia just liked working away from home. We preferred the smaller Reading Room to the big library and usually headed down after a quick cuppa and snack in the Ref.

Week seven Maia sat back and nodded across the central void of the circular reading area. 'Isn't it odd Conor sits in Modern History when he's in? Not that he's in often…'

'So? We usually sit here, same place usually.'

'Yes, but we're in science, near books we might need.' She was staring over at him.

I didn't care. There was too much work to do. We needed to re-write lecture notes supplemented by info from the textbooks for later revision. I had to do this immediately after a lecture or I couldn't read, never mind understand, my writing. Ralph's Swahili and Rosie's hieroglyphs were worse. Jean's neat and concise notes were a boon for missed buses. But getting the textbooks for writing up was problematic too. The University bookseller offered twenty copies at start of term (for 200 students) and took months to fulfil orders. Lending library copies went off-shelf early, some legitimately borrowed, some filched illegally (avoiding return deadlines and penalties) via rear toilet windows. Best bet, as its books couldn't be checked out-and it had no rear windows – was the Reading Room. Yet even first thing many books were not on their designated shelves. A mystery.

I watched Conor amble out of Modern History, lay a book on his chosen desk and saunter along the corridor. In a flash, Maia was off like a rocket. She whizzed back triumphantly.

'That Chemistry book we couldn't find? He had it! Two can play at that game.'

Shooting up the aisle beside us, Maia returned to sit primly and lift her new biro (it took six weeks for her to ditch her time-wasting fountain pen). She looked smug.

'Maia, what on earth are you doing?'

She whispered. 'The Chemistry book's now in Botany, shelf 401.26: I'll tell the girls. It makes me mad. He can afford to buy books - how dare he hide them from those that can't?'

'Oh, he doesn't care. I expect he thinks it's all a joke. He prefers splashing out cash on women and booze at weekends rather than books. Yousef says he blew a fortune last Saturday.'

'I like Yousef. I couldn't understand why he's pals with Conor, but Henry says it's because he's one of the few students with money to burn. They're always at clubs and the casino. Henry says Conor has 'the morals of an alley cat.' But I've seen him at Mass – how does he have the gall?'

Maia and Rosie were the first Catholics I'd met- if you discounted Conor, which I tended to do. Scotland's had a sectarian school system, meaning my school saw visiting Imams and Rabbis as well as Presbyterian ministers, but never priests. Catholics had their own schools. In time, I appreciated Catholicism had benefits: sin, confess, do penance, take communion and carry on sinning. Handy. I wondered why spoilsports Calvin and Knox bothered.

Five

Chaplaincy & Cheating

As Conor walks up University Avenue, week seven, eight am, he decides this will be the last time he'll go to Friday Mass in the Chaplaincy. It's been worthwhile: Liam's had a good shag or two. He'd been right, that's all it's taken to cure his old school chum's depression. When Liam had complained about the lack of talent in his Law classes, Conor had chided him, passing on his father's advice (dispensed with his first condoms) that recreational women are best kept transient and distant. Keep your dick outside of your immediate work/social circle to minimise unwelcome repercussions once you've had enough. Casual fun's best with strangers. Despite starting as a joke, the Chaplaincy had been profitable. Girls from single-sex boarding schools had proved especially satisfying conquests. But available stock was dwindling. Time to bail out. Might keep up with Father Kieran, have the odd pint. A nice young guy, if oddly disinterested in sex. Fancy having to live without it. At least with a partner.

Conor knows that if he stops coming he'll have to lie to his mother. She's a worry since she can't stand unaided now, and her arms are weaker. Sister Joseph has to hold the phone. A bitch of a disease, MS. Doesn't help that his bloody father is as absent and indifferent as ever and hasn't been to the nursing home for weeks. He'd like to go more himself, but it's a drive out to Lanark. Tricky.

Friday nights are the Curler's for drinking, Saturdays have rugby mornings and late bevvies in the Casino which fuck up Sundays. Wednesday afternoon maybe? Means missing circuit training, but hey, the abs should take it!

Roll on tomorrow night: free Casino passes from Rosie. What a girl. Knows a few tricks. That long golden hair like Lady Godiva riding him in his narrow hall bed. Well up for it. Unusual girl: fancy her saying after a few dates there's not much else to do but bonk! And he'd managed first base, first night. Result! Though now she was blowing hot and cold. He couldn't be bothered with it. Plenty more women about. Two last week. That blonde MA from the Curler's could down the pints. And down on him ... an artist! He stirs at a frisson of remembrance. Pity she hadn't worn knickers – ruined the collection. Maybe he should start a catalogue, like in the book which gave him the idea, with name, descriptions, date and positions perhaps? He laughs. A passing girl frowns at him. Bit of a dog: likely wears baggy cotton M&S. He licks his lips. Winks. She blushes. He wouldn't have her on a plate, but there's few women he couldn't get if he wanted – and their knickers, discarded recklessly as he moves into action. Seduction is his true vocation. Roll on the wards. Nurses. Sexy, starchy uniforms!

Now that Wendy Tuffnall-Brown is seriously sexy. Dark. Usually he goes for blondes, but she is class. Finally pulled her on Saturday. Weird she doesn't drink. Possibly not had a boyfriend. Definitely a virgin. Needs going easy, playing slowly. Rosie could go hang. Anyway, Rosie's family? Nutters! How could her mother stay married to a queer? Had she married him after Rosie's real father went? Or had she hung on after he 'came out' because of the money? Conor shudders: gay sex. Common at school amongst both pupils and teachers, but he'd been left alone. Probably his tough rugby reputation. And he could spot a poofter a mile off. Pushing open the door, he can't see Liam, but Frank is there, sitting with a boy he hasn't seen before.

'Hey, Con. This is James, my kid brother, doing Law.'

'Hi James.' Olive-skinned, muscular, very unlike pale slim Frank. Different fathers? He wouldn't mind finding out he had a different father. 'Law? Do you know Liam O'Farrell?'

'No,' says James. 'But I'm in Second, is he in First?'

Conor nods. 'Usually here. Hates Law. Says it's dead boring.'

'It is.'

'So, why are you doing it?'

'Not much choice. Frankie-boy screwed his 'A' levels so he's doing a Med Science BSc to try for grad entry to medicine. That's three years' extra fees, so the old Judge was pissed off and refused me six-year medicine. It was Law like him or Divinity like his brother the 'Bish.'

Conor whistles. 'Your dad's a judge? And your uncle's a bishop? I've only known one bishop, a right fucker. Trollied every night at Lourdes with the school. Used to put him to bed. Shite of a school mine. The day Liam and I left we burned our blazers under the bishop's nose!'

'Really? St Joseph's was pretty OK.'

Frank shifts in his seat mumbling.

James shrugs. 'At least C of E priests can marry, so mibbe they're a bit more normal.'

Frank bites a rag-nail. 'No priests are normal, James, they're all buggers.'

'Kentigern's was pretty big on buggery. And belting. Daily targets – what a game! Boarding school survival meant back to the wall and head down at all times. *Gentle Jesus,* my ass. Religion's a load of pish!'

'Too right, Conor! Daily religious doggerel at a bloody unnatural all-male priest's college would have done my head in!'

'So, if you're C of E, boys, why come to RC Mass?' ·

James laughs. 'Frank's here for his soul! It's the nearest mass, but I've come for these Chaplaincy Challenges he tells me about. Sounds fun. How about her?' James nods to his right.

'Maia? She's in our class. Goody, goody. Quiet wee mouse. A

Grade 3B: Bad Bed Bet!' Conor sniggers. 'Shoosh. Here's Father Kieran.'

'The Lord be with us...'

The student group responds, 'And also with you.'

Conor offers 'and also up you.' Frank snorts. James sniggers. The enticing smell of bacon wafts from the scullery. Conor wonders that they get bacon. The Old Testament forbids pork totally and most priests insist Friday's for fish. He remembers hearing somewhere though, that mediaeval monks won dispensation to eat duck and beavers' tails, them being aquatic. Not that you'd get beaver in Safeway's ... Conor laughs. Heads rise disapprovingly. Fuck them! A least Friday Chaplaincy saves him cooking his own breakfast. And confession provides a nice clean slate for the weekend: all sins forgiven. The ones he's confessed to, that is.

◆

From first term I have nothing to confess, I just studied hard with the odd chaste night out. Perhaps I should confess to some inconsiderate flippancy though, like with poor old Gordon in the final week. While my relationship with Ralph relationship was low key, no strings assumed, Gordon wanted the opposite. Novels always portray women as the ones seeking commitment. Wrong. Gordon was pretty needy and expected a permanent future with long-standing girlfriend Heather. Normally he wore a cheerful lop-sided grin, but that Monday morning in first term he looked like Eeyore: doleful, drooping, huddling into a stripy scarf. I sat beside him.

'What's up, Gordon?'

'Heather dumped me at the disco on Saturday.'

'Oh, I'm sorry. Did she say why?'

'I work too much, apparently. Think more of studying. She doesn't understand our pressure.'

'Well, her teacher training's probably not so intense.'

'The worst thing was, she waited till I took her home ...' He trailed off.

'Why did that matter?' Then I answered myself. 'Ah, of course! If she'd done it earlier you could've got off with someone else.'

He sobbed, making me realise my comment was crass. My excuse was fatigue. I'd been awake half the night worrying about unfinished lab reports. I was upset. Gordon was the first boy I'd ever made cry.

'After four years, how could she?' he sniffed.

I was holding back my next question – '*So, does she have someone else?*' when Yousef arrived. He didn't help.

'Oh Gordon, that friend of Rosie's I got off with on Saturday – what a girl!'

Having realised Yousef changed girls like socks, my interest in moustaches had soon waned. Released from home cultural restrictions, the Egyptian pursued everything female, fair-skinned and free. Then Wendy bounced in. More wound salt.

'Super disco, Saturday, guys. Beth – you missed yourself. Why didn't you come?'

'Sore throat,' I lied. (Always uncool to admit you're catching up with work).

I swopped seats with Yousef who'd started leaning across me trying to make amends by asking Gordon out to some dog-racing track. (I didn't know Glasgow had any).

'So, why was it super, Wendy?' She was rattling: top speed, top volume though it wasn't yet nine. And I hadn't slept.

'I'll get to that in a minute. Must tell you first, I had lunch with Rosie yesterday.'

'Oh?' My mind wandered to my Physics lab write-up.

'She lives in a fabulous house, well, estate, really. Super tennis courts, humungous modern indoor pool, bigger than ours. You been to Thorntonhall? It's out in the country. Pity she's there alone so much, though she's got Mrs McGregor and marvellous shaggy rabbits…'

My thoughts scrambled. Mrs McGregor? Mr McGregor? Rabbits? Beatrix Potter? Were hers shaggy? I was losing my mind.

'And Minnie, the talking Mynah. Trumpet the cockatoo, a spaniel and Persian pussies.'

Not my cup of tea: fluttering feathers freaked me out since horror-film buff Ruth dragged me to *The Birds* and furry things made me sneeze. My attention drifted to the whirrs and clicks of Maddox, the lecturer, checking the orientation of his slides, mostly upside down and mostly big monkeys with grinning teeth and shiny red behinds.

Wendy rabbited on. 'I think, by the way, that I know why she flirts with anything on legs. I mean, it's unnatural for a girl to want so much ...' She paused, blushing.

I interjected 'Sex?'

'Right, yes. So, well, the thing is, Rosie hasn't got role models. I mean, her Dad, don't you know... He's, well... he doesn't mind Rosie's mum's affairs – and she's apparently had lots of them – because he has them himself with ... er ... boyfriends! Currently one Rollo, who works in Fraser's Perfume Department! I mean, r- r-r-really!'

I re-engaged with Wendy. God, how boring was my life? Mum, Dad, young Alice and I, wee three-apartment, one-up tenement flat in Govan. No mansions, gay Dads or socialite mums with lovers like Rosie. No fortunes like Wendy. She'd even done a cover for the Tatler – who could compete? 'So, Rosie's Dad is gay? Gosh!' I shook my head.

Wendy grinned. 'Don't look so startled, darling, I'm sure it's commoner than we think. Oh, by the way, I got off with Con on Saturday night. Such a lark.' She dropped a decibel. 'Quite the kisser...' then resumed full volume. 'He's taking me to London for that V&A exhibition I mentioned. We'll go down the week after the exams and there's a concert at the Albert Hall – always wanted to go there. Con's much more mature than we've given him credit for. His antics are all bluster for the boys!'

She hugged me. The lights dimmed. Maddox started lecturing in a monotone. My, I thought, Conor was moving in fast. But

Wendy didn't see anything wrong with these precipitous plans, so who was I to say? Oh well, London would be nice. Not sure about the inevitable shared hotel room. Nor was he remotely a 'lark.' A carrion crow maybe.

A troop of gorillas filled the screen. Doc Maddox burbled about alpha males. The door squeaked open and shut. I looked down as Conor passed behind Maddox raising a two-finger 'V' sign into the light beam. Maddox's magnified head shadow grew horns on the opposite wall. Laughter tittered, to Maddox's bewilderment. Conor slunk off into the shadows. I looked at Wendy, sitting all bouncy, shoulders shrugged up like a wee girl on Christmas morning. She hadn't noticed the creeping Conor. How could she think him mature? A bible verse popped into my head. '*There is none so blind as those who will not see.*' I tried to switch my thoughts from religion and the minefield that was sexual attraction to concentrate on the slides. Some hope. The apes were bonking away on the screen. Seems the strongest mates with whomsoever he fancies, the females have little choice. That dominant male was an ugly big brute.

◆

Last day of term Conor signs the attendance book and struts into the Physics lab. Tommy McCain is the only supervisor on.

'Hi Tommy. Would you like these tickets for the hospitality suite at Celtic Park on Saturday?'

Tommy accepts enthusiastically, shaking Conor's hand. With a father on Celtic Park's Board, Con has useful access to complimentary tickets. Day one he'd recognised Tommy's tie: St Francis old boy. A catholic school, bound to be a Celtic football club supporter.

Conor checks the experiment is the same as last year before unloading a battered foolscap notebook at his spot beside Malky as evidence of 'temporary' absence. He knows Malky will pick it up when he leaves; he's already got his hospitality free-booze tickets for Saturday's game. As Conor slopes off, Malky works on taking readings. Con chuckles. Loser. He hasn't got an old completed lab book to crib from.

Conor heads down Kelvin Walk towards the Lorne. He's had enough of restrictive single hall beds. The hotel double is adequate. As he moves in on Ingrid's neck, he senses a new and alluring fragrance. Chanel, Ingrid says. A gift. She doesn't say from whom. He doesn't care. They only have till seven when her shift starts.

Sex in the afternoon always seems more daring, like doing it al fresco. Nookie is best naked, but not necessarily at night time. He closes his eyes, smiling, visualising Wendy as his rhythm quickens. It'll take time to get her in this position but it'll be worth it. Will she be as experimentally acquiescent in bed as Ingrid? Perhaps given time. He knows the moves. Even on top isn't bad. He's on top of the work too. He stops thinking and gives himself to the job in hand, exclaiming loudly in triumph as he comes. Rolling off, he lights a fag and smiles again in extra satisfaction, thinking of his classmates toiling away in boring Physics. As Ingrid heads for the bathroom, he drains the champagne and switches on the TV.

◆

We girls worked well in our groups. Jean was organised, Maia meticulous and Rosie kept me amused. Knowing short cuts for presenting results, Rosie also tutored me in report fiddling- how to massage readings to fit the lab book graph illustrations and fudge possible error estimates which we were meant to insert above and below the graph line of our readings. These were supposed to be worked out by complex calculations, but we just 'guessed,' putting what looked 'sort-of-right.' Though slightly anxious this was cheating, I consoled myself that no one died. Rosie's expensive co-ed boarding school had majored her in Darwinian classroom survival techniques. 'Pragmatic Adaptation,' she called it.

She'd also majored in seduction. I'd never met anyone like her. Her social life was scandalous. She changed results several times a week and boyfriends as often. Not sure how much time she spent on her back during dates, but afterwards she spent a lot on her knees. Her priest must have needed a counsellor (though not sure we had them this side of the Atlantic then). Her tally matched many of the boys. Her peak performance so far had been Friday week seven when she'd lined up four boys in different places. My diary lists them: Byres Road Jake (for a drink in the Curler's), Odeon Bobby (for some Carry On film), Boots-corner-of-Argyle-Street Alistair (for an O Sole Mio risotto) and QMU Ronnie (for cheap drink and snacks). I suspect she chose the cash-strapped Ronnie. She had a big heart.

Six

Journals & Jumpers

Most of us girls kept diaries in the sixties. I have Maia and Wendy's journals. Wendy had started hers at fourteen, prompted by a Child Psychiatrist she'd been sent to when briefly contemplating joining her departed mother. He'd suggested unburdening anxious thoughts at nightfall would aid deep and dreamless sleep. She kept her locked, tooled-leather diary in a lingerie drawer in a Chippendale chest hidden from prying fatherly eyes. My Woolworth's jotter I kept under my pillow. Hers is poignant and witty. Mine isn't, containing as it does gems like *'Sausages for tea'* and *'Ruth got off with Findlay on Saturday – what is she thinking of?'* Yet, four weeks later I paired off with him at another school dance: attraction is a fickle emotion in your teens. Wendy logged more serious considerations.

Dear Diary,

Only one week of term to go. First weekend home. Couldn't avoid it. Mum's anniversary. I'll never understand why she felt she had to jump off a viaduct. Seems more than ten years ago. Can't picture her face anymore and can't find a single photo. Bloody Dad.

He's done the 'usual' tonight – single malt oblivion. Choice when he lectures me on the evils of drink and drugs! Not sure I believe this guff about 'genetically-inherited addictive tendency.' Surely it wasn't just genes that drove Mum to opiates? Why wasn't a pregnancy enough reason for living? Might've been a boy after three lost girls. Dad's never forgiven her. No heir and spare. Just useless me.

Gramps keeps saying it's a shame I can't get the title, but since I don't even use 'The Hon. Gwendoline,' I'd hardly want that baggage. Hugo is welcome to it and the umpteen thousand acres. Though I agree with Gramps – young Alex would be a safer pair of hands. Cousin Hugo has about as much between the ears as Grandma's poodle. Gramps blames 'inbreeding.' Not sure re wee barky Sasha, but certainly Hugo and Alex's parents are first cousins of first cousins. Gramps urges me to marry new blood, someone of 'good breeding stock!' Suggests 'The Season.' Poor outdated darling!

Plenty talent in the year. Just started walking out with a dark, handsome rugby buff whose people have money from 'steel tubes.' Hates his Dad, a serial womaniser. Sounds a horror. His poor Mum's an invalid. Con likes the good life. Bit naughty. Not sure Gramps would approve. Another fanciable chap is Ralph. Tall, blonde, from Somerset horsey-bloodstock people. Gramps would approve, but he's going out with Beth, a great new chum whose

Dad works in a shipyard, but lovely.

Work is relentless, exhausting. No time to get depressed, though some wobbly mornings. Determined not to go back on anti-depressants. Must prove I can do this. Dad was so against it, I can't fail. Only a week till first Class Exams. So much to do! Maybe squash in some piano practice tonight though. How I miss it in Halls! Goodbye Diary. Am leaving you here. New start, new life. The Honourable Gwendoline Tuffnall-Brown is signing out. X

◆

I knew back then she'd had an eye for Ralph, but not about her mother's suicide, her own depression nor the reason she shunned drink. But would knowing have helped me to help her?

◆

Henry's confessions about family stresses helped him. He found love, mostly due to a boiled jumper. After my disco Cupid attempts, he'd flirted vaguely with Maia, but nothing came of it. Then one Monday he walked into a lecture like a tortured marionette. It was a wonder he'd got into such a shrunken, matted, Fair Isle woolly.

'What in heaven's name is that?' I asked.

'It's a jumper my Aunt Elizabeth knitted. It's wrecked but I had to wear it, I couldn't find anything else.'

Maia giggled. 'Did you wash it on a boil wash?'

'What's a boil wash? It came out of the dryer like this.'

Maia shrieked with laughter. 'You don't put jumpers in a tumble dryer, silly! You'll need to come home with me to learn about laundry. That jumper's only fit for the bin. There are sales on just now- maybe we could go late night shopping on Thursday?'

After a successful jumper-buying trip, next night Maia took Henry home. Her father was at his Bowling Club, but her mother welcomed him and his washing. As the machine whirred in the kitchen, they left Olga engrossed in Women's Own and headed for the sofa.

'Shame Tomacz is out, Henry. You'd like him.'

'Tomacz?'

'My big brother. I had a younger one too, Pieter, but sadly, he died. Anyway, I don't understand why you've never done any washing. Tomacz does his. Mum showed him how.'

'Well, my aunts do everything since mum's illness.'

'You stay with your aunts?'

'Yeh, Mum's had depression for years. I was only a baby when Dad died, and she had a breakdown. Her sisters took us in.'

'That's terrible. What happened?'

'Dad died in 1950 in a place called Pyong Yang. He was a medic with the UN Forces in Korea. The aunts mean well, but gosh, I'm not allowed to do anything for myself except eat. Food is love to them. That's why I'm so fat.'

'You're not fat.' Maia gave him a hug, though her arms could not encircle him. He kissed her until she drew back hesitantly.

'But I didn't think you stayed at home, Henry, I thought you went to boarding school?'

'Yes, thank God for the Forces Benevolent Fund! Having three mums was a bit much. Mum was a medic too, you know, but she's never practised. She's still seeing psychiatrists. Pyong Yang has a lot to answer for.'

'I've never heard of it.'

'Funnily enough, it came up at my interview: Sir James McPhater's brother died there too. Kinda weird. So was McPhater. Did you get him, the surgical prof in the hideous tweed suit and bow tie?'

'Don't remember. I went straight out to be sick after mine. A tweed suit? How horribly scratchy. Promise you'll not wear one when you're a Professor of Surgery!'

Henry laughed and kissed her again.

Maia appeared next day looking more alive than I'd seen her. Good old boiled jumper!

After that, they were inseparable. Friday nights in Maryhill became a regular thing. Maia's father even allowed him to take her to discos, but by the last Saturday morning of term, she was on edge. We were in the Wimpy downtown after studying.

'We nearly did 'it' last night!'

'What?' I paused drinking my milk-shake.

'Mum and Dad went to the Club and Tomacz was out…'

The straw fell from my lips.

'Luckily we heard Tomacz's key in the lock and he went into the kitchen first so Henry had time to …' I barely caught, 'his trousers.' She was as pink as my strawberry shake. Maia and Henry had reached what she called the 'Point of No Return!' Almost. Who'd have thought Fair Isle could be such an aphrodisiac?

◆

I have no diary entries for exam week. Each day I was shattered after mind-churning, tossing, turning nights. Maia woke vomiting, couldn't eat. At one exam hall door she froze and was frog-marched in by Jean and me. Unlike ultra-calm Rosie, seen filing a broken nail with half an hour to go in Chemistry. After the last exam I slept for 12 hours then went with the girls to see *Far from the Madding Crowd*.

Jean was distracted, even ignoring a proffered Rolo. It was Josh's anniversary. I had that post-exam restlessness from not-being-sure-what-you-used-to-do-before-when-you-weren't-studying. Misty rural England didn't grip me, though if I'd been Bathsheba, I'd have plumped for Alan Bates. The cinema was usually a refuge of mindless escape, better than novels, for we'd had enough of books. I liked its comforting darkness and solitude and, because unlike in pubs and discos, you didn't need to expend energy chatting and being witty (or trying to be). My one recollection of watching that film was my recurring thought: 'What if I fail?'

Perhaps medicine was a mistake. It was much too hard.

◆

End of term results night, it was 6.30pm when the secretary closed the glass cabinet in the quad archway. As she fought her way back through the gathering melee of students, Maia charged in. Being small and nimble, she was back in a jiffy, beaming. 'I've passed, Beth! You and Dan are top. Rosie, and Jean are only a few marks behind.'

'Really, Maia? Are you sure?'

Ralph emerged at my side to confirm he'd passed too. Setting down his case, he hugged me. 'What a relief. So, that's me off, darling. Train's at seven. Have a good holiday. I'll phone.'

As he left, Conor emerged. I had to ask. 'How did you get on?'

'Fine. No point in killing yourself till the degrees!' He moved off.

Maia whispered, 'Sour grapes, if you ask me – he barely got 50s.'

Conor heard and turned. His icy stare made her lower her eyes, flustered, till Henry emerged to kiss her. 'Aren't we clever? This calls for the pub! Coming, Beth?'

'No thanks. Meeting Ruth. She got her results this afternoon. Can't believe how easy her term's been – three free afternoons and one whole day off every week!'

'Lucky her!' Henry kissed me, breathing Tennant's. The pubs hadn't been open long, so it must have been off-licence Dutch courage downed in Halls. He sashayed off, humming 'All You Need is Love.' That's a vivid memory: a dancing Henry and a beaming Maia, my shining friend. One term down, seventeen to go. We hadn't lost anyone. Yet.

◆

New Year, 1968. New term. New stresses: electromagnetism and lover's tiffs.

'Stop worrying Maia,' said Jean, connecting wires that buzzed as lights flashed. 'You could do better, you know.'

'He's avoiding me. Not sure what I'll do without him.' Tears flowed. As I offered her a crumpled Kleenex, Wendy came over.

'Jean's right. You could do better, darling. You don't realise how pretty you are. Henry's, well, a bit wimpy, truth be told. And on the chubby side.

I had to intervene. 'Don't listen to them: Henry's lovely. But there's plenty of time for other boyfriends. Rosie's had dozens.' I nodded over to her, idly chatting up Malky Taylor who should have been at the far side with Conor. Wendy too, stood doing nothing. Only Jean and I were working, she fiddling with electrical connections, I logging ammeter readings.

Maia gave a huge sigh. 'Still, Dad'll be pleased. Says Henry's a distraction.'

Jean abruptly pulled a plug. 'Och, never mind your Dad, he's much too controlling. Mind you, mine's the opposite – couldn't care less. We're victims of our dead brothers, you know. Your Dad wants you to be a medic to compensate for losing Pieter. Mine ignores me 'cos I'm not Josh. But we need to be ourselves – do what we want. We've only got one life, then we're dead too.'

Wendy looked flustered. 'Too much death and psychology at this table, sweethearts. I'm off. You have to get over death, don't you know – it's a fact of life.' With this enigmatic utterance, she abruptly left. Rosie left to help Malky (the reason I suspect, that he'd come over) and I watched Conor leave them to it. As they started switching on plugs at the bench, he ushered Wendy out, arm round her shoulders, eyes scanning the room.

'There's ownership, not affection in that arm.' I hadn't realised I'd spoken out loud until Jean scolded me.

'Wendy's an adult. You're always on about him, Beth, give it a rest. OK, he's smug, but if I didn't know better, I'd think that deep down you fancy him!'

I shrugged off her hug, annoyed. She shook her head and switched off everything.

'Come on, I'm only teasing! Let's go.'

I grudgingly went, feeling sad. I'm a sponge for misery. These poor girls, losing brothers: Pieter from a tonsil op, Josh from a tumour. I couldn't imagine such grief. I'd never lost anyone.

◆

Second term thereafter is a blur. Ralph and I dated. Wendy kept disappearing with Con. Henry and Maia were together but I worried her neediness and constant insecurity about him might scupper the relationship. Rosie went out with God-knows-how-many blokes. Jean just worked. The exams seemed easier second time round. I gained some confidence. Conor had shedloads.

◆

Conor turned from the second term results board. 'Fine: straight 50s.'

Wendy confronted him, hands on hips, tight-lipped and pale. Her marks had plummeted from high sixties to borderline.

'I can't believe I let you persuade me to go out so much. A good degree means more to me than you do. That's it!' Her eyes blazed.

'Please yourself! More fish in the sea, madam!'

As he swaggered off, Ralph muttered, 'And he never stops fishing.'

Rosie added, 'Well at least she's seen through him at last!'

I looked at the sobbing Wendy and prayed she had.

◆

After Easter we returned to start panicking about the looming, important, Professional Exams. Even Conor frequented the Library. Whenever I tried to avoid him, Ralph chided me. Like the majority, he saw Conor then as a hilarious one of the 'in' crowd, the witty, raucous centre of anything happening. But we all have Achilles heels.

◆

Friday of week eight, Ralph found Conor slumped on a bench in front of the Faculty building staring down at the panorama of Glasgow below. He didn't flinch when starling poo splattered his leather sleeve from the noisy flock overhead, swooping from Gilmorehill's gothic towers down to the West end steeples. Wiping mess from the wooden seat, Ralph sat down.

'What's up, man? You OK?'

'No, Ralph. My mother's dying. But the real problem's my father. He's a dick.'

'Why?'

'Oh, he hasn't been to see her. The nuns say she's … She hasn't got long.'

'It's MS she's got, isn't it?'

'Yeh. She can't cough now and she's got pneumonia. She's had practically every antibiotic. It's lucky for us she's still conscious, but maybe not for her. She keeps asking for Dad. Aisling and I are sick of making excuses.'

'I'm sorry Conor. It must be hard on you and your sister.'

'The fucking bastard's banging his secretary, you know. Has been for years. And the rest! He's wiped mum out of his life. We're not in it much either. Not that that's much loss.'

Ralph said nothing, thinking of his close family.

'He had us shunted off to boarding school the minute he put mum away. He was never at home for the holidays, just palmed us off to Uncle Tom Cobbley or bloody camps. There was always a 'crisis'. I ask you – for steel tubes? More like corporate jollies to Gleneagles or dirty weekends away. I've no bloody illusions about J.C. Towmey. He's a fucking arse! That's why I'm in medicine. Once I get the degree, the money licence, I'll be free of him.'

'Oh, Con, I'm sorry. Want to come for a pint? It's after five.'

'No. I'm going to Lanark tonight. But thanks. I'm praying she hangs on till after the finals. Only two weeks now. Can't believe it.'

'Come home with me for a bit after the exams. Dad's got a boat on the Avon – we could go off?' Ralph stood up.

'Maybe.' Conor wiped his wet eyes on his stained sleeve.

◆

The last week in June I fought out from the rugby scrum at the foot of the Medical Faculty stairs. I was joyous: two Distinctions. Sadly, Ralph had a Chemistry re-sit.

'So much for yer high-powered A-levels, Semple!' Malky gloated. Ralph glowered.

'Fancy being shown up by your girlfriend!' Conor's barb hit home. Ralph left abruptly.

Maia was thrilled she'd passed. 'It's fantastic!' she bubbled. 'And Henry's asked me to stay with his family for a month.'

◆

Next night, at the end of term disco, I was jostled at the mirror. Not sure why we bothered. Most boys were too drunk to notice smudged mascara and it was very dark in the White Elephant Club in Sauchiehall Street that we'd hired.

'I'm worried, Beth. What about Points of No Return in Essex?'

'Listen Maia, these aunts sound so "in your face" I doubt there'll be an opportunity for rampant sex!' Suddenly I had space. At the mention of sex my neighbour ceased mascara- twirling and backed off. Rosie behind chipped in, smacking her pointlessly pale lipstick.

'Well, if all else fails, there's always Sister Immaculata's advice.'

'What's that?' I asked.

'When faced with temptation, try mental arithmetic.'

Maia giggled. 'What?'

'It's impossible to think about Sin if you're doing long division, apparently. Or maybe complex fractions might be better for avoiding Eternal Damnation? Seriously though, I could go to Boots for some Durex? But I'm sure Henry's quite prepared.'

Maia looked horrified. 'You'd ask an assistant for condoms?' Rosie's laugh rang out.

It had taken all of Ralph's persuasive powers to get Conor to go that night. His mother was still poorly. Wendy offered a sympathetic ear. He took it and Wendy home. It was the beginning of Wendy and Conor again. But the End of Us.

'Sorry, it's too early to get serious with one girl' said Ralph, pecking me on the cheek and patting my arm before leaving me standing on the dance floor.

I walked away stunned and found Jean. She commiserated, but I just shrugged. 'Who wants a moody boyfriend who can't take a tease?' and went home early. I feared I might cry in public, having realised he meant more to me than I liked to admit. But my Dad was so thrilled at my results that I bucked up and convinced myself

Ralph simply wasn't reliable, though I had to acknowledge how good he was to Conor when his mum died a few days later. Even I gave him a hug when I met him in Byres Road looking distraught. Then Ralph took him home.

Hawkbridge House
Somerset
1st July 1968

Father,

I can't put 'Dear' on a letter to you. Were the plumed-horse-hearse, the walking Victorian mourners and those ridiculous over-the-top flowers a salve to your conscience – eh? Mum hated fuss. I'm glad I slapped your ugly mug at the hotel. My hand had been itching since the grave-side. I'm amazed you found time in your busy whoring schedule to take time off. You had no right to criticise my booking of Cartland Bridge Hotel as Mum wanted. It was much easier for her friends than poncy Glasgow Central Hotel. Consideration was never your strong point, was it? Nor compassion. Shameful you didn't have the courage to visit her at the end. It was pitiful how she asked for you every time.

The lawyers tell me I have sole charge of my Trust fund as I'm eighteen. If you don't take care of Aisling properly till she gets access to her money when she turns eighteen (that's August next year in case you've forgotten) I'll kill you. Am staying with Ralph. His father has been very decent and has suggested a financial adviser. Aisling will arrange for my stuff to be sent on when I get a flat. You no longer have a son. Go to Hell.

Conor

By early July we dispersed. Rosie took Wendy to her family's Marbella villa for a couple of weeks then volunteered in a Calcutta school. Jean went as a leader to a kid's camp in Oregon with the

British Universities' North America Club. I found a job in John Smith's bookshop and spent the summer reading. Eventually I stopped seething at Ralph, reckoning the fewer the distractions the better. Second was acknowledged as the hardest year. Anatomy was the killer subject set to sort the men from the boys. And girls.

Seven

Corpses, Wee Willies & Other Worries

For me, good dreams and happy memories run in technicolour reels. Sad and unhappy ones come frozen as monochrome stills. First day, second year, is a monochrome sepia still of a subterranean room looking like a post-disaster press photo of dead bodies. You know the thing – the deceased laid out in rows awaiting identification by distraught relatives. But no one was coming to claim these corpses: they were all ours.

The body is where it all happens, disease, so we needed to understand its construction and learn the terminology necessary to sound erudite, like 'lateral', 'superficial', or 'sagittal cross-section'. But Anatomy was horrible, an overwhelming assault on the senses, its stench ten times worse than dogfish. Cloying, acrid, stinging fumes burned throats and watered eyes, while barely masking the stale, earthy smell of death and decay. Dissection was a different assault, not on the senses but on the emotions. Sticking scalpels into dead bodies, dissecting and unravelling innards is ghoulish by any civilised standards. It needs a certain mind-set. Not all of us possessed it.

◆

Wendy froze in the doorway. 'I can't do this, Beth, it's too ghastly!'

'Of course you can!' I wasn't too keen myself- but needs must.

Distress etched her ashen face. 'They made me kiss my mother …' she whispered.

I was appalled: she'd been eight. Now she stood, hands in prayer position with her thumbs pressing tightly on her lips, eyes closed. Conor barged past with a proprietorial squeeze of her buttock. I pushed him off and coaxed her in.

'Where's Table Six?' I asked calm, composed Jean. She pointed. We followed.

An Anatomy Room isn't a morgue. No corpses lurk in fridges, they're all out. More bodies, more formalin fumes. More oppressive. An existential wake-up, a first confrontation with death for most of us. Behind an innocent unmarked door in the quad corner, this sepulchral laboratory held rows of steel trolleys lying under strip lights, each hosting a body shrouded in a crisp white sheet. I held my breath. Could I detach my emotions and deconstruct my humanity enough to consider these mere biological specimens? My stomach lurched. This wasn't chopping up dead fish, this was slicing into the flesh of humans who'd breathed, laughed and loved. The white sheets offering a modicum of dignity were whipped off. We were surprised by their size (mostly small), their colour (grey-green), and their consistency (that of tanned leather). I stood wondering who these people had been whose remains lay cold, exposed and naked on a dreich October morning.

We girls clustered round our allotted body in an offshoot of the big hall with other female students including embryo dentists. The boys were in the main area.

Wendy shrugged off my arm to stand with a fixed, joyless smile reminiscent of cyanide rictus (my summer had been spent reading Agatha and Ngaio). Holding her head high, nostrils flaring, she said, 'Let's call him Fred!'

'Fred?' I squeaked. 'Why call him anything?'

'Oh, Beth, darling, we're here for three terms picking over his bits. We should call him *something*!'

'Hasn't he got a wee willie?' Rosie peered at the cadaver's flaccid hapless member.

'What?' I spluttered.

'Haven't you seen one?' Rosie's left eyebrow rose.

'Well, actually ...'

'Not even your father's?' Wendy's shrug wafted perfume towards me: Nina Ricci's L'Air du Temps, now forever associated with death. Like her purple chiffon scarves. Always immaculate, Wendy, believing that you never knew when Mr Right might appear. I doubted He'd choose an Anatomy room and prayed that, for her, He wasn't Conor.

'Pa doesn't wear PJs. He parades around commando in the summer, doesn't yours?'

I was horrified! My Dad trooping about naked? However well-bred the Honourable Gwendoline was, incest and other stuff sprang to mind. I'd met her ramrod-backed ex-Guards officer Dad and couldn't imagine him wandering trouser-less. None of my school friends had hinted at naked fathers. Was this a feature of Lothian high society? Along with taking back an evening dress you'd worn (though not actually paid for, it being on your Dad's account) or buying four pairs of the same shoes in different colours courtesy of a Trust fund? Wendy had everything I hadn't, but I liked her immensely. Not an ounce of malice in her. Didn't deserve what happened. I stood gaping. Rosie wouldn't let it go.

'Come on girls, you must've seen a few peckers? You're not telling me you haven't *done* it, are you?' Rosie's beautifully-plucked eyebrows shot into her shaggy blonde fringe. 'What else d'you do after a few dates? I mean after you've sussed out he's not a serial killer, or worse, find out he's really, really boring?'

'We can't all be the bicycle of the year,' muttered Jean, frowning over her specs, donned in haste as she couldn't tolerate her contact lenses in the stinging atmosphere. She looked crossly at Rosie. She considered her a frivolous lightweight who barely broke into her social life to open a book. In truth, Rosie was super-smart, needing to study less than Jean who worked like a dog. I'd sensed tension when Jean found herself in Rosie's group again. Thankfully, Rosie missed the bicycle jibe. I sighed. They'd have to cope with each other. Easier than coping with formalin. I dabbed my eyes as Adonis arrived.

'Morning ladies! I am Bill Lothian, your Anatomy demonstrator!'

Rosie fluttered everything: sooty eyelashes, blonde hair and shocking pink nails. I curled my bitten, ink-stained ones. Bill drew himself to attention at our table. Rosie drank him in grinning, head tilted to one side, admiring his neat bum as he donned his white lab coat. Muscles did it for her. Bill was late twenties, curly blonde hair, piercing cobalt eyes. Good looking. And he knew it.

'Good Morning!' More vintage Rosie: the smile, eyes lowered, lips licked. Bill beamed, as men did. Jean rolled her eyes, folding her arms with a disgusted shrug.

'Right, troops, let's get started!' Adonis rubbed his hands together.

I was sitting looking at the body. 'Do we know who he is? Where he's from?'

'For goodness sake, Beth,' said Jean, shaking her head. 'It's a body. We don't need to know who he was or what he liked for breakfast, we just have to chop him up, see what goes where, from under what. Like, where the hip bone connects to the thigh bone, sort of thing!'

'Quite,' said Bill. 'To answer your question, most bodies are donations to medical science, but some are from India. Bought or donated, I dunno.'

'Bought?' I was appalled. 'Do we know how he died?'

Maia, surprised me. 'Oh, Beth, does it matter? We can't tell what race he is, since he's green. Nor his age, since he's shrivelled. But he's definitely dead. We can't help him, so let's get on.' Only her tremulous hand betrayed her true emotion.

Our body was dark, malnourished. A Calcutta slum, maybe?

Shouldn't he have had a funeral pyre by the Ganges? If he was Hindu, would he be denied re-incarnation if he hadn't been cremated? Or was that Buddhism? I was miles away. Bill coughed.

'Attention! Enough hearts and flowers, let's start. Abdomen first. Got your Wyburn's *Concise Anatomy*? A textbook actually written by this August Department! The score is, read the book, follow the directions to dissect the area we tell you each week. Flag the muscles, nerves and so forth with their names and each Monday morning we'll have a Viva.' Bill nodded at us sitting on stools around the body.

'Viva?' asked Rosie.

'An oral exam on the week's dissection, graded by me. The usual alpha, beta etc.'

'An exam EVERY Monday morning?' shrieked Rosie.

'Yes. Someone's life in the future could depend on your knowledge. You can't just miss out an area one day to get your hair done!'

Jean met my gaze. *Hair indeed!* My hackles rose. 'Why are we in same sex groups here? In other labs we aren't now. And why shunted in a corner like we're second class citizens?'

'If you look closely, you'll see the gentlemen largely have female, and the ladies, male, cadavers. Having same sex groups avoids embarrassment, I suppose.'

How very Victorian – and he didn't answer my question on us being side-lined.

'Right, let me check off your names.' He read them out, grinning at Rosie Scott, nodding at Jean Shaw and jotting down something at my name, probably 'T' for troublemaker. He smirked at Wendy's 'Tuffnall-Brown,' but made a gratifying hash of Maia's tongue twisting Szakolczai. Then he nodded at Fred. 'Right! Page 9. Start. I'll be back to see how you're getting on.'

Picking up my canvas kit, already grotty from a year of dissecting lesser creatures, I selected my scalpel and made the first abdominal incision. No way would he be able to think us girls squeamish!

'Well done, Miss Slater! Off you go!'

Most demonstrators were embryo surgeons doing Anatomy MDs. A tough career, where bravado may be of protective advantage, but there's a fine line between it and arrogance. He left with a wink at Rosie. We got a dismissive wave from a tell-tale ring finger. Rosie had a blind spot for those.

Our vivas were marked archaically with 'alphas' (as excellent) and 'gammas' (as failed). That term Rosie enjoyed alphas and beta-pluses from her paramour Bill. However, the next term, Martinmas, Bill vanished. Rumour was the Prof was displeased at his 'over-familiarity' with a student at the Christmas Party. It couldn't have been Rosie, absent at a charity ball with her parents. Mr William Lothian emerged years later in London as an eminent transplant surgeon. Friends down there hint that he still has a reputation, and query whether all conquests have been willing, but disappointingly, he has not faced censure. I'd have hoped that with their greater numbers, modern girls would feel more empowered. In our time, however, even some of the boys weren't all that tough.

◆

Frank inhales appreciatively. 'Great fags, Con. Where d'you get these?'

'Present from Yousef. Duty Free Sobrani cocktail cigarettes. Cool, uh?'

'Yeh. Take the smell of bloody death out of your nose.' Frank flicks ash onto the steps outside the Anatomy room.

Conor straightens up from slumping over the railings. 'You OK, mate? You look pale.' He doesn't mention Frank's retching at the cadaver's uncovering or exit as Dan unravelled yards of green bowel.

Frank raises the thin brown cigarette for a drag. 'I'm fine. But makes you think a bit, this place, doesn't it? Like the stuff we've been taught, Resurrection and the rest. You're buggered if you're cremated, but how does it go if you've been dissected? D'you miss heaven and go to purgatory or what?'

'For fuck's sake Frankie-boy, these are carcasses, not people! You'll go mental thinking about it. Priests are wankers. Why, we even had one that thought he was bloody Elvis. Couldn't get enough gold-embroidered white satin and big rings. Right poof!'

This comic deviation doesn't engage Frank, shakily taking a last puff before tossing and grinding the butt. 'Our priests were all poofs. Right arses. Liked arses too, those bible buggers. Fucked us up, big time. In the Name of the Father. Come to Papa, Frances Xavier...'

The faltering whisper alarms Conor who shivers. Dead leaves swirl round the quad though the sun is shining. 'Enough!' He laughs, slapping Frank's back. 'Who needs fathers?'

'You have no idea, Con. Hope those priests rot in Hell. And my father.'

Conor has had enough and throws his spent cigarette over the railing.

'Forget it! Hell's an invention to keep the masses in check! Let's go back in, finish up and go for a drink.'

Steering Frank through the door, Conor wonders if his friend is ill: so slight and gaunt. He said he was excused competitive sport at school. Had he had asthma? Or something else? Today Frank looks out of it and has tiny pupils. From medication? Or something non-prescribed? He suspects Frank doesn't have the bottle for medicine, never mind for doing surgery as he aims. The pressure and responsibility could get to folk. Like Colin something-or-other, whose place Frank had slotted into. He'd tried to hang himself over re-sits. Stupid cunt fucked his suicide too, ending up brain-damaged and doolally in a locked ward. Medicine needed a thick skin, a scheming brain and connections if you were to survive. He had all three. Like that Physics Pass/Fail Oral exam end of First when he'd spotted the external examiner's St Kentigern's tie and guessed correctly the Edinburgh Prof had been a peer of his godfather. Cue a chat about Nudger's family and stock-broking success and bingo, wasted time! He smiles, slicing through a muscle. He has what it takes. But Frankie-boy?

◆

Maia loved Anatomy, being strangely unfazed by dissecting the dead and delighted by the subject's logic and orderly classification. She won a First Class Certificate of Merit which her Dad proudly framed. Our other second year subjects were Physiology and Biochemistry: heavy and hard. I took to revising on the bus, envying those who'd moved into flats near the University. Though they had a stress I didn't – flatmates. The hall lads and girls had moved into rented flats at the start of Second. With his mother's legacy, Conor bought a flat in Hyndland Road and moved in Frank, James and Ralph as paying guests. They seemed to rub along. I was only in the flat once, in final year. The memory still makes me shiver.

Eight

Unexpected Adversities

Three weeks into first term of Second, Jean was removing a test tube from the spectrometer with tongs to set in a rack at odour-reducing distance.

'This liver mush is disgusting!'

'No wonder, it's been fermenting for weeks. But we can bin it after today.' Rosie jotted down Jean's readings into her Biochemistry lab book.

'I'm never going to have liver pate again!' Jean screwed up her nose.

'You should become vegetarian.' Ralph spoke from across the bench.

'Oh, no- live without bacon? So how come you're veggie, is it a family thing?'

'Dad sent my pet lamb for slaughter when I was six and I've never eaten meat since!'

'Thought your folk had horses?'

'Oh, we have lots of other animals – sheep, ducks – even a few goats.'

'But isn't it hard to be vegetarian? You must be sick of salad.' Jean shook her new time-saving bob and looked over to him.

'There's veg, lentils, rice, eggs, chips, baked potatoes, beans – it's not that hard.'

'Have you converted your flatmates?'

Ralph laughed. 'No. Conor's a dyed-in-the-wool bacon roll man. Frank and James live on beer and Fray Bentos tinned pies.'

'Heard your flat in Hyndland Road is great.' Jean pipetted and squirted. 'Dan told us Conor *bought* it. Lucky him. I see he isn't in today.'

'Yeh, well we give him rent. Works out OK. Not sure where he is. Had a set-to with his father last night. Surprised. The old boy gave him an account with Campbell, Stewart and MacDonald to order stuff – like classy leather sofas and comfy beds.'

Dan chipped in above the din of Ralph's tubes spinning in the centrifuge.

'Unlike ours! We'll be lucky if they last the term. Though Henry and I *do* have air-conditioning – the wind whistles through the windows! Mind you, it's better than the drag of coming in every day by train. Thank goodness the Biology Bursary's let me rent.'

Maia smiled. 'Well deserved! You're a lucky duck living five minutes away in Otago Street. No wasting time at bus stops like Beth and me. And you can do what you like!'

'It's not all sweetness and light, staying in flats, though, is it?' Jean winked at Rosie.

To my surprise, Jean had asked Rosie to move into her flat in nearby Barrington Drive after her flat-sharing old school friend Megan had proved a disaster. A few weeks into term the drug-taking party-loving chum ran off with a rock musician to a commune in the Borders.

'It'll be fine as long as Rosie doesn't bring home strange guys, keeps her rubbish in her room and doesn't leave coffee cups breeding penicillin under the sofa.'

She looked sternly at Rosie who went pink and changed the subject. 'Wendy says Nessa's real untidy. She's used to having a maid.'

We looked over to Nessa's bench. She waved. I'd only got to know Nessa Rosenbaum after she moved next to us in labs, replacing a 'drop out.' With her blue-black hair piled high, aquiline nose and slender neck, I saw her as Nefertiti. But she was the Jewish daughter of a war-time Austrian refugee, now a prosperous London silversmith. He'd only agreed to her coming to Glasgow if she lodged with her Aunt Miriam in Newton Mearns on the south of the city. Miriam was a lovely lady whose lavish hospitality we enjoyed frequently during our student days. In '68 we thought needing a chaperone was quaint, but seeing how things turned out for Nessa, it was probably wise. Boys lusted after her, but she usually socialised accompanied by her cousin, Sam.

'Surprised Nessa's Dad let her move out of Miriam's.' Ralph looked over from his bench at Rosie.

'Och, Miriam persuaded Mr Rosenbaum she'd be living with an Earl's granddaughter in a listed gorgeous flat. It is fabulous, by the way- up in Great Western Road near the Botanic Gardens.'

'Oh, yuck!' Jean held her nose and poured her cloudy potion down the Biochemistry sink: glycogen successfully isolated from rat liver. (Relevance? *Pass!*)

'But have you seen the Shamoun boys' flat in Novar Drive?' Dan whistled. 'It's like something from the Ideal Home Exhibition! His dad hired an interior designer. Yousef's at the dentist this morning but said to tell you lot they're having a house-warming on Saturday. Everyone's invited. Nine till midnight. Booze provided. Request for shoes off at the door – they've got a cream shag pile!'

One up, 33 Novar Drive, was in a red sandstone terrace of smart pre-Great War tenements. It had a stained-glass panelled front door, two bedrooms, ornate high-ceilings, black leather couches, purple and gold Liberty wallpaper, deep-pile carpets and a chandelier. There was a state-of-the-art kitchen, though neither boy could cook. On offer at the party were sophisticated fizzy Lambrusco and cheese cubes on sticks with pineapple cubes and olives. Drinks came in proper glasses, not plastic cups. Yousef's brother had finally joined him after two years of trying to get into Strathclyde University Business School. Butros was two years older, taller, slimmer and smoother. And was immediately drawn to Nessa.

'So where have you been all my life beautiful lady?'

I groaned: he sounded like a B-movie gigolo. But Nessa had had a sheltered upbringing and fell for Butros with a clatter. By eleven she was off in his dark green MGB GT. Lovely Sam went home alone, loyally staying schtum for Aunt Miriam. Next day we heard of a 120 mile an hour race through Glencoe after midnight.

'Gosh, the speed! What a thrill! He's quite a guy. Going to expand his father's business internationally. Full of ideas!'

I'll bet. She had that shining-eye-look seen in adolescent pop fans. Or kids in Disney movies. Or someone on a drug-high. Apart from the occasional lecture appearance extolling the wonders of Butros, she vanished for most of first term. A Strathclyde BA obviously wasn't taxing Butros. Jean and I worried; we couldn't afford to miss anything. Overhearing us (one of his specialities) in a Biochemistry lecture, Conor added his tuppence worth.

'Believe me, it'll not be much loss if she drops out – she's a basket case. Only wants a fun life – not interested in medicine.'

He wasn't the one to talk.

◆

After Christmas came peering down microscopes to draw a book of all the body's cells, well, one of each type. The fun of using colouring pencils like at primary school soon palled. Pointless, tedious and probably unhelpful in practice- would a backache patient ever want to see a drawing of a muscle cell finely sliced and dyed pink on a slide? Yet we spent hours on it. Most of us.

Nessa was out on the town with Butros, so Wendy invited Conor over and made him his beloved pork fillet in cider. Conor offered no thanks for it, despite the hassle it had been to conceal the pork from Jewish Nessa with all the fridge subterfuge and air freshener. Wendy was cross. She decided the evening was now her own.

'I'm not going to the pub, I'm off to the lab to finish the renal slides.'

'You're a fool. I've paid a first year Med Sciences guy to do mine.'

'But Con, how'll you recognise the cells in the Spot Exam?'

'God, I'll look at the book the night before – don't fuss! You only need 40% in Class Exams. It's a game. Life's too short. Don't do anything you don't have to do – Conor's Law!'

Wendy attempted to throw her big Guyton Physiology book at him but it was too heavy.

'OK, Miss Prim, forget it. I'm off to the pub.'

Next day she told me he was a lazy ungrateful bastard and it was over. Halleluiah.

◆

Now Physiology, like most of Second Year, involved death and sacrifice. Quite nice otherwise. We worked in self-selected groups. Amiable Henry was chief executioner, becoming swift and deadly at murdering frogs and mice to order using a swift bang on the head. Speed was of the essence. Frog's hearts had to be cut out still beating so we could drip chemicals on them to measure voltages and heart rates. And to frog's legs we gave tetanus. (Relevance? Pass). It was worse at Harvard. Wendy's cousin Sara (one of only six girls) had to anesthetise and cut out bits of living dogs.

Henry rejoiced to find a scientific law bearing his name. Henry's Law was something to do with partial pressures of oxygen dissolved in liquids. Conor boasted he'd get immortality by having a surgical instrument named after him. Frank suggested a vaginal speculum, along with some lewd proposals for what could be done to whom with such a device. Dan and Conor hooted. Jean erupted.

'Oh, shove it, Frank! The only thing which should be named after Conor is a windbag! How did they let you two in? You're a disgrace.'

Frank growled, 'Well no one'd want to stick it up you, anyway!' His lewd gesture was ignored by the passing male lab supervisor: no change there.

Jean was my partner. Mid-term we had an experiment of practical value for a change: taking blood pressures. Unable to hear a thing through my stethoscope, I consulted the manual. 'Apertures should face forward and down, corresponding with the inclination of the external auditory meatus.' Ah! My earpieces were pointing backwards. I turned them.

'Eureka!'

Jean laughed. 'Maybe we should read the manual more often.'

It was a standing joke. They even posed an exam question on it: 'You have been provided with a laboratory manual in order to *A) Carry to and from the laboratory in the hope of developing manual dexterity later useful in Surgery or B) Read, digest and carry out the experiments as indicated or C) Wipe your instruments on.*' At least the Physiology Department had a sense of humour. I loved Physiology. Until that Thursday.

With a correctly inserted stethoscope, I put the BP cuff on Jean's arm and pumped it up. Deflating it gave me 200/130. Everyone else had around 120/75. I repeated it, and got 200/130.

'Dr Graham?' I called over our new lady supervisor.

She repeated it and looked at Jean. 'How are you feeling?'

'Fine.'

'Headaches? Visual upset? Water works problems?'

'Bit headachy at Christmas, the family doc said my pressure was up a bit then, probably stress after exams. But I'm fine. I played squash at lunchtime.'

'Sorry, my dear, this is more than stress, needs looking into.' Dr Joyce Graham fetched an ophthalmoscope to peer in Jean's eyes. 'I think you should see your GP.'

'Mine's in Dundee.'

'I'll phone Student Health. Take it easy till we check this out.' Her smile was barely there. Jean shrugged. Joyce returned with an appointment for five. I went along, worrying. Jean was thinner, eating poorly and looked increasingly tired, I'd thought due to excess sport though I'd not commented for fear she'd get mad. She emerged mad anyway.

'I've to go to the hospital tomorrow! How can I tell Dad?'

'Don't be daft, just phone him. You'll get pills.'

'Not so sure. Idiot says I need blood, urine tests, kidney X-rays. It's down from earlier, but he says there must be a reason for it at my age. And no sport. Crap!' Close to tears, she shrugged off my offer to walk her home. 'No. And don't tell the others!'

I looked up hypertension and kidney disease that night but didn't know enough to make head nor tail of it.

◆

By week seven she was in hospital. Friday lunch break Rosie, Maia and I visited in time to see our Surgical and Medical Profs, McPhater and Killin, emerging from her room with a stooping red-haired chap between them whom Rosie identified as Jean's Dad. Prof Killin had his arm round Professor Shaw's shoulders, guiding him along to his room. My heart sank.

Rosie breezed in and unstacked chairs. Jean had been lying curled on the bed facing the windows, but sat up as we sat down. She looked smaller, dimmer. Even her hair.

'How are things?' I asked.

'I've got Renal Carcinoma.'

We were shocked into silence. Cancer: a deadly enemy. Not expected at our age.

'They tell me I'll lose a kidney, but you only need one and

the other looks OK. I'll maybe need radiotherapy afterwards too, depending on the biopsy.'

'Gosh.' Rosie was wide-eyed.

'At least they say it's early and it hasn't spread.' She took a deep breath. 'I'm not giving up, you know. I'm carrying on.'

The door opened to Dan, clutching a brown paper bag.

'Hi, Dan!' Jean looked pleased.

'I've brought you some Kit Kats and soap, Bronnley's Fern. Mum suggested soap.'

He looked like a little boy lost, a knock-kneed schoolboy, though without the short pants. Jean thanked him and patted the bed for him to sit. He did, looking as if he felt it was going to give way any minute. We left them to it and were surprised when only minutes later he caught up with us on the way to Biochemistry lab.

'She will be all right, won't she?'

'Sure, Dan!' Rosie hugged him. We walked on. But she had no idea. Nor had I.

◆

Jean had her nephrectomy two days later and went home for six weeks convalescence which took her into the Easter holidays. Yousef drove me in his car up to Dundee on the few remaining term Saturdays to give her lecture notes and lab results. The Dean was accommodating, arranging for some intensive personal teaching sessions in Anatomy at the end of the holidays, and lab work tutorials. He suggested she miss the June exams and take the re-sits. On our visit she looked pretty good. She took the work stuff then requested gossip. I obliged.

'Wendy is still with Conor, though they're like a faulty light switch: off and on!'

Jean sat up on the sofa and sipped her tea. 'It's bound to end in tears. He's a waster. So, what's everyone else up to?'

'Well, I'm sorry to say, Nessa's besotted with my brother. I don't see a happy ending there either.' I was glad Yousef had said it.

'They're both intelligent women. It's up to them.' Jean sighed.

'They say love is blind, don't they? I can't comment, having never been *in love*.' She looked wistful.

My heart skipped a beat: would she get a chance? I hadn't considered the possibility she might not make it. 'Maia is still with Henry,' I added, by way of light relief.

'Great. And Rosie?'

'Ah, amazing record – four months with that vet student Nigel Fraser and by the way, I mustn't forget, Frank sends his love.'

Jean groaned. 'Oh God! Can't he take a hint? Worst date in the world, banging on about the importance of 'finding yourself' and things 'acceptable between consenting adults' – save me! I should have listened to you, Beth, but I felt sorry for him. I tell you, I miss you lot loads, but God save me from Frank the Wank!'

We rocked with laughter. The nickname stuck. Like Con the Plonker.

'Won't be long till you're back. And I'm sure you'll manage. You've got plenty of time to study in the holidays. Heavens – that the time? We'll need to dash.'

We hugged her and left. Her mum Janet always fed us. Gave us doggy bags too. Lovely woman. We never met her dad, always working even on Saturdays. As were we, apart from a few discos and the odd Wimpy or Chinese carry-out in someone's flat. Second Term exams flew by. We all passed.

Third term. Now to meet our first real, live patients. Patients. That was what a medical career was all about, wasn't it?

Nine

First Combat

The challenges of a medical career involve more than book knowl-edge, there's also developing rapport with patients and relation-ships with colleagues. Some of us were more naturally predisposed to that than others, which became obvious when we started train-ing in the wards.

Depressing grey and cream décor underpinned by cracked lino dominated NHS hospitals in the sixties. On our first clinic morn-ing at St Mungo's Hospital, a grim-faced nurse ushered Henry and I into a side room which contained two enamelled tubular bed-steads (chipped), two bedside tables (swollen-edged chipboard), orange bed curtains (frayed) and a stack of maroon leatherette chairs (cracked). Consumer comfort hadn't yet reached the NHS. The main wards were Florence Nightingales: noisy, lacking patient privacy but staff-convenient as nurses could easily see all the pa-tients billeted in rows down each side like in an army barracks. I was beginning to feel like an army recruit myself. Second year was a tough battle. I hoped meeting real patients would re-enthuse me.

Lovely Gordon was in there already. He'd arrived early and was encircling the made-up bed with chairs. As his Dad was a sur-geon, he knew the score. Our Surgeon was dapper: silver-haired, pin-striped and sporting a silk tie and carnation. As befitting a consultant God, he wore no white coat, unlike us. Mine was newly laundered, though un-ironed. No time.

'Good morning, boys and girls, I am Mr J.T. Baker, Consultant Surgeon. I hope you'll enjoy your term here.' A charming smile. 'These initial sessions will be short, but don't be afraid to ask ques-tions. If you don't ask you'll never learn! This is ... a patient!' He stepped aside to reveal an elderly gentleman. 'Pop on to the bed, Mr Donald. Let's start from first principles, boys and girls. How do you address him?'

Rosie, first as ever, flashed a smile. 'Good morning, Mr Donald?'

'Excellent. Always check records for a patient's correct name and use 'Mr or Mrs. Be polite and professional. What next?'

'What brought you into hospital?' Rosie again: coquettish, head tilted. Impossible girl. A few heads shook.

'Yes, I agree with your colleagues,' said JT. 'The answer's liable to be 'an ambulance' or 'a taxi!' Any other suggestions?'

'What's wrong with you?' suggested Ralph.

'Ah! That invites "You tell me – you're the doctor!"'

'How about just, "How are you?"' Yousef offered.

'Better, but you might get, "Ill – that's why I'm here!" Anyone else?'

Mr Donald lay back grinning, hands behind his head.

Henry groaned. 'What can we say without risking a smart-alec answer back?'

'How about "How can I be of help?" or "What seems to be the trouble?" Keep it general. Think before you open your mouth in case something you say might be misconstrued. And introduce yourself – patients have the right to know your name, especially if you're going to examine them intimately. Let's start with you telling me your names and why you're doing medicine. It might help to concentrate your mind. Starting here.' He pointed at Yousef.

'I'm Yousef Shamoun from Luxor. I want to be a surgeon...'

'I'm Beth Slater from Govan. I'm not sure what speciality ...'

'I'm Henry Thompson from Essex. I've always wanted to be a surgeon.'

'Ralph Semple, from Somerset, wanting to be a physician or a GP.'

'I am Frank Hutton and I wish to be a surgeon.'

'I'm Rosie Scott and think paediatrics might be fun, but maybe I'll wait till after Finals and see who'll have me.' She twisted her ponytail and chewed today's red lips.

'I'm Conor Towmey from Lanarkshire and I'd be happy to have Rosie now and not wait till after Finals!'

JT glared. 'Humour may help get you through the ordeal of a medical education, but sexual innuendo has no place in clinical medicine. Please refrain from any more remarks of that nature concerning ladies, especially when patients are around. This is not the Union Bar.'

'Sorry. It was only a joke. I plan on being a surgeon ...'

'Indeed?' Giving Conor a withering look, he turned to the rest of us. 'Remember 90% of diagnosis comes from a good history, 9% from the examination and only 1% from today's expensive fancy diagnostic tests. In my view tests should merely confirm what a good doctor has already diagnosed at the bedside. Miss Slater, could you could take this patient's history?'

I gulped. 'Good morning Mr Donald, so what is troubling you today?'

'Excellent, my dear.' Behind Baker's back, Conor stuck a finger in his mouth aping a vomit.

'It's the bike. I've trouble riding it.'

'Because of pain?'

'Oh no, it's the swelling.'

'Where? On your foot?'

'No, it's a bit more delicate than that.'

'Er, is it ...' I swallowed, 'your penis?' I flushed. The boys grinned. Old Mr Donald, bless him, saved the day.

'It's the wedding tackle, Miss. Swelled up, it did, got bigger and bigger. Got the fright of my life. Like a melon – didn't know which side of the bar to put it on going to the shops!'

'And have you had treatment for it?'

'Hang on Miss Slater! Don't jump the gun. Right, it's a swelling but we're still not sure *exactly* where. We've an idea of its size, but did anything happen to cause it? Does anything make it worse? Needs put in context, lots more questions! Anyway, for today's purposes, let's take a look. The lurid curtains were drawn while

72

Mr Donald disrobed helped by Nurse Frosty-Face, all smiles with JT while we mere recruits hadn't merited the time of day. Minutes later we gazed at a supine Mr Donald minus his trousers.

'Perhaps Mr Towmey would care to examine? Let's see if he is as smart as he thinks he is.' He beckoned Conor. 'Describe swellings by site, size, colour, consistency, mobility, translucency – revise that in Hutcheson's Clinical Methods. Well, boy?'

'Swelling, left ball, size of a cricket one.' He clutched the testicle. 'Tense and solid.'

'Indeed? What are you thinking of, Mr Towmey? Would you like me to grab you by the privates? The correct nomenclature for balls in medical circles is *testicles*. And you might have sought permission before assaulting Mr Donald by asking 'May I examine you?' Always ask if it is tender first. And how do you know it's solid? Did you shine a torch through it, or are you blessed with X-ray vision? This mass seems a bit large for bowling at stumps. Most Scots are more familiar with fruit than cricket. As the patient said, this was a melon and has now shrunk to a grapefruit.'

'Sorry, Sir.' Conor looked anything but.

JT stepped up to shine a torch under the swelling, demonstrating its translucency.

'This is a hydrocele, a collection of fluid formed round the testicle especially common in older men. We have drained it but it has recurred. Unfortunately, definitive surgery is contraindicated by the patient's heart condition. Thank you, Mr Donald.' He closed the curtains and led us out into the corridor. 'So, you've seen your first real 'live' patient presenting with a swelling. Lumps and bumps are common with many possible diagnoses. Look up conditions of the testicle. Order your mind like a textbook from the beginning. It will stand you in good stead throughout your career, especially in the wee small hours when your brain is half-dead. Conditions can be from infection, inflammation, vascular causes, cancer and so on, as you'll learn in Pathology next year. On Wednesday we will consider breast lumps. I trust Mr Towmey will have grown up by then and can desist from inane schoolboy humour.' Conor was scarlet. 'Today's main lessons? Order your thinking. Examine gently. Try to treat all patients as if they were your mother or friend.' J.T. Baker waggled a finger at Conor. 'And Towmey, you may see twenty or more patients a morning, but you may be the only doctor they see that day. They'll remember more of your conversation than you of theirs and can be upset, enraged or embarrassed by a flippant remark. They may even sue. They certainly are unlikely to share your humour. Good morning.' Taking a pipe out of his pocket to pack with tobacco, he left.

'That old buffer's past it,' Con snapped at Ralph. 'The future's in diagnostics, not prehistoric bedside manners!'

He went for lunch alone. The afternoon was spent practising mouth-to-mouth artificial respiration on a manikin in a Physiology lab. I expected smart remarks from Conor about 'who he'd like to give it to.' But for once he was silent.

◆

Two weeks later Jean was back in Barrington Drive with Rosie. I went over.

'You feeling OK? You're still looking a bit peaky.'

'Och, don't fuss! The nephrectomy scar's itchy but otherwise I'm fine.'

'Have they decided about radiotherapy?' I poured out tea.

'They can do it over the summer to let me have a bash at the June Degrees. Think I'll leave Anatomy till the re-sits though.' The doorbell went. 'That'll be Dan.'

'Getting serious? Mm-mm?' Rosie's eyes narrowed. She shrugged suggestively.

'No, just friends!' Jean laughed. 'We're only going for a walk in the park. But he is sweet. Came up to Dundee in the train every weekend. And amazingly, it's the first time I've seen Dad take an interest in any of my boyfriends – said he's a 'sound lad with great ambition!'

'That's not what Beth thought!' Rosie nudged me.

Jean rose. 'He's sobered up now and a nice person to chat with. Really quite shy.'

◆

I was feeling similarly about Gordon. He was a nice person to chat with. I'd been enjoying Saturday drinks and visits to the pictures with him. We started 'dating' after he'd been devastated to hear Heather *did* have someone else: she'd announced her engagement. I'd asked him out (bold for me!) really to cheer him up, but he was good amusing company. He read a lot, was interested in the arts and world events and not just football or rugby. Plus, he had a car for weekend escapes to country pubs. A semi-platonic relationship suited me. Workload gave enough pressure. Anatomy was like a telephone directory: so much to learn, so much never used later. Like 'Corpora Quadrigemina' and 'Column of Fornix' which linger bafflingly. Poor Henry developed panic attacks. His eczema went mental. Steroid tablets helped his skin but dropped his mood. One day, overhearing from behind a pillar in the Ref, I realised how bad he was feeling.

'I'm sorry, Maia, but I think we should stop… I mean I can't give you the time…'

'Oh, don't be silly, Henry!' Maia sounded cross.

'I'm really sorry, but I need to concentrate on work. Let's cool it for a bit, OK?'

I saw him leave looking flushed and miserable. At a consolation session with Maia in the Ladies, Wendy didn't help.

'Forget him Maia. As I've said before, you deserve better.'

Maia wept on my shoulder but soon surprised us all. After a few days she didn't mention Henry, though greeted him politely in class. A pattern many of us followed over the years: glossing over break-ups after a few awkward days. Unlike at school, where tensions seethed for months. All good practice for the trials and tribulations of our later careers: a life of picking yourself up and starting all over again when floored. I became good at that.

◆

Rosie had learned how to move on early. Her life was her own. She did what she wanted and slept with whom she chose, though her admission that she'd slept with Adonis appalled me. In my Calvinist eyes, adultery was a dreadful sin. Her only concern was avoiding pregnancy after a private termination she'd had done while at school when it was still illegal. Since then, she'd taken the pill and reckoned since she enjoyed sex she might as well carry on. Rosie was one of life's survivors. My 'worry' energy transferred to Nessa, whose passion for Yousef's sleazy brother, Butros, baffled me more than Rosie's promiscuity.

He'd arrive after morning lectures.

'The car's up the road.' He'd jerk his head towards the MG.

Nessa would trot after him. 'Where to today?'

'Edinburgh.'

Miles away. Bang went afternoon classes. Butros called? She jumped. I also began to suspect he hit her, though she insisted a black eye was from a 'fall.' In our view, she was far too deferential to him, too accepting of the clandestine nature of their relationship. When Mr Shamoun visited at Easter to berate spendthrift Butros, she stayed away. Aunt Miriam was still in the dark. I became so worried I had to say something.

'If you keep missing classes, Nessa, you'll fail.'

'Oh, Beth! Stop worrying! He's everything I've dreamed of, you know. So handsome! We're flying to the Paris Fashion Shows, imagine? And he's clever. Soon he'll be in charge of his father's luxury hotel chain.' Her eyes were distant. 'To get free of Dad I need a man of substance!'

God, she sounded like a deranged Austen (or should it be Galsworthy?) heroine!

'This is my chance to fly the coop!'

I'd seen photos of her palatial home in Mill Hill, London: it bore no resemblance to a hen house. 'But what about your degree, Nessa?'

'Oh, Beth, you've never been in love like this – it's amazing!'

She wafted off. Beautiful but nuts. I couldn't have taken such passionate distraction. Work needed all my energies.

◆

Second Year was classes, labs, notes, books. And comfort food. Henry ate chips, I, chocolate. There were occasional boozy nights out. Some folk, like Dan and Conor, dispersed stress by circuit training, running or rugby. But by third term even Con ditched them. Wherever possible though, the boys went to Saturday matches. They rarely travelled home. But one Friday near Second Year Professional exams, Dan met Henry coming out of the Library.

'That an overnight bag, Henry?'

'Sorry Dan. Have to go home.'

'That's a bit sudden!'

'Mum's in hospital. Just ran here with some very overdue books. Off for the sleeper. Didn't think I'd catch you so left a message on the kitchen table. Sorry won't make the match tomorrow'

'What's wrong?'

'Oh, Mum's depressed again. All my fault. Told her about the six weeks' camp in July as part of the Army Scholarship. Idea of me in the Forces brought all the Dad stuff back. Think I'll have to pass it up.'

'Tough.'

'Yeh, I'd like the money.'

'Know what you mean. I'm passing up on the intercalated B.Sc. they've offered. Can't afford an extra year.'

'What about Beth, she doing that Biochemistry one?'

'No. It's worse – two years extra. She told Jean last night it's too long. Anyway, mustn't make you miss your train. Hope your mum perks up. See you Sunday night. Bye.'

◆

The Degree Exams went well. Wendy did fine after red-carding Conor at term end. Dan got a Distinction, another Bursary and a Hunter Physiology Medal. Remarkably, Jean passed Physiology in June, and Anatomy and Biochemistry at September re-sits. Not remarkably, Conor slithered through a Pass/Fail Anatomy Oral.

Dan met Conor exiting his Oral, smirking.

'Hey, definitely pays to have an unusual surname!'

Dan looked puzzled. 'What?'

'Turns out the external examiner was an old friend of the parents from way back. Must have fancied mum- he looked devastated when I said she'd died. Only asked me the course of the ulnar nerve and to identify a liver cell. Piece of piss!'

Dan raged. Conor through Anatomy on a nod? And him wanting to be a surgeon.

◆

The year ended with the usual disco, this time in Queen Margaret Union. Waiting in the foyer for Maia, I was accosted by Frank who was combing his hair without a mirror and leering at passing girls. His Brut could take on all comers.

'So, what are you up to in the holidays, Beth?'

'I've got a job at the Royal Southern's Haematology lab. What about you?'

'Gordon's dad has got us porter jobs. Good money. Malky's going to the Eastern General with Gordon, as you probably know, while Con and I are at St Mungo's. Then end of August we're all heading for the Costa Brava!'

'Right.' Gordon had told me about the job, but not the holiday. Och, well, maybe they'd just decided ... I wondered how Frank was going to manage as a porter, him being such a lightweight. They had to hump patients on and off trolleys.

Maia emerged from the loo with a giggling Patricia Bonham. She looked 'out of it.' I wondered if she'd taken some drugs: I'd heard rumours Frank was selling. She was a diminutive, pretty girl who made even Frank look tall. She, having a 'B' surname, wasn't someone I knew well, but Frank obviously did. He grabbed her by the wrist and sucked at her neck (it couldn't be described as a kiss- a hickey was developing as I watched) before marching her to the bar, hand clamped on her bottom.

'Something about him!' Maia shivered. 'Always grabbing somebody's backside.'

'Yep. Jean's right – he is Frank the Wank!'

Maia didn't smile.

'Hey, it's *Yellow River*, come on, I love this!' I steered Maia through to dance as the disco blared. After a bit, we stood singing with Gordon and Henry. Some of the twenty who'd failed anatomy were drowning their sorrows. Most hadn't come. Maia was tired and left before midnight, but I stayed till one, leaving Rosie doing a 'Moonie' wrapped round her Nigel, and Dan sitting with his arm around Jean. We were all happy to have survived Second Year, the major battle of our campaign to become doctors. I began to hope we might all make it.

Ten

Capitulation

January 4th 1971, two years later

The night has been interminable. Her mother hasn't stirred. The morning paper flops onto the mat. The Glasgow Herald front page is distressing. The death toll is over sixty. So many families grieving because of a football match. Her father never missed the New Year's Day match, the annual derby between Old Firm rivals Rangers and Celtic. Rangers' Ibrox Park stadium was just up the road. The roar from the crowds had formed a backdrop to her childhood Saturdays.

She reads explanations for the carnage. Collapsed crush barriers. Mayhem on fateful Stairway 13, site of previous fatalities. No lessons learned. That poor footballer must feel devastated, his last-minute injury time goal causing that roar, the crowds turning back to see if it was a Rangers equaliser. How he must be suffering. She feels guilty: it's for the dead she should save her pity, for lives extinguished in crushing panic amongst the swirling mass of leavers and returners. So many families having to live on without loved ones.

The paper is fat for a Monday, its pages filled with photos of the dead. Margaret Ferguson is the only girl. A heart flutter: it could have been her if she hadn't been working in Casualty. Or young Allie. She scans the eye witness reports. Rescuers arrived promptly but couldn't force their way through the crowds. She tries to read. Tears well. She thinks of the lifeless blue man in the resuscitation room they'd tried so hard to save and the weeping fans outside in the corridor, rivals embracing as they sat on the floor united in grief. The battlefield that was Casualty. Her first major disaster and it will be her last. Anatomy dissection hasn't toughened her at all. That had involved old bodies, from lives that had been lived. These casualties had been young, vital, loved. She puts down the paper and puts on the kettle.

Yesterday is a blur, merging into the frenetic one before. Should she phone the hospital? Is there anything she should be doing now? Like ask when Uncle Jim can come home? His concussion is a worry. But ribs will heal. Dad's side are tough cookies. He'll mend. Unlike some. She catches her breath. Morgues. One in Glasgow's Saltmarket yesterday, one in a hospital basement on the other side of the world. The guilt of being alive. The aching emptiness of being left. Life can never be the same. Her eyes fill. She sits down.

'Toast?' Her friend comes into the kitchen and opens the bread bin. 'Or do you have cornflakes?' She lifts the newspaper out of the way,

setting out four places.
'Toast's fine.'
Life has to go on. But a medical degree doesn't.
She's decided she can't do it. Can't deal with losing patients. Not now.

Eleven

Disease, Death & Demons

October 1969. Third Year started amongst death. Pathology tutorials took place surrounded by chilling Victorian bell jars. Worst were the pickled two-headed foetus and the lumpy disembodied head of a Neurofibromatosis victim: an Elephant Man. Little better were pots of tarry tumorous lungs and swollen fatty alcoholic livers, not that they deterred the dissolute chain-smoking boozers amongst us. Nor did a tutorial on destructive syphilis deter sexual activities. Week four Conor was treating us to graphic details of his weekend exploits, probably aimed at shocking Maia who moved her chair to squash in between Jean and me.

'I'm going to tell Wendy. He's disgusting!'

'Save your breath, Maia. She'll laugh, just say he's winding you up.'

I was more worried about Jean, currently slumped on Dan's shoulder. She'd returned too soon. But Maia was drooping too, her exuberant hair scrunched tightly into a severe low ponytail. Though she didn't mention Henry, I knew she was still hurting. He was also looking down, exhausted with the workload and going home every weekend to see his mum. Only Rosie bubbled on cheerily, oblivious to the pots of diseased organs, pre-occupied by the Love-of-her-Life, Nigel Fraser. A nice chap. Unlike Wendy's beloved Conor Towmey.

◆

Wendy was sitting on the sofa in Conor's Hyndland Road flat copying out notes when he nudged her. 'Gonna get me a coffee?'

They were alone. Ralph, James and Frank were at the library. She irritably moved Conor's feet from the coffee table where he'd dumped them on the open textbook she was using. Her brow furrowed. 'Get it yourself. I'm busy.'

'Come on, take a break! It's weeks till the exams. Let's go for a drink. I'm bored!'

'You nearly made me fail last year. I only came tonight because you said you were working. This shirking will catch up with you one day, mark my words!'

'Don't whinge! Let's go to bed then. Or why not do it here? The sofa has interesting possibilities … It's only eight and the boys won't be back till ten.'

'There's more to life than sex.'

'Is there?' he laughed. 'Nothing wrong with something that makes you feel good.'

'Speak for yourself. You never take your time to make sure I enjoy it. Selfish in and out of bed, that's you!'

Conor sat up. 'That's a bit below the belt. I've never had complaints before.'

'Surprising. Anyway, I bet you don't have any Durex, so it's not on.'

'Condoms? Why? You're on the pill!'

'I'm not one of your 'on demand' bits on the side.'

'Oh, come on, you know I'm faithful now. There is only you!'

'Hmm... Not sure I believe that. And you never listen to me. I told you yesterday, I'm off the pill. My BP's up. Student Health offered me Durex but I think you should take some responsibility, so if you want sex you'll have to get some.'

'I don't like them. They're too tight, like eating a sweetie with the paper on it.'

'So, you're more of a man than the rest of the population, is that it? Durex too wee? Hurt the big man? What a joke!'

'Come on, you've just finished your period, it'll be all right.'

'No!' She batted off a hand attempting to cup her breast. 'I'm beginning to think Beth's right. You're a selfish bastard.' Slamming her books shut, she stuffed them into her bag and before Conor could think of a smart reply, left.

Moments later a key turned in the door. Ralph walked in. 'Where are you going?' he asked, seeing Conor lifting his coat from the hall rack. 'I just passed Wendy on the stairs crying. What's up?'

'Oh, nothing. She's being a tit. You want to come for a drink? Why are you back now? The Reading Room shut early?'

'No. I'm hungry and had no cash on me. I've some beans here …'

'Think I'll go see if any of the Casino girls are off at ten. Haven't seen Ingrid for weeks. You wanna come? I'll buy you something there.' Conor put on his coat.

Ralph carried on into the kitchen. 'No thanks,' he called over his shoulder. 'Beans on toast will do me. I want to go over that Path stuff. I need coffee, not booze.'

'God – surrounded by boring swots! I'm off.'

It was half an hour before Ralph realised the reason he felt freezing sitting studying in the lounge was because Conor hadn't closed the front door.

◆

The next night at nine Dan waited outside the library for Jean who'd promised him a drink before closing time. She came out with a pile of folders under one arm and an empty shoulder bag over the other. Looking down at the binders in puzzlement, she clumsily tried to balance her bag on the wall and put the books into it, not noticing Dan only yards away. As he stepped forward to help, she staggered.

'Hey, you OK?'

'Got a headache. Bit dizzy. Mibbe we shouldn't … what was it we were going to do? Let's just go home. Can I have your arm?'

He put her bag over his shoulder and walked slowly down University Avenue, Jean clinging to him. Every so often she'd stop, close her eyes, take a deep breath and swallow. Dan wasn't sure how he got her along to Woodlands Road and round into Barrington Drive. The stairs to her first floor flat were a challenge. By the time they reached the front door he was holding her up. Concerned she would collapse, he didn't rummage for her key but rang the bell. Rosie opened the door and Jean lurched past her to the bathroom. At the sound of vomiting, Rosie followed. Jean was slumped between toilet and washbasin, clutching her head and looking seriously unwell. They dialled 999. Rosie was cross with the Ambulance switchboard.

'No, she's not drunk, she's recently had surgery and radiotherapy.' She slammed the phone down. 'Arrogant bastards, assuming all students are drunks!'

Dan looked distraught. 'I bought her a burger at lunchtime. D'you think it's that?'

'I doubt it. She's been up in the middle of the night leaving empty paracetamol packets around. And this morning she couldn't get her lenses in, kept dropping them. Then she was repeatedly cleaning her glasses, I'm not sure she could see properly, but she wouldn't let me take her to Casualty.'

'Oh, no! Do you think its meningitis? Does she have a rash?'

Rosie knew she didn't. She didn't suspect food poisoning or infection, but seeing Dan's face, she didn't say what she thought.

◆

Two weeks later I sat in St Mungo's Hospital across the bed from Professor Shaw. He'd been crying. I wasn't far off it myself. Jean wore a white jersey turban. The last of her fiery hair had gone. The least of her worries, she was deeply unconscious. A nurse took her temperature and blood pressure. 'Wouldn't you like to go for a cup of tea, Dr Shaw, as Jean has another visitor?'

'No, I'll stay. Thanks.' She left. Ian Shaw looked across the bed.

'Thanks for visiting Jean so faithfully. It's kept her spirits up.'

'It's no big deal, Professor. We all love her. She's a great girl,' I said softly, one eye on Jean, immobile and as white as the sheets on which she lay. Such a deterioration in 24 hours. Yesterday she'd been talking.

'You know, I don't think I've ever told her how much I love her. She's been such a great support to Janet over the years since Josh. And I don't think she knows how proud I …' He sighed. 'Now it's too late. You know the prognosis, Beth?'

I saw his eyes fill.

'We're surprised, thought the radiotherapy would have …'

'It was an undifferentiated tumour. They can be especially tricky.'

'Sister said metastases now,' I whispered, turning my back to Jean, for we'd been taught hearing is the last sense to go. Since he, of all people, was discussing this in front of her, I considered it ominous. 'Are they sure there's nothing …?'

'How's Dan? Haven't seen him.' The Prof's change in conversation said it all.

'He doesn't do sick visiting …' I laughed nervously. 'I know it's odd in a medical student, but maybe it's because he loves her and can't take seeing her like this. Feels powerless he can't fix her.' *I have spent a lifetime apologising for Dan.*

'I'm cross she didn't say about the latest headaches. Perhaps if she'd said earlier there might have been a chance of… well, a bit longer. It's unbelievable, losing another child.' His voice broke.

I had nothing to offer except my grief, burgeoning as it absorbed his. 'I'd give anything to get back the time I've missed, working so much. She's my life.' I left quietly, hoping Jean could hear him. In the corridor Janet Shaw had a half-empty cup of cold tea spilling in her lap. I took it from her to place on the floor. She was staring into space.

'How are you?' I asked. Stupid question.

'Quite peaceful, isn't she? Thank God for morphine. Won't be long. We'll delay the funeral till after the exams if need be. Start tomorrow, don't they? You've all been so good…' She trailed off, staring again, switching inwards. I went to my lecture. They were the first parents I sat with who were losing a child. It never got any easier.

◆

It was a freezing December Saturday when Yousef drove us up to Dundee in a hired minibus. St Paul's Episcopal Cathedral was packed with her old school mates, orchestra chums, her National Hockey Team, family and student colleagues. I saw her Dad's old friend, our medical Professor, Brian Killin. Her old choir sang. The eulogy reminded us how much she'd packed into a short life. Jean's sudden departure shocked and sobered us. Our first 'casualty' to leave the battlefield. Sobering.

Funerals can bring out the best in people. I watched Conor consoling Wendy. They'd sat apart, having arrived late. On the church steps as we were leaving, Nessa collared her. Relations had been strained between them all term, with Nessa accusing Wendy of doing nothing in the flat and Wendy accusing her of being a prima donna. Nessa had been phoning me concerned about Wendy's disappearance, but in the emotion of the day her concern exploded into anger.

'Where've you been? When the boys said you weren't in Conor's flat I was worried sick – even phoned your Dad. It's been four days. I was about to call the police.'

'Conor and I went for a break, so?' she snapped. 'Why did you bother my father? That's it, Nessa. We're finished. You can move out!'

But when after Christmas, Wendy returned to Great Western Road, so did Nessa. No more was said, according to Nessa, but relationships between Wendy and the rest of us were strained. We felt powerless. It's hard when you see a friend blindly heading for disaster.

◆

Over the holidays Wendy phoned several times, trying to build bridges. I was unconvinced by her argument that, despite being occasionally bossy and difficult, Con was a 'pet.'

'You have to understand what an awful life he's had, his mum dying and his father being an indifferent monster. And he's so sweet to his sister, Aisling.'

Didn't convince me he was a safe bet for a life-partner. She sounded fragile. I didn't disclose any of the boys' stories about Conor's womanising: she'd only deny them. I couldn't understand her blinkers. It's only now I know abused women can become self-delusional. Then, I only thought she was depressed.

'But all that doesn't explain the way he treats you, Wendy. I mean ...'

'Oh, you don't understand how I need Con! Dad wouldn't let me go to Austria skiing with him and Ralph's family. And you don't know how horrible it is here. I'm all alone in this beastly, big cold house while Dad's at his Edinburgh club, or drunk in the study. It's really getting me down. I'm so fed up, darling. Not sure I can go on.'

I knew the remedy but could only urge her to see her GP for an anti-depressant.

◆

Second term started with Prof Killin's 'Christmas' sherry party, postponed until after the holidays because of Jean. Apart from his friendship with her father, he knew folk wouldn't have felt like partying. As I sipped the ritual brown goo, he surprised me.

'Miss Slater. How would you like to go to Sydney?'

'Gosh! I'd love to!'

'I'd like to send girls on the Exchange Scholarship this year. It's to the Sydney Royal with Prof Mitchell. A nice chap, did medicine at Glasgow with me after demob.'

'Sounds great! But will it be expensive?'

'You need £100 for the airfare, but room, board and an allowance are provided for eight weeks in hospital and a two weeks holiday bonus. The English Speaking Union run it to encourage graduates in Medicine, Dentistry and Engineering to emigrate after qualifying, but no strings are attached.'

'Great! So, who else is going?'

'I'm wondering about Maia. I don't want to pressure her, but I feel she'd benefit from stretching her wings.'

I felt a bit disloyal saying that money might be a problem for Maia. It wasn't, in the end. Her godmother gave her the £100 in a flash. Before I knew it, I had a passport, and my visa application was on its way. Maia already had a passport from trips with her godmother. Her dad was ecstatic: a scholarship for his girl!

◆

Dan was anything but ecstatic that term. After Jean's funeral he dropped out of sight. When no one had seen him for 24 hours, Henry and Ralph went looking and found him in a Byres' road pub looking like a tramp. Getting him back to the run-down flat he shared with Henry, they tried to put him to bed, but he hit out.

'Get the fuck out of ma life, ye nancy-boy! You Henry, wi' yer curly-wurly hair an' yir big fat belly, who are you tae tell me whit to do? Ye should be sellin' yersel' doon Blythswood Square wi' all thae ither shirt-lifting poofters!'

Despite being English, Ralph and Henry got the gist of Dan's drunken relapse to West of Scotland playground vernacular. Henry, not taking lightly to the 'poofter' comment, swung a punch. Dan fell back on to the bed, blood spurting. Luckily, he was already swaying bed-ward when the blow came so his nose wasn't broken. Fingering the trickling blood, Dan gazed at his hand. Tears came.

'You of all peepul... I thocht you cared aboot me!' he wailed. 'See me? Ah was gonnae marry Jean, set ma eyes on her at oor interviews. She wus bonny, an' clever – everythin' a man cud want- but ah thocht she wus tae good fur me, an' a bottled it, ah nivver told her proper! Ah never said goodbye!' Dan sobbed, bleeding onto Ralph's shoulder.

They stayed up all night pouring coffee, sense and orange juice into Dan. Having seen drunks woken up in Casualty by fructose drips, Henry thought fructose-rich orange juice might help. It did, and was thereafter adopted by us for hangovers. Next day, Dan turned up for lectures sober and clean, albeit blood encrusted. At the weekend, Henry sent Dan home to Clydeside and enlisted Rosie and me to help clear his room. The door had been closed all term. It took three hours and six bin bags to dispose of furry banana skins, crushed beer cans, empty cider bottles and chip-shop wrappers. He hadn't gone home for Christmas since his mother had gone to the US courtesy of a small Littlewoods pools win. We dumped the bags and sent the salvageable bedding and clothes to the launderette. Dan returned suitably grateful and apologetic. Ralph convinced him there are times you need to face reality: Tennant's Lager only multiplies demons. Wendy offered a kindly ear and made excuses for him, even his inability to visit Jean in hospital, but I felt the whole thing bizarre. Doctors visit the sick! Anyway, their chats were mutually beneficial and Wendy brightened up. I hoped they might get together.

◆

Often on Sunday nights we girls went to Nessa's Aunt Miriam for a grand supper and grand piano. Wendy played brilliantly. Maia said she was concert level, and Miriam suggested to Wendy that if she was unhappy in medicine maybe she should change to music? Wendy considered it, but every time she phoned home to discuss it, her father was too drunk. I counted my blessings.

Not all doom and gloom though. Third was the year of twenty-firsts. Conor had a weekend boys-only-Rugby-and-Rose-Street-pub-crawl party first term which saw Frank and Liam unconscious on drips in Edinburgh Royal after a drinking game. They survived, but with permanent bars from a few of the capital's hostelries. We never heard the full story. I doubt they remember. Ralph recalls some time spent in a police station while Frank and Liam went in the ambulance. Fortunately, no one was arrested. Then.

Rosie's Valentine's night birthday party was more sophisticated. Maia declined, but Nessa, Wendy, Ruth, I and some of Rosie's old school chums hit the town. It was an evening of firsts for me: roulette at the riverside Casino, a Tequila Sunrise, a prawn cocktail, fillet steak and champagne. Later a limo whisked us to her mansion home where we didn't go to bed but danced, sang and played silly games. Overnight it snowed heavily so at dawn we made snowmen and snowballs, fighting on the lawn in anoraks, evening dresses and wellies. Borderline insanity. Happy days. We forgot about medicine for a few hours.

Learning medicine dominated our lives and altered our brains. Some of us imagined we had the illnesses we were being taught. A little knowledge is dangerous to a med student: every cough is TB, every lump cancer. Conor self-diagnosed 'meningitis' (actually tension headache and heat rash). Dan hounded ENT for a laryngoscopy fearing throat cancer (inflamed vocal cords from screaming at the Welsh in freezing, wet Murrayfield). Headaches worried everyone, after Jean. I didn't have time for imaginary illness, being too anxious about failing. So many subjects. We'd done Anatomy to understand body structure, Physiology to understand organ function and Biochemistry to understand how cell chemical reactions kept us alive. In Third, Pathology and Microbiology gave us what disease looked like (ugly) and what caused it (bugs, genes and lifestyle), while Materia Medica (another telephone directory) taught us potential cures. Miraculously, we mastered these and passed first go. Except Conor who had a Pass /Fail Oral in Pathology. This time he didn't know the examiner, but he bragged he'd 'nailed it' by time-wasting discussions about the relative cirrhosis-inducing properties of different alcoholic drinks. That boy always morphed his disasters into triumphs.

◆

The last Theta disco of third saw Wendy storm off from Conor again. I can't recall whether they were actually together at its start. With reason, Dan dubbed them our 'Burton and Taylor.'

Drunk Conor left with a gang to go up Byres Road for chips

and ended up in Maryhill Police Station. Once sober, he dialled Malky's home. Tom Taylor QC listened to Conor's diatribe on police vindictiveness. He remembered this cocky lad from his son's twenty-first and knew his wealthy father was currently waging a lucrative law suit through Taylor and Eliot. By six am Tom had dispatched a junior. By seven Conor was out. By noon the bill was despatched to Towmey Holdings.

Conor laughed all the way home in the taxi. What was the problem with knocking off a bobby's hat and having a wizz up a Byres' Road alley? Everyone did it! Lucky he'd fallen and bashed his nose. The lawyer assumed 'the polis' had done it. He didn't disavow him of the idea. No worries.

The rest of us had had a less eventful night. Rosie danced with Nigel, Nessa with Butros, who was leaving early for his flight home. Dan and Ralph squired some nurses. Gordon and I left late. A happy night of dancing, snogging and singing to Mungo Jerry's 'In the Summertime'… 'the livin' was fine.' We'd battled half-way.

The boys headed to US internships. Maia and I set off with Qantas to Sydney. By way of fateful synchronicity, at Heathrow we met Wendy, heading for San Francisco and Rosie bound for Botswana.

Only three of us returned.

Twelve

Foreign Deployment

God, it's a long way to Australia, especially accompanied by wailing kids from families on the Government's £10-a-head Assisted Passage Migration Scheme off to start new lives Down Under. I thought this sounded exciting. Maia didn't.

'Imagine going all that way not knowing when, or even if, you'll see your extended family again? I couldn't do it. Awful!'

I was beginning to wonder if I'd done the right thing agreeing to go on this jaunt with Maia. At the departure gate she'd panicked and I'd had to push her up the gangway. When the doors closed she became rigid. By take-off she'd clutched my hand so tightly my fingers went white. It didn't help my own anxiety. This was my first flight. She'd at least flown to Europe with her godmother. I had to take the window seat as she couldn't bear to see the earth so far below. When we exited briefly in Teheran for re-fuelling, she moaned about the manky cramped bus which took us past dusty grey buildings standing in dusty grey desert. Then held her nose in the dusty grey hangar decked out as a Kasbah shopping opportunity. The machine-gun-toting soldiers, scudding jeeps and ominous parked fighter jets signifying the Shah's days were numbered made us both tense. With a taciturn Maia, it was a long flight.

◆

Thankfully, a warm welcome and waiting car greeted us at Sydney Airport to whisk us to our home for the next eight weeks, the nurses' home in Sydney General. We weren't allowed to stay in the all-male Medical Residency. The only other female intern stayed locally. I was miffed at being lumped in with nurses, already weary of folk's assumption that if I said I worked in a hospital, I must be a nurse. Not that there's anything wrong with being a nurse, it's just the presumption. But being in the home had compensations. It was high on the hill above the hospital with lovely gardens of bougainvillea and frangipani. The season might have been their winter, but it was a warm springtime to us, even though the Prof's wife greeted us in a fur coat. (I suppose it's all relative).

The other internship students were Aussies in their 'winter' break who hosted barbecues, beach trips, cinema outings – and pizzas.

'You've never had a pizza?' Rebecca was incredulous.

'No. We've got Italians in Scotland since the war, but they do ice cream.'

I got laughter from my working partner Ned. 'Isn't it too cold for ice cream?'

'It's never too cold for ice cream!' laughed Maia.

◆

Weekdays were spent in wards, operating theatres, clinics and even autopsy rooms. Fantastic experience. Maia relaxed a bit, though was still exceedingly quiet. I tried to make allowances. New situations unsettled her. We muddled along. But four weeks in came our first serious row. Ned asked Maia out. She turned him down.

'You're an idiot, Maia! He's gorgeous!'

'Then you go out with him!'

Our second row came two weeks later. He invited us for a holiday with his family at the end of the internship. Queensland had tropical sun, palm-fringed beaches and pineapple plantations. His family home on the Gold Coast had a pool. I accepted avidly. Maia left the dining hall without a word. Later we had a heated exchange.

'Maia, why did you stomp off?'

'I've got stomach ache.'

'Really? It looked so rude.'

'Couldn't help it. I was sick this morning and felt sick again. You could be more sympathetic.'

'Are you really sick? It was very convenient to let you off the hook. We're going to Queensland though. It's a great idea.'

'I don't want to go...'

'Why not? You can't pass up on a free holiday! Is it because you're scared Ned's keen on you? For he is ...'

'Oh, sod off!' She slammed the door. Totally unreasonable. We had two free weeks and scant cash: this was a gift. Besides, Ned was nice. For the second week, Prof Mitchell's sister had invited us to Adelaide. The Aussies were a generous and friendly lot. Maia grumbled, but I accepted both invites. Returning to the hospital for tea alone, I wondered if Maia had PMT, despite previously denying its existence. On my return, I heard her throwing up in the bathroom, and again next morning. Oh, well, she probably had a bug. But I was still mad and left without speaking. She missed morning class.

'She's got the Wog,' Ned asserted.

'What the heck's that?' I asked.

'Aussie vomiting bug. You might call it gastric flu.'

'You're having me on – "the Wog"?'

'No. Right up! It's viral. Australia's paradise for viruses. You know like "Q fever," first isolated in Queensland?'

'Really? So how d'you treat this Wog?'

'Plain biscuits, flat Cola or lemonade. You should take her some over this arvo'. Works every time you're crook!' Aussie is a foreign language.

I trotted out at lunch time to buy his suggestions. Maia accepted Ned's prescriptions gratefully, promising to buck up. By Sunday week seven, she'd agreed to Queensland. Ned's Dad would collect us on the last Saturday and drive us up the scenic coast. I couldn't wait. On the Wednesday Prof Mitchell held a farewell barbie at his lovely waterside home. Maia sat with Ned chatting freely about her family and laughing at his jokes. Bit late, but she was finally socialising instead of endlessly scribbling. My only scribbling was brief notes to mum and Gordon, who was having a whale of a time in New England. Maia was always scribbling in her diary. One night in frustration I'd yelled 'Diaries are no substitute for life'. That provoked a slammed door, but perhaps it had hit home.

Ned confided he was very taken with Maia, but he held back. At least she hugged him when we left the party, giving him a peck on the cheek and looking relaxed for the first time in weeks. What a lot of time they wasted. Ned was shy (rare in Oz) and tall, lean, tanned and well-groomed. Even his shorts had a knife-edge crease. She could've done worse. I couldn't wait to go to Surfer's Paradise for sun, sand and sea.

◆

The San Francisco summer was baking. The melted road tar wafted acrid fumes which nauseated Wendy as she boarded the limo with her male cousins, all dressed to the nines, not a sweat-shirt or trainer in sight. The cars had been air-conditioned, the open-air meal tempered by the Oceanside breeze, but back here in her bedroom the whirring ceiling fan was ineffectual. The window's panoramic view of the Bay and Bridge held no more interest for her than the day's events. Discarding her nightdress, she lay naked. It was 3am.

Cousin Sara's wedding to a Senator's son had been in a Country Club outside the city. A lavish affair. Coral co-ordinating napkins, flowers, candles and the eight bridesmaid's dresses. The jollity had accentuated her misery, even though her father had turned up, danced with her and told her how lovely she looked. But now he was Jack-Daniel-unconscious next door. She felt so alone. Four weeks with no word. Then on the hall table she'd found the white envelope post-marked New Jersey which now lay crumpled on the floor. She remembered Conor's face as he swore undying love. She'd believed him when he smilingly agreed to her proposal and afterwards, made love even more passionately. He'd promised to write. She wished he hadn't.

◆

Summit, New Jersey,
July 14th, 1970

Dear Wendy,
Taken me a bit to get round to this. There's nothing for it but to say it straight out. I'm not getting engaged. No way am I ready to settle down. And definitely not with you. I've found someone who isn't as needy. You can be too clingy. It's wearing. Being so desperate isn't appealing. Time you sorted yourself out, my girl. I'm not a psychiatrist, but at times I think you come over as a bit of a

basket case. Sorry about your mum and all that, but we
have no future together. Never did, if I am honest. Can't
make it clearer.

Hope you've had a nice time in America.
Love, Conor.

Love? How could he put that? She should never have told him of
her mother's suicide, nor her depression. Nor suggested marriage-
what had she been thinking of? She wished she'd never met him.
His betrayal with someone else was like a physical wound. She
feared he'd delight in broadcasting that he'd turned her down. How
could she go back to face everyone? The bridge was silhouetted
against the dark star-studded sky. Dawn wasn't far off. She sat up.

◆

Nine thousand miles away a thin blue airmail was being penned.

> *St Xavier's Mission, Botswana,*
> *August 14th 1970*

Dear Beth,
Sorry I haven't written. Been very hectic – bed at dusk
and up at dawn. No slacking. I've lost weight – busy and
tight rations. The need here is unbelievable. They even
re-use rubber gloves. One of the nuns hangs the washed
ones up alternate colours on the line, blue Church and
cream UN. When I arrived, I thought it was bunting!
They find humour wherever they can. There's hardly any
medicine. People walk thirty miles carrying the sick – old
and young. I feel so helpless. Dozens of children are dying
from malaria. I'm a bit fevered, myself. Trouble keeping
my eyes open ... wondering if it's sleeping sickness... De-
spite mosquito repellent I'm covered in bites. And I've

thrown up some malaria tabs. Not good. Missed a period too. Especially not good.

    I've had a 'Dear John' letter from Nigel. I admit it was a worry when he went to New Zealand for his post-grad year, but he's fallen for some floozie after only four weeks – four!! Apparently, he's 'in love.' God that was speedy. I'm mortified. I know you think I've had a lot of guys, but he was the first I really thought I'd stay with. Pretty demanding as a lover though. Asked for some odd things. Frankly I think he's spent too much time in farmyards ... I'm now off the opposite sex completely. Beginning to think nuns have it easy. As if that wasn't bad enough, Scruff is dead. My lovely spaniel. Run over by a taxi. Mum just had him put down, didn't try the Vet school or anything! I'd had him since I was 10. He was my best pal, especially since Gran's gone. To cap it all, it's her anniversary today. Life's a bitch. It all seems too much. Wrote to Dad but no reply. Probably off cavorting with Rollo in Marbella.

    One of the docs is taking us on a weekend safari to Kwhai Bridge. With any luck the minibus will be better than the train on the last trip: animal poo has no place in a passenger carriage! Anyway, hope you and Maia are having a fab time. Sister Catherine is going to post this in Gaborone tomorrow. She's taking a cerebral malaria kid to the big hospital. Think he's a goner. Have you ever felt you want to run away? Life's a bitch. Have I said that already?

    Miss you, Rosie xxx

On the twenty seventh of August, I woke at four. Unusual for sleepy-head me, but I did get back to sleep. When I woke again, I shot out of bed. It was 8.20. Stupidly, I hadn't set my alarm after returning from a party. Excess 'grog,' as the Aussies say. I'd gone alone to the party as Maia had pulled a 'sickie.' Doubtless she'd be up already, which made me cross. She could have woken me. Probably sulking again. I knocked on her door: no reply. She must have gone on ahead. I grabbed a handful of Lamingtons from the kitchen and just caught the 8.30 lecture. Full house. Topic? Leprosy. Not much use in the Gorbals, but fascinating. Afterwards I sped off with Ned to an ECG tutorial. I didn't see Maia nor her current 'surgical' partner, Rebecca. They'd been quick off the mark. After lunch, Ned and I strolled in the sunshine before spending the afternoon taking bloods. At teatime in the canteen, no Maia. No one had seen her all day. Not even Rebecca.

I ran back to the Nurses Home. She must have been lying in bed ill all day and I was a terrible, neglectful friend. Her bed was pristine, her clothes neatly folded, but there was no Maia. I rushed round the home. The warden, Mrs Jackson, said she'd looked fine last night. She'd picked up her mail and said she was off for an early night with a book. Mrs J suggested she might be homesick, needing time on her own. Perhaps she'd gone off for a bit of peace and quiet? Rebecca suggested the Mall or the pictures, yet a creeping chill gathered in my gut: she hadn't left a note- something was wrong. Still, with no sign of her bag or new book in her room, I mustn't panic. She'd gone off to read. Or shop. Or scribble.

The gardens had quiet spots. No sign. Back in the lounge, her room, no sign. Ned and Rebecca came to see if I'd found her. They'd phoned a number they'd got for the intern secretary in case Maia had phoned in sick or said she was going somewhere: she hadn't. No one in the hospital had seen her. Everyone knew us from the photos David Mitchell's secretary had put up before we arrived: *Scottish Interns – be nice!* They were, so nice. Ned even asked in the snack bar across the road where we bought doughnuts. They hadn't seen her. Rebecca went home. I tried to stay up in case Maia returned but dozed off, only to wake with a start at 2am. I rushed next door; still no Maia. The warden had gone home. Should I call the police? What was their number? Was I being hysterical? Would they mock me? What to do?

I went back to my room, undressed and lay down exhausted. When I woke it was with a start: my clock showed almost four like yesterday. But this time I could hear a gentle ringing from next door. I went in. Maia's little travelling alarm was 20 minutes slow. Its tinny bell was ringing. Unlike mine, the alarm repeats daily unless switched off at the back. Had this woken me yesterday? Had Maia cancelled it with the top button but not switched off the repeater? Why in Hell had she set an alarm for 3.30am? Where was she?

By nine the warden appeared followed by the police. I'd called Ned and he'd called his father. A friend of his in the Sydney police came personally to question us. We'd seen no strangers. She hadn't told anyone she was going off. I said I'd no idea where she might be or why she'd disappeared. Yet I had a secret I couldn't share; didn't want to share.

Lying on Maia's bed at 4am with tears in my eyes, I'd felt a lump inside the pillowcase: her beloved diary- surely she wouldn't mind if I looked? I scrabbled in her drawers for the key before remembering she'd made a point of telling me she kept it in a little silk packet inside her toilet bag, the psychedelic toilet bag sitting prominently on the dressing table.

The diary had some torn pages. Confetti fragments fell to the floor as I flattened the remaining recent pages and read them in disbelief. My heart swelled. My brain whirled. Could I keep this to myself as she asked?

I knew it was too late.

Thirteen

Guilt & Grief

On the second of September, I sat in Professor David Mitchell's office in Sydney Royal. Mr Szakolczai opposite looked like Jean's father had done nine months before: shell-shocked, automatically accepting pleasantries and returning them. After Maia had been missing for 24 hours he'd flown out to Australia.

Ned's Mum and Dad had come down from Brisbane and checked into a nearby hotel. I don't know what I would have done without them. My mother couldn't speak on the phone for weeping. They knew I couldn't go home until I found out what had happened to Maia and my Mum and Dad certainly couldn't afford to fly out to me. Mum spoke to Matt, Ned's police inspector dad, who assured her everything possible was being done and that they'd look after me.

The papers were reporting the disappearance as a possible abduction. No other theories were offered. We speculated she'd had an accident or fallen into a coma somewhere. It was my first experience of being involved in a media circus and I was shocked at the misinformation and downright lies in the papers. Ned took them from me and binned them. We stopped switching on the TV. His theory was she'd run off for some time alone and would re-appear any minute, contrite at the upset she'd caused. I didn't tell him the truth.

I was wallowing in guilt: I should have seen the signs. Now having done Psychiatry, I know it can be difficult. Once someone decides they've had enough, they will find a way. And before they go, they might appear suddenly relaxed and happy, for they've resolved their problem, made their decision. But I found it almost unbearably hard. I blamed myself, wanted to shout out in despair. The guiltier I felt, the less I felt inclined to bring up the diary. I rationalised that the only thing I could do for Maia now was to keep her secret, be faithful to her memory. I knew now she was a memory. When a solemn woman in a black suit came into the hotel lounge with two uniformed police, I knew. A body downstream. Someone had reported a 'jumper' from the Sydney Harbour Bridge two days before. The timing was right.

◆

After formal identification and more police interviews, I flew home with Mr Szakolczai. Maia would follow later. Kristoff, as he insisted I called him, sat wringing his hands. Olga had been admitted to hospital with chest pain and his son Tomacz had urged him to come home. He immediately booked a flight rather than waiting for the post-mortem results. I didn't say much on the journey. Food trays came and left untouched. Kristoff recounted stories of Maia.

'Such a clever girl. She could have become a professional musician, you know, but she wanted to serve humanity.' He blew his nose.

I was silent. True, she had wanted to help the sick, but her main driving ambition had been to please him.

'But I do not understand, Bethany, why would she commit suicide? The police insist she took her own life and are so sure no one else was involved...' *Well, not at the time she jumped.* 'Why did she not say to you? She always said she'd never had a friend like you!'

I wanted to scream, 'But I failed her!'

'We have to look after the living now.' He patted my hand. 'Olga needs me. My one consolation is that Maia was a good girl who died in purity, a state of grace.'

I felt sick. What did he mean? Purity from no sin or sex? From confession? She hadn't been to Mass since we'd been away: that should have warned me. Her diary lay in the hold wrapped in an orange beach towel beside presents I'd bought for my family from a holiday of a lifetime that had become a nightmare. For the rest of the journey I pretended to sleep. I did drift off once or twice, into a heady maelstrom of alarm clocks, bridges and water heading towards me at breakneck speed. How could a girl so scared of heights she couldn't even climb Edinburgh's Scott Monument jump off a high bridge? She must have been distraught.

At Heathrow, Mum and Dad met me. We went to a hotel. I slept for over 24 hours and they had to book a second night. We hardly spoke on the way back to Glasgow in the train. There was nothing to say.

◆

The next week we went to visit Maia's family to discuss funeral arrangements. Mum and Dad came for support. I was glad. Olga, newly discharged from Coronary Care, sat pale and drained in the pristine lounge of their bungalow. Tomacz made tea. Kristoff was still querying the Australian Police's verdict of suicide.

Olga silently dabbed her eyes. 'They say the balance of her mind must have been disturbed. How can that happen?'

I said, 'I can't imagine.'

The same questions we'd covered on the plane home were re-visited. There were no answers to his questions. Or certainly, none I could give.

'Perhaps you would like to see this?' He offered me a large envelope. 'We've decided not to read it. We've been told she drowned. It is enough. This will be in Medical English we will not understand, but I thought perhaps you might…' He looked out of the window. 'They say she looks very peaceful. Of course she was embalmed for the journey home.'

I breathed in deeply to prevent myself being sick. Oh God, embalming. Formalin. Only weeks since we'd worked side by side in that Sydney mortuary, cutting up bodies: someone else's daughter, someone else's friend. I realised the last two years hadn't hardened me, made me professionally detached about death. Sweating, with racing heart and shaking hands, I took the hospital-crested envelope with its Sydney Police red stamp. Maia's father was talking.

'She comes home on Monday. The funeral will be Friday. Of

course, she will lie in church on Thursday night for the Vigil. Details will be in The Herald and Evening Times but please tell her friends. Would you do a reading, Beth? Anything you choose.'

I shifted in my seat, moved a chintz cushion, thought of some Psalm about healing the broken-hearted, binding wounds. Then I realised that that would be for me, not Maia. I wasn't religious. Dad would find something.

'Of course, I'd be happy to.' I looked through the open door to Maia's bedroom. How often we'd sat there, laughing. Above her bed was the Anatomy Certificate of Merit. And her Hungarian grandmother's wooden crucifix. I swallowed hard. Her parents were now sitting erect and still. Beyond crying. My eyes moved to the photo on the piano of a cheeky looking Pieter at his First Communion. Two lost children. Like Jean's family. Unbearable. I felt compelled to un-gum the envelope in my lap and remove three sheets of familiar typewritten pro-forma. Maia and I had done several. On bodies annihilated by disease, not cruelty. On people who'd lived their lives.

'*Cause of Death: Drowning.*' I skimmed the general stuff. '*Compatible with … No signs of external force or injury. No defence wounds …*' My eyes slowed at the foot of page two. '*Not virgo intacta but no sign of recent sexual activity.*' It was buried in screeds of prose. I hoped he really hadn't read it, or if he had, didn't understand it. I slipped the pages back into the envelope and re-sealed it, cheeks burning. The report also said 'Nulliparous'- never been pregnant, she'd been so wrong! But she'd mentioned missing two periods, so it must have happened before we left. Was there any way I could find out who it was? And get him punished?

Dad was now engaging Maia's dad in reminiscences, admiring old family photos set symmetrically on the piano. He had a gift of putting people at ease. I'm glad that he was there that day. Tomacz arrived with the tray. As my mother poured, she looked at me oddly, doubtless curious at my high colour. I expected her to challenge me in the car on the way home. I'm glad she didn't.

How can you talk to your mother about rape?

Fourteen

The Diary

We started Fourth Year in a state of shock. The papers reported Maia's death. Everyone knew about it, though only I knew why she'd died. First day back Professor Killin called me in. He rose to greet me and took my hand in his.

'I'm sorry things turned out the way they did.'

As I sat down, he patted my shoulder; such a gentle, nice man, unbelievably approachable for an eminent Professor of Medicine.

'It's been hard to accept she's gone. I feel I should have suspected something.'

'Well, Beth, any doctor will tell you they feel guilty about suicides on their watch. None of her teachers here, or according to David Mitchell in Sydney, had any inkling she was so depressed.'

'It wasn't work...'

'What? David didn't mention any note. Nor did any of the news reports here. In fact, some insinuated that it was some kind of accident, although her father said the Sydney Police were adamant it was suicide.'

'Her diary.' I swallowed. 'I read her diary. She meant me to, even told me where the key was. She didn't want anyone to know, but she was raped end of term and thought she was pregnant. But she wasn't. I read the post-mortem report.' It sounded so stark, staccato.

The Professor's eyes widened. He paled and covered his mouth with a closed hand for a moment, elbow on desk. 'Did you tell the police?'

'She told me not to.'

'Did she say who did it? I assume it was a student and not staff?'

'Staff? I hadn't thought … No. She said nothing identifying who, or where, it happened.'

The prof took off his glasses, laid them on the desk and closed his eyes before massaging his temples and running his fingers through his silver hair. He leaned back. I felt some of my burden crossing the desk. He sat silently for several minutes.

'I'm glad you felt you could share this with me.'

'It's preying on my mind. Should I do something?'

He looked up to his right, thinking. 'Beth, in all honesty, look at the facts. We have no firm evidence pointing to anyone, nor indeed that a rape definitely took place. She could have invented a cover story for a regrettable liaison she thought had made her pregnant.'

I protested. 'Maia would never lie …'

'None the less, we have to consider how the police would view this. There is no one to corroborate her story. As you rightly say, we have no idea where or when, never mind who. Perhaps your silence has been wise.'

I sighed. Tears weren't far away.

'I've spoken to her father at length, offered the university's condolences. Her mother's health is frail. I think they've been through enough. On balance, perhaps it's best to keep this between us at present. I know it will be terribly hard, but you must try to put this behind you.'

'But what if it's someone in the Year?'

'I sincerely hope not. I shall take some confidential legal advice. If I need the Diary, I'll be in touch.' He rose. 'You'll make a good doctor, Beth. I know you'll find the strength to go on. This is a vital year, of course, Fourth Professionals being Part One of the Finals, as you know.'

I didn't! That news abruptly distracted me from my obsession with the Diary. It also obliterated his compliment so I didn't thank him for his kind words.

'Remember I'm always here, and there's a Student Welfare Officer if you need to talk.'

'I'm fine, sir.' I shook his hand and went to my clinic. The others were so appalled about Maia they asked few questions about my summer. I was grateful.

◆

This fourth 'Integrated Year' was when all our knowledge in Medicine and Surgery was supposed to come together. The coursework was immense, the recommended clinical books dauntingly massive. The 'inside trackers' with medical families headed instead for summary books like the 'Shorter Textbook of' series. The rest of us quickly cottoned on, though I had a sneaking love for Bailey and Love's *Short* Textbook of Surgery (a mere 1500 pages) with its quirky biographical footnotes on those who'd had diseases, instruments and ops named after them. I hoped Conor would never feature. Easier books were but one advantage of having a medical pedigree, like that of gentle Gordon who was my native guide.

Medicine is a strategy career. Open ears, chats and advice swopping with colleagues and antecedents is essential: 'networking' they'd call it now. Form a rapport with someone? They might be useful later. Antagonise someone? A potential career saboteur. As some of us found out. Same everywhere, I suppose. My biggest shock was realising this year's exams were part of the Finals. But then came another one. Even if I passed I might be left behind in the rat race.

The morning after seeing Killin, I told Gordon I hadn't known this year's exams were part of the finals.

'Of course! Important year all round. Got your Residencies fixed up?'

'What?' Unease gripped me. Residencies were our first pre-registration jobs after graduation.

'I've fixed up JHO surgery at the Royal Southern and medicine at the Vale.'

'Heavens! I'm behind in career planning before I knew I had a career to plan!'

'Don't worry, there's a ballot in Sixth for remaining places.'

'Does it matter where you go?' I wasn't getting how this worked.

'It's easier to get a good Senior House Officer post if you've managed a good teaching unit resident Junior House Officer one pre-registration. You know after SHO there's Registrar and Senior Registrar before Consultancy?' I nodded. 'A teaching hospital's best for your CV and best for learning since there's more time for tutoring with the extra staff on tap and educational departmental meetings. Extra staff mean less punishing rotas too, so more study-ing time for membership exams. But if you just want experience in a speciality you're not going on with, a peripheral hospital's fine, though you are on call more. But the proposed new overtime pay might compensate for lack of sleep. You do know, at present, you get the same money whether you're on '1 in 2' or '1 in 4?'

God it was so complicated. 'Och, I'm not bothered. I'll just take the leftovers.'

'See Brian Killin, Beth. He'll likes you and he's upset about the Maia business.'

Our consultant arrived then to teach us about ulcers, I think. My mind was somewhere else. At lunch I discovered to my horror that most folk had sorted jobs already. Even Henry.

'Sir James called offering me a residency. It's probably due to his brother being in Dad's old regiment, but I'm grateful.'

Big ears Conor couldn't resist a jibe. 'I expect I'll see you there. The old man's bank-rolling the Prof's new research fund. Should be a shoe-in.'

Frank laughed. 'Thought your father was a bastard?'

Conor didn't respond, but as we left, Henry was incandescent. 'All I need,' he muttered, 'working with Conor!'

Ralph shook his head. 'He shouldn't bank on it. McPhater's picky. And pally with JT Baker. When he offered me a job he told me to tell 'that comic Towmey' he needn't apply.'

All this made me anxious, so the next day I made an appointment with Prof Killin, who looked relieved when I asked him for job advice. I think he was worried I'd decided go to the police about Maia's rape which might reflect badly on the University's reputation. Charming as ever, he offered me a job in his unit for the first six months and got me an interview in Paediatric Surgery for the second. Weird being interviewed for a job in a subject I hadn't yet done, but Killin's friend, Mr Grantham, offered me a post. Gordon laughed when I told him Grantham preferred female JHOs. 'He says we're more conscientious!'

'Ha! Watch out, Beth! He's got a reputation!'

No matter, I'd cope. Jobs sorted, I tried to relax and concentrate on work. But the Diary persistently encroached my leisure time. I read and re-read Maia's last entry looking for clues.

◆

27th August 1970

Dear Diary, or should I say Dear Beth,

I know you'll read this. Writing everything down has helped me decide what to do but I've destroyed most of it. Too upsetting for anyone else to read.

In brief, it was the worst kind of nightmare. He was so strong. I couldn't stop him. It hurt. It was the end of term in a grotty cupboard. So much for imagining my first time on honeymoon with silk sheets and romantic music. It was over a dirty table. The worst thing was his triumph, like he'd won a medal! He even laughed, as if it was a joke. Then he told me he did it for a bet – a bet! You have no idea how bad I feel. Sick. Ashamed.

Now I've missed two periods. The vomiting's stopped, but I'm seedy all the time. Definitely pregnant. I wondered about trying to see someone, but I don't know about abortions over here and worry they might just send me home. Everyone would know. I couldn't bear it. And if I wait till we get back I might be too far gone.

Life's always been a battle, pleasing everyone. If it had worked out with Henry then I wouldn't have been alone that night. But I'm damaged goods now. No one will have me. Even if I got an abortion, Dad would wonder why I wasn't going to Mass anymore; if I confessed I'd be ex-communicated. Anyway, recently I've decided there is no God. Nor Heaven. Nor Hell.

I'm praying they won't find my body. No one must know. You must destroy this. I only wanted you to know why I did it so you knew it wasn't anything to do with you. You're the best friend I've ever had. Don't grieve for me, I'll be at peace. You know, apart from a few months with Henry, I don't ever remember being happy. It's all too much. I can't go on. Sorry.
Maia, xxx

◆

I had few clues about this horror. Firstly, it had happened at the end of term, in a cupboard. The QM Union disco? The 'would have been with Henry' made that likely. Secondly, it was someone who laughed and mocked her. Thirdly, the bastard liked a bet.

Likeliest culprits were, one, Conor. But she couldn't stand him, how could he have got her into a cupboard? And surely someone would have seen it if he'd bundled her off?

Number two, Butros. We knew he was a cocky rampant stud, despite Nessa's passionate defence of him. He was as muscular and strong as rugby-fit Conor. But again, would she have allowed herself to be alone with him – in a cupboard? Made no sense.

Number three, Frank. Not as strong as the other two, but recently addicted to squash. Did that give him strong arms? Maia was very slight. I regarded Frank as an arch weirdo, a possible sadist who joked about bondage and submission. Did his taste run to rape as well? Did 'no' mean 'yes' to him? I remembered Maia's jibe as he bundled off Pat Bonham. 'Always grabbing someone's backside!' Frank had split with Pat and was rumoured to be dabbling in drugs. But if he'd given Maia something to bundle her off, surely she'd have mentioned feeling odd? Or could a spiked drink just have lowered her guard?

For a time, I even doubted Dan – with a drink in him quite capable of acting Jack the Lad. But in my heart of hearts I felt that if he'd drunkenly forced himself on a girl he'd have been sorry afterwards, not laughed. Or would he? I hadn't indulged with him, so I couldn't say. Dan was certainly a gambler, like Conor. Might someone have made a bet with him for big stakes and he'd been drunkenly led on, thinking it a joke? But surely not with wee Maia. He hadn't really dated since Jean and I doubted he could be sexually aggressive. No. he'd never have sex for a bet. But could Dan have *made* the bet?

Then there was Killin's suggestion of a staff member. There were Union barmen, waiters and janitors, many of whom were familiars. I was going mad. It was hopeless. It could be anyone. I had no one to discuss it with. Only Prof Killin knew, but didn't want to. Any hints to the others would expose Maia's secret, arouse suspicion about her death. To my shame, I did nothing. Other events overtook me.

Fifteen

Staircase 13

In Fourth Year, there were various ways to learn: tape/slide presentations in booths for personal study, lectures and tutorials. I even learned to play bridge at lunchtimes, though was rubbish at remembering the cards played. Luckily, I was better at acquiring practical medical skills. We were welcomed any time in theatre or

Casualty, so I took to hanging about at the Royal Southern near home, where great teams did a hard job with humour and efficiency, even when the place resembled a battlefield. They taught me suturing, bandaging, wound dressing, drip insertion, history taking and result interpretation. The Sister, Sandra Barbour, I'd known from her time nursing Jean. Much of my Christmas holidays was spent with Sandra. Saturday nights in Casualty were especially chaotic. Saturday afternoons quieter. Usually.

◆

On Saturday the 2nd of January 1971, I found myself amongst mayhem. Ambulances shuttled patients to hospitals all over Glasgow from Ibrox Stadium. That Saturday, the Glasgow Ranger's Football Club ground was the scene of a dreadful disaster. Almost at the final whistle, fans were leaving an 'Old Firm' local derby match with Celtic Football Club as the score was 1-0 for Celtic. The later Inquiry found a crush of excited Ranger's fans surged back to see what caused the crowd's roar in the final seconds. Rangers' Colin Stein had scored an equaliser. Hundreds trying to leave early thinking the match was lost, clashed with returners. In the crush, there were heavy fatalities. Hundreds were injured, and men, women and children were suffocated in the seething mass of bodies trapped in a confined space. All over the city ambulance sirens screamed.

I was with a team in the resuscitation room of the Royal Southern's Casualty Department when a blue patient was rushed in. My first cardiac arrest. I put in a drip cannula (my second), fetched a litre of saline to attach, trotted as ordered to grab things from the crash trolley, opened ampoules for injections and ran with cross-matching blood samples to a waiting porter who ran to the lab. I listened to the practised exchange of orders, instructions and encouragement between these dedicated doctors and nurses trying to save this cyanosed patient's life as they called out the time at intervals till it was time to give up. Brain death was inevitable. A nurse had barely filled in a chart with his name and date of birth,

He was a handsome devil of forty-eight: much too early to be snatched. He'd merely gone to a football match with his brother as he'd done every Saturday in the winter since a boy. I wasn't the only one in tears but went out to the corridor and sank to the floor. The seats had been commandeered for the waiting room, where by now people were even sitting on the floor.

Sandra appeared. 'Well done! You were a great help. We needed every pair of hands there. I know it's hard. Is this your first death?'

'No,' I answered.

'You can't sit down there – come on! The waiting room's full.' She put out a hand to me.

'Can I have a minute with him?'

'Oh, God! Do you know him? You should have said!'

'He's my father.'

Sandra wept with me.

◆

The eventual Death Certificate said *Asphyxiation due to Crush Injury.* Sixty-six people died, including children and teenagers. It was a black, black day for Glasgow. And me. A big hole had opened up in my life: a black, black hole. You think your parents will always be there. Dad was our provider, our organiser, our rock and our clown. Calm in a crisis, slow to anger. My supporter-in-chief. My best friend. I left the hospital quivering with adrenaline, ready to explode. This was medicine in the raw. At the sharp end. I didn't think I could take it anymore.

Next day, Rosie came from Barrington Drive and stayed over. Though I felt I had to be strong for Mum and Alice because Dad would have wanted it, I let Rosie take charge. Mum didn't get out of bed. A trail of bemused friends and relatives washed through our flat in a sea of tea brewed by Rosie. Even very old friends turned up. I heard a queer note in Rosie's voice when she opened the door to one. 'Oh, hello! And who are you?'

'I'm Findlay. A friend of Beth's.' The voice which years ago had quickened my heartbeat now sounded formal, distant.

'Come in!' Looking aside at him as she shut the door, Rosie grinned and winked. First light moment of the day.

'How's your mum?' Findlay hugged me. Like a sister.

'Pretty awful.'

'Had to come. Mum and Dad send love. If there's anything we can do?'

'Thanks.' That was beginning to make me want to scream inside. The only thing we wanted was to have Dad back. Not Findlay's fault. It's just what you say at bereavements, isn't it? Like 'Time's a great healer' or 'Life must go on.' My mum always took the grieving a casserole because she felt they needed to eat but wouldn't feel like cooking. All she got from folk were platitudes, however well meant. Rosie ushered Findlay into the living room then fetched tea and Blue Ribands. Alice came in. Findlay hugged her. She cried. I was past tears. Alice and I sat mute. Rosie blethered. She came back from walking him to the close mouth.

'You never said he was so gorgeous! Why did you let him go? For two pins I'd ...'

Oh, Rosie! Always flirting, despite now professing undying love for James Hutton, Frank's brother, though fortunately more normal. I didn't understand her need for relationships. They were too much hassle for me.

Gordon came over but I didn't kiss him: anything sexual seemed inappropriate. I took a hug- acceptable physical comfort in any situation. We had slowly become closer, but I found myself wanting to tell him I'd had enough, both of him and medicine. I couldn't. Next night I told my mother. She'd come through for tea, still in her dressing gown.

'I've decided to leave medicine.'

'What? After all the work you've done? Why on earth would you do that?'

'I can't face it. I can't go to another resuscitation. I can't bear the thought I might fail to save someone else.'

She was angry, angrier than I'd ever seen her and fled back to bed weeping. I felt worse. I blamed myself for Dad's death. Maybe I should have done something differently? I couldn't face the thought of going near a hospital. I was wretched.

'You go home Rosie. I'll manage. And don't worry, I won't lose touch.'

Rosie erupted, her eyes blazing. 'How can you think of giving up? Your Dad would have been livid! Don't you see this awful situation gives you all the more reason for graduating?'

We stayed up all night talking, emptying a whole tin of Quality Street and mum's Hogmanay leftover Harvey's Bristol Cream. Sherry made me think of the Prof's party. Maia. More guilt.

'I should have saved Maia! If I hadn't persuaded her to go to Australia she might still be here …'

'You've flipped Beth! If she wanted to kill herself she'd have done it wherever she was.'

I was as near to telling her about Maia's rape as I had been, but stopped myself: I'd made a vow to keep her secret, respect her wishes. Instead I wept buckets on Rosie's slight shoulder. Tears for Maia, but also tears for me and the injustice of life. For the first time I almost understood how Maia must have felt. Everything was too much. But not for me a final bridge to jump off; I wanted a dark corner. We went to bed at three.

Next morning Rosie marched into the kitchen and headed straight for the bin. She came to the table and plonked Monday's paper on top of my Weetabix. Flicking through the pages, she aggressively pointed at the victim photos.

'Look at all these people, their stories.'

'I wonder where they got that pic of Dad? Not from us. The shipyard maybe?

'It's terrible. But see these?' She tapped the next page. 'These injured folk might have died too if it hadn't been for doctors. You can't leave medicine. You've got the brains and ability and you'll be letting your Dad down if you quit. He was so proud of you.'

Rosie made me feel guilty about feeling guilty: a true Presbyterian sentiment.

'I really can't go back and face everyone. I must have a break.'

'Maybe you should see that nice Assistant Dean, Bill Simpson, and arrange a year out? Then if you feel the same way, OK. Expect your mum would accept it then.'

Rosie went home the next day. I cruised on autopilot. Alice just cried, especially on her fifteenth birthday the following Friday. If she hadn't had a cold she might have been at the match as well. It didn't bear thinking about. Mum eventually got up and dressed to have occasional monosyllabic conversations with the doctor, the police. And me.

It took a while to organise the funeral with the delay in releasing Dad's body. His brother Jim was a great help. He'd been carried along a passageway for 20 yards with three people on top of him and more underneath. One might have been Dad. Uncle Jim had nightmares for years, as have I about that day. And Maia. I began to think the dead have it easier. They've escaped horror and pain. It's the people left behind who suffer. Guilty they're still here, grieving for things never said, distraught they can never say them now. I panicked every night at the point of falling over to sleep. What if I died? Was there a Heaven? Or might I never see Dad again? Oddly, today, with death imminent, I'm not panicking. Not a damn thing I can do about it but have faith in my doctors and live for now. To the max. There are no second chances.

But at least we had a body to grieve over, say a final ritual goodbye to. If someone disappears and you don't know whether they are alive or dead it must be completely unbearable. A nightmare.

Sixteen

Suspects, Shesheta & Sangria

Conor wasn't all bad. The week we returned after Christmas break he gave me a hug, the only physical contact with him I can recall. Stepping back, he looked me in the eye.

'Sorry to hear about your Dad, Beth. Heard you were there too. Terrible.'

'Thanks.'

'At least when I lost my mother I'd had time to get used to the idea. Anyway, Wendy says your Dad was great. You were lucky. Mine's a bastard.' He carried on into the lecture.

I'd taken Rosie's advice and been to see the Assistant Dean, Professor Simpson. Like Rosie, he insisted I'd more reason than ever to carry on. And he dismissed the 'year out' idea. Why add the strain of getting to know another set of students when my current year seemed to be a particularly nice bunch? I found his arguments persuasive.

But Gordon was driving me mad, constantly asking if I was all right- of course I wasn't! I now understood Henry dumping Maia. The work was enough strain. Gordon accepted it well. Though steering clear of relationships, but I did become close to Yousef that term, not in a romantic sense, more in a 'car' kind of sense. The Powers-that-Be scattered us every morning all over the city at clinics but expected us back for lectures at Gilmorehill ten minutes later. Asking Gordon for a lift wasn't 'on' now, so Yousef offered. My bus stopped outside his flat, good. But getting him out in the morning? Not so good. A late-bedder, he'd greet me at 8am unshaven and bleary-eyed. Getting him, a fastidious dresser, ready in time was tricky. He needed a different floral tie and coloured jacket each day and had more shoes than any girl. Coaxing him out by 8.30 needed effort. Still, he was a good listener and made me laugh. Today I laugh at us all in 1971 photos: shaggy-locked boys in double-breasted jackets, long-fringed, pasty-faced girls with spider lashes and bare knees. Yet while the peacock boys and scantily skirted girls went uncriticised, a girl in trousers was sent home to change by a consultant for being 'unsuitably dressed.' How times change.

Clinics were the best thing on our course and usually started around 9.15 after consultant's rounds. One clinic stands out.

Frank strolled in fifteen minutes late, hands in pockets, exuding Brut. Eminent Scottish surgeon Mr Dick Stewart paused his teaching spiel.

'You are late! Name, boy?'

'Frances Hutton. Sorry, sir. My watch must be slow.' He smiled, like it was no big deal.

'Wipe that smirk off your face!' Frank's eyes sparked. 'So, since you've drawn attention to yourself, let's give you more limelight. Take a history and examine this man. And don't ever be late for me again!'

'Slow watch, my ass! More like hungover,' Dan muttered to me sideways. 'Henry left him still downing in his room at two!'

As Dan turned to look at me, his eyes widened. He nodded to indicate I should look behind me. Cricking my neck to follow his line of sight, I caught Stewart's tall, dashing registrar, Graeme Donaldson standing in the doorway hugging case notes -and blowing a kiss at Frank! What was that all about? Conor sniggered. It didn't amuse me. Little did then.

Rosie tried to distract me with trips to the University Café, films and walks by the River Kelvin. Most Fridays, James went out with the boys so Rosie came home with me for tea. Alice was at Guides and mum at the Women's Guild. Rosie mightn't have been aware of it then, but she's a born psychiatrist. Her persistent quizzing about the reason for my doldrums eventually made me produce the Diary.

She read the passage I indicated before closing the book and wiping a tear.

'Oh God, I'd no idea! And you've kept this to yourself?'

'I've only told Killin – not that he'll do anything. You know, I think it must have happened at the June disco. I've racked my brains trying to think if anything odd happened, but it's hard remembering a particular night.'

'Well, I remember Butros had an early flight, so Nessa and he were leaving at eleven. I saw Maia after, so it isn't him. But, can we be sure it was that night?'

'Can't think when else. She didn't go out much. And it must have been some place large, like the Queen Margaret Union, to have a cupboard big enough for a table.' I shuddered.

Rosie rested her head on her hand and an elbow on our kitchen table, thinking hard. 'Dan was there till late. It'd never be him though, surely?'

'Och, I doubt it. The boys were all at the bar, stocious – probably incapable, Malky especially.'

'But Malky's a groper – remember Ruth, our first disco? And a gambler. Seen him come out the Byres Road bookies. Definitely a candidate. Why didn't Maia go home with you as usual?'

'Oh, she booked a QMU room for overnight, saying she felt she'd imposed too much on me, staying over so often. Silly. I'm sure I last saw her with that quiet Chaplaincy friend, Mary, around 11.30-ish. But I can't ask Mary anything. She'd want to know why.'

Rosie sighed. 'It's pretty hopeless, Beth.'

'It's terrible to be so suspicious of everyone.' I sobbed with frustration.

Rosie sat back. 'I saw Maia late on, I'm sure. Conor, Liam, Frank and Dan left before us for chips, midnight-ish. Loud and annoying. Con even had a stray kitten at one point!'

'What? Dan said Conor spent that night at Maryhill police station for being drunk, peeing in Byres Road and punching a bobby, did you hear?'

'Is that true or just one of his big stories? He can't have been charged or he'd have been out of medicine like a shot!'

'Dan's sure he was banged up. Thinks some barrister got him off.'

'You know, Beth, we simply have no idea. Does it even have to be one of our lot? Could have been a staff bloke.'

'That's what Killin said.'

'I think we'll have to forget it, though it's the most horrible thing I've ever heard.'

'It's been such a burden. I wish I'd never read this bloody diary. I still wonder about going to the police.'

'What with?' said Rosie, 'It's too long ago and there's no real evidence. Maia should have gone, but she didn't even want to name him to you.'

'I keep wondering why. She must have known the rapist and the punter making the bet. Maybe that made it more embarrassing for her to go to the police.'

'I don't think she'd have gone either way, too shy. Besides, I think the police don't take girls seriously. She'd have put herself through a lot for nothing.' Rosie shook her head.

'I just wish there was *something* we could do. He shouldn't get away with it! What if he does it to someone else?'

'You can't help it, Beth. Oh, what kind of bastard could do that to a sweetie like her?'

◆

Butros might have had an alibi, but I still disliked him. Yet Nessa remained besotted. In late February, she got glandular fever and moved back to Aunt Miriam's for a couple of weeks. Wendy felt nervous on her own in the big flat, so I stayed over, partly to save time and bus fares, but also as a break from home where I constantly felt I should be doing something for Mum: no idea what. Sharing a bedroom with Alice wasn't easy either. Her anxiety had given her tidy-mania. She kept moving my paperwork study piles. I have a system. It's just not obvious.

Even before Nessa went off sick, I worried about her. She'd spend ages in the Ladies and would sit distractedly in class replacing lipstick all the time and brushing her hair. When we visited her at Aunt Miriam's she looked ill and exhausted. Butros hadn't been in touch apart from one cryptic 'Get Well' card she hid under her pillow. She made endless excuses for him, though Yousef told me Butros was still out partying. Nessa returned to her flat end of week four. Wendy and I were arguing in the kitchen about pasta cooking time when Butros arrived.

'You not ready?' He confronted Nessa.

'I am!' She smiled.

'I don't think so!' He looked her up and down. 'What's that you've got on? Is it your grandmother's?'

Nessa's smile vanished.

I wasn't taking this. 'I think it's lovely. Green suits you.'

'I didn't ask you!' Butros turned his back. 'Go put on that dress I bought you.'

Nessa sped off to the bedroom, emerging in a black dress which made her look older. She was a stunning girl: long black hair cascading from a centre parting, appealing large eyes. But that night her olive-skin looked ashen. The fever had taken its toll. That had been another gift from Butros. Yousef informed me that over Christmas his brother had contracted glandular fever. With swollen neck glands and mild jaundice, it's caused by Epstein Barr virus, saliva-contagious and often called the 'kissing disease.' Butros did plenty of that on his all-night trawls. Yousef told me he'd stopped accompanying him after getting gonorrhoea (not what I'd expect a guy to share, but then he regarded me as one of the boys). Butros only behaved on Saturdays when Wendy stayed over. Yousef worried he was missing classes. I worried he was making Nessa more ill.

As she put on her coat, I hugged her. 'Have a nice time. Maybe not be back too late? You look tired.'

Butros glared, violently snatching up his car keys. 'She'll be home when she's home. Enjoy your boring evening, girls. Let's move it!' He pushed Nessa out, slamming the door.

We looked at each other. Wendy had seen the light with Conor, but Nessa was blind to Butros's bullying. Yet, he was considerate of his sister.

◆

The brothers Shamoun had a younger sister, Shesheta who visited from Egypt second term as she was considering a Glasgow Languages MA. For 'propriety' Yousef asked Rosie if she could stay with her in Barrington Drive which I thought funny: more guys went in and out of her flat than his! Early one Thursday evening during her visit, Frank turned up. With Class Exams on the Monday, he must have known Rosie would be at the library.

'Hello Shesheta. Is Rosie in? I want to borrow a book.'

'No. I'll tell her you called.'

'Likely she won't be long. I'll just come in and wait.'

Unable to prevent his entry, Shesheta shrugged and asked if he'd like a coffee.

'Lovely.' Frank sat down in the kitchen. Shesheta gave him a mug then turned to carry on making the sandwich his arrival had interrupted.

'How old are you?'

'Seventeen,' she replied, not turning around, not hearing Frank get up.

'What are you doing?' She tried to lift his head off her neck.

'You're gorgeous! Come on, let's have a bit of fun!'

She managed to turn. His beery breath made her recoil in disgust. He pushed her back over the worktop, his left hand clutched her back at shoulder height, his right hand grabbing her skirt hem, modest by contemporary standards but still short. Pressing his lips on her mouth to silence her, he moved tack, raising his right hand to grope her breasts and try for the buttons on her blouse. A swift glance made her realise the knife block was out of reach, but with supreme effort, as he moved his left hand down her back, she grabbed his long hair sharply with her left hand and achieved enough distance to slap him hard with her right before, shouting in rage, she raised her knee to forcibly crush his testicles. He buckled, gasping, but advanced again laughing. A ferocious right hook cracked his nose. She hadn't grown up with two brothers for nothing. Her father shouldn't have chastised her for fighting as a child: it was a useful skill for a girl. The ball-breaking knee jerk was her first, but she'd seen Butros do it. As Frank looked ready to move in again, she seized a knife from the block and hissed, 'Get out!' He did.

Half an hour later Butros arrived to take her to the cinema. At her tale he left abruptly.

Next day, Conor regaled us with Frank's injuries which he'd catalogued for the Casualty Officer. Epistaxis (bloody nose: Shesheta), peri-orbital haematomae (black eyes: Butros), a raised weal on left cheek (slap: Shesheta) and testicular bruising (bull's-eye knee: Shesheta).

'Didn't think Frankie had it in him!' chortled Conor. 'He's usually last in line to move in on a girl. Weak stomach, too- vomited in Anatomy and all along the corridor to St Mungo's morgue last summer trundling a corpse!' He laughed- yet this was his friend? As I walked off, he threw in, 'And he nearly shit himself when we fed Pathology body parts into the incinerator. Shook like a girl. Prat.'

Frank was off for a few days. His nose wasn't completely broken, but relations with Yousef were. Shesheta returned to Luxor, never to return. After hearing this tale from Conor my imagination was in overdrive: was Shesheta just luckier or better prepared than Maia had been for a sexual assault by Frances Xavier Hutton?

◆

Beginning of third term in Fourth, we gathered in Yousef's flat in Novar Drive. With its nice sofas, fresh décor and spacious tidy rooms, it was a good place to hang out on Saturday nights. No one else had velvet curtains and crystal lamps. Butros was out. Dinner was lasagne and Chianti courtesy of Rosie. Henry and Dan kept going to the loo. After their third visit in an hour, I had to ask. 'What's wrong with you two?'

Dan laughed. 'It's the drugs!'

'Drugs? What drugs?'

'Not what you think: we're on a Drug Trial. You take a pill each day for a month and keep a diary. We got enrolled by Mick Shaw, the Mat Med guy. It's quite safe. They've been tested on animals and humans already. It's just to see how common any side effects are, the time it takes to work, and so on. You randomly get the real pill or a placebo – you don't know which. This trial's a diuretic. We think we've got the real thing!'

'I should say! You're peeing for Britain! How much are they paying?'

It was a lot of money for diary-keeping. My thoughts turned to the summer. Rosie had invited me to her family's place in Marbella in July with the girls, but I couldn't afford the flight and had refused to let her pay. I got Mick's number from Dan. By the next weekend I was guinea pig number 125, enrolled testing a beta blocker. I was warmly welcomed as there were few female volunteers, for you couldn't take part if on the pill (it interfered with drug metabolism) or were in a relationship (risk of pregnancy/foetal damage). Neither applied to me. From coursework I knew beta blockers might cause slow pulse, dizziness or tiredness but with no symptoms, I assumed I'd pulled placebo. Diary and blood checks done, I was paid in pounds, shillings and pennies on April 30th and spent it on an air ticket at Student Travel on May 3rd in new decimal pounds and pence. Odd what triggers memories: old money means lovely half-crowns. Half-crowns mean Saturday morning pocket money and going out with Dad to spend it. Happy days.

◆

Everyone, Conor included, passed Fourth Professionals first go. From that term Yousef and Frank never spoke again except when forced to by work. Nessa's infatuation with Butros was unwavering. Wendy, Dan, Henry and I stayed single. Rosie clung to James Hutton. With a shorter summer break after Fourth, most folk didn't get jobs, though Conor and Yousef went to New York for a month externship with Yousef's uncle. I enjoyed two lazy weeks in sunny Marbella. Rosie was a great hostess, apart from lying that Sangria was mildly alcoholic fruit juice. Waking at four in brain-expanding agony wanting to die, I vowed to stay off alcohol for ever. (That particular vow lasted all of 48 hours.)

The second week Nessa joined us. Lying by the pool she told us Butros was working.

'Why? He doesn't usually,' I put down my Jackie Collins.

'He told his dad he's with an accountant,' she laughed, 'but he's in Ladbrokes.'

'Well, they are Turf Accountants!' Rosie sniggered.

'He hasn't gone home this year at all. His father's still mad at the plane ticket fiasco.'

'What fiasco?' I asked, turning over on the lounger to sun my back.

'Oh, we fell out last year at the end of term disco. I went home and left him. He got so drunk he missed his London connecting flight and re-booked with his Dad's Amex but via Vegas! He stayed over and lost a packet. Caused fireworks. But he's promised to stop gambling now.' Elegantly anointing herself with Ambre Solaire, she donned her sunglasses and lay back.

I turned to sit up. So Butros hadn't left the disco early? With his arrogant sexuality, gambling and habitual mockery he could well be Maia's rapist. I was burning, not only from the noonday sun. I dived into the pool, shaded by over-hanging bougainvillea and welcomingly chilly, to lie floating, brain cooling, thoughts swirling. Butros the rapist? But then, Ralph had recently mentioned Conor bragging his father had paid off a girl. Why? Paternity? Or assault? Conor was still in the frame. And Frank with that Shesheta carry-on. But my gut instinct nailed Butros. Could I prove it? At least he wasn't going to be a doctor like them. Oh God, what kind of medics were they going to be? I swam madly up and down the pool.

Seventeen

Bomb Disposal

A year later, basement, St Mungo's Hospital

How long does it take a body to burn? He has no idea. That's almost four hours now. He's turned the furnace up to max but with no viewing window available, it's hard to know if anything recognisable might remain. His watch says 5.30. Is it safe to leave? Maintenance staff arrive at eight. He must be well away by then.

God it's hot and claustrophobic down here. How can folk work in this boiler room for days on end? A right Victorian dump. Previously he's only been in for a few minutes at a time, bringing rubbish and organ bits for disposal from theatres and pathology. That was a lousy summer job, being ordered about as a menial gofer, but it's proved useful. He knew about this incinerator. It had been gruesome stuff, disposing of body parts from road accidents or ops. They were small though, compared to this. It had been a struggle getting the body in. Good thing Pat was slight. Getting Gee in would have meant chopping something off. Even he would baulk at that. Fleetingly he acknowledges that it's as well Pat lived alone. With luck it might be a few days before anyone twigged.

The blood should have cleaned up OK. Lucky the mattress was wrapped in one of those red rubber covers, easy to wipe. Gee had sprinted up the back stairs with the sheets to stuff them in a theatre laundry basket. Wouldn't give cause for concern or arouse suspicion: so much blood-stained linen from the afternoon lists ay up there uncollected till next morning: more inside info from the portering. He wonders if he should nip back for the rope and pulley from the bed. It was pretty spattered. Not that Ortho ward 7A would be in use for some weeks. No sign of the decorators yet. He'd been surprised at the blood. So much from nose and mouth. spurting everywhere. Reminded him of that woman with burst oesophageal varices in Casualty last month. Blood just kept coming, more purple than crimson. Venous. She'd died too. His shirt isn't bad, should wash, but Gee will have to destroy his. He'd been daft to attempt CPR. Life was extinct by the time they'd taken off the bag.

He is surprised how calm he feels now. Amazing how quickly he's come down. Half an hour ago they'd been high as kites. It had been a stupid idea. All Gee's. The closed ward: the pulley rigged up: the auto caper trial. The trick lay in cutting off some oxygen, just enough, to heighten a climax. Gee had suggested trying it first in company in case anything went wrong. Christ, didn't it just? The poppers had been too much, really only needed for one-on-one. Some of it was down to Pat though, being stupid, over-excited, swallowing some amyl, not just inhaling. God, turning so purple... Another mistake was having no knife to cut the rope and using more weights than they could counteract in time. He could still smell the blood. Jesus knows what had ruptured. A stunt not for repeating.

He's pretty sure they can't pin anything on them. He's confident Pat wouldn't have broadcast their plans. He'd been so pleased to be invited, up for it, loving the whole idea and the illicit, clandestine, naughty location. No, Pat would have kept schtum. Been dead chuffed to be asked to the threesome. He smiles. Huh, dead certainly. And chuffed on the way. Went happy!

They'll just have to put it behind them. Carry on regardless. Getting rid of the body is definitely the best thing. Couldn't leave the remains. A ticking bomb. Fleetingly he wonders about a wee prayer. What might be appropriate? Wasn't in the school curricu-

*lum, prayers for the incinerator! No matter. He's not even sure Pat
was a left-footer.*

*His heart rate normalises. Only four hours to shower and get
some shut-eye before Icabod's session. Last clinic of Fifth. Prof Crane's
a bit of a stickler wouldn't do to be late for his Orthopaedic Clinic.
Christ, after today he'll certainly give Orthopaedics a wide berth.
Putting his hands in his pockets, he saunters back along the dark
corridor. Feeble strip lights barely illuminate the bare brick walls and
fat silver-pipe-clad ceiling. Cockroaches scurry, crunchy underfoot.
He decides the pulley cords aren't worth bothering about. By the
time the ward's used they'll only show a few faded rusty splatters.
No body? No case.*

*Out of the cobwebbed fire door the main road is quiet. Chilly for
May. He's hungry. Might there still be bacon in the fridge? Or would
someone have finished it after the pub last night?*

Eighteen

Mania & Exam Marathons

If Fourth Year was a steady reconnaissance of gaps in our knowledge, Fifth was a rapid call to battle stations. Specialist subjects
assaulted us on all sides. After morning clinics we'd skirmish round
Skins, Eyes and Ear, Nose and Throat, fight a rear-guard action
with Medical Jurisprudence (gory murder and malpractice) and
tackle Epidemiology (Public Health stats and barmy sociology).
How I envied Ruth her post-grad Journalism course – two lectures
and one tutorial a week. Despite returning 'recharged' from my
Spanish holiday, within weeks I was flagging. Psychiatry was especially harrowing with folk baring their souls. Like Trixie, whom

we observed through a two-way mirror.

'So, how often *do* you wash your hands?' The consultant nodded encouragingly.

'Well, I'm not sure. My husband tries to stop me, but you've got to be clean – there's so many germs about.'

'So, when do you do it?'

'Em, after the lavatory, of course. In the kitchen, of course. After touching someone and door handles, the TV ... the hoover. I use that a lot.'

'It sounds tiring and time-consuming. And if you're out of the house, how's that?'

She fidgeted. 'I don't go out, except to come here. Not even to get my daughter from school. My friend goes.'

'Stupid bitch!' Conor was laughing. 'Needs to get a grip!'

We glared at him, worried Trixie might hear us even if she couldn't see us. Frank and he cracked jokes throughout the interview. Afterwards, the psychiatrist dismissed Conor's suggestion Trixie could get a grip.

'Impossible. She needs intensive psychotherapy.'

'How long will that take?' asked Rosie.

'The longer you leave Obsessive Compulsive Disorder, the harder it is to treat. She took a while to seek help so she's a difficult case.'

As we collected our coats, I grabbed Wendy. 'That's Nessa, isn't it? She's got OCD!'

Conor tutted at me. 'Told you they shouldn't let in girls. She's a basket case.'

'Stuff it, Conor.' Wendy pushed me past him. 'It's bloody Butros! Dr Mann says its stress induced.'

'You know at first I thought the kitchen scrubbing was a sort of Jewish thing.'

'No, it's not, and if she was strictly Kosher, Beth, she wouldn't be living with me. You might have seen the cleaning and hand-washing, but there's other rituals. Like aligning study pens, sorting socks in rows, folding and re-folding laundry, switch-checking before going out – that's a biggie.'

'I didn't know she did all that!'

'Yes. I've been hoping it'd stop, but it's getting worse.' Wendy sighed.

'What can we do? Couldn't you mention this patient, hint she needs to see someone?'

Wendy looked doubtful. 'I'll try.'

During the first week in November, Wendy heard Nessa in the bathroom at midnight. The taps ran for 45 minutes. At breakfast Wendy went for it.

'Have you seen any OCD patients yet, Wendy? We did … I was wondering … I mean we're all pretty stressed … d'you think you might have it- a bit? I mean, those taps running at night for so long …'

'I'm not obsessive!'

'But the taps for 45 minutes – are you taking baths?'

'Don't be silly – in the middle of the night? You're imagining things!' She stormed off, for once without checking switches. That was the week she stopped going out with us, and visiting Aunt Miriam, even for Shabbat, though she still trailed after Butros several nights a week. Getting ready took longer and longer, food was left largely untouched, dark haloes surrounded her eyes and her face became gaunt. She dismissed our concerns. 'You all eat too much. Butros feels I'm getting thick in the hips.' She was late for class – when she came at all. The checking increased. Week six everything imploded.

It was a Sunday night. Rosie and I were with Wendy in her flat attempting to make revising ENT 'fun.' Rosie read out 'Causes of tinnitus – that's ringing in the ears – include …' Cue doorbell ringing, imperiously. We laughed. It rang again. Then again. Then continuously. Rosie angrily opened the door, ready to shout at the suspected male joker. She didn't. She shouted for us. 'Oh, Heavens, girls, help!'

I moved to the hall. Rosie stood in the doorway supporting

Nessa, a chalk-white disaster with staring eyes, tear and mascara-stained cheeks and tousled hair, coatless despite the freezing wet night. A torrent of sound rushed from her. She ranted, rambled, rhymed, sobbed and laughed. We had trouble piecing together the story.

'Beth, phone Student Travel. Need a flight! I'm right. He loves me- not Ingrid, see … She's not his girl. It's a whirl! Babies! Rabies!' She looked round at us. 'Rosie! Posy!' She smiled, like she'd had a brainwave. 'Airport! Fairport! Can't delay. Not fair play! Doomsday!'

Sobs punctuated wild tangents of punning speech.

'Stop, Nessa, sit down. You're not well!' Rosie led her to the sofa, whose velvet arm she clutched so tightly that her handprint could be seen next day.

'Don't say I'm not well. Kiss and tell, ring the bell.' Her eyes darted about the room, never engaging with ours, scarily miles away. She shook her head as if to clear it. 'I've given up my family! He wouldn't just leave me – that bastard's taken him away, kidnapped him! Don't you see – he wouldn't go without me!' She wailed. 'Keep out. Keep me out … it's a conspiracy! They're after me – diddly dee, can they see me?' She looked about fearfully. 'Butros and me… Wedding bell, death knells. No. Here...' She put her hand inside her sodden jumper and pulled out a chain. 'We're getting married! I've got a ring – here! He's mine! All fine.' She laughed: high pitched, cackling, heart-wrenching. I unclasped her palm and saw an engagement ring on the chain. The bastard, I thought, he's done a bunk.

'Oh, he's not gone … away to Spain, it isn't plain …' She looked puzzled and stopped as if having a momentary flash of sanity. 'No, he's … I'm …Where am I? I need a drink!'

Rosie fetched a glass of water. Nessa took the drink but looked at it as if she wasn't sure what to do with it. 'No, he's gone home!' She moaned. 'Get me a plane!'

The doorbell rang. Rosie met Yousef on the doorstep with Nessa's bag and coat.

'Nessa ran off. I thought she'd come back up for her coat and I'd run her home, but she didn't. I'm worried.'

'She's here – in some state! What happened?'

'Dad drove up from London in a fury. He jumped on a plane in Luxor when Strathclyde returned his course cheque for Butros, saying he was no longer a student. And his debts are hellish – the casino, horses, dogs …' He was shaking his head. 'It's my parents' fault, you know, spoiling him the Egyptian way, not chastising the first-born, like they're a God or something. He's hopeless. I'm so sorry.'

'It's not your fault.'

'Maybe not. But there's worse.' Yousef looked very upset. 'Ingrid's pregnant, and as Wendy came in she was leaving – shouting about having his bastard.'

'Jesus!' Rosie's hand fled to her mouth in shock. 'I thought she was Conor's…'

'Well she was pretty free and easy. Anyway, Dad's paid her off to stop her going to the police after Butros hit her. He called her a slut – said it wasn't his. He called Wendy a slut too. She got hysterical. Dad bundled Butros downstairs. Then she ran off.' Yousef was close to tears. 'I was worried she'd do something silly, like jump in the Kelvin.'

In my view she was beyond doing anything, silly or otherwise, having parted company with reality. The emergency doctor came and arranged admission to the Psychiatric Unit. While Wendy called Nessa's Aunt Miriam, I went in the ambulance to give her admission history. She couldn't. The receiving Psychiatrist pronounced her hypomanic.

'I'm sorry but since she won't agree to stay in we'll have to Section her under the Mental Health Act…'

Miriam signed the form as we sat in the Day Room, its psychedelic orange and green curtains and stale cigarette smoke exacerbating my stress. Surprisingly Aunt Miriam took the sectioning of her niece with equanimity, having known about Butros all along but hoping it was just a passing phase. She blamed herself for not trying to do something earlier. The staff brought us tea and biscuits. The psychiatrist reassured us they'd sort Nessa out.

They did, though she didn't return that term. The only person who laughed was Conor.

'I told you all along she was a nutter. Good riddance!'

Compassion? Not in his bones. How in Hell's name was this guy ever going to be any kind of medic? He was bound to come a cropper, surely?

♦

We accepted Nessa was mentally ill: she'd clearly lost reason. But there were surprising conditions considered illnesses in those days. Like homosexuality. It featured in our Psychological Medicine exam. *Please discuss a) nocturnal enuresis b) prefrontal leucotomy c) anorexia nervosa and d) homosexuality.* Odd now to lump homosexuality as a disease along with bed-wetting and anorexia. Times have changed. Even then pre-frontal leucotomy was passé, thank God. We'd seen a patient whose past leucotomy (done by drilling into his skull to inject alcohol and destroy his frontal lobe) intended to 'cure' his homosexuality, had meant perpetual insomnia and suicidal intent meriting permanent hospital admission. Yet Moniz got a Nobel Prize for leucotomy. You can't trust all doctors.

On the subject of homosexuality, however, in the seventies we were conditioned to think it abnormal. It was rarely mentioned and bisexuality never, even by our bonkers Medical Jurisprudence lecturer Fanshaw, who delighted in showing us gratuitous slides of 'buggery-in-action' (Conor's terminology – who else). Fanshaw lectured on the illegal practice of sodomy but never mentioned 'swinging both ways.' Dan's homosexual jibe at Henry during his melt-down had shocked me. I was appalled to hear it was commonplace in boarding schools. The first homosexual I encountered was Frank. Homosexuality was still illegal in 1971 Scotland. That didn't bother Frank.

Late one evening, I sauntered into the surgical unit Duty Room to write up a case to present at the next day's ward round. Frank didn't see me, but I saw a lot more of him than I'd have liked to. The boldness of a sex act in a potentially public space left me speechless: the perpetrator was the Registrar, Graeme Donaldson, thankfully at least he had his trousers on. While I now realised he had definitely been blowing kisses at Frank in the clinic, it was something different he was blowing this time. At lunch next day I told Ralph. He shrugged.

'Not surprised. Frank's said Pat Bonham would be his last woman. Say, haven't seen her lately. Is it true she's been sectioned?'

'I haven't heard, but do know she threatened to kill herself when Frank dumped her, though Rosie told her she was lucky.'

'Frank gave her uppers all the time. Poor girl was like a budgie. Anyhow, Frank's idea is it takes a man to know what a man likes. Can't see it, myself. He's a nutter.'

Ralph went off with his plate of egg and chips. I was a bit off food, myself.

◆

After three weeks in hospital, Nessa returned to Aunt Miriam's before heading home to London and I met her at Wendy's for tea. Though a bit flat from her sedatives, she was pretty much her 'pre-Butros' self and had just come from an interview with the Dean.

'He was lovely. I told him I knew I'd been an idiot, but now had my priorities sorted. He said he's had psychiatric reports and they say I'm fine to repeat fifth. The Dean even said my experience as a patient might make me a better doctor. Not sure I agree, but anyway he said I must put it behind me. The OCD counselling's going well too.'

We hugged her, relieved. Wendy said how much she looked forward to her returning in October. For Nessa, Butros was history. But I dwelled on him: was he the rapist? Or, in view of recent developments, was it Frank? Had a girl threatening to kill herself after he'd dumped her and one who did so after he'd raped her put him off girls and on to guys?

As for poor old Pat Bonham, rumours circulated. Oddly, no one had her phone number or her exact address, only knowing she had a bed-sit off Byres Road. We were shocked to realise how little we knew about her. Yousef could tell us she'd had two brothers killed in a car crash and that Conor dated her once. I wouldn't have thought her his type: too small, dark and slim. But my 'who-is-Maia's-rapist?' fixation continued. Overhearing Conor boasting he'd had as many lays as curry, and that no one would refuse him, he jumped again to top of the list. But Ralph's replying banter 'I bet you couldn't go a week without nookie!' and 'bet you can't get her?' while pointing at a girl at the Ref made me doubt him too. The Maia question suppurated away no matter how hard I tried to staunch it. I slept poorly. I even stopped alcohol, feeling it exacerbated the nightmares. I longed for a whole night's oblivion from the exhausting, crowded waking days.

◆

Fifth was the Year of the Exam Marathon. Looking at the papers I can't believe I answered any of them. In the morning- *'Name drugs used in dermatitis herpetiformis'* (what?) In the afternoon- *'Discuss the contribution of sociology to the study of doctors and patients' behaviour'* (yawn). Next day- *'Tabulate the signs, symptoms and management of acute antral infection'* (sinusitis- for once useful!) Next day- *'Discuss the treatment of manic depression'* (no problem after Nessa). With nine exams in five days we became zombies. Even knowing where they were held was stressful, for they could be all over the Uni in halls or even churches round campus. Henry was especially anxious. Huddling wearily one day outside a still-locked hall, he suddenly asked, 'What exam is this?'

Wendy frowned. 'Orthopaedics, of course!'

'Oh, God! I revised Dermatology last night!'

Henry got a sympathetic hug. I was almost a basket case myself by the end of Fifth. I tried not to show it, but as I'd learned from Maia, you never know what's going on in someone's head. Or when they might flip.

◆

The woman was weeping into a handkerchief, the husband speaking.

'John, if you hear this please let us know you're all right. Whatever has been worrying you, we can work it out. You're not in any trouble. Please come home!' The man rose with heaving shoulders and left the press conference. A braided policeman continued.

'Any information leading to the whereabouts of...' A photo filled the TV screen.

'Can you put that off please?'

Mum obliged. I knew how those parents on the BBC News felt. Someone was missing: I'd been there. I also knew the lad. We'd all been interviewed about John, a medic in the year below, known to me only by sight as a polite boy who opened doors. Wendy had heard him sing solo, beautifully, at a Cecilian Society concert. No one else had spoken to him. Prof Crane gave us a talk on seeing Student Health if we felt depressed. Someone at Argyle Street bus station reported seeing John board a bus to Drymen. Rumours spread he'd had an accident in the Campsie hills. A small injury might have been serious for someone with von Willebrand's Disease, a bleeding disorder. The police quizzed his classmates and scoured his usual haunts. The Herald reported he'd been on anti-depressants so the buzz shifted to a lethal, lonely mountain-top overdose. Con reckoned he'd jumped off a ridge. Tragic. This medical course demanded so much of us, set its standards so high. But life went on.

We all passed. No re-sits.

◆

The end of term disco, as usual, saw an altercation involving Conor, but this time not with Wendy. She'd steered well clear after Nessa's experience. It was with Frank.

Conor growled, 'Forget it! I'm not going away with you!'

'Why not? Walking in the Lake District's fantastic. There's great pubs and the Youth Hostels are posh now. They'll be full of foreign talent. You never know who you might meet!'

'Depends who you want to meet and who you want to risk sharing a room with. The gorgeous Graeme coming, eh?'

'No. Just a few of the old guys from Halls, Con. I thought we were friends?'

'Forget it, Frank. I'm not your type. Malky and I are off in the train round Europe.' Conor pushed past him and barged towards the front of the bar. Frank sauntered off.

'What was that all about?' Henry asked Dan, who exchanged a brief knowing look with me as we queued to buy a drink to celebrate our Distinctions in Psychiatry.

'Beats me,' said Dan, shrugging. But we knew. Conor had obviously sussed Frank's involvement with Graeme too. He was like a ferret.

Henry carried over my martini and Yousef arrived balancing baskets of scampi and chips. As I sat tucking into the feast, I tried my best to banish any thoughts of my duty room encounter with a trouser-less Frank.

Nineteen

Pregnancies, Pawing & Pharmaceuticals

Henry ladled HP sauce on to his second bacon roll as I dolloped Heinz Ketchup on a fried egg. Rosie was on her tenth fag. It was noon, lunch Byres Road's University Café, likely our last one together for some time. Sixth Year meant assignments all over the city in Obstetrics, Gynaecology and Paediatrics.

'Where's Dan and Ralph?' asked Rosie. Her newly cropped hair made her look older.

'Circuit training. They say it helps them think,' mumbled Henry chomping, looking more like a teddy bear than ever in a brown fleece.

'Better swigging Irn-Bru!' laughed Gordon. 'Caffeine, that's the stuff. Great for hangovers!'

'Goodness knows what it does to your innards though – it stains dreadfully!' Wendy was unconvinced about Scotland's 'other National Drink' claiming to be 'made from girders.'

'But I love it!' Rosie also loved coffee, nicotine and Coke. Anything with a kick. Most of us indulged, except Nessa, avoiding all stimulants since her breakdown. She'd returned to the year below. We were three down now: Jean, Maia and Nessa. I hoped I wouldn't be the next casualty.

◆

I was paired with Conor for Paediatrics. To my surprise he attended regularly, positively exuding bonhomie. He could be found sitting on the floor playing Lego or reading Dr Seuss to young patients. Amazing. I'd never seen him laugh before except at someone else's expense. A new caring Conor, saints be praised.

Obstetrics was next, living in a maternity unit for eight weeks to witness as many deliveries as possible. I had Conor again, diluted by Rosie, Wendy, Ralph, Dan, Frank and a quiet girl, Stella Hubbard, who'd come into our year after a PhD in 'wound healing.' Conor showed he hadn't completely reformed by mocking her as a 'dowdy frump.' Maybe she wasn't snazzily dressed and didn't wear make-up, but I liked her. She loathed Conor. On sight.

First day in the unit Stella, Conor and I shadowed Dr Obanaya, a jolly Kenyan with disturbingly large hands for an obstetrician. We saw a wee, thin girl with an acne-pitted face and bleach-damaged hair screwed back in a rubber band. Obanaya spoke softly.

'When was your last period, dear?'

Twisting a cotton hanky, she hung her head. So young looking for an ante-natal clinic.

'Not sure. Think I've missed a couple,' she whispered.

'Mr Towmey, please examine this patient.'

Conor did so. 'God's sake, you've missed more than two. Your belly's up to twenty-four weeks at least!' He laughed. She burst into tears.

'Outside!' ordered Obanaya.

Minutes later, Conor returned to apologise. Over lunch he was bombastic.

'Hey guys, saw a wee hairy from Gorbals trying to say she was two months gone. Huh, she was at least six!'

'Yes, and you made her cry!' said Stella crossly.

'Rubbish! She was trying it on – probably wanted an abortion, stupid cow!'

'Obanaya didn't think so. I heard him tear you off a strip. What was it he said? "If I hear you speak to a patient like that again you'll be off this course as quick as a flash, boy. Respect. All patients. All the time. Got it?" And he was quite right!'

Conor left, glaring at Stella. I liked her even more. Gentle, considerate, kind. Like with me when I became upset after seeing a patient who brought back Maia.

This girl was a young red-head admitted with contraction pains. She had a swollen stomach, yet ultrasound scan showed no foetus for she was suffering from Pseudocyesis, a delusional condition where the patient imagines pregnancy and her body mimics it. I hadn't realised it was a recognised disease.

Otherwise, 'living in' for Obstetrics was fun for me, being unused to having a social life on my doorstep instead of across the city. The only bugbear was Frank, whose spectral presence was inescapable.

◆

I'd tried to keep a distance since witnessing him 'being done' (as Ralph put it) in that duty room. In Sixth he behaved strangely: one minute, life-and-soul-pumping-your-hand jolly, the next, moody-taciturn-ignoring you. If he came at all to class functions, he often brought a 'friend,' usually stylish, slim, silent and male. Only one spoke to me when abandoned by Frank going to the loo.

The friend smiled at me. 'Hello, what's your name?'

He had a cultured European accent. His eyelashes suggested this wasn't a chat-up line, but a polite overture as we stood alone together at the Union Bar door. I noticed he wore nice Italian kid shoes. I smiled back. 'Beth. And you are?'

'Dieter. May I get you a drink?'

'It's all right, my friend Dan is at the bar.'

'Would you like something to brighten your weekend?' Dieter raised a brow.

'Pardon?' I stammered, uncomprehendingly, as he wrote on a slip of paper which he tucked into my blouse breast pocket. A bold move, but I didn't take offence, doubting it was a sexual gambit. Not from a youth with blue eyeshadow.

'That's my number if you need anything. You know… uppers, for studying, keeping you awake for the finals, yes? Good quality, from Hamburg. Or something calming. Valium, perhaps or some reefers?'

As Dan sidled up with a Martini and lemonade (I was currently between abstention vows), Dieter backed off, bowing. Dan jerked his head at him.

'Who's he? What'd he want?'

'Frank's mate. Wanting to sell me … Forget it – did you see his mascara? Amazing.'

'Mascara? He's a bloke! Sell what?' Dan looked vacant. 'Fags? Handbags?'

I laughed. 'Fags? Ha, punny! No. Drugs- uppers, downers…'

'God, bloody fools! Frank's definitely on amphetamines and boasting about it, idiot. Conor smoked pot in the residency, you could smell it. Worried they'll think we're all at it!'

'Did the warden catch him?'

'Mrs Frankenstein?' (Harsh, but she had a wee bitty of an evil look and the boys said she was always lurking). 'No. Conor's impossible. Ralph's glad of the break from him while he's here. Did you know Conor's asked Frank to leave? Ralph says the tension between them is bad. Now James is off to Edinburgh for his Law Apprenticeship, Ralph wants to move out.'

◆

In class Frank mostly now socialised with Henry, whom I suspected coped with his moods because of his experience with his mother. Dan worried Frank had designs on Henry, but by Christmas, I stopped worrying about anyone as I counted the weeks to the Finals. I worked every night except Saturdays when the Ruby (Rubaiyat) Pub became a favourite watering hole. Rosie collared me one night in the Ladies near closing time.

'Oh my God! You met Ralph's new girl?'

'No. Just got here. We've been to the pictures.'

'She's your spitting image. Green eyes even. She could be your twin!'

'Where's she from?'

'She's an oncology nurse. Bright. Doing a Masters.'

'Hope they'll be very happy.' I didn't care. Ralph was history. I was back with Dan. So much for my old vow, but this time it was an intense, sudden physical and passionate attraction. Sixth Year was generally intense. Perhaps the constant studying distorted my hormones, for by date four we passed Maia's Point of No Return. Sex was amazing: I'd never imagined anything like it. I got the pill from Student Health as my old GP didn't approve of pre-marital sex. After all the hard work, I wasn't trusting condoms. By Easter we were engaged. Both mothers were ecstatic. Dan pushed for a wedding after the Finals and I was carried along in a ridiculous sea of bliss. Apart from choosing dresses and flowers for myself and bridesmaids, Ruth and Alice, I left mum to organise everything. Rosie and James also got engaged. I was a bit lukewarm. Hard to say exactly why – he wasn't Butros or Conor.

'I hope you're doing the right thing,' I said.

Rosie frowned. 'You don't know James well enough, he isn't

140

like Frank. And anyway, at least I've been going out with him for years – you're jumping off a cliff! How come you've changed your mind about Dan so much in a few months?'

I was wounded, though felt a tiny frisson of disquiet. Our engagement *was* precipitous. But I felt certain I could trust Dan completely. Could Rosie trust James?

A few nights later my James fears were fuelled when I saw him leaving the Odeon with a brunette. Dan, returning from the Gents, dismissed me as mistaken. But I'm as sure today as I was then, that it was James with another girl. I didn't tell Rosie. Not sure why. My current view is that during Sixth we were in no fit state to make good personal decisions. Being highly stressed and emotional, it was easier to accept comfort from one another and dismiss doubts about relationships rather than consider potential problems. We took things at face value. There was no time to analyse people's intentions and motives. Some folk were lucky, discovering infidelity early enough to save heartbreak.

◆

One Saturday, Rosie and I took Stella in hand by visiting Rosie's hairdresser and having a shopping spree in Lewis's. We decided she needed a make-over for a date with her new beau, a handsome young consultant whizz-kid, Monty Thirlwall. It went swimmingly. Till one Saturday when I spied him in Great Western Road. I waited till the Monday.

'You're not going to like what I have to tell you, Stella.'

Stella looked up from her lunch. 'What?'

'Monty.'

'What about Monty?' She smiled wistfully.

'He's married.'

'What? Why do you say that?'

'Have you been to his home?'

'No. He has two straight-laced flatmates. They don't take girls back.'

'That's what he told you? I'm sorry, but he's married. I saw him

141

with his wife and child on Saturday morning. He kissed her. They went off arm in arm.'

Stella paled. I recounted Monty coming out of a shop with groceries he put in a basket beneath a pushchair containing a cherubic toddler (his spitting image) and kissing a pretty girl wearing a wedding ring. Like his.

'I've not seen him wear a ring.'

'No? I wonder why?' I left it at that.

Stella didn't. She said she enjoyed confronting him and felt vindicated when several people on the ward witnessed the slap, including Conor. There would be other slaps.

◆

Unlike Stella, I'm not one for public scenes, though there are times … Our Final Year Dinner was one. To this big January bash at the four-star Grosvenor Hotel, we invited consultants and tutors we admired, plus a few we 'had to.' Most teachers were excellent, many inspirational, but that chilly January night Lady Luck dealt me a bum hand with the table companion from Hell. There were no other girls at my table, so when trouble came I was completely unsupported. To my left was an amusing Dermatologist who entertained during the starter, but turned to his left for the main course (Good Manners according to The Honourable Wendy Tuffnall-Brown). With Chicken a la King came the attention of my other table companion, a new medical consultant with a nasal voice. And paws.

'Call me Tarquin, my dear! So, what are your career plans?'

'I'm not sure …'

'Well, if you fancy it, there's always room in my team for a bright female SHO!' He patted my knee. I drew it away. He boasted about his extensive achievements, occasionally asked fatuous questions while gripping my arm so often my chicken was congealing on the plate. Surreptitiously, his left hand descended to the small of my back, then further to squeeze my buttock, at which point my right thigh received his hot right hand slowly advancing over my thin crepe ball gown towards my crotch. In panic I looked around. Though he was practically across my lap, face level with my cleavage, no one noticed except Frank opposite, laughing. I was used to being treated as a second-class citizen, but this blatant sexual harassment in public was intolerable.

'That's my boyfriend,' I pointed, elbowing Tarquin's right arm off as I did so. Dan waved back from afar, happily boozed-up already. Tarquin continued squeezing my buttock with his left hand and breathing nauseating stale whisky breath. I suddenly stiffened, stood up and tipped my seat to extricate myself. Nowadays I'd have removed his hand and slapped him, but then I fled to the loo to sit tearfully in a cubicle, seething. Gathering courage to return for the speeches, I moved my chair to face the top table – out of grabbing zone. My barely-touched chicken was long removed, my meringue glace out of reach. Bloody Tarquin. Did men have nothing on their minds other than sex?

Later in the bar, Dan thought it hilarious. He didn't see that being tipsy is no excuse for groping, especially by that kind of bully in a position of power with a sense of entitlement who thinks they're irresistible. But I survived. Sixth Year went on.

Twenty

Knocked Up & the Knickers

If in fifth year our Psychiatric teaching was mirrored by Nessa's misadventure, in sixth it was Obstetrics which was reflected in our lives. Again, an ill-advised sexual relationship was to blame, but this problem had feet. Just after Christmas, Conor had homed in again on Wendy whilst they worked together.

Come early April I found her in the University Café. Conor had barged past me as I'd come in. Wendy sat alone, her hand covering a quivering lip.

'What's wrong?'

'I'm late.'

'For what?'

'Time of the month, you ass!'

'Thought you were on that new pill?'

'It can fail if you have diarrhoea. Remember that curry?'

Wendy had told me Conor wouldn't use Durex, so she'd got a new kind of contraceptive pill with only one hormone, progester-one, suitable for people like her with labile blood pressure.

'Gosh!' I said. 'Have you had a test?'

'No. I thought Con might go with me…'

'Forget that. Rosie and I will come.'

The Family Planning Clinic at Charing Cross confirmed a pregnancy caused by that dodgy Korma. Diarrhoea had stopped the pill's absorption, allowing a foetus to implant. After much tearful angst, Wendy felt she'd no choice but termination. The clinic doctor suggested the anonymity of the British Pregnancy Advisory Bureau Clinic in Liverpool, adding 'it might affect your career if you had it done up here.'

I seethed. So much for patient confidentiality!

'Worth "Bugger all,"' Rosie said crossly.

So, Wendy went to Liverpool for the weekend, accompanied by experienced Rosie. At least abortion was legal now. Wendy used her Trust Fund to pay BPAS so she didn't have to tell her father. But foolishly, she decided she had to tell Conor. A mistake.

'What makes you think it's mine? Bet I'm not the only one who's been up there, Miss Prim and Proper. Up the duff? Your mess- have it seen to.'

Rosie and I were in his hall, having let Wendy go with him into the lounge. His mocking laugh came through the wall before he stormed out past us as if he'd forgotten it was his flat. We thought his response no bad thing: Wendy was finally over him. Though Rosie and I kept the secret, Wendy confided in Henry, soon to be her residency partner at the Northern.

'He's so supportive. I wish I'd had a big brother like him!'

Henry was certainly big. Sixth Year stress had increased his chip consumption and waist circumference accordingly. If Henry hugged you, you knew it.

◆

By April, pressure was on to excel in Class Exams to get exemption from the degree ones. If you bagged high enough marks in Paediatrics and Obs & Gynae, then you only had Medicine and Surgery to cram for in June. I found myself aping Conor by cutting short oral exams. Not on purpose, though.

During my Gynaecology exam we retired to the Day Room to discuss the patient. My examiner threw himself into a chair, managing 'Now, Miss Slater …' before a muffled expletive. His soles rose to greet me. I did know the webbing in that chair was dodgy, but hadn't managed to say anything in time. I commiserated and helped him up. Restoring his composure and wiping blood from his tooth-bitten lip, he asked only two cursory questions. I passed. Paediatrics was even more Norman Wisdom. I dropped a heavy iron cot-side on the Prof's foot. (Well, the catch slipped). The infant patient chortled as the grey-haired Prof hopped and hummed with a forced smile. Again, two brief questions before he limped off. Another Exemption. Conor would have been proud.

◆

It was end of third term that I found myself in Conor's bedroom. I'd never have dreamt of being there – it was Ralph's fault. Cardiology isn't my forte and having missed a revision class, I asked to borrow Ralph's notes. He took me back for a coffee to get them. Then asked my advice on proposing to Kitty. A novel idea, asking your ex that. I'll never understand men. My only suggestion was to let her choose the ring. He blethered on anxiously then looked at his watch and jumped up.

'Blast! Kitty gets off at four. Right, the notes!' He rushed round the room, lifting and laying things, then stopped. 'Ah! Conor borrowed them. They'll be in his room. Go and grab them: green folder. I'll just dash to the loo!'

Conor's room was flamboyant and disorderly: laundry discarded in a corner, books in a pile and the walls hung with posters of Mungo Jerry, the Stones, Ursula Andress and Twiggy. (She was a surprise: no boobs to speak of). The black furry bedcover, satin cushions, red lamp and mirror above the bed spoke volumes. No green folder in sight. A chest of drawers lay half-closed, contents spilling out. My eye caught pink lace. Intrigued I pulled the drawer open and found dozens of pairs of knickers: lacy, black, striped, conventional. My stomach lurched. I saw a distinctive purple pair with lace daisies, a tiny pink bow, size 10. I'd bought Maia a set of lingerie before Oz while I'd been treating myself in Fraser's sale with prize money. She'd had so few nice things. I racked my brain to remember if they'd been amongst the belongings I'd packed up to bring home? No. My chest was tight. What was he doing with this stuff? Was he a kleptomaniac? Or a cross-dresser? No, most were small ... I checked the wardrobe: no dresses. Deep breathing. The knickers could be anyone's. I stuffed them into my pocket. The loo flushed. Ralph appeared to spy the folder peeking out from under the other side of the bed.

'There it is dopey!'

I retrieved it and we headed off. I had to ask. 'Ralph, why does Con have lacy knickers hanging out of his drawers?'

Ralph laughed. 'Oh, that's his trophy collection. Says girls throw them off in such abandon and can't remember where they've landed so he nicks them. He has quite a collection!'

'What?'

'Yeh. He's disappointed if they're not wearing any. Can't say I've ever met anyone without undies, but then I'm not going after the same class of totty!'

He ran off to propose, leaving me wondering how many girls

146

had risked West of Scotland frost-bite going home knicker-less. And who had owned the ones in my pocket.

◆

The actual Finals are a blur. I do remember waiting for the oral surgical exam and running constantly to the loo while my fellow examinees-in-waiting sat impassive and continent. I didn't know that, along with poor Henry (scratching for Britain), I was one of the few not on Valium from their doc. My knotted stomach, tingling arms, racing heart and spinning mind were a walking aide memoire for panic attacks. I didn't maim any visiting Professors, though if I'd pulled Tarquin I'd have been tempted to inflict more than a bloodied lip and bruised foot.

We all passed. First time. Now to become Dr Slater! And then Mrs Sheehan.

Twenty-One

Passing Out & Signing Up

I am ashamed to say my graduation memories are clouded by post-alcohol amnesia, but the 30th of June 1973 was a glorious day, both in weather and achievement. The boys looked unchar-acteristically smart in suits. The girls wore black dresses or skirts with white shirts under hired voluminous black gowns and red-satin-lined MBChB. hoods. I came by bus, stepping off as Wendy's elegant legs emerged from her dad's Bentley. We met in the quad grinning like mad things, amazed we'd made it. It was great seeing all the relatives I'd heard about over the years. Henry managed tickets for his mother and both aunts, who clucked exactly as he'd described. Rosie had fiancé James, a mother dressed ready for Ascot and a Dad conventionally dressed in a suit (no sequins). Conor had sister Aisling with fiancé, Ritchie. He hadn't told his father the date. My mum wore her Sunday best. Alice had a new dress and was even more excited than I. They sat with Dan's mum.

We trooped into some room under Bute Hall to recite the Graduation Oath. In the Hippocratic tradition I promised to '…exercise my profession to the best of my knowledge and ability etc.' I'm a bit vague on the details. Afterwards we walked up alphabetically for our diplomas to the endless applause of proud relatives. If the Hall, large, panelled, gilded and historic, gave the event gravitas, the Oath made us sober up to our future responsibilities. But afterwards I was far from sober. As usual when excited, I'd missed breakfast, so drinking countless glasses of deceptively innocuous fizzy stuff at the post-graduation reception Prof Killin gave for the prize-winners had an inevitable result. I wafted home in a taxi and slept till noon the next day when realisation dawned. I was now on the Provisional List of the General Medical Council and signed up to the Medical and Dental Defence Society of Scotland in case someone sued me. Dad's 'wee Beth' had made it. He'd have been so proud. The big scary wards loomed. But first we had weddings: Rosie and James in the University Chapel on the Tuesday after graduation. And three days later, Dan and I.

◆

On July 3rd, 1973, unconventional bride Rosie Scott wore a cream chiffon mini dress with ribbons criss-crossing the bodice and a circlet of vivid-pink Zinnia daisies in her hair matching her bouquet. Wendy wore a pale blue version, looking more like a Greek goddess than a bridesmaid with her upswept hair. Groom James Hutton looked handsome in his morning suit, standing at the University Chapel with brother Frank soberly at his side. Rosie's father wore the same, though with added pink silk handkerchief. Her mother, Laura was in a shocking-pink coat dress with an extravagantly feathered hat and Everest-high heels. My dress was some hideously 70's-purple-patterned maxi-dress. After the wedding ceremony, a coach took us to Rosie's splendid home outside Glasgow in Thorntonhall. The day's most vivid memories are the scent of hundreds of roses in the marquee. And Mrs Hutton.

A 'Scottish Field' snapper was taking endless permutations of the bridal party and guests. I thought it odd I'd be seeing Rosie amongst its grouse shoots and big house balls in my dentist's waiting room (the only place I'd ever seen a copy). After she'd done her posing for family groups, the groom's mother caught me alone. Her eyes scanned me from foot to head before she deigned to speak. I felt exposed, naked. She didn't comment on my hippy dress.

'Can she cook?' Her voice had a nasal, clipped, pre-War BBC Received Pronunciation whine. She nodded towards Rosie.

'What?' I asked.

'Does she cook well? I presume there must be some extra attraction...'

'Er, yes. But she's a sweetie, Rosie. And gorgeous in that dress, isn't she?'

'Well, I would have liked there to be a little more of it.' Lips compressed.

'It's a Marian Donaldson!' The popular Glasgow designer obviously meant nothing to her. 'They're in love- isn't that what marriage is all about?' I was cross.

'Oh no, my dear, it's security and stability, and of course sex. At least to begin with.'

'What?' I couldn't fathom this woman.

'My boys are like their father. The physical attraction will wane and they'll be off to pastures new. Cooking might help maintain ...' She closed her eyes, inhaling then breathing out forcibly she carried on. 'Such a pity it's James at the winning post. Not quite the thing for the younger brother, marrying first.'

'What?' I'd lost the capacity to speak any other word. Imagine having this for a mother-in-law? Poor Rosie. I was tempted to say, 'You'll have a long wait for Frank to marry.' I didn't.

'Frank has been, well, somewhat of a disappointment. Despite the Judge's discipline, he lacks mettle. Quite useless at sport. His father played a Test, did you know?' I didn't. 'And as for him becoming a surgeon? Frankly, I doubt he has it in him.'

'But he plays squash … I'm sure …' I stopped. Her attention had wandered to scan the garden, which was the size of a park, and the turreted ivy-clad house, the size of a small country hotel. She returned to me.

'Still, at least Rosemary comes from money. And is well-educated. No finishing school, sadly, but she should know how to behave.'

My face crimson, I turned my back to compose myself. Boarding school must have been a welcome relief for James and Frank. A passing waiter proffered a tray. I sighed. This was a wedding, not a time for disagreement. I lifted glasses of champagne and gave her one. She took it and sniffed, elevating her nose. Her flared nostrils twitched like a squirrel. Or a pig. In a farm yard. Muck. I suppressed laughter. Lady Muck sipped, blinked and looked surprised.

'Oh! It's quite decent!'

A shadow fell across us. The considerable bulk of Judge Hutton hove alongside.

'See you've managed to get a drink, Cynthia. Well done you! Jolly good.'

'It is quite decent, Hubert.' She graciously handed the glass to her husband. I fetched her another. Then slipped off. Gladly.

◆

Two nights later, Dan was on a hillside looking over the Clyde Firth, standing amongst waving willow herb, nettles and fluttering litter of chippy wrappers, crisp pokes, loose Racing News pages and rainbows of plastic bags. He kicked an empty Tennant's can between bent iron spikes atop a concrete block left from the demolition of old flats. This was his world: the end of his road, the beginning of his journey into medicine- a fall onto a broken El Dorado bottle. Bloody ironic, calling cheap plonk 'City of Gold!' the gash had meant his first stitches in Casualty. He'd been smitten:

the drama, white-coated docs, guys looked up to, respected. Guys with status. And motors, even GPs had Jags. And he'd done it! He wouldn't be stuck here on drugs and drink, having quickies up a close with a willing lassie on Saturday nights. The degree and the Medals were his. Tomorrow the next stage of the life plan: a wedding. Then a nice car, nice house, kids. No repeating of his father's mistakes. Mum was happier than he'd ever seen her. She loved Beth. Pity Elaine couldn't manage over. He'd send her some money. Soon.

◆

The sixth of July 1973 was a wonderful day, apart from the acute lack of Dad which at times overtook me. Uncle Jim did a grand job replacing him, walking me down the aisle, making a funny speech. The University Chapel was historic and grand and splendid. We made our solemn vows, signing up for a lifetime together. Mum wore a gorgeous blue outfit and pearl-encrusted hat, very Queen Mum. Alice and Ruth were serene in purple: no wishy-washy pastels for us! My dress had a scoop neck, high waist and long sleeves with frilly lace cuffs. Mum had married in the War and was determined ours would be a proper wedding with cars, flowers, an iced cake and a dance: 'The Works.' Mum had only cardboard on her cake: rationing meant no icing sugar. Dan's mum couldn't contribute financially, but helped in all the planning. She looked well. Dan's best man, brother Iain, looked handsome in his dress uniform. Elaine sent a telegram: kid number four was imminent. Randy had departed. I fleetingly felt a pang. How awful for her, especially so far away.

Our reception was in Govan Town Hall. Uncle Jim provided the caterers, sparkling Cava and lots of beer. To keep costs down, University friends came in the evening to the dance. The band were ace, the atmosphere heavy with love and laughter. A grand party.

We had ten days of sunny honeymoon on the Isle of Arran, hill-walking and beach picnicking, talking endlessly and doing lots of the other thing newly-weds do. I didn't realise there were so many ways. Dan's repertoire, he said, came from the Kama Sutra, apparently a post-pub Friday reading ritual with the boys. I was surprised he'd remembered anything after nights in the Curler's. He'd never suggested being inventive before, but now we had time … Life was great. Before we knew it, it was the first of August. We were pre-registration year residents, Junior House Officers, entrusted with the power over life and death. I couldn't wait.

Twenty-two

Mrs MacKay & the Non-clinical Use of ESRs

During residency my main companions were Fatigue, mind-numbing fatigue, and Hunger, extreme stomach-gnawing hunger – especially in the wee small hours of that first month. Pre-registration house jobs were tougher than any exam. My first six months in Prof Killin's Medical Unit was in familiar territory, but with unfamiliar responsibility. The killers were overnight 'receiving' stints for emergencies. Peak stress came at three am, the body's nadir for cortisol and adrenaline production accompanied by low energy, weariness and fuzzy thinking. I hadn't been to bed when Mrs MacKay came in, the seminal patient of my residency.

I'd had a thickly-accented phone call about her. She arrived with a scribbled note on a blank prescription sheet. *'Agnes MacKay. CVA. Admit.'*

A CVA was a stroke, a cerebrovascular accident. Mrs Mac was pale, clammy, cold and looked dead but wasn't: she had a pulse. But she didn't have the brisk reflexes or up-curling toes from stroking her soles you get in a CVA. I baulked at ringing my supervising registrar again. He'd just returned grumpily to bed after seeing a bolshie academic who'd demanded I get a senior despite his diagnosis being indigestion, not a heart attack. Leaving Sister Pearson checking Mrs Mac's BP and temperature I consulted Mr MacKay, sitting outside in Bryl-cremed splendour.

'Hello, Mr MacKay. Can you tell me what's been happening?'

'I woke at midnight, doctor, and thought she'd passed so I called the doctor.'

'Was she unwell before- slurred or dizzy?'

'No.'

'Any headaches or arm weakness? Falls?'

'No. But she was sick.'

'Right. Any illnesses? Tablets?'

'No.'

'Did she respond to the doctor tonight?'

'Oh, he didn't examine her, could see from the bedroom door she'd had a stroke.'

I returned to a sister proffering lancets and glucose testing strips.

'You'll be wanting to check the blood sugar, doctor?'

I looked behind me to see which doctor she was speaking to, then remembered I'd been Doctor Slater for a whole week now! Stabbing Mrs Mac's finger, I squeezed blood on a strip and found her blood sugar was very low. Sister Pearson pointed out the tummy scarring (fat atrophy from insulin use) and handed me a glucose-filled syringe. As I injected it into a vein, the 'corpse' rose like a zombie in a Boris Karloff movie- the most dramatic cure, ever!

'Where am I? What're you doing?' She was fighting (folk do with hypoglycaemia).

'You're in hospital, Mrs MacKay. I'm giving you a sugar injection …'

'I mustn't have sugar! I'm diabetic!' Sister lay across her to let me finish, whereupon Agnes put her free right hand to her head and screamed. God, was she having a brain haemorrhage after all?

'My rollers! Bert should've taken them out!'

I laughed. Luckily Agnes did too. We finished her recovery with tea and toast. Because she'd vomited her meal, her blood sugar had plummeted since she'd had her insulin. Anyway, her recovery delighted me. Her husband didn't. I returned to the corridor bench.

'Why didn't you tell me Agnes was diabetic? You said she didn't take medicine!'

'Insulin isn't a medicine, it's a hormone.' He looked smug. 'The doctor told her to get on with her life, not think of diabetes as an illness. It's a deficiency.'

I gave up but learned several salutary lessons. One, ask very specific questions about medicines, injections and medical ailments especially from Bryl-cremed pedantic relatives in Army-shiny shoes, collar and tie after midnight. Two, keep in with Sister: she's seen it all and can cover your back. Treat her badly? You're on your own, as Conor learned to his cost. But mostly, believe in yourself, don't trust the opinion of someone who can't be bothered to examine a patient or write a proper note. Mrs Mac sent me a huge bouquet of flowers which I guiltily gave to Sister. My co-resident Yousef was impressed by the story. We were a good team. For Dan, it was a different story.

◆

Over at Dr Todd's Medical Unit at the Northern, Dan was partnering Frank, unhappily. He had mastered the art of absence coupled with the ability to miraculously re-appear should the boss come in. Then he'd scurry around like an indispensable terrier. And nothing was ever his fault. Like failing to read ESRs. An Erythrocyte Sedimentation Rate test (ESR) is where blood is forced up to a mark in a glass tube and checked in an hour: the faster red cells fall, the more likely the patient has inflammation somewhere. Todd used them for reassurance when trying to discharge patients expediently. One day, despite knowing Dan was busy at an emergency elsewhere, Frank left the ESRs and waltzed off for breakfast. Returning for the ward round, he blamed (still absent) Dan for failing to read them. This pattern repeated itself. For six months

Dan did the lion's share of work. Being hell-bent on surgery, Frank didn't care that much about a medical reference from Todd, but Dan did, so decided to hold his tongue. Dan got his reference for his coveted Cardiology SHO post, but Todd was no fool. On his last day he told Frank never to darken his door again.

♦

After a few months we adapted to lack of sleep, stealing it when we could. One midnight things looked quiet as Yousef drained his glass of milk (the only sustenance available on the ward).

'Shall we take a chance and try for a nap, Beth?'

'No one else expected and no acute problems now, are there?' I stretched my limbs.

'No.' Yousef counted the temporary case files on the duty room desk. 'Twelve women and eight men. Surely that's it? Let's go for a rest.' He nodded at a figure sidling past. 'See Towmey's in. After that blonde staff nurse. He doesn't change!'

'I don't understand how he got into McCaig's Unit with his results -that's a prime job! The only good marks he got were Surgical Finals.'

'Ah, well, McCaig was a friend of his mum's. He's even been to his house for tea.'

Yousef was filing case sheets into the trolley alphabetically. I'd fix them into handier bed order later...

'God, how does he know so many people? Dan says he's seeing his Dad again too – thought he hated him?'

'He's blown his mother's trust fund, Beth, even tried borrowing from me. But he's got his Dad donating to McPhater's Surgical Unit Research Fund again, thinks that while it didn't work for Residency this year, it might for SHO next with a McCaig's reference.'

'Oh Yousef! How can we compete? He's even joined a Lodge. I saw him giving the funny Masonic handshake to Mr Grieve at the joint clinical meeting last week, making them instant pals. Lodges don't take women though.'

'An Orange Lodge, like in Ireland? Aren't they to do with the

IRA? How will that help?'

'Different. My Dad was a Mason. It's more a charity/mutual help, thing. They're not all Protestant. There's Catholic ones too.'

'Is there a Coptic Christian one? I'll need all the help I can get. There aren't many foreigners or non-whites who've become consultant surgeons round here!'

'Oh, don't be silly! You got the Surgical Medal. And Gordon's Dad will help after you've worked with him at the Southern. Aren't you going home eventually?'

'Dad's nagging about the US, but I like Glasgow – even the rain!'

I laughed and stuck the last case sheet in, deciding alphabetical order would do. Sleep was more important. We got a few rare hours of it.

◆

Apart from worrying about making mistakes in the ward and future career steps, there were other pressures: 'interpersonal' you'd call them now. Dan and I had rented a flat in Radnor Street near the hospital to spend time off together. Mostly we slept. The idea was that the flat had a lovely king-size bed, unlike the residency narrow singles. But Residency was like bromide, suppressing even newly-wed sexual desire. Medics become habituated to exhaustion. Non-medics can't imagine it.

Rosie was in a peripheral hospital pairing Gordon in an onerous medical job. New husband James was back in a Glasgow solicitor's firm doing a part-time English Law post-grad conversion degree. We hadn't seen them since their wedding, but on Burns Night, Dan's birthday, I threw a party (sans haggis – which neither of us could abide). Before the drink flowed, work-talk dominated the chat. Dan enthused about the recent South African heart transplants. I was sceptical.

'It's pretty poor show if someone has to die to cure someone else.'

Dan disagreed. 'Oh, come on – it's exciting stuff!'

'Morbid,' I said. Others demurred. Too heavy for me. I headed for a drink, but at the door I hesitated, hearing an angry voice.

'Why can't you ask for more time off?' James.

'I can't just take days off willy-nilly. You have to ask for annual leave in advance. Residency rotas are the worst. It'll be better next year.' Rosie sounded upset.

'Frank's got much more time off than you- and he's home by five.'

'He's one in four, not my one in two. Anyway, if he's home by five, he can't be doing his job properly. You can't just "clock off" leaving sick people.'

'Well, don't expect to find me always waiting when you deign to grace our home with your presence ...'

He went into the bedroom, snatched his coat and slammed the front door leaving Rosie in tears. I ushered her into the empty kitchen.

'It's awful, Beth! I'm sorry I got married. James wants me there all the time, and a baby, now. That used to be what I wanted, but I'm not ready. Why can't he understand?'

We sat in the kitchen for the rest of the night. My Bacardi bottle had vanished, so we drank Conor's Asti Spumante and a Blue Nun. Everyone else was in high spirits. Gordon and Heather had reconciled and were marrying at Christmas. Ralph was with nurse fiancé Kitty. Conor was asleep in the corner with his current blonde. I'd been against inviting him, but Dan did it anyway, saying he wouldn't bother Wendy. He didn't. She was laughing at Henry's tale of a patient streaking out of his ward at midnight pursued by aliens. Poor chap. Still, black humour got us through. Eventually, everyone left bar Rosie, who showed no inclination to follow James home. Dan wobbled through about two and took Rosie to the close mouth for her taxi. He downed several more Tennant's, became unintelligible and collapsed snoring over the table. I forgave him. We hadn't relaxed for weeks.

I missed Yousef who was on call, like Frank. I didn't miss him.

He was distancing himself. Dan had seen him being picked up and kissed by Graeme, now a Northern SR. We didn't spread this. Homosexuality was still illegal. 'Outing' would be career suicide. Reluctant to go to bed, I poured a Bacardi and Coke, having found the rum in the loo under the crocheted ballerina spare-loo-roll-holder Dan's mum had gifted us. Sadly, only enough remained for one measure as the thief had almost emptied it. And the coke was flat, it's top missing, which reminded me of Maia, who always left them off, loathing fizz. My hopes of finding her rapist were dimming, though I still pondered suspects and still had the Diary and knickers in poly bags in my sweater drawer. Dan wanted them binned, but it seemed disloyal. Sighing, I left snoring Dan and went to bed. At least that night's party had been better than the last one we'd attended.

Twenty-three

Love-ins & Lightning Strikes

Sean McCafferty was bold in blarney, bow-tie, manner and voice. More like a Dublin car salesman than a physician. First week in January had seen me in his room at St Mungo's asking for a reference. I'd been quite happy to bumble on just enjoying being qualified, but now four months into my first job, Prof Killin was urging me to apply for the St Mungo's three-year Senior House Officer Rotation starting the following August. To him, it was the crème de la crème of jobs, guaranteeing me a trajectory to a top-notch consultant post. He suggested I ask Sean to be second referee, saying McCafferty had spoken highly of me after my Sixth-Year attachment to his unit.

In Sean's chaotic office I stood waiting to be asked to take a seat. Eventually I slid a case sheet bundle onto a heap already adorning the floor and sat anyway.

'Ah, Miss Slater, isn't it? Hello there!'

'Actually, I'm Sheehan now … Anyway, I'm here to ask if you'd act as a referee for me? I'm applying for the Medical Rotation.'

'Reference? Mmmm, right.' He tilted back in his chair, lifting long limbs up over the desk to expose lurid yellow-striped socks – evidence he'd been appointed by an outside body, not the local conservative medical hierarchy. In my experience physicians tended to be sober-sides, surgeons being more likely to be of the colourfully-eccentric brigade. Academics have their own ideas on appropriate attire. Sean was an academic peacock. And more.

'Yes. Well, you know, I think you are probably a girl who should be given a chance.'

My blood boiled – so most girls *shouldn't be given a chance*? I regret to say, however, that by then I'd become so pragmatically downtrodden I let it go. But I needed to hear him confirm he *would* supply a reference, not just '*probably give me a chance.*'

'Fine, so can I put your name down?'

'Sure! And by the way, there's a little party here tomorrow night. A leaving 'do' for Gavin, remember Gavin? Off to St George's. Come along, why don't you? Bring your husband – more the merrier! Kick off around eight. It'll be informal, relaxed, easy.'

Later I remembered the 'easy.' I thanked him for my reference and accepted the invite. We were both off. Dan wouldn't turn down free booze. Plus, I liked Gavin who'd taught me a lot. But there was more to learn.

When we turned up at nine, the room was pretty full with a motley group: unit doctors, senior nurses and friends of Gavin's, mostly louche English academics and a selected few juniors, mainly girls. Sean welcomed us in and introduced his wife who smiled like a rabbit with a smell up its nose. I repeated her name and nodded, only to be chided.

'Not Amelia my dear, Amalia – quite, quite different!'

Shades of Cynthia Hutton. She abruptly turned away. I should have left then.

Couples were dancing to Chuck Berry's 'My Ding a Ling.' Some sat about, entwined. Drink flowed: good wine I didn't recognise then, Fleurie and Chevrey Chambertin, not our cheap Black Tower or Mateuse Rose. Dan was happy with a can of Tennant's. The music slowed. The lights dimmed. Couples drifted off. I concluded academics favoured early nights. Dan was leaning on a wall breathing heavily over a female cardiac registrar he knew vaguely when Sean side-lined me to an adjacent room, arm affably round my back. This time he invited me to sit and appeared more subdued than usual. I thought this an odd occasion for private career advice. The next-door music changed to Quadrophenia, an improvement, if a deafening one. Sean's lips were only millimetres away from my ear. His breath was warm, his voice quiet. I thought I'd misheard. 'I beg your pardon?' He repeated his whisper. I hadn't.

'How about it? We swing here, you know. With research patients only admitted Monday to Friday we have the side rooms… for swinging…'

At only two drinks down, I wasn't squiffy, but I was tired. Why should it matter that this ward was empty on weekends? And 'swinging'? Odd word associations romped in my befuddled brain: swing jazz, or club, racket? Play park rope swing? I must have gazed at him like an imbecile.

He narrowed his eyes. 'Do you believe in Free Love?'

Then it hit. Jesus, the rapt attention on his face wasn't a gaze, but a leer. Oh God, he meant couples swinging, changing partners. Sex with strangers! I was horrified. Not only that this old beer-gutted lecher wanted to get his hands on me, but that I'd just put his name on a job application. Was he presuming then that he was on a sure thing? What to do? Run or cry?

'Free? Well, I wouldn't ever pay for it!' That unnatural sounding laughter must be mine. Sean looked puzzled.

'I'm sorry. It's the time of the month,' I mumbled. It wasn't, but I thought it a reasonably off-putting excuse. I downed a gulp of wine deserving of better treatment.

'Never matter! The Jews think sex during menstruation is like Christmas ...'

I doubted Jewish lads ever considered *anything* was like Christmas and have never got around to asking Nessa if they have a thing about menstrual sex, but God, I realised he wasn't taking 'No' as an answer. My stomach somersaulted. Retreat called for.

'I'm sorry. I've an early start!' I stood up, snatched a startled, semi-sozzled Dan from next door and exited. Stunned, I didn't tell him till next day. He didn't believe me.

'Casting couches are for Hollywood, pet. You must've misheard.'

I wondered who ended up with Amalia. Perhaps she was a satyr's delight, but I couldn't see it. I feared my exit might queer my Rotation ambitions, but whether Sean drunkenly forgot I'd spurned him or worried I'd blab about their weekend revelries on hospital property, I got my reference. The interview came a few months later, a sexist patronising interview, but at least devoid of seedy propositions.

◆

The Board Room was stifling. No one had opened its windows for years and even on that sunny May day, the heaters seemed on full.

'So, what are your plans, Miss Slater?' The moustache didn't introduce himself, but I knew the type: never call a JHO, 'doctor' – they're not fully registered.

'It's Mrs Sheehan, actually.'

'So, Mrs Sheehan, do you plan children soon?' The jowl-cheeked Buffoon next to Moustache sucked on an unlit pipe while twirling his ridiculous bow tie. I suspect he didn't recall me, but I recalled his paws ruining my final year dinner. He got worse.

'Are you on the pill?'

In a sagging chair, facing six sagging males (plus lovely Killin as Chairman) sitting on higher thrones around a shiny Board Room table, I sat up straight. Time to make a stand.

'I'm sorry, but would you ask a man about birth control? If I was planning a child, why would I apply for a difficult 3-year training programme?' My face was hot. Sweat trickled down my cleavage. My rage was hard to control.

Prof Killin interjected. 'Quite right, my dear! You mustn't ask that, Tarquin. Now, which medical speciality appeals to you, Beth?' He smiled.

'General Medicine with Haematology or Dermatology? I'm not sure yet.'

'Haematology requires the M.R.C.Path. Exam too – that's three more years after your M.R.C.P- a long haul for a girl.' Greg Morton, the Haematology Consultant smiled.

God, that sounded a long haul for anyone! I'd no idea haematology needed two exams.

Killin then asked about my experiences in Australia and about Sixth Year locums. My answers were as advised by Gordon (my mentor in all things career), enthusiastic but measured, avoiding anything risking possible lines of questioning on unprepared topics. Gordon's dad tutored him, he tutored me. Pitfalls abounded. Interviews were such a strain. After thirty minutes of grilling I left, being told I'd hear their decision in 'due course.'

◆

Dan's Cardiology SHO interview lasted ten minutes and mainly concerned the joys of Clyde sailing. His prospective consultant kept a boat in Dan's home area. Candidates were told the result in two hours. Dan was in. Four days later I received my offer. We were on our way.

Going home that night along Byres Road I met Henry whom I hadn't seen for weeks. He was beaming. 'I've got it!'

'What?'

'The St Mungo Prof's Surgical Rotation! I was *so* worried after the interview, felt I'd rambled. Mind you, they knew I'd been up all night, elbow deep in gore from that pile up on the switchback.

Two ruptured spleens. Did you hear?

'Enough, Henry! Sorry, no. Poor things. Still, great you've got your first choice.' I hugged him. His reciprocal greeting was breath-taking: how carb-laden residencies had taken their toll on his frame. I disentangled myself to tell him my news. 'I've got the Rotation here. Dan's got his Cardio SHO. Any word of the others?'

'Frank's got the Eastern for Surgery. I really bombed my interview there ...'

'But then that's a lucky escape for you – Frank led Dan a merry dance last year.'

'Well, Beth, you know, he's got his problems.'

'You don't say?'

'He'd a terrible time at school, you wouldn't believe the buggery. No one cared. His Dad's a sadistic bully. Beat him. Locked him in a cupboard for crying afterwards. His mum's a cold fish.' Henry shook his head.

I knew all about Mrs Hutton. I also knew Conor was going to the Prof's Unit but didn't have the heart to dampen Henry's enthusiasm. He'd find out soon enough. 'Anyway, well done! Say, are you off tomorrow night? We both are, for once.'

'Yep.'

'Great. Let's meet for a drink to celebrate. Curler's at seven?'

Henry agreed before scuttling off to phone his mum. I was barely home when Rosie phoned.

'I've got Obstetrics at the Royal Southern and Wendy's got Paediatrics there too.'

'Fantastic! You free tomorrow night? Meet us and Henry at the Curler's, seven?'

Rosie was.

◆

We ended up with quite a party at The Curler's Rest. Ralph and Kitty made it too. The mood mirrored the night the results went up, but without the Union's blaring disco. The background folk singer murdering James Taylor's *You've Got a Friend* was ignorable: we could hear ourselves talk. Another difference was that some of us didn't need to pool our pennies for drinks. We could afford whole rounds each now. The excited chat centred on our next career moves as 'proper' registered doctors.' Dan brought one damper.

'Yousef's got surgery at the Eastern- with Frank.'

'Wonder how that'll go?' Rosie blew a whistle.

'Sparks, I should think! Yousef's not forgiven him for Shesheta.' Dan shrugged.

My stomach lurched. Shesheta. Frank. Assaults. Maia. Dan said I was like the Ancient Mariner. Maia was my albatross, around my neck for eternity. I sighed as Gordon swept in, grinning.

'I've got a place on the Royal Southern GP Rotation!'

'When did you hear?' said Ralph, paling.

'On the mat when I went home,' said Gordon. Ralph rushed off alone.

Kitty laughed. 'I'm not leaving my Bacardi and Coke. He'll be back soon!'

Ralph returned clutching an acceptance letter for a place beside Gordon. We had another round and went back to Yousef's till four. Luckily Dan and I were off next day.

◆

By this time, I was in my second Resident's job. The first few days at Sick Kids had been horrific, trying to secure rubber bands round squirming baby's tiny heads to swell up veins for blood-taking. Being responsible for neonates was worse than adults: babies can't tell you anything. Here, support from experienced nursing staff was even more vital. Lots of new skills came from examining babies. Nappy changing for instance, an art necessitating the ability to predict baby-boy urine spurts. Spotting incipient vomiting was another. Twister skills were also acquired, aided by Day Room tutorials from junior convalescents. But my most heart-warming lesson was an appreciation of how adaptable children were, even after months lying flat in orthopaedic spinal plasters or trussed up by pulleys straightening twisted limbs. Long-stay orthopaedic kids were stars. Dan was a great co-conspirator on nights off, bringing in chips for midnight feasts to whoops of joy. He was great with kids. Those kids. And the nurses were great: except one.

◆

Shattered after a 36-hour stint, I was called to X-ray when a truculent nurse accompanying a car accident victim had thrown in the towel. Little Carla had good reason for screaming. Her mum was in a different hospital and she couldn't get painkillers till she'd been properly assessed for head injury. Nurse Impatient-and-wanting-off-duty-Simpkin's scolding hadn't helped, so the radiographer sent for me. I held Carla's hand, coaxing, pacifying her. The technician ran in and out replacing plates for multiple views of legs, head, chest and pelvis.

'All done!' she called brightly. Then she emerged from behind her screen. Her smile faded. Her shocked face stopped my drooling contemplation of scrambled eggs on toast in the canteen.

'Where's your apron?'

'What apron?' I had on a white coat, why did I need an apron? There was no blood.

'The orange rubber one with the lead in it,' she said.

'The nurse didn't give me it.'

'Well, I hope you're not pregnant! That's a lot of radiation you've had.'

'No, I'm not pregnant.' I was too tired to take in the implications. And hungry.

'Oh well, I'll need to get you to fill in a form for inadvertent radiation exposure. I'll leave one out for you.'

'I'll pick it up later.' I didn't. Nor did I lose any sleep over it. Then.

◆

While at Sick Kids, Nessa was seconded to my ward for her Final Year placement. She was in good form, though a bad example for the kids, being a desperate cheat at snakes and ladders. I disallowed her move up a snake.

'Not fair!' she shrieked. 'I'm nearly Home!'

'I'm gonna win now!' Polly-with-the-pigtails, despite a sling and a steel-plated arm with protruding bolts, threw the dice so enthusiastically that it went across the room to fall at the feet of Dr Abraham Zeigler. He was an Israeli Registrar on research exchange who had appeared in search of his tutorial group, which included Nessa. She stooped for the dice.

My memory proffers a rare full-colour still image: Nessa in a green mini, white coat, jet hair tied in velvet ribbon and with flashing eyes. Yet Abe maintains it was her smile which captured him. Dedicated and six years older, he was a strong handsome chap with a trim beard and, this time, someone worthy of her. He attended parties at Aunt Miriam's. She delightedly swept him into the family, although he did not officially 'date' Nessa until after the Finals. Nessa got a Paediatric Distinction which delighted me, knowing she felt she'd a lot to prove. We celebrated in the Curler's. Even Conor congratulated her. He wasn't all bad. We celebrated a bit too much. It was the night before Ralph's wedding, at which only teetotal Abe felt splendid. I vowed never to drink again. Again.

◆

It was a glorious day, the ninth of July 1974. We were in Kelso down in the Borders.

'Doesn't she look lovely?' Rosie looked dreamily at Kitty coming down the aisle on her beaming father's arm.

My stomach fluttered. Kitty was uncannily like me.

'Stunning dress,' Rosie added.

'More to the point, doesn't she look happy?' I said.

'I hope she is. Marriage isn't all a bed of roses, is it?'

It was too public to ask what she meant. I'd hoped things would have settled down with her now being 'on' less often, but she was without James, coming 'later.'

'How do you feel about this, Beth? I mean, you and Ralph were ...'

'Long time ago. Wrong place, wrong time. I'm happy for them. And happy with Dan.' I looked towards him fidgeting on my other side, finger in shirt collar, hating being 'dressed up.'

The service in the Cathedral was a Nuptial Mass. After forty minutes of chanting, bells, smells, and getting up and down, I muttered that I didn't have the knees to be Catholic. At least that made Rosie laugh. Buses took us back to Kitty's large family mansion. Seeing the pink champagne, I, of course, ditched my abstinence vow and had several. It was followed by oysters which came on trays. With a surprise.

'Oyster madam?'

'Findlay!' He was standing before me with a tray he'd swiped from a waitress. 'What are you doing here?'

'Kitty's my rich cousin. Isn't it a small world? Well, Beth, how do you like oysters?'

I gagged, whispering 'Gross!' not wanting to upset any of Kitty's family within earshot.

'That's my girl. Always honest!' Findlay passed on the tray and clasped me to his chest, whirling me round and planting a full kiss on my lips. A few nearby folk raised eyebrows at his ebullience. Despite circumstances forcing us apart, there was still a bond of a kind between us. Shared history lives in a world of its own, surrounding us with an impenetrable wall that outsiders can't breach. He stepped back grasping my two hands. I queasily feared another whirl after three glasses of fizz.

'Who'd have thought, Beth, eh? Do you know, it's seven years since we left school? And here's you a real doctor and me on the way to being a QC!'

At that point, James rolled up to greet Findlay like a long-lost friend. Findlay was less effusive. My buddy was a man worth knowing: name in the Scotsman, someone going places. At dinner, I sat with him, Dan, James and Rosie. Later as we danced, Findlay spoke quietly.

'Rosie is really lovely. Tell me, how did she end up with that idiot James?'

'What do you mean?' My stomach knotted.

'Hutton's a randy bugger. Divorcees a speciality. A reputation for sailing close to the wind too. Villains love him. He's hot on technical dismissals, dodgy deals – even money laundering, they say. Keep it quiet though. He'd sue me at the drop of a hat! My boss calls him the Master of Fornication and Malfeasance.'

'Och, I tried warning her before she married, but she didn't want to know.'

The band stopped. I returned to my table and tried to block out this conversation and enjoy myself. Such a lovely day otherwise, filled with sun, laughter, lashings of champagne and great food. And Dan stayed sober: relatively. Conor disappeared early. A teenage bridesmaid's seat became empty around the same time, silly lass. Still, an unforgettable happy day for the rest of us. I cherish them now.

Suddenly it was August 1974. We were fully registered doctors standing on the threshold of glittering careers of altruistic service to humanity. Well, some of us were.

Twenty-four

Saboteurs: A Vamp, a Snail, a Liar & a Loss

If my primal fear as a new medical student was that I couldn't possibly learn enough to pass finals, my over-riding fear as a newly qualified doctor in August '74 was that someone would discover that I hadn't graduated. In my nightmares, Maia's face was replaced by a bushy-eyed GMC Chairman accusing me of practising without a diploma. I'd wake sweating in the wee small hours while Dan slumbered. At work I was permanently tense, finding little consolation in knowing I had a resident below me knowing less than I, but some from knowing I had a Registrar, Paul, and a Senior Registrar, Bob, above me for navigating difficulties. Of which there were many. Not all concerned patients.

There was Sophia 38GG, I can't recall her surname. She occupied a 'free-floating' extra post in the unit. At first, I thought her amusing, but she was a viper. In breathy, sultry voice she'd defer in all things to Paul, a gentle, conscientious lad who made up the rota. He assigned fewer slots to Sophia than I, always putting himself on with her. I protested.

'Well, you know, Beth, she's not as confident as you, needs a bit of hand-holding.'

I doubted it was her hand Paul wanted to hold. She could milk helplessness, standing close to the guys, looking down demurely, directing their eyes. For three months I did double her work for the same pay until she jumped ship to an unwarranted promoted post in Edinburgh. She must have projected confidence to the interviewers as fervently as she'd done vulnerability to poor Paul. He was devastated. I was pretty unchuffed myself at her accelerated advancement. Dan suggested mammoplasty as a career move. I wasn't amused. OK, so everyone uses what they have, but I'd have to sink or swim on my own merits. Silicon wasn't an appealing option.

I also sparred with Terry Maguire JHO, who'd obviously never met J.T. Taylor. His mind was unordered, his common sense absent, and snails were speedier. Each emergency patient was clerked in with dogged pedantry, copperplate writing and requests for every esoteric test available. Terry couldn't see common sparrow conditions for fear of missing a hummingbird. Patients risked anaemia.

'Terry, that lassie in bed four doesn't need a lumbar puncture – she's been epileptic ten years. Neurology did a full work-up on her. If they've not found anything, we sure as Hell bloody won't!'

And stop ordering so many bloody blood tests. You'll be wanting a bloody serum rhubarb level next!' Lack of food and sleep were taking their toll on me.

'What a lot of bloodies, Dr Sheehan!'

Killin would walk in at that point. He summoned Paul to arbitrate. The number of obscure tests diminished, but Terry remained slothful. He's a pathologist now. At least there's no rush to make a diagnosis in the mortuary.

Another thorn in the flesh was Jonathon Bridgewater, especially with his antics at a lunchtime Case Conference, April sometime, 1975. With our hours of work, study time was short, so such inter-departmental patient discussions helped us learn from seniors and one another, sharing knowledge. Like Mrs McKay, that Wednesday was an epiphany. I realised some of my peers held a different view of medicine to mine, not regarding it as just being all about patients, but more a contest to promote yourself, make your mark, strive up the career ladder.

I presented a case of Insulinoma (a rare pancreatic tumour). I outlined the tests, differential diagnoses and treatment plan I'd formed, only to be shot down in flames by fellow SHO Jonathon. He criticized everything, confidently citing papers and authorities that I hadn't mentioned, suggesting I'd made wrong assumptions and ignored recent treatment evidence. I felt crushed. Two weary evenings later, assisted by helpful librarians trawling Index Medicus, I discovered the reason I hadn't found and quoted his 'Taylor et al, 1973' and 'Suttie and Caldwell, 1974' was that they didn't exist! I thought an unbelievably risky gambit, but the next day Stella, popping in for a cuppa from her nearby surgical ward, shrugged.

'Typical Jon. Killin's away. Insulinoma's a rare thing and he's reckoned no one else would be confident enough to call his bluff, but they'd just think he's on the ball.'

'I despair! Are the surgeons any better?'

'Not much. I work away, invisible. Beginning to think I'll not make it in surgery. I don't have a Y chromosome and a golf bag!'

'Oh dear. Here, they've started toadying for the third-year specialist jobs. Jon wants Endocrine and Kevin Gastro. Nick favours Geriatrics cos it has quieter nights which shocked Jon as it doesn't have private work!' I sighed. 'Third year? Not sure I even want a second. I hate hospitals.'

'Well, to do surgery I have no choice!' Stella laughed. 'I'm realising there's very little support for girls in surgery. Even passing the Membership first go, I didn't get any '*congratulations*." All I got was, "*Fancy a girl passing first time?*" Face it, Beth, it's a man's world. Anyway, when are your exam results out?'

'Tomorrow. The multi-choice was OK, but the slides were tough.'

'You'll have walked it!' Stella hugged me.

Next day, I was the one giving hugs. To Henry, whom I met in the corridor, distraught.

◆

He couldn't believe there was no sign of it. Maggie had said she'd leave it on his desk, but today he only found lab results and discharge letters for signing. A search of the adjacent secretaries' room proved fruitless: no copies, hand-written or typed. A whole year's work gone. When Conor arrived, tossing down his case-notes and recording tape, he saw Henry on his hands and knees.

'What *are* you doing?'

'Looking for my paper. Was going to tackle McPhater about publishing it.'

'Where did you leave it?'

'Maggie was typing it night before last. She was at the end, on the references, when I was bleeped for Casualty. She said she'd leave it in the duty room. But I got caught up with that motorway minibus RTA. Mangled teenagers. Hellish. Should be a law about seatbelts. Two of them were DOA, one just sixteen.'

Conor switched off. *Dead on arrivals? Ten a penny.* 'Jesus, don't get so het up Henry, it'll be here. Are you sure you didn't take it yesterday and file it? You looked wasted.'

'I was. No sleep two nights running. Hey, by the way, the Prof just asked me where I was yesterday. Thought you said he told you to send me home?'

'Oh? I thought he did.' Conor looked away. 'So, you don't have another copy?'

'No, didn't think I'd need one.' Henry scratched his neck furiously. 'I'll look again.'

Conor helped search the secretary's drawers, bookcase, the corner table, the back of the desks and the duty room. Again nothing.

'Maybe Maggie took it home? She was off yesterday but she should be in soon.'

Conor left. Henry was grateful he'd helped. They were getting on surprisingly well. That 'go home' message business though? Probably a misunderstanding. At nine Sir James returned to start the Friday morning round, eager to discharge as many patients as possible for the weekend receiving. Henry couldn't concentrate, found himself rifling through case notes for results he'd normally reel off pat. The Prof was tetchy. Conor helpfully pushed the trolley between patients, asked erudite questions, found case notes. Henry was grateful.

◆

I was munching a bacon roll in the Cafeteria when Henry arrived.

'It's all gone, Beth. Months of work.'

'What?'

'My research paper.'

'Oh, dear.'

'Even Conor tried to help me look for it. He was surprisingly supportive.'

'Conor supportive? Wouldn't trust him an inch! He'll have hidden your paper for a lark. Remember his track record hiding library books. Be careful, Henry.'

◆

In the afternoon there was still no sign of Maggie. Henry knew she'd been going to the doctor on Wednesday night, perhaps he'd put her off sick? Staff nurse helpfully told him Maggie had taken Thursday off to get her boiler fixed. Her co-secretary, Lynne, was dismissive. She found this chubby overweight English boy irritating: always scratching, pushing specs up his snub nose. What a fuss about a bit of paper! Now, that Conor Towmey? Dishy. Opened doors. Kept his dictation short. Always up for a gossip...

Monday morning came a bombshell. Maggie was in Neurosurgery at the Royal Southern. A plumber calling Thursday saw her on the floor and phoned the police and ambulance. The Prof said she'd ruptured a cerebral aneurysm and the prognosis was guarded. Sister sent flowers. Henry was devastated. She'd be off for ages. His research was gone. But immediately he felt guilty. The poor girl was at death's door. Then Conor offered a lifeline.

'Was thinking over the weekend – was it a grey folder? There was one in the secretaries' waste bin on Thursday morning.'

'Yes!'

'Maybe it fell in by mistake or she threw it in, confused, the aneurysm working on her?'

Henry knew brain haemorrhages didn't 'work' on you, they were sudden catastrophes. None the less...The bin was empty. He found the ward maid, Annie. She hadn't been in on Thursday but found the girl who had. Trish hadn't seen any folder. A cold trail. All those long hours, poring over case records, collating data, matching patients as controls. All those evenings and Sunday mornings in the dusty basement Records Office: wasted. Henry's skin erupted red, raw and weeping on his neck, elbows and behind his knees.

Frances Blix the Dermatologist gave him potent steroid cream.

'If it doesn't settle I'll give you prednisolone. I expect it'll settle after the Exam.'

Henry declined the steroid tablets, remembering the depressed spiral they'd sent him into before, that time when he'd broken up with Maia. Poor soul. Perhaps if he'd been more supportive she mightn't have … He sighed. Life was a bitch. His elation at finding an inverse link between allergy and breast cancer dwindled to despair. It was probably rubbish anyway. He could never face doing all that work again.

The next month was his Primary Exam for the Royal College of Surgeons: two papers of two hours on Applied Basic Science and Principles of Surgery in General. Henry's skin was on fire, but he couldn't risk taking drowsy-making antihistamines. Worse, his hands, usually spared, were now dry and cracked. Contact dermatitis was developing on top of his eczema. He tried to hide his hands from the Prof by arriving early to scrub up and don his gloves.

Four weeks later he heard he'd passed the Primary, as had Yousef and Frank. Conor planned to sit his in London in June. But despite Exam success, Henry felt down, even without steroids. Mr Jackson was the final straw.

◆

It was 2am. Henry was 'scrubbed up,' assisting Sir James as he operated on a Steven Jackson, whom Henry had sent home the day before with 'backache.' But at midnight he'd reappeared at Casualty, very ill, and was seen by McPhater's Senior Registrar since Henry was busy elsewhere. Now Jackson lay on the table bleeding internally from a ruptured main artery, an aortic aneurysm.

'You do know, Thompson, your incompetence has grossly reduced this man's chance of survival?' the Prof sliced and sewed. 'Bleeder!' Henry diathermied a spurting artery. 'Not to mention your chance of good references! Swab!' Henry swabbed. 'Forceps!' The theatre sister slammed them handle first into his impatient hand. 'Bad enough that you missed this diagnosis, but I'd gone to bed when you phoned. Suture! Christ, all this blood! It's right through!'

Henry swabbed, clamped, cauterised bleeding points and held back tears. His skin was hot, itchy and inflamed under his mask. Scratching was impossible: his blood-stained gloves were inside a dying man's abdomen.

'I find it hard to believe you missed this. Folk have ended up in front of the GMC for less. Makes us a laughing stock. The physicians know we missed it first time. They saw the tell-tale widening mediastinum in the X-ray. Lucky for you Terry was there.' He nodded towards the Registrar. 'And Jackson's wife's an MP- couldn't be worse!'

Steven Jackson was wheeled to ITU. Henry went to the changing room toilets and sobbed. This was the death of his hopes. The Prof would bin him. The Jackson family would sue and complain to the GMC. His skin was on fire as he wearily changed out of his scrubs. He knew he'd have to give up surgery.

◆

At his appointment a week later, dermatologist Dr Blix agreed sympathetically.

'You're right Henry, surgery isn't for you. You'll have to avoid anything needing lots of scrubbing-up. What about Dermatology? It's good, less night work.' He grinned.

'Oh, I don't know. Can't think today…' Henry sighed.

'Anyway, meantime I'll speak to James McPhater. He'll need to be told about your skin. Scrub only with Hibitane, avoid Betadine, its Iodine may be an aggravator.'

'I've cocked it up with McPhater anyway.' Henry recounted the Jackson disaster.

'He's a bit of a blusterer, old James. We were residents together. I remember him being a grumpy bugger without sleep. He's quick to flare up, but he's fair. And you're conscientious, so you'll get references. Everyone makes mistakes – that's how we learn.'

'Thanks. I'll consider Dermatology. I've certainly got experience with how skin disease fucks up your life.'

Blix sat back. 'Actually, Henry, one of this August's SHO's has pulled out. Why not come here? Think on it. But let me know soon. If you don't want it, I'll have to advertise.'

Henry went for tea to the Cafeteria and met Beth. 'You stalking me?' He challenged.

'As if Henry! I'm here for survival. I've had "nil by mouth" for hours!'

He told her about Blix's offer.

'Why not? It's interesting and has good scope for private work. I know you worry about helping your mum out.'

Two days later Henry was summoned by Sir James who commiserated with him over his skin and, astonishingly, told him he'd had the makings of a good surgeon. References weren't a problem. The Prof wished him well.

'The Jacksons have complained to the GMC, but we'll handle it. By the way, sorry to hear about your missing paper.'

But Henry no longer cared.

Twenty-five

Court Martial

1989

The Chairman of the General Medical Council Fitness to Practice Committee places her tortoiseshell glasses on the end of her nose and looks towards the legal teams, the members of the public and the press.

'As outlined in the Determination of Facts which have been presented to the Counsels, the Panel have found the facts proven. In respect of the Determinations of Misconduct, which we have also been given, it is our opinion that the defendant's actions amounted to Misconduct at the serious end of the spectrum and as a consequence his Fitness to Practice is currently impaired. In reaching its

decision on Impairment, the Panel has come to its own independent judgement. It has borne in mind its responsibility to protect the public interest and in particular to protect patients, to maintain public confidence in the profession and to declare and uphold proper standards of conduct and behaviour. The Defendant is deemed to have brought the profession into disrepute, breaching fundamental tenets of his profession such that his competence and integrity cannot be relied upon. Accordingly, this day we instruct that his name be erased from the List of Medical Practitioners of Great Britain and Northern Ireland. He has 28 days to appeal against this decision.'

The defending barrister looks stricken. He dreads telling his client. But perhaps fate may intervene: the word is not good. Still, even in that eventuality, there is his own sister to face. She will not be pleased.

Twenty-six

True Colours

Conor parks the case-note trolley in the duty room and muses about the joys of living alone. Old flat mate James has gone to Edinburgh, with Rosie following in August. Lucky sod, James, bagging Rosie. Conor feels himself stir recalling that Lady Godiva night in First. He doesn't miss bloody Frank, now in a flat in Jordanhill with his disgusting boyfriend, but he does Ralph, away since marrying Kitty and always the best flatmate, washing dishes, changing his bed, appreciating the nice stuff in Hyndland Road. Like the Slumberland beds, joyous compared to the Residency's crappy, noisy singles- incompatible with good sex! Next month though, they'll be in in the new St Mungo' hospital.

The new JHOs won't have bare floorboards, naked light bulbs or cracked wash-basins- and they'll enjoy gleaming theatres, airy duty rooms and wards.

This Prof's surgical SHO job is a gas. Plenty of juniors, light rota. Required research project is in hand, as is blonde buxom Staff Nurse Jenny. Cool she's followed him from the Medical Unit. Useful too: seniors tend to forget nurses are about, so all the ward gossip is his! Jenny's becoming a liability though, lingering at Beaverbrooks' window last Saturday: rings! End of first year SHO isn't the time to saddle yourself with a fiancé. Drinking his coffee, he decides – one last fuck on Saturday, then *finito*.

McPhater enters to pour himself a coffee. 'I hear you're thinking of tying the knot, Towmey.'

Jesus, who'd told him that? 'No, sir!'

'Oh? I heard you and Staff Nurse Wilson.'

'Just friends, sir.'

'Pity. Married registrars are focussed, steady.' Draining his cup, he lifts a biscuit before collecting his case-note bundle. 'Well, carry on! See you at nine tomorrow.'

That afternoon Conor sits, feet on desk, reading the Express. Sir Jimmy has a cheek advising marriage: the present Lady McPhater is wife number three! None the less, perhaps he should be on the look-out. Grocer's daughter Jenny is not consultant-wife material. Now, Wendy? Ideal. Classy, presentable, well-connected. Pity he fucked that up. Those eyes, those breasts... Shit, chest drains! Best check today's post-ops. The Boss is especially testy. Word's out the Jacksons are at the GMC. Henry's days in medicine may be numbered.

Next day's round goes satisfyingly quickly. All results proffered promptly, all drains draining into their vacuum bottles, all patients docile and uncomplaining. Henry is rabbiting, Conor nods sagely. He's mastered the Art of Efficiency: stand nodding, move swiftly, hold a clipboard. Frank called it 'arse-licking.' Conor shudders. Frank. Arses. Queers.

Henry is talking. 'Last patient is Mr Jacobsen, a fifty-two-year-old man presenting with a large painful right inguinal hernia and angina.'

Henry is sent to arrange an ECG and a physician's opinion about fitness for surgery, the kind of menial task Conor avoids whenever possible. The Professor leads him into the duty room as the ward maid brings in tea and biscuits.

'How would you like to accompany me to the Breast Conference in London next week, Towmey? You're down for the Primary anyway, aren't you? Be good experience.'

At last! Evidence of true patronage from Sir James after months of acting keen as mustard, copying the old man, even acquiring a tweed jacket and bow-tie. He knows he cuts it in the corridors: stethoscope slung sideways round the neck, walking briskly, attracting admiring glances from nurses. A young clinician, going places. But sod nurses. Classier game needed.

◆

The next week Conor is wondering why he's been called in for a surgical opinion on Jessie Turnbull, an eighty-year-old admitted with confusion and a urine infection. So what if her toes are going blue? Her arteries are shot. Finishing his cursory examination of the deaf, uncooperative old lady, he heads for the duty room, but pauses on the threshold at hearing Beth's unmistakable Glasgow voice saying, 'Wendy.'

◆

'Wendy says the death duties are a quarter of a million alone! She doesn't even know how much the whole estate's worth. She'll get half, though she's already got a big Trust Fund from her mother.'

'If my Grandpa left me that, Beth, I'd not be working a hundred hours plus a week – I'd be off to the Caribbean with a designer wardrobe!'

'What? When did you lasts buy clothes, Stella?' That slipped out: I wouldn't have hurt her for the world, but since the Monty episode she'd never bothered about her appearance. Luckily, she laughed, pretending to sway like a model on a catwalk. Then Conor breezed in.

'Ola, jolly senoritas! Doctor Conor Towmey, surgico extraordinario, at your service!'

We didn't smile. Nor did we comment on his 'recent-holiday-in-Spain' tan.

'Mrs Turnbull, Cooper Ward – got her notes?'

'So, you're the surgical opinion we requested?' I frowned, handing him the bulging folder.

Flourishing a pen plucked from his top pocket he nodded sagely. 'Like the Mont Blanc pen? Present from a grateful patient. Yes, I'm the surgical opinion, you lucky ladies! Diagnosis? Old Crumble, with blue gungy toes that might fall off. Prognosis? Hopeless. Treatment? Why bother?'

'You're a callous bastard Conor,' said Stella. 'If I'd been asked for a surgical opinion on a geriatric with compromised circulation, I'd recommend a phenol block to help the pain.'

'Oh well, but your surgical unit isn't an elite vascular unit like mine, is it? Suppose a quick injection in the back might be worth a try, but certainly it's not worth scrubbing up a theatre for. Order an arteriogram and Jimmy's SR will see her tomorrow. He's at an interview today, so I was the only one around to send.'

'More's the pity,' I muttered, scanning his scribbled entry. Illegible.

◆

Time was getting on. Frank had to speak to him today. Application closing dates were next week. Things had started well in his surgical SHO job at the Eastern General. He'd ingratiated himself by volunteering for extra rota slots when a colleague broke his leg. When he passed Primary Surgical Exam first go, Mr Nixon had looked pleased. but ten months on, Frank was worried. It might be his imagination, but whenever he came into the duty or scrub room, he thought Nixon tended to scurry off. Not being on a secure three-year tenure like jammy Conor at St Mungo's, he needed to know if he could bank on a second year with Nixon or had to apply elsewhere. Finally, he managed to corner the consultant alone in the secretary's room.

'Can I have a word, sir?'

'If you're quick, Hutton!'

The unit secretary entered. Frank looked at her crossly and indicated with a nod she should leave.

'Spit it out, boy! Jean knows everything that goes on here, often before I do.'

'Well, I was wondering about a second year here?' Frank smiled. Nixon didn't.

'Come to my room, Hutton.' Nixon turned on his heel and marched out of the door. Frank had to run along the corridor to keep up. The Chief shut his door, leaned against it and glared.

'I decided not to terminate your current contract, but be assured there's no question of you continuing in my firm. It has been brought to my attention that you are a sexual deviant who has importuned a young student. This will not happen again on my watch. Do you understand?'

Frank was speechless.

'You will get a reference for your work, which is mostly satisfactory, but there it ends.'

Shit, he'd been right: Nixon had been avoiding him. 'Why, sir, importuning students? Who says so? It's not true!'

'Enough, Hutton! I've said my piece. I suggest you consider repentance of your abhorrent deviance.' Nixon opened the door, waved Frank out and closed it, firmly.

In the corridor Frank fumed: Toby! That little bastard, was gay, only scared to admit it. Fancy running to the Chief? But there couldn't have been any witnesses, the scrub room was empty. He toyed with complaining to higher authorities, but mud sticks. Any hint of homosexuality might attract attention. He sighed, consoling himself Nixon didn't have long to go. Influence waned rapidly for guys dropping off the career ladder into pensioned oblivion. He'd have to get on with applications for a second year elsewhere. Perhaps the Royal Southern or St Mungo's? Eugene loved St Mungo's. Great guy, the American theatre orderly. Graeme and he had picked him up in the Muscular Arms and they'd become a fun threesome. Pity Graeme was off to the Big Smoke as SR to Nixon's old buddy at St Thomas's. Though he'd been a bit distant lately. A sinking thought: he'd seen him last week cosily closeted with Nixon in the Day Room. They'd clammed up when he'd entered. Young Toby wouldn't know that Nixon was a bible-thumping Free Kirk Elder ripe for homophobic arousal, but Graeme would. Graeme was the only one he'd told about the boy, had he shopped him? Why? After everything he'd done for him, the risks he'd taken- what a bastard!

He marched off to teach his Fourth-Year student group. One girl had bawled last week. Ninny shouldn't be doing medicine if she couldn't take it. Medicine was like school: give it or get it. In the afternoon he'd skip off to draft some applications.

◆

Ten months into first-year SHO and I was flagging. I was pleased I'd passed Part One of the Royal College of Physicians Exam, but my peers' continual one-upmanship and jockeying was getting to me. Admissions came relentlessly, my pager went incessantly and I was tethered to the ward from eight till six or seven most days. After an overnight, I rarely got my scheduled half-day off. I'd forgotten what it was like to go for a walk in the park. Or to read a novel without nodding off. There was only alternate Sunday nights for relaxing, dozing on the sofa with wine watching TV. Dan was concerned.

'If you hate it so much, pet, do something about it. These Sunday Night Blues are becoming pathological!'

Cardiac Arrests were the worst of all. Even after a successful resuscitation, it took fifteen minutes in the duty room for my tremor and palpitations to settle. I confessed to Dan. He insisted I see the Prof.

Prof Killin looked at me baffled. 'Sorry Beth, why do you think you're in the wrong place?'

'I hate being trapped in the hospital all day, and only seeing a patient for a few days in the ward or ten minutes in the clinic before they're gone and I've no idea what happens to them because when they return to the clinic I'm rotated somewhere else. I think I'd prefer to be a GP, with just me and the patient long-term, so I can follow them over time.'

'Surely not, Beth? It's harder than you think. My wife's a GP. She thinks we specialists have it easy. They see dozens of patients a day, never knowing what might come in next. Much of it's only social problems, you'd be wasted there. And it's pressurised too, you often have to guess at treatment as you don't have access to instant blood and X-ray results.'

'But I'd be using clinical acumen all the time. I've realised I'm not interested in doing some silly research just to publish papers or having to constantly worry who to impress to get on.' I paused, the Prof looked hurt. 'I mean, your seniors are great, but I've decided I don't want an academic career, I just want to help people!' I groaned inwardly: it sounded so wet, but it was the best I could do.

Prof Killin put down his pen, took off his specs and rubbed his closed eyes before looking directly at me. 'You're probably right. I've published dozens of papers, I'm a Regius Professor with gongs and Chairmanships, but, still, it's the patients that make it worthwhile, isn't it?'

I nodded. He'd got it.

'If you're serious, make an appointment at the new GP Deanery. I'll speak to the Dean. Let me know how you get on, but keep it quiet.

'Why?'

'You might change your mind, and it doesn't do to be seen as half-hearted around here.'

Perhaps given time, I might have overcome my 'crash team'

phobia and joined in the politics, but in truth I was thinking about kids and saw no hope of a career break in hospital medicine. I'd met a pregnant SHO from the Eastern General whose request for maternity leave was met with ridicule. 'We don't do *that* here, Dr Jamieson! You'll have to leave.'

She did. Even when the Sex Discrimination Act arrived that year (1975) most girls wanting a career didn't challenge chauvinism. They left.

◆

On a rare Friday night out in the Curler's, Gordon told me some of his rotation had already changed specialities. One girl, aghast at the 'intimacy' of being a GP, went to Radiology.

'Gosh, that's hardly less intimate – all that new contrast stuff they're doing, injecting up bums or into groins!'

'I don't think she dislikes physical intimacy, more the emotional thing, getting close to patient's miserable lives.'

'Funny, that's what I like Gordon!'

'Same goes for me, Beth. We're all different.'

'I think you need a bit of ruthlessness to climb to consultancy. Dan's got it, I haven't.'

'My father's mad I've chosen 'lowly' General Practice. He wanted me to be a surgeon like him, but it's my life.'

Dan eventually appeared to hand Gordon and I our drinks.

'Wait till you hear what Conor just told me! Stella slapped him today, accused him of slagging her off to her boss and lying she was AWOL while on call. He thought it a gas. Malky heard her screaming about Conor sending her off chasing a non-existent patient. Conor denies that, but I know whose version I believe!'

'Fancy bragging about being slapped! Conor's something else!'

'Seems Sir Jimmy came in and she got it in the neck for being a hysterical female. Conor thinks it's hilarious.'

'He would.' I swigged my rum and coke. 'That's exactly why I want out of hospital. Independence, continuity and satisfaction, yes, but save me from chancers like Conor!'

Chancers. One of Dad's favourite words. He met a lot of chancers in the yards, he said. I'd have loved to discuss moving jobs with him. He'd have understood. Mum didn't. She was appalled I wanted to leave a prestigious post. But I was resolved. My appointment with the General Practice Dean was booked for Monday. By August 1975 I'd be out.

◆

Wendy was at Sick Kids doing a punishing one-in-two rota with little free time. I couldn't understand how it happened, but it did.

On a drizzly July night, Dan and I arrived at the BMA Summer Ball to a shock. There was Wendy, welcome drink in one hand, Conor in the other. Later, in our usual male-free sanctuary, the conversation was heated at the mirror.

'What are you thinking of Wendy? After the way he treated you? He's a swine!' I hissed.

'You're so wrong about Con! We've had a great six weeks. He's reformed. Practically teetotal, working hard. He was second in the London Exam and doing so well the Prof's put him in charge of the Unit research and promised to get him a London job after...'

I cut in. 'You're mad. You'll rue the day. Dan spilled his drink when he saw you with Conor. How did he get to you again?'

'Oh, he wrote so prettily after Gramps died. I was very low. We went for quiet drinks. It went on from there. Dad likes him. He's been giving him lessons so he can ride with the hounds. And he's great with animals, so changed. A perfect gentleman now, truly.'

Truly? For God's Sake, I thought, looking at her in the Ladies' mirror, a beautiful picture in a low-cut red satin gown and sparklers. She caught my eye, dolefully, seeking an approval I couldn't give. *Truly* the Honourable Gwendoline Tuffnall-Brown was gorgeous, if insane. *Truly,* Conor was a handsome devil. They'd turned heads crossing the dance floor. But '*truly*,' I doubted he'd changed a whit. It would end in tears. '*Truly*.'

'Just make sure you don't get pregnant this time for pity's sake!'

'Oh, I won't. I've got a Dalkon Shield from Family Planning.'

There was a lot more I could have, should have said, though I knew she wouldn't listen. The Dalkon mention diverted me. After some Family Planning training in preparation for my career swerve, I'd heard rumblings about them. 'Are you sure it's OK?'

'It's fine, stop worrying!' She waved dismissively. 'So, how's General Practice?'

I muttered, 'All right.' As a woman pushed between us I took advantage and left.

'She's impossible!' I told Dan.

'You can't live her life, Beth.' As he steered me to dance, I looked over. Conor bobbed up and down, pulling out chairs, fetching drinks, introducing Wendy to senior BMA grandees, working the room, making the President of the Royal College of Surgeons laugh.

'Her is ignoring us,' I said to Dan, who laughed.

'No wonder, seeing your face!'

We left early. Donning my wrap at the top of the stairs I saw Conor going down to shake hands with Malky Taylor coming up.

'That's weird, Dan. They've been sitting together all night!'

Dan snorted. 'Oh, Malky's probably gone to get him something for the weekend.'

Slow in the uptake, once outside I asked 'Condoms?'

Dan hailed a taxi. 'No, pet! Hash, uppers. Or something stronger. Idiots.'

◆

My last few hospital months flew by with Nessa rotated in as my JHO. We'd enjoyed her wedding to Abe, which had been my first Jewish one. Very different. Men and women segregated during the service but a very jolly after-party. She was off to do Paediatrics in Israel after Registration Year and very happy. Till one Monday.

'I can't go!' Tears flowed.

'What do you mean, you can't go?'

'Mental health issues bar me from training. Conor was right when he said years ago being certified would finish me as a doctor.'

'What does he know? It was a one off. The Dean took you back and you're fine now. It was all bloody Butros!'

'Abe's angry my GP won't fudge it. And if Abe doesn't get a visa to stay here, it's a disaster!'

'Does the form have to be done by your GP? Do they ask for actual copies of your medical records, hospital letters and such?'

'No. Just a doctor's certificate.'

'Why don't you bring the forms round tonight?'

Nessa looked at me sideways. 'You wouldn't?'

'Why not? I've got a GMC registration number and can say I've known you eight years.'

'Not sure I could let you do that, Beth. You'd have to lie.'

'Och, a wee white lie never hurt!'

That night Dan and I sat with Nessa, Abe and the forms. I, Dr Bethany Slater, certified Nessa Zeigler, nee Rosenbaum, as 'of sound mind and free from physical disability.' Then I put a diagonal line across the section asking 'Past Mental Health History.' I didn't actually write 'None.' We sealed the ceremony with Bacardi and Coke, smashing the glasses in the fire-place, a cathartic ritual borrowed from their wedding. Never mind doing it in remembrance of some temple destruction, it seals any ceremony so well, being both reckless and satisfying at the same time. Even if it meant a trip to Woollies for more glasses, Nessa was on her way. And soon, so would I. August 1975, Bearsden GP Training Practice here I come!

I thought.

Twenty-seven

A New Posting & Swelling of the Ranks

I've never been for a dirty weekend with a married man, nor had an argument with a tree. But the Bearsden GP trainee I was meant to replace did. Her hospitalisation after a midnight crash involving a tree, a bend and alcohol scuppered my first GP training post. The trouble was that she was on the way back from a naughty night with her trainer when his BMW came off the Loch Lomond road on a bend. The medical grapevine is unforgiving, as was the trainer's wife returning from her sister's to find him in hospital strung up with a broken leg. Only his first black eye was from the accident. His training licence was revoked and I was assigned to practice further out of town in the village of Milngavie. A lovely place.

I'd done some crashing myself to pass my test in six weeks. Driving is essential for GPs. Planning to proudly show off my 'new' orange Volkswagen Beetle, I invited Rosie for Sunday lunch. Her brand-new gleaming Scimitar beat my wee wheels, but it was great to see her. I missed the gossip of hospital camaraderie, for being the only female medic in the area, I was surrounded by golf-mad colleagues and young girls with very different interests, like TV programmes I'd never seen.

Rosie had also changed specialities, to Psychiatry and James had passed his Bar Exams and English Law conversion degree and was anxious to move south. Rosie wanted to wait till after her post-grad exams before moving. I foresaw fireworks.

Dan handed Rosie a gin and tonic.

'Beth's trainer Jimmy Nesbitt says mixing drinks is a vital skill for GP spouses.'

Rosie laughed as she took the large wedding-present crystal tumbler.

'So, how's being a shrink, Rosie? Better than Obstetrics?'

'Definitely, Dan. Less on-call, more sleep. And really interesting.'

'I think it's ideal for you. Takes a 'nutter' to know one!'

'Hah! But the laugh's on me. Did you know psychiatrists can retire at 55?'

'Why?' Dan raised eyebrows.

'I suppose they think it's stressful.'

I objected. 'What about those exhausted peripheral hospital obstetricians doing alternate nights into their sixties? They should be able to go early!'

'And,' said Dan, 'Psychiatry's just talking to people, who don't listen to you anyway!'

Rosie punched Dan. James laughed. He looked different with his short-cropped hair and cigarette-less hand. I still found him supercilious, yet Rosie seemed happier.

'Say, have you heard from Nessa?' I asked. 'I've not been able to get hold of her.'

Before Rosie could reply, the hall phone shrilled.

'That'll be her!' Dan went out laughing but returned ashen. 'It's Nessa!'

I sat disbelieving. He yanked me up. 'Go get it! Phoning from Israel costs a fortune.'

Nessa sounded buoyant. 'Hi Beth, how are you?'

'Nessa! We were just talking about you!'

'How strange! I wanted to tell you that I'm having a baby though I'm still coming to London to sit Paediatrics Membership afterwards. Studying hard now and I'll use maternity leave to cram as much as I can.'

'That's great!'

'I'll be in London for a bit with Mum and Dad. Maybe you can get the girls together to come for the weekend.'

'Love to. Will you bring the baby?'

'Probably not. Abe's mum's moving here and Miriam can come

189

if I need her. Sadly, Mum's poorly with arthritis.'

'I'm sorry about your mum, but I'm delighted for you.'

'Looking forward to the baby so much. Life's great. I can't thank you enough for getting me out here to Haifa. And your support during Fifth.' Her voice was breaking.

'Sorry, Ness, I smell dinner burning! Stay well – speak soon.'

We ate slightly charred boeuf en croute, drank wine and discussed babies and careers. The guys watched a match on TV. James fell asleep on the sofa. They spent the night.

◆

Frankly, babies weren't my favourite topic. I'd just completed a compulsory 'live-in' Maternity month to get on the GP Obstetric List. Filling my log book of 'personally-delivered' sprogs meant staying up all night, for otherwise, by the time I got a call, it was so late that I'd find a smug nurse putting a child in a mum's arms. Infuriating, the games they played. Even as students we girls took the whole eight weeks to log our twelve deliveries. The boys? Two. Mental. But the biggest surprise I got that month was seeing how many women faced motherhood alone. I couldn't imagine it. Then.

Overall, I liked General Practice more than hospital. It had lots of intellectual challenge and insight into people's relationships and fears. Sometimes, however, their reported symptoms were bewildering. Take dapper banker Jeremy, who saw Jesus Christ in Sauchiehall Street. He was alarmed. I was puzzled. He didn't do drugs, nor have schizophrenia, epilepsy or a tumour. My trainer suggested phoning the Bishop which made me worry more about Jimmy than Jeremy! I mention this case as illustration of the randomness of General Practice: anyone can come in the door. Even someone life changing.

Anyway, I decided to stay in practice, sat the Royal College of General Practitioners Exam and passed first go, before gleefully accepted a nearby Bearsden partnership in August '76. We moved to a semi. The mums fretted about the mortgage. My mum, Peggy, felt the prevalent 15% interest alarming. 'Still, you'll not be out of a job, I suppose, Beth.'

Dan's mother worried that we took my salary into account for the loan. 'Oh dear, what if you "fall," Beth?' An awful West of Scotland term, like women were always doomed to 'fall!' And ironic for Katherine to say that. She worked throughout Dan's childhood. I dismissed their worries, not intending babies yet. But I had to give up the pill due to migraine.

One Monday the smell of dry tea nauseated me. Next day I couldn't keep anything down. Three days later a lab colleague phoned confirming my pregnancy. All it took was one night when we couldn't find the Durex …

I felt guilty, having just signed a Partnership Contract giving me paid baby leave. A boon, for the new Employment Protection Act guaranteeing maternity pay didn't cover GPs, being self-employed. I knew colleagues who'd had to take unpaid leave *and* pay for their own locum, but I secured thirteen weeks maternity leave and could add on any due holiday weeks. Dan was happy. His mum was thrilled, having missed the infancies of her US grandkids. Around this time Dan published his first paper on the new echocardiogram. By New Year 1977 he'd landed a registrar post in the prestigious Eastern Hospital's Professorial Unit. Life was good for us.

Twenty-eight

Happy Families

By Easter 1977, Frank was feeling twitchy as he arranged the notes in the trolley for Mr Chin's round at St Mungo's. Though colo-rectal wasn't his favourite speciality, this was a good teaching hospital post, albeit won by bullshitting about the 'social implications' of colostomy, quoting umpteen papers, some he'd read and some non-existent. He'd even invented 'patients,' like an old lady put in a home, her daughter unable to cope with her faecal leaking, and a woman divorced by a husband who strayed after she had an ileostomy bag. Frank had claimed his ambitions lay in developing new reversal techniques. The interview panel had lapped it up, along with his assertion that good surgery meant treating the *whole* patient, though in truth he felt it was more to do with the scalpel's power over life and death. And private practice.

He worked diligently (in his view) and re-took his surgical Primary exams, consoling himself that many failed first time. The exam result letter lay in his pocket all morning before he retired to a cubicle in the Gents to tear it open. Stifling a scream, he crumpled it and flushed it. Part Two failed again! That bloody homophobic Nixon's fault, still around examining like a dinosaur. Should've been put out to pasture with his pension. He'd not tell his mother. Anyway, he only phoned monthly now.

Perhaps it was time to move on. The Vale perhaps? Graeme was there, returned from London. Might he put in a good word? They'd hooked up occasionally again, though he suspected it might be only when Graeme didn't have a better offer. He still had lingering doubts however, about Graeme and that Toby business. In the Duty Room, he sat back drumming his fingers on the desk. Such a lot to consider. Could he face that exam a third time, swotting the same old stuff? Embarrassing if he failed again. And was surgery really for him? The buzz, the midnight drama of charging about saving lives on the operating table, was palling. Money from private work or the much-vaunted new overtime Units of Medical Time payments was no longer a factor. He and James were now awash with cash. Who'd have thought the Judge had been so loaded? If he'd known he might've been tempted him to take him out, painfully. Disappointing that old Hubert had died peacefully in his sleep. The bastard.

Next night a party at Eugene's gingered him up. Someone brought Jock Selman, a charming Public Health guru often seen on TV during health scares. He made his speciality sound a cake walk. No nights. Rapid promotion. Much less competitive than surgery. With Graeme unreliable and Staff Nurse Eugene heading back to Detroit, it was a no brainer: Frank accepted Jock's dinner invitation.

'I want out of surgery,' Frank told Jock on their date the following Saturday.

'What do you fancy?' The older man sipped claret.

'Not medicine. Standing at the bottom of a bed dithering about whether to tweak a dose or send for another test? Would do my head in.'

'Quite,' said Jock, clicking his gold lighter.

'ENT or Ophthalmology means more clinical exams. I've had it with them.'

'Who could be bothered?' Jock blew slow smoke rings.

'GP's the usual cop out, but constant nights, new patients every five minutes? No way!'

'Never fancied it myself,' Jock mumbled, chewing foie gras on toast.

'I was thinking about what you said last week; NHS re-organisation needing more planners. Do you think Public Health offers good opportunities?'

'Indeed!' Jock waved for another bottle of Merlot. 'You know if you're serious, there's a training programme starting August. You should apply.'

'Wouldn't they think it odd swapping from surgery?'

'Oh, no, the broader your experience, the better. Lot of us are ex-hospital.'

'I'll seriously consider it, Jock.'

'Splendid! Back to my place for a dram, Frank? Wife's away with the kids.'

'Fine. Good meal, wasn't it?'

'Malmaison's always reliable. Central Hotel upstairs is pretty decent too.' He winked.

'Grand.' Frank paid the bill.

Jock Selman was an inventive lover not indifferent to augmentation of sensation by pharmaceutical means. It'd been five years since Frank had indulged. He'd hesitated, hoping Jock's supplier was safer than some he'd known previously. It was a spectacular evening. And with Jock, Frank saw a family way of life he'd never experienced nor considered. Jock was married with two teenage boys. Over the following months Frank enjoyed accompanying them to rugby and football matches and realised their worth in maintaining appearances and circumventing the social and legal complications of homosexuality. Under Jock's coaching, Frank sailed through his application and interview. Mr Chin presented him with a Good Luck card and a bottle of cheap sherry. Wanker. Frank was on his way in Public Health.

◆

Having a baby was much harder than I'd expected – despite my maternity training! It didn't help that Dan was absent when Julia was born on 30th of June 1977, though he was very attentive two days later when he brought us home. The patients showered me with knitting and flowers. Julia was adorable.

While I was still on leave, Henry came to visit. A new calm, confident, three-stones-lighter Henry, beaming behind a massive pink teddy bear. After a year in Skins in Glasgow, he'd moved to Bristol, taken up running and was happy. His eczema was history.

Henry was vexed Wendy hadn't replied to his letters. I wasn't surprised.

'Not sure she wants to keep in touch. We haven't heard from her either.'

While he stayed, we invited Rosie, Gordon and Ralph with partners. Julia went from knee to knee gurgling, though her daytime placidity belied her night-time fiendishness. Dan saw firsthand my legendary sleep-deprived grumpiness of residencies.

Ralph brought photos of Wendy's July wedding, to which only he had been invited. St Mary's Episcopal Cathedral in Edinburgh overflowed with flowers as later did the Great Hall of Wendy's ancestral home. Her elaborate hair held a family tiara, while her crystal-encrusted gown's long train was tended by six white bridesmaids sporting pink satin sashes. I recognised Aisling, Conor's sister, looking lovely. And Conor, looking smug.

'He's marrying Wendy as a career move,' said Dan. 'She's society.'

Ralph hesitated before saying quietly. 'In the bar he boasted that she was worth marrying just for her bank balance.'

'He actually said that?' Rosie was aghast. 'I was upset she didn't ask any of us, especially after...' She paused, meeting my eyes, forgetting only we and Henry knew of the abortion.

Ralph shook his head. 'I don't think she has much choice about anything.'

'I wonder if that's part of the attraction. She doesn't like responsibility, you know.' Rosie wore her serious psychiatric look.

'Worse, he maintained one consultant in the family was enough, so he aims to have her 'up the duff' soon as!'

Rosie stood, picking up glasses. 'She'll need to get a coil. He'll dump her Pill.'

I remembered her BMA Ball disclosure. Dalkon Shields had now been recalled after causing septic miscarriages. I hoped she knew.

Everyone left at midnight, but I lay awake. Rosie didn't want to move south: Wendy was ensnared in a foolish marriage. Maia and Jean had gone. How lucky was I?

The baby slept all night. Typical.

◆

Conor is wasted by the time the car arrives. It takes Liam and Ralph's best efforts to get him into the limo and doorman assistance at the Balmoral to get him up to his suite. Wendy spends her first night of married life lying awake beside a snoring drunk.

Eventually, Conor calls to her, groaning. 'Get me some Brufen!'

'Do you think that's wise after all that whisky? Paracetamol might be safer for your stomach than non-steroidals.' Wendy comes from the bathroom, offering two tablets and a glass of water. Conor strikes her hand away.

'Brufen I said!'

'Get it yourself then!'

It's almost ten. She's been dressed for an hour and she's hungry. What a waste of a honeymoon suite! The airport car will be here at twelve. He'll have to get himself together by then. Hopefully, two weeks in the Italian Lakes will banish this relapse to old selfish, hungover Con. Now that he's *Mr* Towmey, with his FRCS Part Two and a prime registrar's job at St Mungo's Breast Unit, he'll be fine, settle down. She grabs her bag and heads for the dining room.

Eating toast she's liberally spread with butter, she decides some of Con's grumpiness might be post-booze low blood sugar and summons a waitress.

'Would it be possible to send some coffee and croissants up to the Lomond Suite for Mr Towmey, please?' The girl bustles off. As she wipes crumbs from her blouse, Wendy decides she'll keep Tuffnall-Brown professionally: it has a nicer ring to it. She doesn't like to admit it, but maybe school friend Sally's remarks at the wedding had hit home.

'Fancy you becoming a Towmey? It's an Irish tinker name!'

Wendy had walked away annoyed. Sally was definitely off the Christmas card list, especially with her allegation that Conor had groped her dancing: he didn't do that nowadays. During the two years of probation she'd stipulated before setting a ceremony date there'd been no straying. It had been a fun two years. It would be fun again. Still, she'll not say she's keeping her name till after Sirmione. Nor mention the changed Trust Fund conditions.

◆

After my mini-reunion with Henry and co, Rosie sent a letter apologising for James. I admit before they left he'd upset me, recounting a rape case where he'd defended a guy by demolishing the girl as a tart. Next day I'd almost phoned Rosie to disclose Findlay's 'Fornication and Malfeasance' allegations about James. Dan stopped me.

'Never bother. He'll be away south soon.'

That wasn't the point, Rosie's happiness was. We heard nothing further till February, when Rosie phoned.

'We've decided not to leave Edinburgh and have found a lovely Victorian House near Kirknewton, half an hour from James' chambers. Sadly though, it's the wrong side of the city for a registrar job I've been offered. James wants me to give up work to supervise the renovations. If all I can get are these frustrating locums with no continuity of care, I might.'

'Has your offer for the house been accepted?' I asked.

'We'll know tomorrow. James wheedled out the opposition's offer and topped it. House has land, stables and a paddock. James says I can have horses and he can make them tax-deductible! Anyway, once we're fixed up, you must come through. There's eight bedrooms!'

She moved on to the Edinburgh Law Ball and the Jenner's ball gown James had chosen for her. I slipped out of the flow. Till I became aware of silence.

'You still there Beth?'

'Sorry, yes.'

'Anyway, looking forward to the move. If I'm not working, perhaps the stork will visit. I'd like three kids. You know how I hated being an 'only.'

'Yes.'

'Mind you, James will have to curtail his late-night networking dinners to be home ready for it.'

She was obviously still clueless about James's gambling and high sexual appetite alluded to by Findlay. Thoughts flitted: Maia had liked James. He made her laugh – and went to our discos. Might she have gone with him? Pointless speculation. I sighed. Wendy now sounded upset.

'One last thing, Dad's lost weight, been coughing and has an effusion on chest X-ray. Laura thinks its cancer, all those smoky nightclubs, but I'm worried it's Gay Related Immune Deficiency. As yet, though, he hasn't got sarcoma lumps or fungal infections.'

'That's awful, Rosie. Tell him I'm asking for him. And let me know about the house.'

I came off pleased Rosie was staying in Scotland but thinking how odd it was that she always called her mother Laura, like a sister. She had an odd family all together. But I shouldn't talk: my family life wasn't perfect. Though if I kept my problems to myself they didn't seem so real. The Ostrich Solution.

◆

It was eight o'clock. I'd just sat down with a cuppa. The phone rang, Gordon. I was pleased.

'How are you Beth?'

'Fine! Dan's on call, Julia's asleep and I have my feet up.'

'Enjoy the rest. Phoned to tell you Heather's expecting again in July.'

Gregor was only six months old, yet Gordon sounded pleased at the prospect of more sleepless nights.

'And I've got that retirement vacancy in Bishopbriggs, so we wondered if you and Dan would come and celebrate next weekend or the one after?'

'That's tremendous, Gordon. Congratulations. I'll get Dan to check his rota and let you know. And by the way I'm due too, Hallowe'en.'

'Lots to celebrate. See you whatever Saturday is best. Night, Beth.'

I hung up. Gordon: so enthusiastic about another child. Unlike Dan who was proving an odd sort of dad. How I missed mine, longing to ask him for suggestions which might help Dan, encourage him to think another child was good news. Wendy was back in contact, but she had enough on her plate with Conor. I couldn't turn to old-pal Ruth or little sister Alice, both pregnant, nor Rosie, never a fan of me marrying Dan. Not for the first time, I wished I had a big brother. Like Henry, everyone's ideal big brother! But he was on holiday in France. Then I remembered Yousef, albeit in far-off California, always a wise, sympathetic friend. Time we were in touch. I sought a pen and paper.

Twenty-nine

Confrontation & Dereliction of Duty

Gentle Yousef was such a contrast to his egotistical brother Butros. Nature and nurture are, I suppose, the basis of this story, being responsible for the variations in our capacities to respond to adversity. And survive. Or falter. Yousef replied immediately to my letter.

◆

San Diego, California May 1978, 2am.

Dear Beth,

Thanks for your note. Congrats on the baby. I'm sure Dan is really delighted, he'll just be pre-occupied with work. I know what it's like. Here I start with breakfast meetings at seven then it's OR sometimes till midnight. I'm grateful Uncle Omar sponsored me. The ECFMG diploma and Royal College Membership weren't enough to get me a Californian Plastic Surgery Internship. Am doing Maxillo-Facial plastics, so slogging at dentistry too, but love it. Just as well, I think, that the Prof sent me to London for a year and I was frozen out of Glasgow afterwards. Suppose I wasn't surprised my promised job went to the St Kentigern's guy: the consultants were all R.C. Out here there's no religious discrimination, but there are no black medics in my hospital. And guess what? No females!

Buying a house on the shore and getting married in November. Was hoping you and Dan could fly out, but you'll just have to come later with the babes. Dan will like Fay. She's a cardio nurse. Her Dad's a lawyer, made Dad happy – he says you can't have too many lawyers in the family! Mum kept on match-making but now accepts and loves Fay. Who wouldn't? Dark, curvy and legs going on forever. Remember I said I'd never be content with one woman? So wrong. And like you, she lets me away with nothing! Hoping for kids soon. Your Julia looks a darling. Shesheta's had a son. Her husband helps Dad with the business. Butros is casino managing in Beirut, escaping Dad, debts, women and angry fathers. Still arrogant. Don't hear from him. He's worse than Towmey. By the way, saw his Lancet paper on Breast Cancer last Christmas. Reminded me of research Henry did. Maybe he gave it to Conor when he left? Say 'Hi!' to Henry. Lost his address.

My aim is to do pro-bono facial reconstructive work funded by female cosmetic procedures. You've no idea how much you should value the NHS. Loads of folk here can't afford any treatment. It's only the Land of the Free if you have a job and insurance. Enough – bedtime! Keep bearing up, girl. No bearing down till you're in labour! Your affectionate friend,
Yousef Shamoun, F.R.C.S, M.D. (nearly), B.D.S. (sometime), US citizen (one day!)

◆

Things got worse. There are no words to describe sitting by the bed of your unconscious child. Julia has meningitis. She is nine months old and I am four months pregnant with another baby. Dan is working, hasn't visited or phoned. It's two am. Rosie is in Marbella. Neither Gordon nor Ruth answer my calls, Henry does. I feed coins into the Sick Kids' lobby phone, weeping about Julia's sudden vomiting, rash and drowsiness. I've forgotten about Yousef's letter abandoned on my mantelpiece. Henry reassures me Julia will be better soon and offers to come up. I mustn't hesitate to phone him, anytime. I thank him for listening and return to sleep beside the cot, troubled by my stress dreams of Maia. When I wake Julia blinks, cries, raises her arms for a cuddle. A miracle.

Next day I phone Dan to take us home. He comes, all smiles, apologetic. I now accept he cannot 'do' sickness in the family and accept that he is a complex and fickle character.

◆

Dan lifted his whisky from the bar. 'Here's to baby Susan! You'll not forget her birthday, Gordon, the Twelfth of July. There'll always be an Orange Walk to remind you!'

Gordon laughed. 'Thanks for meeting me, Dan. Thought we could have a quick one here since it's just down from the Queen Mum's Hospital. Didn't we have some rare nights here as students?'

'God, aye! Never understood why this pub is called the Stirling Castle – it's nowhere near Stirling! Well, here's to Heather. Sorry she had such a hard time.'

Gordon swigged his Guinness. 'Wee besom came out face first – typical thrawn woman. Thank God for epidurals. Heather was in agony till it kicked in.'

'Were you there?'

'Of course! Weren't you with Beth?'

'No. I was on call.'

'Surely you could have got cover?'

'Giving birth's women's stuff. But Beth wants me there for number two. I'll try. She's had a time of it this year, what with Julia's meningitis.'

'She hasn't any sequelae – brain damage or blindness or anything?'

'No, thank God!'

'You should go to the delivery. I wouldn't have missed ours for the world.' Gordon looked at his watch 'Must dash. Time for the mother-in-law's casserole before reading Greg a bedtime story. You'll be wanting home to Beth, anyway, won't you? Cheers Dan!'

Gordon empties his glass and leaves. Dan nods at the barman. 'Another whisky, a double Bell's.'

◆

The midwife triumphantly raised the wriggling pink baby by her feet. 'Another girl, Beth!'

I was pretty woozy with the gas and air, but lifted her, letting go of Dan's hand. He'd been surprisingly supportive, urging with contractions then exclaiming in wonder as Katy shot out. Despite seeing deliveries as a student, this was different. I was delighted he'd come – the first time he'd ever been to hospital with me for anything. And although I knew he'd hoped for a boy, he looked delighted. We'd decided on Katherine Rose. After his mum.

'Well, hello, Miss Katherine Sheehan. Welcome to the world!'

As Dan cradled her in a little cotton shawl, she yawned, arched and stretched out her arm from her wrappings to grasp his finger tightly. A bond, I thought. Fireworks exploded outside. It was Guy Fawkes 1978. At least Dan might remember Katy's birthday. He never remembered mine.

◆

We knew she was dying. I couldn't believe Dan took it so badly when she passed. It was a blessing in the end. The pain was terrible, her morphine dosage insufficient. I felt non-steroidal drugs would have been better for her secondary bone pain, but her GP didn't like them and wouldn't increase the morphine. I was cross: addiction wasn't an issue with only weeks to go. Dan stayed with her for the last fortnight, taking annual leave. During then he didn't phone. I did, to get him to speak to the girls. I'd suggested bringing Katherine up to Milngavie but he said she was too ill. It suited him to be alone with her: the favourite son. Elaine managed home for the last 48 hours. She'd become a US citizen, which made

Dan cross, God knows why. His brother Iain got compassionate leave from the Army at the end, but I knew Dan thought this was his bag, his burden, his duty. They'd grown apart as a family. As had we.

She died on the 31st of July 1981, but it was five days before he came home, the night before the funeral. He returned to work the day after. Julia and Katy didn't grasp what was going on. At four and two, death is difficult to explain. After the service I took them straight to the Tontine Hotel wake, thinking it wasn't appropriate to take them to the graveside. Dan expressed no opinion.

I hoped things might return to normal after the internment, but Dan spent longer and longer at work, less and less at home and practically nil with the girls. They were in bed when he left and when he came home. After eight weeks of this I confronted him, gently.

'Dan, I was wondering if we should plan a break with the girls – maybe down to the Lakes for a few days? They haven't seen much of you and…'

He cut me short. 'No, not just now. I've taken enough leave lately.'

'Dan, your mother has died, her suffering's over. I know how much you miss her, but you have a family. It's not disrespectful to her memory to spend time with us. She'd have wanted you to. You know how pleased she was you had kids, especially after your father…'

'Don't talk about him. If you keep nagging, mibbe I'll begin to see what he felt.'

That took me offside. 'What? I don't believe I'm hearing this! I'm not nagging, just suggesting a break. You're working too hard, you've had an emotional time and you won't connect with us. I think you're depressed. You need to talk to someone. If it isn't to be me, then someone professional!'

'Oh, goin' all psychological now, are we, doctor? At least you've still got a mother!'

'Yes, and I had to help her through the loss of my wonderful father who went to a football match one lunchtime and never came back! I'm not completely without sympathy, but your girls need you – I need you! Please come back to us Dan, or just let us in, occasionally.'

'You finished? I'm gonnae go to bed. Big presentation the 'morra frae Smithfield, the high heed yin at Guy's. Night.'

Slurring into the dialect of his childhood, Dan left the sofa. And five empty cans. I'd only seen him with two small scotches. That was the first night he slept in the spare room. I didn't pursue him. Maybe I should have. Perhaps the problem was that he never cried. Except once: I heard him weeping in his sleep. We muddled on. I did force a break in the Lake District and a year on I thought things were improving. When in August 1982 he was made a consultant, I was delighted and threw a party.

'Well done, Dan! You must be chuffed. Your dream job – and so early. Ace!'

'Thanks, Gordon. Bit touch and go with that Edinburgh guy in the running.'

'They're doing transplants over there now, aren't they?'

'Believe so, but I think it'd be better to invest in state-of-the-art diagnostic equipment in every NHS hospital instead of splurging on that glory-seeking transplant carnival. We'd save a lot more lives with prevention and earlier diagnosis.'

Passing at this point to pour wine into Gordon's glass, I smiled at hearing Dan echoing my views from years before, but didn't comment. Still walking on eggshells.

'Come on you two! Don't stand around talking shop. Get me a lemonade!' Heather poked Gordon before sitting down heavily.

I couldn't believe she was having number three, though Nessa was currently leading in the baby stakes by expecting a fourth. Two were all I could cope with so I'd been sterilised. I knew Dan didn't want more kids and wouldn't countenance manhood-impinging vasectomy, so I didn't ask. But that was a good night: Dan danced and held me close. We spent the night in the same bed. Finally, he was over Katherine's death. I was sad she hadn't lived to see him a consultant, but pleased he was drinking less.

Then he started seeing private patients at the Nuffield Hospital and his working day lengthened. He came home late, ate and went straight to the study. On Christmas Eve 1982, a letter arrived postmarked Toronto which I left on the study desk. It wasn't mentioned at dinner, nor at breakfast the next day. Dan lightened up for Christmas dinner, read out cracker jokes, assembled Julia's Barbie House and returned to our bed. An improvement. But no mention of The Letter. I was damned if I was going to ask what it was about. Slowly the chasm between us grew again. Physical relations dwindled to nothing. His priority was work. Mine was survival. I was shattered: working, ferrying the girls to nursery, school, dancing and music classes, plus shopping, cooking, cleaning, homework supervision, bath-time and bedtime stories. The girls stopped asking when Daddy would take them out. When he left they barely noticed.

◆

It was a month later, Burns' Night 1983. His birthday. I woke at 7.00am in an empty bed. Across the landing the girls' door was open and I saw Dan shaved and fully dressed, looking silently down on the sleeping girls. As I entered, he bent down to kiss them. A taxi hooted outside. Downstairs our large family suitcase stood heavy at the door. He said the Canadian job was too good an opportunity to pass up: superb equipment, research possibilities. Money, substantial money, would be in the bank each month.

'It's a one-year contract, like a sabbatical, and my job's guaranteed when I get back.'

I stared.

'First leave's in three months. I think we need a break from one other. When I come back, we can try to work things out.'

'Dan, what do we have to work out? Have you stopped loving us?'

'Of course, not.' He kissed my cheek and left, shutting the door behind him.

I knew he'd never go to Marriage Guidance or Bereavement Counselling. I hadn't asked. In my heart I felt he'd decided the only way he could cope with his depression was to leave. Like father, like son? I took the girls to school and phoned in sick. By eleven, when I'd stopped sobbing, I phoned mum.

'He's gone!'

'Oh. Did the vet put him down?' I realised she thought I meant the hamster who'd been ill. He died naturally the day after Dan left. A bit of me died first.

'Not Harry, Dan!'

'What do you mean, *gone*?'

'Packed up, gone. To Canada.'

'That's a shock. So, when are you and the girls leaving?'

'I haven't been asked.' I broke down.

'I'll be over as soon as I've packed a bag!'

Peggy was there within an hour: mums know when you need them. I got very drunk that night – even took a whisky. But the next Monday I went to work, business as usual. Except it was the girls and me, on our own, with Mum as back up.

Dan had only been an NHS cardiology consultant for months. Colleagues thought he was following the money, I knew he was running away. When the first substantial pay cheque came through, I realized I could afford a part-time live-in nanny. With the fabulous Shirley covering on-call nights and after school I settled down to the life of a single mother. Mum came and went as needed. It was a while before I told people. I felt as if he'd torn off a bit of me and thrown it away. Or like I'd been bereaved, yet a body was still there, alive but ignoring me, disinterested in my grief. Interested in another woman?

I almost wished he'd just taken to drink and stayed.

Thirty

Re-grouping

The previous February, Conor was buttoning his white coat and taking his stethoscope from across his shoulders to roll into his white-coat pocket. Looking in the Gents' mirror, he lined up his top-pocket pens and straightened his red and gold striped BMA tie, chosen as he doubted anyone in St Jasper's would recognise a Glasgow University one. His new shorter hair and sideburns he feels, add gravitas. He's come far since graduation. Senior Registrar in a London teaching hospital! Consultancy must follow soon. He smiles and marches out into the corridor.

The Professor, tall, lean, and haughty, had missed Conor's selection interview due to a family bereavement and still looks in mourning. 'Towmey, I presume?' he grunts.

'Yes, good morning, sir!'

The great man strides off purposefully into the ward without a backward glance, leading a posse of juniors and students, Conor follows the other Senior Registrar, a hook-nosed, cool Englishman, all watery smile and cold eyes. St Jasper's isn't very welcoming, but he'll win them round. That stacked staff nurse at the nurses' station will give him the gen. He'll give her something in return. Wendy isn't coming south for a month.

◆

For a few months after Dan left I worked on pretending all was well. On April Fools' Day 1983, I stood on Gordon's doorstep in Kirkintilloch ringing his bell and feeling a fool: always advising everyone how to live their lives but unable to manage my own. I'd missed the last Theta Committee meeting in October as Dan had been on call and I'd no babysitter. Tonight I had Shirley. This meeting was important. The Ten-Year Reunion was only six months away.

Gordon opened the door and handed me a drink. The others were already there. Henry gave me a hug before sitting back down beside Ralph who regarded me intently. I felt everything was in slow motion, and hoped I was behaving normally. These were my oldest friends, did they sense an elephant in the room? Gordon read out Dan's apologies, but none from Conor. He never came. The agenda was full, the venue chosen, but menus and quotes needed decisions. We drafted an invitation letter, checked lists of addresses and divided up the work. I tried to concentrate. Business over, I helped Heather to bring in trays of sandwiches. As I put them down, I felt unable to ignore Ralph's piercing gaze any longer. I sat down, taking a deep breath.

'I'm sorry to say Dan and I have separated. He went to Toronto in January and hasn't been in touch since. I saw a lawyer yesterday.' Tears flowed.

Rosie looked stricken. Henry put his hand on mine.

'Gosh! Silly boy!'

I slumped onto Gordon beside me. Heather nearly spilled the coffee pot when she returned to see me crying on her husband's shoulder. Gordon explained.

'Dan's left Beth. I wondered what was up. I haven't heard from him apart from that answer machine message about tonight. He never mentioned being overseas.'

'Bloody fool!' Ralph shook his head. 'Why did he say he went?'

'Opportunity, equipment...' I was over making excuses. 'Och, he just wanted free.'

'He's depressed, delayed grief reaction. Needs a psychiatrist,' said Rosie.

'I tried. He wouldn't go, just bottled it all up and buggered off. I've got to consider the girls and get things on a legal footing, because if he stops sending money we can't stay in the house. I don't want to uproot them. It's been bad enough.'

'Is there anything we can do to help?' asked Stella. Since Conor had defaulted, Gordon had drafted her efficient presence into the committee. I hadn't looked at her, sitting quietly in the corner in a stylish black dress, earrings, red lipstick. Then I saw it. The ring.

'Stella! You're engaged! That's great! When's the Big Day?'

A welcome diversion. Her fiancé, Jackson, was a hospital pharmacist. And she had now finally succeeded in becoming a Surgical Senior Registrar. We chatted for another hour or so till Gordon wound up, scheduling another meeting for those of us living nearby to send out invitations soon. By the end I was relieved. Sharing the loss had somehow made it official and final. Dan had gone. I left first but Henry caught me up at my car.

'Call me any time, Beth, if there's anything I can do.'

'Thanks, but there's nothing, really.'

'I'm sorry, I thought you two were made for each other, from day one.'

'Well, perhaps Dan would have been happier with Jean. But he's gone now and I'll just need to get on with it.'

Henry stepped forward with a hug before saying, 'By the way I've got a BMJ paper coming out!'

'Well done! That reminds me. Yousef asked. Did you give Conor your research to put in the Lancet? I wouldn't have!'

'What?' Henry paled.

'Yousef saw one on Breast Cancer which looked like something you did …'

Henry was purple. 'The bloody devil! You warned me he was "at it!" That was the one that disappeared, remember? The secretary typing it got sick. Bastard!'

'Oh, of course! How could I have forgotten?'

'Bloody Conor *helped* me look for it, but he must've had it all the time! I stopped reading surgical stuff when I went into skins. When was it published?'

'Not sure. Christmas the year after you went south maybe? Certainly before I was pregnant, sick and in hospital with Julia's meningitis. I think I might have actually phoned you the night I got his letter, but so much was happening. When I did remember,

I told Dan who said forget it, but then his mum died and...'

'Hell, Dan's right. Forget it. Who cares! How could I prove it was mine? Conor's not the first person publishing someone else's work. Besides, I've got papers of my own now. The new one's on light treatment for Psoriasis.'

'Sounds interesting. I'll look out for it.'

Henry wrinkled his brow. 'You know, Conor's a rat, Beth. I hope someone in London susses him out. God knows who else he's suckered to get on. I'm glad Stella's got promoted, Conor tried everything to wreck her career by spreading rumours about her 'instability.' Like saying she threw tantrums in theatres and fled once in hysterics- all bullshit. He'd better not come to the Reunion, I swear I won't be responsible. And the way he used to talk about women? Disgraceful, taking bets on whom he could bed, boasting who he'd stolen knickers from – brains in his balls.'

I froze, key half-turned in the lock of my new Escort Ghia (Matilda the Volkswagen's big end finally went). 'What? Bets on him bedding women?' Words were hard to form.

'Yep! Sliding scale, like a tenner for 'least likely' or a quid for a 'pushover.' Mainly between him and Frank, till Frankie decided women weren't enough and swung off to the boys. You were the only one he never bet on, he called you a stroppy dyke, actually. Most targets were first years or nurses. Why am I telling you all this? Forget him!'

'I'm sure he did Maia, you know.'

'What? Did what?'

'Raped her. She killed herself thinking she was pregnant.'

'Jesus! Surely not? How do you know?'

'From her diary. She didn't name the guy, just said he'd laughed, maintained he'd done it for a bet. I found knickers like hers in Conor's room. But it's all circumstantial, as they say, no proof.'

'Like my research. I've no proof, no original. Oh, Beth!'

I hugged him. He was still a substantial hug, though he was more muscular than in the chocolate and chips days.

He shrugged. 'Sod him. Life goes on. Right, bring the girls down at Easter. I've got loads of room. We can go to Cheddar Gorge and Bath. And they'll love Pinky and Perky. My neighbour feeds them when I'm away, or at home, I suspect- they're fat wee moggies!'

'Ridiculous names for cats Henry! The girls will love them. But the holidays are very soon, they're off from the 14th, is that OK?'

'Sure! I'll take leave. Promotion interview next week. Did you know by the way, I didn't get an interview as promised for Blix's Glasgow job? Was in the end the usual pre-arranged stitch-up, like you say Yousef faced- old boys' network.'

'Och, but Bristol's got less rain! Anyway, Henry, you're on, I could do with a break.'

I went home happier than I'd come. But overnight, resentment and anger simmered. Maia. Stella. Henry. Could nothing be done about Conor?

At the next Theta meeting for posting reunion invites, Gordon announced Towmey had got some new prestigious SR job at St Anthony's in London. He was seemingly unstoppable.

◆

Conor is scrubbed, assisting The Great Man of St Anthony's.

'Get that bleeder Towie!'

Conor diathermies a spurting arteriole the surgeon's just nicked. He no longer corrects his boss for dropping the 'M' from his name. He likes it. Zippier... bit transatlantic?

'Retract!'

Conor pulls back the tissue flaps. Moving to this elite unit is like being a medical student again, but worth tolerating for the honour of working with Sir Roger Vincent, a straddler of the world stage. Conor's Glasgow references for his job in St Jasper's had been good enough, but landing this plum post had required extra effort. Like 'augmenting' his CV a tad and egging on Roger's brother to put in a word. Handy he was a pal of Malky's who needed help with gambling debts. Anyway, Conor felt he deserved this post. And he got on well with Sir Roger.

'Good paper.'

'What?' Conor mops, pulls and fries, trying to keep up with Roger's rapid dissection.

'I said good paper, Towie!'

Conor nods. 'Thanks.' He knew his Five-Year-Follow-Up paper on breast cases was well-crafted and completed in record time. Pity his name was third down the authors' list. That was how it went: higher the rank, higher the billing and the less actual graft put into the paper.

'Our results compare to the best, even the Yanks.' Roger pauses, looking down. 'This doesn't match…' He peers at the mammogram film fixed to its light box high on the wall, then at the gaping wound. 'Oh, dear, don't like the look of this, do you? Mind you, film's three months old. She's been bumped off a few times for bed shortages. Aggressive tumour, eh?'

Conor silently seals a bleeding vessel in the sinister knot of exposed tissue on the patient's chest.

'It'll have to be a Radical. A lumpectomy offers no chance. It'll be in the glands now.'

Conor agrees, despite hating Radical Mastectomies, desecrations of womanhood where breast tissue, underlying muscle and all armpit glands are cleared, leaving the risk of a leaden, swollen arm. He wonders if a female surgeon could do one. Something gung-ho, macho about the op. Unusual for him to be squeamish. Boobs though, important.

Roger's sharp scalpel cuts a swathe round the tumour, removing a wide safety margin of normal breast tissue and muscle.

They were like Gods: the power of life and death in their hands. Dice and slice. Conor winces as the knife extends to her armpit. Axillary glands can't be left or tumour will spread body-wide, if it hasn't already done so while the woman languished on the NHS waiting list. Blood seeping over the green theatre sheets triggered memories: watching a butcher as a child, marvelling at the swift sharp knife carving a hanging carcass in Coatbridge. He shudders looking at the flesh in front of him. Is he getting soft, doubting a surgeon's power or entitlement? With a consultancy in his grasp, this isn't a time for hesitancy. And it's not just any consultancy. Roger is offering a golf outing.

'There'll be a couple of chaps from St Mary's. You know Ginger's retiring from there soon? Might be able to swing it for you. Their next-in-line, Senior Registrar Arvind, is an overseas fellow, competent enough, but… while Harley Street boys might favour him as less competition – not Anglo-Saxon, get my drift – in practical terms it's not on. One's patients mightn't be happy covered by him should one have to go to St Andrew's or the Algarve. Now, *you'd* be ideal. So, OK for this Sunday, Towie?'

Conor meets the Chief's eyes, framed in their web of tapes and green linen, and enthusiastically accepts. He holds out a stainless-steel basin for the large lump of tissue now orphaned from this woman and destined for pathology. Never again would Mrs Y see a lover gazing at her creamy bosom in desire, not with a huge ugly scar across her flat, deformed chest.

'Hang on, Conor, we're going to try something.'

His chief slices an ellipse of skin round the woman's nipple, leaving it attached to a strip of skin which he swings round, stretching, to re-attach in her arm pit. Conor looks wide-eyed, but says nothing. Biting his tongue is now second nature.

'New technique! Going to give this lass a re-construction and implant. The NHS doesn't run to them so I'll magnanimously bring an implant meself from the Wellington. Do a dummy run here before trying it there. This filly could be wearing a 36D soon! And if the nipple graft re-vascularizes nicely, with a bit of luck it'll be sewn back on target after reconstruction. She'll have proper sensitivity then, according to Simmonds in Boston. Now, close her up.'

Sir Roger stands back and jerks his elbow to his head, indicating he needs his brow mopped. A nurse jumps to attention. Conor smiles at her as he sews.

'Take a bit more care! You're not sewing up a mattress!' the Chief snaps.

Conor winces and concentrates. Discomfiting, nipples in armpits. He's seen some tattooed nipples after re-constructions: fools no one, no erectile tissue, hopeless for givers or acceptors of pleasure. Perfecting this it would be a huge money-spinner.

'Remember on Harley Street patients will want it to look as though they haven't had surgery. Tiny stitches, no puckering. Practise in here on the NHS peasants.'

The nurse frowns. Conor thinks this a bit much himself. Roger wouldn't have risked saying that in front of the Panorama team in earlier filming.

'Here...' Sir Roger takes the suture needle, demonstrating a different technique. 'Harley Street style, see? Why don't you come with me Friday? See how it works? Best suit, clean nails, silk tie.'

Conor thanks him profusely.

'Carry on finishing the list. Nothing else of interest to me today. All in your capable hands. Be in my room if you need me.'

'Yes, sir.' Conor stitches, mops, snips.

'And do tomorrows round for me, eh? Got a Maharaja's wife who can't come Saturdays. Should manage a Caribbean cruise this winter!' He chortles and wheezes off.

Moving to the new Breast Unit at St Jasper's has been so worth it. This firm is more dynamic and welcoming. Conor has found London surprisingly lonely. Wendy is always doing lunches, riding or buggering about with silly clinics since she's swopped to School Health. With a consultancy looming, it might be a good time to expand the socialising though they couldn't host parties with the likes of Sir Roger in the current Peckham pad. Wendy understands that sort of entertaining. If he finds a house with a stable she should cough up. Mean bitch. Why leave the Earl's money in the bank? And why shouldn't she book a posh suite for the coming reunion? Get her on it tonight.

London hasn't all been bad. Malky's been here for years and

is now a consultant obstetrician. An awful speciality – always on bloody call and delving into women's plumbing. Lucrative, though. Earned him a new nose and a swish Wimbledon house. Hysterectomies were like caviar he said, solved all a girl's problems in one swoop: periods and pregnancies. Malky was still single, but had useful contacts for everything a bored married man needed. Like willing women and other mind-altering delights.

◆

1983 was a busy year. I couldn't have managed full-time practice and two young kids without Mum. I tried to support her too. In August I went with her to a funeral. Duncan was an old family friend – and Findlay's father.

By four o'clock only Findlay, his wife Sandra, mum and I remained as stragglers in the Queen's Park Hotel. Staff cleared away uneaten sausage rolls as Sandra disclosed she was a psychiatric SR in Edinburgh – and worked beside Rosie.

'Have you heard when she'll be back from Marbella, Beth?'

'Sorry, Sandra, I've no idea. It must be months since her Dad died.'

'Yes. She's had two months unpaid leave. Must've been awful watching her Dad die with AIDs.' Hoovers throbbed nearby.

'I haven't seen her since the funeral,' I said.

Findlay's eyes narrowed. 'I hope it's only grief she's suffering from? How much does she know about that philandering arse of a husband of hers?'

Sandra answered, 'Oh, I think she suspects.'

I sipped cold tea. 'I thought things were better, I mean, she was trying for a family...'

'Never mind a baby, I'd worry he'd give her something else from Edinburgh's saunas and whorehouses.' Findlay looked fierce.

Whorehouse did it. My mother rose. 'Time to go, Beth.' The staff looked relieved.

In the car she raged. 'Poor Rosie. James sounds an evil rat!'

I could think of a few worse, but diverted her.

'Fancy coming with me to Catherine's of Partick on Saturday, mum?'

Of course she did: her favourite shop. I decided I'd treat her while looking for a dress for myself. Bit of pressure, reunions. You don't want to look over-the-hill. Still they're interesting for seeing where everyone's got to. Maia came to mind again. What would she have become? Though deep in my heart I feared we'd never find who was responsible, I still ruminated on Frank or Conor as being responsible for the tragedy. Guiltily, I moved on to a more pressing problem: what kind of dress might make me feel confident for Dunkeld, my first big un-partnered event? I sighed. Doubtless Frank and Conor would be there. Fortunately, Dan wouldn't.

Thirty-one

Revelations

Dunkeld House was a charming hotel in the Perthshire hills. I was delighted so many of our old year had booked rooms for the Reunion. September 9th, 1983 was a time to renew old friendships – and see who'd done what. Some classmates were now consultants, many not where they'd intended. Some were divorced, or like me, solo. As Mum moved in chez Sheehan for the weekend, I took Friday afternoon off. On arriving at the hotel, I immediately ran into Wendy in the lobby.

'Wendy! Great to see you!' Clasping her in a bear hug, I was shocked at her bony frame. Her face was puffy and caked in thick makeup with desperate red lipstick, though she still looked smart in a stylish trouser suit and 'brothel' heels (Dan's term for stilettos). Dan, still popping daily into my thoughts. It would have to stop.

Wendy smiled. It didn't reach her eyes.

'No Conor?' I gave my booking letter to the receptionist.

'No. His Prof's in Hong Kong and the other consultant has slipped a disc at squash. He might manage Sunday but I said not to bother. He's mad – I booked a suite!'

'Good for you! I've got a single, probably overlooking the bins.'

'Let's have a drink before dinner. I've brought champagne.' She turned to the receptionist. 'Say, could you put notes in with the keys for those people I asked about?'

'Certainly, madam.'

Wendy borrowed a pen. The helpful girl took the scribbled notes. Wendy turned to me again. 'So, Beth, who's all coming?'

'I looked at the final list this morning: Rosie and James, Gordon and Heather, Henry, on his tod, Ralph solo too. No Nessa. Her new babe Malachi has Gaucher's. I looked it up, an awful, rare disease, mostly affecting Jewish families.'

'Oh no! They won't have him long. Tragic. It causes progressive mental and physical deterioration. How are your two?'

'Four and six. Healthy, happy and infuriating! Katy's going to be a politician – has an answer and argument for everything.'

'Lucky old you! I'm first floor, Glamis Suite. See you at half six?' She teetered off, towing a smart Vuitton. I collected my key and trailed my battered M & S trolley-bag to my first ever single hotel room: top floor at the back as suspected. I'd been single now eight months with no word from Dan. I was glad Ralph, Henry, and Wendy were also here alone.

◆

In the end, it was only I who joined Wendy. I had but one glass of champagne, yet the bottle was left upturned in the bucket. On the way into dinner we laughed at Rosie's notice board: photos of mini-skirted girls and lanky long-haired boys on a hill-walk and awful fashions at some drunken ball. The evening passed quickly. The chatter ran high. Wendy talked of life in London's fast lane with brittle laughter, re-filling her glass between attentive Henry's top-ups. Frequently heading for the loo, she'd return with perfectly re-applied lipstick. But by midnight those sorties, returning via the bar, were taking their toll. Wafts of brandy gave the game away. She swayed to her feet. Henry caught her arm and guided her upstairs. My mood plunged. Topping up with spirits out of sight: a tell-tale sign of dependency. The party was breaking up. Many had come great distances and were tired.

Next morning, returning from a swim, I met Henry in the corridor. He grinned at my Medusa head.

'Don't laugh! I didn't take a hairbrush to the pool – didn't expect to meet anyone!'

'You don't look half as bad as Wendy did last night when all that war paint came off!'

'What do you mean?'

'She had a black eye under her make-up.'

'Oh dear!'

'She cried on my shoulder for ages. I made coffee and helped her into bed – she was so wasted! She's got fingertip bruises on her upper arms too, just like in those old Jurisprudence abuse slides.'

'Conor?'

'Who else? She still excuses him, but eventually she admitted he hits her. Last week when she refused him more gambling money, she had to lock herself in the spare room.'

'Why does she stay?'

'Scared? Afraid of being alone? Of admitting she's been foolish? Who knows. He's even threatened to have her certified as mad from booze and drugs like her mum if she files for divorce. All rubbish, but she's scared so hasn't seen anyone when she's been hurt. His current wheeze is pestering her to buy him private practice rooms in Harley Street.'

'She shouldn't take that crap – and drinking isn't the answer.'

'Yeh, she admits to a bottle of wine a day. Probably a lot more. She's buggering her liver, has loads of spider naevi. Needs to get liver functions done. But I don't think she'll stop drinking while she's with that bastard.'

'Good God! What else can Conor do to us all?' As I walked away, a thought occurred. 'I didn't see any naevi, Henry, must be slipping. Are they on her back?'

Henry blushed. 'The red liver spots are on her breasts and tummy. But her liver isn't enlarged yet, I checked... Actually, I slept with her.'

'Henry!'

'She was scared on her own. Needed support. We didn't do anything till this morning...'

'Enough Henry – too much information!'

Henry gave a shy smile. 'I've loved her for years. I won't let him away with this. The research theft was one thing, but ...'

So, there it was. Poor Wendy. I had my own survival to think about. I summoned the lift to return to my attic garret for a brush and hairdryer. On the top floor there was another surprise, standing at the door of the room next to mine.

◆

Dan had a room towel draped over his arm, a not-unattractive sun-tanned arm.

'You don't need a towel, the pool has its own,' I said. Not *where have you been for eight months, you bastard?*

'Oh, well, I've got one anyway. Can we meet for a coffee in the lounge, say at ten?'

'Fine.'

I rushed inside to shower, tame my hair, apply make-up and squirt perfume, then sauntered down to the lounge. Dan soon arrived. His slicked back hair reminded me of my father at tea-time. The waitress brought coffee. Dan poured. He'd never poured me anything before.

'I'm sorry Beth, the way things worked out.'

I didn't reply.

He smiled. 'I've done a lot of thinking. I'd like to come home. I miss you and the girls.'

Still my tongue didn't work. Annoyingly, I felt my anger dissipating, my resolve crumbling. He looked… different: less Scottish, more film-star-ish. Sexual attraction defies logic.

'I do love you, you mustn't doubt it. I wasn't myself, Beth.'

He held out his hand. I took it. The coffee lay untouched. We kissed gently in the lift going upstairs. On my bed his ardour grew with extraordinary passion. He cradled my head, smothering me with kisses and eliminating all thoughts- even of eight empty months. When he started undressing me, I didn't object. I'd resisted sex for years before marriage, but it's like a drug once you've tried it. There was some suppressed anger in this session. I did bite his ear and rake his back with my nails. His 'Oh Beth's! were the only words spoken. My utterances were not convertible into language. We stayed in my bed till noon, then exchanged our single rooms for a suite. Dan told me he'd been seeing a counsellor, had talked over his problems, especially about his childhood, and was taking antidepressants. I was amazed.

'There's four months left of the contract, Beth. Then I'd like to come home if you'll have me. I've agreed to a job at the Eastern. Can I come to see the girls before going back?'

I nodded, but decided I wouldn't warn Mum. If she made a scene, he'd have to take it on the chin. I briefly wondered if I was as bad as Wendy, not that I'd been physically battered, more emotionally. But Dan had been unwell. Conor was just a bad bastard.

We lay on the capacious king-size bed and made love again, more slowly. News from the past months tumbled out as we dressed.

'Conor's hitting Wendy. She's in a right state. Drinking.'

'That's awful.'

'Henry shagged her this morning.'

'What?' Dan stopped with one leg in the air and half a foot in a sock. 'Never heard you use that word before!'

'Seems appropriate, though. And I told Henry about that Lancet paper. He didn't give research to Conor. I remember now, it

220

disappeared from the ward and Con helped him look for it. But I warned Henry at the time, helping's not Con's style!'

'What Lancet paper?'

How could he have forgotten? We'd discussed it at length. Or rather I had, he then being liable to tune me out, being impervious to my distress. 'The one Yousef wrote to me about. A Lancet one Conor published which Yousef thought was Henry's stuff.'

'Oh, yes, I remember. No surprise. Con's usually at the bottom of anything underhand.'

'Like Maia. I'm sure it was him.' Emotionally heightened, I got upset at that point, thinking of her. Dan standing in boxers, open shirt and one sock, clasped me as I stood in my top and no knickers. As he gently kissed me, trying to stop me crying, I fleetingly wondered what particular medication had been powerful enough to change him into someone as empathic as this. We fell to the floor. The clothes flew off again. I was glad I'd never sent that divorce letter. We walked into the village for lunch on our own. Late.

◆

That night's Gala Dinner was dire. Conor made a Grand Entrance an hour late, strolling in wearing a grey lounge suit though we were 'dickied' up in full evening garb. He swept in like he owned the place. Waiters scurried to set an extra place at our table.

'Decided I couldn't let you be here all alone, beloved! Did you miss me?' He blew Wendy an extravagant kiss across the table. She said nothing. Henry glared. 'Found a locum for 24 hours and jumped in the Aston. Fairly hoovers up the miles!'

God, Conor, lover of clichés. Even his words were stolen from other people. Wendy gave him a wavering smile. Henry sat bolt upright beside her, opposite Conor. Ralph, on Wendy's other side, glared at him tight-lipped. Rosie, next to Henry, was sending me daggers as I sat with Dan's arm round my shoulders. It was a dinner swirling with undercurrents.

In the bar we waited whilst the tables were cleared for the dance. Once Dan headed for the Gents, Rosie rounded on me.

'Can't believe he's just waltzed back like nothing's happened. What are you doing?'

'He's the father of my kids, Rosie. I love him.'

'Turning up here unannounced? He's done it so you won't make a scene in front of us. But remember, we're here if there's any trouble.' She patted my arm, in full psychiatrist mode. James at her side, nodded, reassuringly. Already glassy-eyed, I doubted he'd be much help with 'trouble.' Dan returned. Stilted small talk passed the age till we could return to a table.

The strain didn't diminish. Ralph sat all night wide-eyed and glazed, never rising to dance, just downing whiskies and intermittently catching my eye with a definite vibe of disapproval. I didn't eat much. It was worse than the Final Year Dinner, though at least I wasn't being groped. Only Conor was full of life, his own mostly. I left the table as often as possible to dance with Dan, away from the wonders of Conor Towmey's prestigious new consultant post in London, his revolutionary breast re-construction techniques with their huge potential market in breast plastic surgery. 'Big tits' were what it was all about, he said. When the bragging started about the actresses and models he'd treated, only James stayed. Ralph and Henry headed to the bar, Rosie to Stella's table. Even with Dan at my side, I felt abandoned. The condemnation of my friends was palpable. But it was my life. I was happy Dan was back. Most of them were in muddled relationships themselves and shouldn't criticise me.

As Dan sat talking with Conor, I fumed, itching to denounce him as a thief and a wife-beater and accuse him of raping Maia. It was all too much. At one o'clock I followed Wendy upstairs, taking a double brandy as a hypnotic. No idea when Dan came to bed. Doubt he knew either. Mixing alcohol and anti-depressants is never a good idea.

Next morning I woke before seven. Since living solo, I'd become a lark, adapting to an early rise to steal time to myself before my heavily-scheduled days. Dan was machine-gun snoring. I'd drunk (fairly) sparingly till my 'medicinal' brandy but he hadn't counted his whisky doubles. I was unsure whether to believe his claim of abstinence when away. At any rate, this was a child-free day which I was going to make the most of with early breakfast and a walk. The dining room held few early birds as I headed for the buffet to select orange juice and a croissant, before sitting down opposite the only other member of our group who had surfaced.

'The reunion's gone well, hasn't it?' Ralph smiled.

'Yes, I think so.'

'So, that's you and Dan back together again?'

'I'm not sure, but I'm prepared to give it a go. After all, there's the girls to consider.'

'Do you love him?'

I thought this a very personal question, especially at 7am. I debated whether to answer and stared at him for a few seconds before glancing down to see that I'd just spread apricot jam on my napkin. Was Ralph looking differently at me? I remembered last April at Gordon's when I felt Ralph was looking into my mind. Thankfully he was now shifting his gaze out at the gardens. The sky was bright. It might be warm enough for a coatless walk.

'I thought I loved Kitty.'

I didn't know if I was up to this; there had already been enough emotional turmoil this weekend. 'So where is Kitty? I didn't get a chance to ask you last night.'

'In London. Got a job there after her Ph.D.'

'And you're still in Somerset?'

'Yes, in Frome. I'm attached to Bristol University's Department of General Practice.'

'Do you two get together at weekends?'

'No. Not now.'

I hadn't got much from this exchange, but persisted. 'Have you broken up?'

'Yes. Some people aren't meant to be married. They don't like giving up independence, taking responsibility for another person, or persons.'

'You mean Kitty?' I could think of others.

'Yes. Kitty's decided she wants a high-powered nursing career. It's fine. When she didn't want to come back from London up to Glasgow I commuted down at weekends for a bit. But when I moved to Bristol to help Dad with Mum's Alzheimer's she decided we'd best call it a day. The divorce is nearly through.'

'I'm sorry, Ralph.'

'No, I'm sorry. I should never have let you go.'

This was getting uncomfortable, especially as I was feeling an uneasy flutter of regret myself, a wisp of nostalgia...

Then Dan walked up, unshaven and grey. He called over a waiter for a pot of strong coffee then staggered towards the buffet. At the other side of the table Ralph rose, car keys in his hand.

'Remember Beth. If you ever need anything, ring me.' He put a card on the table, kissed the top of my head and left. I slipped the card in my jeans pocket.

Dan returned from the buffet with a heaped plate and started munching his bacon, sausage, black pudding and bean mountain with fried eggs swimming on top: the West of Scotland hangover cure. He'd have had Irn-Bru too if it'd been on offer. I sipped my juice, having abandoned my jammy napkin and crumbled croissant.

'You went to bed too early. Frank collared me in the bar late on. You won't believe the things he told me...' Dan went goggle-eyed and shook his head.

I wasn't up for much more in the way of revelations, but on the other hand, after Ralph's declaration of love, neither was I sure my legs were strong enough to take me outside. 'Frank? Not sure I want to know.'

'He burned a body!'

'What?' That got my attention.

'So he says. Mind you, by midnight he was pretty wasted. He thinks he's up for a Public Health consultant job, you know. Sound like very rapid promotion to me, but apparently the competition's weak and he has friends in high places.' He tapped the side of his nose and winked.

I hate winking. 'He's as bad as Conor! Mind you, if he did despatch a body, he's worse. But why should he tell you about it?'

'D'you remember Graeme Galbraith? That surgeon who blew him kisses in the clinic?' Dan pointed his knife at me. Grease dripped onto the white linen tablecloth.

'Yes. Was it him?'

Dan was masticating noisily, mouth half open while talking. I watched fascinated as greasy egg dribbled down his chin. 'No. But he's just died. Of Hepatitis C. Well, so Frank reckons. He had jaundice, liver failure.'

'I don't get this. Frank's nearly a Consultant. He burned a body? Graeme's dead? So?'

'Well Frank and Graeme were homo items for years, so he figures, whatever 'Gee,' as he calls him, got, he might get. He's worried. And his conscience is bothering him, though he maintained he'd no one trustworthy to confide in, hence him using me, thinks I'll keep his confidence, apparently! Poor Frank thinks he's damned or something. Drinking brandy!'

I was puzzled. Not at Frank drinking brandy instead of pints, but at Dan's pride in receiving Frank's revelations. Was it just because *someone* was pleased to see him yesterday?

Sighing, I asked, 'So whose body was he going on about, if not Graeme's?'

'Well,' Dan looked about to see who was listening, then lunged to flatten himself across the table and whisper, 'It's like, well, they used to do threesomes…' I didn't know how much more of this I could take but there was no stopping him. 'And one of them was with that boy in the year under us who disappeared the end of Fifth. Remember it was on TV? The police called him John but he called himself Pat.'

'Pat is John? Or rather John was Pat?'

'Exactly! Patrick was his middle name. He was John Patrick. Good Mick name.'

Vague memories stirred: of asking mum to switch off the TV in our Govan kitchen, of the news story about a bonny blue-eyed boy, a singing hill walker who vanished.

'Anyway, it seems they were up to some auto-erotic thingy involving near-strangling. Well it wouldn't be 'auto' cos Pat wasn't alone – do they have a name for it, if they're helping one another?'

'I have no idea Dan!' I looked round. The room was beginning to fill up. With kids too. I wasn't sure this was the proper place to be having this conversation, if indeed, anywhere was.

'So, the boy snuffed it! Poly bag on the head jobby. Strung up he was, by a rope from a pulley hanging from those hooks you get above ortho beds. Weights and pulleys were involved, he said. Sorry, bit vague on the details.' This was already more detail than I cared to hear but I sat fascinated and despite myself, curious. 'But he didn't suffocate. They were drugged up by all accounts. John Patrick took too much amyl nitrate Frank thinks, dilated some blood vessels and bled out. Remember the press said the boy had a bleeding diathesis?' Dan looked at me expectantly.

'Von Willebrand's,' I ventured.

'It all happened in an empty Orthopaedic ward in St Mungo's, and I think the pulleys...'

'Dan, enough!'

He sped up the narrative. 'So, Frank stuffed him in the basement incinerator he knew about from our time as porters and no one was any the wiser. There!' He finished and sat back, at last wiping his eggy chin with a napkin.

'God, Dan, he saw you coming! Burning a body? What a cock and bull story – how could he move a body from top floor Ortho to the basement without someone seeing? That boy died in the hills. And Frank's never worried about Hell. He always mocked Maia's God-squad for believing in a Sky Fairy!'

'Well, he was pretty bloody convincing! What should we do

about it?'

'What can we do? A known idiot tells you a drunken tale alleging a death what, eleven years ago? And the only other 'witness' is dead? Forget it!'

'But it's such an amazing story …'

I looked at this man in front of me: still a schoolboy, a lover of tall tales in a pub. I never got my walk. Rosie and James arrived with Henry, however Frank, Wendy and Conor didn't appear. Maybe they breakfasted in their rooms.

◆

When I returned to Bearsden with Dan, my mother was terse.

'So, the wanderer returns? You took your time!'

Dan had the grace to look sheepish. We went to bed early for less passionate but more tender sex. After which Dan had palpitations. He dismissed my idea it might be anti-depressants and excess booze. We had a blissful week spoiling the girls and an emotional airport goodbye. He promised to phone regularly and to get a cardio check-up. But there was a final bombshell.

'By the way, I'm taking instruction to become a Catholic like my father.'

'In an Arab state, Dan?' I said, flummoxed. 'Why?'

He left with a wave but no answer, as ever. My complex and fickle husband.

Thirty-two

No Man's Land

1989

The nightmare shows no sign of ending. He can't wake up, he can't move. But he feels peaceful, complete. This is a weird trip. There's humming. Not musical. Electrical? And darkness. Inky, like night. Endless. When was the last sunrise? One day? Two days?

Now there's a rhythmic vibration, a swishing, like wings. Passing birds? But it's warm and there's no breeze. Indoors. Definitely indoors. He feels high, not sublimely but physically. And horizontal, heavy.

Straining, he hears faint distant music, a chorus being almost drowned out by the rhythmic humming and vibrations which are getting louder. Whoomp. Whoomp. Are they angels' wings? Jesus, he's really flipped this time. An overdose or contamination? Not good.

Lights flash and dim, the whoomps lessen. There are still other barely audible sounds: an atonal concerto of clicks, beeps, hums, buzzes. The faint music fades to a voice, talking. A radio! Where is it? Where is he? He tries to recall something which almost flutters into vision before wavering and vanishing leaving only flickering light.

There is peace and pleasure, but no rush of orgasmic experience. This isn't heaven. Sweet Jesus there's a monitor flashing numbers-148, 150… 168. Is it attached to him? Holy Mother! His focus fades as his chest tightens and his ears suffuse with a pressure that eliminates sound. The pain passes. Tensing, he strives to understand. Where is he?

Milliseconds of life flash by. A definitive memory swirls amongst fleeting confused thoughts: a cardio-version. He sees himself from on high on a bed. The vision fades to black with a central glimmer of light: a tunnel. He's falling into it. If this is the end he doesn't care, for he is shrouded in peace and floating down.

Hell! His heart is gripped again. A tear-stained face looms, a cloud of hair, a pale, pale neck. He hears mewling. God, a cat? He hates cats. The girl weeps. The suffocating sensation in his chest worsens. Is this a hallucination? Or a dream? Why her, long forgotten? Why not someone from the present, someone he loves? But what is her name? He can't remember. Panic rises. The peace vanishes. The light is dying. Is he dying? He's never felt so abandoned. That agony pierces again. Forces drag him back. Enough!

The jackals don't hear his silent scream as they circle with their needles and tubes and tapes and wires and paddles and trolleys and barked orders. Damn them. They won't give up. He can't speak for the choking tube. He can't move. The pain subsides. His vision clears. There's a green screen with wildly spiking pulses. Normal PQRS waves vanish into wild Ventricular Tachycardia spikes, the speedway to Armageddon. The vice comes again. His chest can be crushed no further. The palpitations beat uncontrollably. The screen flashes Fibrillation: a heart out of control, failing. Holy Mary, Mother of God. His pulse races, exploding into his head.

That rhythmic clicking is the ventilator! The shrill cacophony is the monitor alarms! The counting is the Crash Team!'

In his consciousness the abyss appears. Black.

God, will someone make sure he has the Last Rites?

Thirty-three

Cilla, Celibacy & Celebrations

Two weeks after the Reunion, Conor rings a bell. Typical bloody Malky, it doesn't work. He lifts the knocker to rap, but the door swings open. He smells cooking. In the kitchen lies a board with cubed steak and sliced mushrooms and a pan with butter-congealed fried onions, but no Malky. He calls out. No answer. The Kensington Mews house is compact. It doesn't take long to look round. The dining room is set for two: candles, wine glasses and, by its nose, a serious claret breathes in a carafe. The bedroom smells less pleasant: grubby sheets, stale sweat and laundry with soiled underpants on the floor. Worse than his old student flat. Back in the hall, the front door opens to admit a tall, smart girl, hair upswept in a tight French roll who strides past to look swiftly through each door off the hall before confronting him.

'Who are you?'

'Conor.'

'What are you doing here? Where's Malky?'

'Don't know. Gone out for some ingredient he's forgotten maybe? He's cooking.'

'That'll be for me.'

Conor wonders how she'll feel when she sees the bedroom. Walking into the kitchen, her eyes sweep the room. She replaces the wall-phone which he hadn't noticed dangling. Impatiently, she upturns the tea caddy, sifts through the teabags then rummages in the refrigerator icebox, pulling out a polythene bag. Con recognises dihydrocodeine and some unidentifiable small red pills in poly packets which she throws into the sink in disgust. She moves to the study, Conor following. As much paperwork lies on the floor as on the desk. He sees a letterhead he recognises and picks it up. She glances over.

'You know he's been reported to the GMC? You a medic too?'

'No,' Conor says. 'He never said last weekend. And yes, I'm a surgeon.' God, this girl was very officious.

'Bloody idiot. Smashed at work. He's been suspended. Alcohol's the least of it, there's huge debts. The stupid bugger's being chased by some heavies.'

Conor is alarmed. 'Should we call the police?'

'Doubt he's been abducted. Raincoat and Triumph keys gone from the hall.'

'Never noticed... so, who are you, exactly?'

She flashes a warrant card. Conor nervously fingers a packet in his pocket. Focussing on the card he gets it: Detective Sergeant Priscilla Taylor. Cilla! Malky's sister. Drug Squad? Bloody ironic or what!

'I'm here for a Council of War to persuade him into a rehab place in Surrey. He was going to cook me dinner to show me he can cope. He can't. I'll wait for him.'

Conor feels dismissed. Nothing to be gained by hanging about here.

Next morning Conor flicks on the TV while eating his corn-flakes. 'Here is the BBC News for November 4th 1983...' Malky's face appears on screen, followed by footage of a Triumph sports car crumpled under a lorry. The newsreader's words jar. 'Head on...wrong way...one-way street...ICU in the Hammersmith... doctors say critical...not expected to...' Chased by dealers or out of his face? Jesus, there but for the Grace of God! The newsreader mentions Malky's GMC case. Conor makes a pact with himself to slow up, sleep more, take less stuff. He astonishes Wendy by taking her up a cup of coffee before leaving for work.

◆

That week Liam was donning his coat in his Kirkintilloch hall when his phone rang.

'How are you Liam? Are you up for a game of badminton next week?'

'Sure, Frank. Sorry I've missed the last few weeks, been hectic. Could do with some exercise. How about Wednesday?'

'Right oh, Wednesday, Sports Centre at six?'

'Well, court in afternoon, so best make it seven.'

'Right, Liam. I'll book it.'

'How's the new consultant post?'

'Pretty good. A few of the usual dross who don't pull their

weight, but still better than the circus of surgery. Didn't envy the surgical lads at the Reunion however hard they tried to mock me.'

'Haven't heard from Conor in yonks. Was he there? How is he?'

'A big cheese, by all accounts. Didn't speak to me, hasn't for a long time. Think he was terrified I was after his body. Admittedly, I used to camp it up a bit, make him squirm. Payback time after years as the butt of his jokes. Thinks he's a London player, but it's all Wendy's money or his father's.'

'Well, that gravy train's done for. Towmey Holdings has crashed.'

'Really?' Frank chortled. 'How the mighty fall!'

'His Dad's filed for bankruptcy and our firm's doing the Receivership.'

'No kidding? Change of subject. I've bought that boat, the thirty-two-footer. Called her the "Gee and Tee" and mooring at Rhu. You'll have to come out for a sail.'

'Love to. Sorry Frank – gotta go. School bonfire's at seven. See you Wednesday.'

Frank replaced the phone and sat back to admire his newly completed East Kilbride penthouse with its velvet Ligne Roset sofa, Tintawn shag-pile, Laura Ashley bedrooms and modern sculptures and paintings. He loved beautiful things. Few people bothered. Graeme had. Liam did, but then his mother was an interior designer. He loved Liam, especially as he'd 'stolen' him from Conor. He had so few other confidants now, Jock having a new protégé, Graeme being dead. He's glad they made up at the end, a terrible end. Swollen, confused and fitting. Now he constantly inspected his eyes for yellowing. The slightest itch might mean liver disease. Hepatitis C had such a long incubation period.

He'd given up sex. Not worth the risk. Once it had been his reason for being, he'd been fixated by climaxes. Why? For affirming he was alive? To escape loneliness? To know some other human being desired, needed him? But with Hep C and 'AIDS' as they called it now, sex could kill. Celibacy was the thing. Frank the philosopher – who'd have thought?

A more imminent worry was his indiscretion in the bar at Dunkeld. Hopefully Dan had been too blootered to remember. And it was all so long ago. There was no body, no evidence, no witnesses left. Poor Pat. A rocket streamed past outside. Bloody Guy Fawkes. Fires and bangs and people enjoying themselves. But they'd all die, every one of them. The trick was to try to forget about it. He swigged his remaining vice: Glenfiddich. Even that would go if he got hepatitis. Fucking life! Or rather a 'no fucking' life! Laughing. He drained his glass and tossed the empty bottle into the bin before going to bed in the arms of Mogadon.

Next morning the bathroom mirror brought another reminder of mortality. Roots. Time for an appointment at Vidal's. Nothing wrong with holding back the sands, but maybe he'd keep a few distinguished silver streaks.

◆

After the reunion, Dan returned to Toronto. He phoned on Katy's birthday and Christmas Day, promising a visit in early February. Instead came a Valentine's letter.

> *Dear Beth,*
>
> *Just to let you know I am moving to Dubai to set up a Cardiology department at the new University. After some thought, I've decided that it would be best if I gave you your freedom so I've started divorce proceedings on the new grounds of irretrievable differences. I'm sure you will agree we are now too far apart…*

I didn't read on. Devastated, I took a few days leave. Mum came. We got tiddly again. She didn't say, 'I told you so.'

The following Sunday, Ralph phoned as he sometimes did. I needed someone to talk to. I couldn't burden pregnant-again Ruth and Rosie wasn't entirely supportive, having made it clear she'd thought me mad to trust Dan again. Ralph started phoning most nights. The next weekend but one he came to visit and Mum headed home for a rest. Ralph and I stayed up talking. He hugged me. I cried. He played with the girls, tucking them up to insane stories about skiing in Switzerland, cuckoo clocks and gnomes. We had separate beds. He didn't ask.

Our telephone calls eased into a daily habit. At Easter I took the girls to Somerset to his pretty cottage amongst daffodils and rolling hills. We ended up in bed. A psychiatrist tutor once told me we should garner endorphins where we can, collect maximum plea-sure chemicals from food, wine, the great outdoors – and sex, even if adulterous. Dr Tobias practised what he preached. He had three wives. Theoretically Ralph and I only committed 'half-adultery', him being divorced. His love-making was different from Dan's: slower and more considerate. We drove around in his big Range Rover and met Henry in Bath for afternoon tea. Julia gorged on cake and threw up on the way home. Ralph was fine about it. We found Dettol and had a great time. Within six months Ralph sold up in Frome, found a post in Glasgow University's Department of General Practice matched with a part-time partnership in the West End and then moved in. Why waste time, we thought? Perhaps I had a premonition. Life isn't endless. Besides, the sex was good.

On Julia's seventh birthday the following year, 1985, watching Ralph light fireworks in the garden and play with the girls, I real-ised how much Dan had missed out on. Ralph wasn't perfect: he couldn't catch a ball for toffee (yet he'd captained a cricket team?) and kept putting his back out trying to master Julia's hula-hoop. When he allowed Katy to christen the dog he bought 'Tiddles' I refused to walk him- fancy calling 'Tiddles come here!' in the park! Eventually I did, of course. Ralph was home by six every night and wasn't a stranger to the oven, the hoover or the iron. Mum loved him. The girls adored him. Divorce papers were finalised. Dan was history. Even the Maia problem faded. Ralph proposed.

September 30th, 1985, nineteen months after Dan called it a day, the small, soulless Glasgow Charing Cross Registry Office was brightened by the girl's infectious enthusiasm. Katy had shrieked and giggled all the way in the taxi. She was so like my father with her laughing personality, fresh complexion, blue eyes and brown hair. A delighted Rosie had helped plan the day, though I had misgivings about the Dallas-style shoulder pads on my cream jersey maxi dress. She'd pinned up my hair with peach roses and helped the girls into frothy short dresses and sparkly shoes. My sister, Alice, was Matron of Honour in a peach dress. Ralph's sister, Cressida, arrived home from Forensic Science studies in the States the week before. A slim, blonde, female version of Ralph, we hit it off immediately. She brought Tim, her partner, a Scotland Yard officer. Useful. Later.

The only hitch was Henry's panic at losing the rings. He eventually found them in his back pocket. The reception in the Grosvenor Hotel was near Nessa and Wendy's old flat. Nessa came from Haifa. I didn't ask Wendy. Ruth and her husband came. And Rosie, without James. Gordon and Heather were away. My family comprised just mum and Alice. Uncle Jim had died. Ralph only had his dad, Cressida and Tim, as his mum had died two months before. Like Dan, Ralph went home for the end. But unlike Dan, he returned immediately after she'd passed. Anyway, on the Day, the debris of the meal had been cleared from our private dining room and coffee had been served when Henry got to his feet, tinkling his wine glass with a teaspoon for attention.

'Ladies and Gentlemen! At last, I give you Mr and Mrs Semple – my best friends who have finally realised they are made for one another!'

There was clapping. Katy shouted 'Hooray!' In horror I noticed Black Forest Gateau spattering her expensive dress.

'Beth and Ralph would like to thank you for coming today to help them celebrate. And I have to thank the bridesmaids. Not sure why – they haven't done much!' Henry blew a kiss to the indignant girls. 'Though they've certainly enjoyed their dinner. I see Katy's taking some home… But Alice, thanks. I know you've been a huge help to Beth. Better than me as best man. First time

I've been asked, and probably be the last…' More laughing and hooting. The warm sun streamed in. 'And Beth says thank you to Rosie, chief fashion co-ordinator. Now, a few telegrams and cards...' After reading out Wendy's, wishing us years of love, respect and support: everything I knew she lacked, he raised his glass. 'Ladies and Gentlemen, the Bride, Groom and Bridesmaids!'

We only had the one speech, no dance. It seemed inappropriate with Ralph's mother so recently gone. The girls went home with Mum. Ralph and I stayed on in the honeymoon suite. Next morning we flew out for two weeks in Yugoslavia. Nothing pertinent to add to the saga there: just sex and sightseeing. And a warning that Slivovitz brandy is on a par with Sangria. You've never had a headache until you've tried Slivovitz.

◆

The day after the wedding, Rosie dumped heavy grocery bags in the hall and lifted the phone.

'Hi, Wendy. You've caught me just back from Safeway's. James buggered off to golf first thing so this is a great time for a chat!' She sat down on the hall chest.

'Con's on the course too. I was just wondering how yesterday went?'

'Quiet, but lovely. Beth was wearing cream, had peach roses. The girls were like wee meringues. You could've eaten them! Katy is Beth's double. Bossy, dashing about and messy!'

'I'm sorry I wasn't there…'

'Well, you know, Beth was worried Conor might turn up even if she only invited you.'

'I know. Henry says she's as angry as him about that thesis.'

'Oh? When did you see him? He didn't mention it yesterday…'

There was a long pause. 'I've seen quite a lot of Henry…'

'You sly old thing! How often?'

'Once a month, roughly…'

'What? Have you? I mean, did you?'

'Oh yes. Lots of rampant sex, oodles of lust! I can't tell you

236

how re-born I feel! We jog, we dance, we fuck ... It's pretty damn marvellous, darling!'

'Wendy Tuffnall-Brown! Do you hear yourself? How do you manage to meet?'

'He phones Fridays when Con's at Harley Street or when he's away at the weekends golfing, shooting, fishing, whatever. Maybe bonking some bitch. Then Henry and I meet up in the Cotswolds, or midway between Bristol and here. His wee house is charming too. Shh!' Rosie heard Wendy's voice become muffled then a whisper, 'There's Con. Early! Bloody typical. Can I phone you later?'

As Rosie hung up, golf clubs clattered in her own hall followed by a chink of glass. The decanter stopper. James, only two o'clock but straight into the study. Her mind returned to Wendy and Henry. She was dying to spread the good news, but not to James, he'd blab to Conor. Beth was on honeymoon. Stella! She'd love this. Her bête noire cuckolded? Time they had a lunch anyway. Tomorrow was Bank Holiday, hopefully she'd be off. Rosie dialled Stella's number.

◆

My first day back from honeymoon was chaotic and held no aura of significance. My mum believes that 'the Lord moves in mysterious ways.' Ralph's mum favoured astrological signs. I saw no heavenly signs of providence or astral crabs, lions or planets bringing luck, but I do believe in the power of cats. If my partner Meg's mum hadn't fallen over her tabby, Meg wouldn't have had to rush her to Casualty with a hip fracture and I wouldn't have had to take her surgery. Then I wouldn't have met her last patient. An insignificant-looking, stoutish, navy-suited, white-bloused, cameo-brooched lady who looked a bit Miss Marple.

'Oh, Dr Beth!'

'Sorry?'

'But Sheehan? That wisnae your name then...'

No bells rang. 'Sorry, have we met?' Actually, I'm not Sheehan now, like on the door, I'm Semple- but I was once Slater.'

She looked as confused as I felt. Her bulging, buff, medical envelope said she was Anne Margaret Hyslop, DOB 22.4.40. Occupation, Typist.

So, how do you know me?'

'Och, St Mungo's Hospital. I was Sir James McPhater's secretary, Maggie Nesbitt then.'

'Maggie!' I yelped. She jumped. 'Amazing you remember me!'

'Och, I mind your lot fine. That lovely Henry. And that Earl's daughter, whit wis her name again? A beauty.'

'Wendy. You remember us? After all this time? It's fourteen years ago!'

'Och, Henry was there a while, lovely lad, aye time for a cuppa and a blether. Ah typed fur him, ye ken. Even that last day afore ah was took ill, had that haemorrhage and that… Ye know I didnae return tae the ward though, all that hassle doin' the professor's stuff, wi' patients' callin' in and that. Off six months, ah was, then ah went back to the typing pool, a bitty easier. So, Henry? Is he a big professor noo? Such a clever boy. Did he publish his research?'

'He's a dermatologist now. And no, he didn't publish. His research paper disappeared. Do you remember what you did with it?'

'Och ah gave it to that cocky wee chap, him always smoochin' up to the nurses.'

'Conor Towmey?' It could only be.

'Aye. An uncou' wee devil. Aye boastin'. Couldnae keep his hands aff the lassies. Ah mind wan cryin' after he'd touched her up in the sluice, the toe-rag. Ah, see men!' She pouted and, patted her hair bun. No third finger ring: a story there for another time.

'Conor published it. Pity we can't prove he stole it.'

'Och, so as we can! Ah've got a copy. Henry had lovely writing.'

'What?'

'Och, I used tae tak' copies o' stuff hame fur mair peace. Filed it aw away.'

'Maggie, d'you still have it?'

'Sure! Ah'll away and rummage. Ma faither always said, 'Keep copies of everything, Maggie. You never know!'

God bless Maggie's Dad! 'Maggie if you could…'

'Ah always thocht that boy was sleekit! The rest of your lot though, braw. Ah mind ye bringin' in fish n chips fur a richt sick wee lassie wi' leukaemia an' ye doin' her hair for a photie wi' her aunty in her weddin' dress. Aye!' Maggie shook her head, reminiscing in a lilting Ayrshire accent broader than I remembered. As was she. She stood up, buttoning her jacket.

'Richt, am off tae look fur it. That poor lad.' She scurried out. As the door shut, I realised I hadn't asked her why she'd come to the surgery.

Shakespeare was wrong, good isn't always interred with bones, kind actions can live on. But the evil that men do certainly lingers. Maggie would always remember Conor for his groping, I for his cheating dishonesty – and abuse of Wendy. But if Maggie had Henry's original manuscript, we might get Conor for *something*. I pulled over a pile of prescriptions to sign as my manager, Ellen, brought tea. It was only when I spilled it that I realised my hand was shaking uncontrollably.

Thirty-four

Picasso, Plans & Sambuca

As Rosie opened the heavy oak door, a November chill rushed in. She kissed Frank on the cheek. She always tried to be welcoming. James had been cool since Frank had 'come out.'

'What gorgeous flowers!' Frank sniffed the lilies on the hall table. 'You well, Rosie?'

'Fine, thanks. James is in the study.' She pointed at the door: it had been ages since he'd visited. 'Coffee?'

'Great! De-caff if you have it.'

Rosie didn't. James had hinted his brother sounded different after three months in California. She'd been sceptical his studies there would help advance health in deprived Lanarkshire, though maybe the Americans had new solutions for curbing smoking, drugs and poor diet. 'I've thawed steaks. Is that OK? James only said today you'd gone veggie.'

'Not completely, Rosie. I eat meat once a week. Trying to get fit. Taken up badminton and yoga – building up muscles so I can learn to relax them, I suppose!' He laughed.

Rosie thought him thinner, not fitter. Sunken-eyed. Jet-lagged maybe?

James came out extending his hand. 'Hi, stranger!'

They'd never been physically demonstrative. Rosie would have been more effusive if she'd had a sibling. Poles apart these boys. Rosie knew James favoured the theory that they were only half-brothers when trying to come to terms with Frank's homosexuality. She'd chided him. 'We are as we are, James!' Today, heading for the kitchen, Rosie worried. Frank looked unwell.

In the study James sat back. 'Long time no see! To what do we owe the pleasure Frankie?'

'Yeh, sorry. Busy! Public Health's not as cushy a number as you'd think. Lots of meetings, research, planning initiatives. Bollocks, mostly. Travelling opportunities good though.' He smiled, mind on that boy at Newport Beach, a tough celibacy test.

'Jammy call, California! Need to tell me all about it. Anyway, a Glen Livet?'

'No thanks, I'm not drinking weekdays.'

'Right, sorry…' James returned the bottle to the cabinet. 'Coffee coming in a minute.'

'James, before dinner, there's something I'd like you to do for me.'

'Sure, Frankie, what?' James looked worried.

'Draw me up a will?'

'A will?'

'Yes.'

James leaned back in his chair, eyebrows raised. 'What's brought this on? You ill?'

'No, but with some friends, recently... Thought I'd like to be prepared.'

'But Frank, sorry, but I wonder... It's just that you've, well, no wife, no children ...'

Frank was amused. Apology, worry, surprise – could he elicit shock and horror from his brother next? Once he'd have enjoyed the baiting, but life had assumed more serious dimensions now. Besides, best not to tell him everything. The manner of Gee's death for one. Their frightful secret for another: might be an unbearable burden for a lawyer, brother or not, who might feel obliged to go to the police. 'I know, James, but I've doubled the Judge's legacy on the market. Got quite a nest egg. I want to make charity bequests and there's the Picasso...'

'Picasso?' James whistled.

'It's only a cartoon, a preparatory sketch, but pretty pricey. I bought it a few years ago in Spain, with Graeme, when we ...'

'Sorry. I heard. You must miss him.'

'Yes, well, we had our ups and downs ...'

'So, what's your wish list?' James opened a drawer but before he'd lifted paper, Frank put down a white envelope.

'It's in here. Maybe you could draft it up properly and I can come to sign it next week?'

'You'd be best to come into the practice so it can be witnessed by someone independent.'

'OK, then. If that's how it works.'

The door opened. Rosie brought in coffee and biscuits. 'Dinner in half an hour, boys.'

Rosie noticed Frank declined her specially-bought Jaffa Cakes. Was he avoiding sugar because of that terrible acne on his jawline? Odd, acne at his age. It didn't help his looks, poor thing. She'd always felt sorry for him, James being tall, even-featured, olive-skinned and athletic Frank being slighter, paler, less handsome. Their only common bond was a hatred of their parents. And boarding school. James vowed they'd never send any child of theirs. If only.

After eleven, James strode across the stone-flagged hall to lock the storm doors. Looking up he saw Rosie yawn at the top of the sweeping Georgian stairs. She looked exhausted. He should get her some help in the house.

'That's Frank away, darling. Thanks for a lovely dinner. Up in a minute.'

Rosie waved. In the study he had an odd sense of unease as he lifted the sealed white envelope. It contained a single sheet of paper dated November 30th 1986. The hand was clear and neat, not Frank's usual demented scrawl. The bulk of his Estate was to go to a Terence Higgins Trust, some to Oxfam and some to PDSA. *Animal welfare – Frank?* Two Russell Flint watercolours to Liam O'Farrell. Conor's friend. *Were they still in touch?* A bronze ballerina to Rosie. *An early fine art buy she'd always admired.* A Picasso drawing, 'Head of a Boy: II,' to Mrs Marjorie Forsyth, 60, Craigends, Castle Douglas. *Who was she?*

As he got into bed, Rosie moved to spoon him, murmuring 'You're lucky to have a brother, you know. I'll have no family when mum goes.'

'I've been thinking about that, Rosie. If you want, we can try Donor Insemination.'

'I'm not sure, James. Think I'm getting too old. And the NHS doesn't fund donor AID.'

'Then let's go private.' His voice was unusually soft. 'Talk about it tomorrow.' He turned around. 'By the way, has Frank ever mentioned a Mrs Forsyth in Dumfries?'

'No, why?'

'He's leaving her something very, very valuable.'

'Didn't you ask him who she was?'

'No. It was on a letter he left. He's changed, hasn't he? Even his writing. It's gone all tiny, neat, sloping backwards.'

'Pre-occupied with inner thoughts, bit depressed maybe? I'm no graphologist, but I know manic writing's the opposite: huge, wild, forward sloping. He has gone all sort of ascetic and health conscious, hasn't he? Wonder why.'

'No idea! Maybe like all of us, he's aware he's not getting any younger. By the way, do you know what the Terence Higgins Trust is?'

Soon, once Rosie had told him about the homosexual support charity, James fell asleep. Rosie didn't. She was touched by James suggesting an infertility clinic. He hadn't wanted to consider it when they'd discovered his lack of sperm. She'd told Frank. He wasn't surprised, and thought it was due to the chlamydia infection James had suffered as a student. But she didn't tell Frank that James could no longer perform in bed. He came home every night now. Still, a test tube baby? Could she carry a stranger's child? How thoughtlessly she'd discarded her teenage pregnancy. That baby would be nineteen now. Her life has not been as she imagined it, with endless time for children later. But a child wouldn't restore their love life. Still, it wasn't everything, sex.

◆

Six months later, Rosie was in a train pulling out of Waverley, en route to a weekend with Wendy whilst Conor was away. It was a mystery to Rosie why Wendy was still with him. Her own problems with James and his women were nothing compared to the belittling, bullying and abuse that Wendy had suffered. Rosie opened The Handmaid's Tale, a present from Frank. Appreciating he was lonely without a partner, lately she'd accompanied him to concerts and galleries. James didn't mind. Frank had also impressed her recently professionally, demonstrating wide clinical knowledge, planning and organisational skills in a Women's Heath Committee to which she'd been seconded. Her new book was absorbing. The journey to King's Cross went quickly.

Wendy picked up Rosie in her Jensen. Flying up the immaculately bordered drive, Rosie was impressed by how gorgeous Wendy's Weybridge mansion was. It would be hard to leave, but was it worth living with Conor for- surely she could afford a place of her own?

'I've booked us a wee place in Soho for dinner and a limo, so we can celebrate and forget all our worries!' Wendy carried in Rosie's bag

Rosie was looking forward to the night out. Edinburgh aspired to sophistication, but London had it. James was furious he couldn't move there. On the way she'd confided in Wendy.

'I suspect the Judge's old enemies blocked James. Hubert was a horror. You should have seen the papers I found clearing out the old house: lots of personal, vitriolic law suits and hate mail from old colleagues as well as criminals he'd sent down. I shredded a lot- didn't want James to see it all.' She didn't say it was the first time she'd felt sorry for him as he broke down after seeing how hated his father had been. 'Mind you, I found nothing to back up the idea he and Frank were half-brothers. In truth, the old judge was equally horrible to both. He should have been thankful he'd had any sons.'

'Are you and James going to have kids?' Wendy had asked.

'I haven't said, but James can't, well, he's wondering about donor insemination. I'm not sure.'

'Maybe worth a go? I doubt I'll have any myself. Certainly not with Conor.'

The subject changed to lighter topics over coffee in the Bauhaus kitchen. Soon it was like old student times, trying on clothes and swopping make-up before going out.

As the driver closed the limo doors, Wendy smiled. 'By the way, I've arranged a few surprises for tonight!'

'What?' Rosie demanded.

'Not telling! Then they wouldn't be surprises!'

My Glasgow train didn't get in to Euston till seven, so I went straight to Amadante, a lovely Kensington Italian restaurant. Redolent with the aroma of garlic, roasted tomatoes and melted mozzarella, it had chequered tiled floors, Tuscan murals, flickering candlelight and tables separated by velvet curtains on brass poles. Handy for clandestine dates but tricky for finding friends. Wendy's throaty laugh gave her away. She was all shining hair and eyes as she rose for a hug, endangering a wax-drenched Chianti bottle.

I exclaimed at her table companions. 'Rosie! Henry! What a surprise!'

Rosie looked delighted to see me. 'I didn't know you were coming either – Wendy didn't say! Nor about Henry.'

'I knew,' said Henry smugly. 'Now, red or white wine?'

We ate, drank, laughed and listened to Wendy and Henry's romantic adventures. Conor wasn't mentioned, but I brought him up. 'Henry,' I pointed a chocolatey spoon at him. 'Did you do anything with that stuff I sent you ages ago? Maggie's still game to make depositions.'

'I saw a lawyer.'

'And?'

'We met the GMC and the Medical Defence people. It'd cost me to sue Conor personally. Though it's cheating, misrepresentation and so on, they weren't sure it'd be enough for court conviction or even GMC censure which needs less proof. He'd have hot-shot QCs.'

'Really? But he stole your work!'

'The defence union says it's common, it even has a name, "research appropriation."'

'So you're just letting it drop?'

'Can't be arsed wasting money. We've got other irons in the fire.'

'So, are you two going to come clean?' I licked my spoon.

'Well, eventually, once Wendy's worked through the legal stuff with Findlay's lot.'

'My Findlay?'

'Yes, your Findlay! His firm was recommended by Dad's Edinburgh people. He's been simply terrific, darling!' I watched Tiramisu melting on Wendy's top lip. Love changes people: she was no longer a conscientious napkin-dabber.

'What's he doing?'

'Tightening Family Trusts, checking Deeds of Variation and things since Dad died in May, moving money offshore. Con's not getting his paws on a thing. You know Coutts has binned him? Caused ructions with his great mentor Sir Roger Vincent who'd recommended him for an account. That's how it works, you know.'

'Surely he earns a bomb with society ladies wanting snipped or tucked?' I asked.

Henry snorted, choking on a truffle. 'Whether they need it or not, I bet!'

'Yes, Henry, but I don't think you've grasped how badly he oozes money, pours it like champagne on horses, blackjack, the Ritz, Langan's. Thousands a night!'

'Wendy,' I had to ask. 'Why have you stayed?'

'Oh, Beth, at first I convinced myself he could change. It was promises, promises. Now? I'm going. But not until I've got the capital and property tied up. There's a truce at home just now. Con knows I've lodged injury photos with a lawyer, though he's cocky enough to think I'll shy off divorce because he'll allege I'm mentally incompetent from booze. But I'm at a good shrink. See my two wee glasses of "controlled drinking" tonight?'

Henry and Rosie had been less controlled and made a raucous toast 'to Divorce.'

In our usual loo 'confessional,' Rosie admitted she'd come to urge Wendy to leave.

'I'm thrilled she's going. Doesn't she look well?' She pressed the hand cream dispenser shooting a glug sideways onto my new dress. Rosie was horrified 'Oops! Sorry, didn't notice it was crusted up!'

'Never mind.' I scrubbed it ineffectively. By then I'd realised there were worse things than stains. As a spasm seized me I started to rummage in my bag.

'You OK, Beth?'

'Just stomach ache. Back playing up too.' I found paracetamol to swig with a palmful of water, arching my back to try to ease the discomfort.

'You're looking pale – promise me you'll see someone? You mustn't neglect yourself!'

I assured Rosie I would. Later, I regretted accepting Wendy's last treat: a Sambuca laced with three flaming coffee beans for health, wealth and happiness. At two am I woke from a Maia nightmare with severe abdominal pain. Sambuca joined Sangria and Slivovitz as poisons to be avoided. Tequila's not much better. S and T- as I said, avoid wherever possible. And if there are any spirits beginning with H, the same goes.

◆

The next month, June 1987, Conor was palpating a breast he knew well. Elizabeth Granger's husband had made the appointment. Lord Aston Granger was the wealthy Chair of the Health Authority. Conor was flattered. His reputation was growing. Aston didn't know Conor was the one who'd brought the lump to her attention. Their affair, sparked at a Society Ball, had caused him to ditch his last squeeze, socialite Victoria Haversham, who despite being loaded and recently widowed, was much less well-connected.

Conor's new nurse Carrie Clark hovered. Propriety was needed.

'Ahem, might be nothing Lady Aston, but we'll need a biopsy.'

'Shall I lose the breast?' A hand clutched her throat.

'Let's not be premature. I'll arrange for a biopsy tomorrow at the Wellington.'

His new nurse Carrie Clark gently helped Elizabeth dress. She was an improvement on his previous opinionated bitch.

The next patient was a Middle Eastern lady whose husband, a substantive gold-bedecked potentate, wanted her breasts enlarged. She sat, eyes downcast, upper torso bared. Conor outlined the procedure, solely addressing the man, even when prodding the woman's breasts. He made a sweep indicating where the incisions would be made, reassuring the husband they'd be unobtrusive. Carrie frowned. This Arab-speaking woman was signing operation consent without any idea what she was agreeing to. Perhaps this Friday job was a mistake. She'd heard rumours from her St Jasper's colleagues that Towmey wasn't the charmer he seemed, but was 'up-himself.' There had also been a veiled warning from her cousin Vicki who'd 'heard things' abut Mr Towmey. Vicki was recovering from a torrid affair with 'a surgeon.' Surely not Towmey? She'd been his patient. Totally unprofessional.

◆

Returning from London, I saw Jack, my GP, who prescribed Gaviscon and a diet sheet, diagnosing 'Dyspepsia.' Unhelpful. It just means 'disordered digestion.' My vague symptoms eventually subsided on small meals and no alcohol, making me popular as a night-out driver. The girls were growing fast and loud. Our house was full of laughter. I imagined this was contentment. But grumbling months of intermittent pain settled to a constant ache. X-rays and blood tests didn't help. My appetite plummeted and then my weight. By December 1988, I was awaiting admission for endoscopy and stomach biopsy. I was off at home when Henry phoned.

'Hello Beth. Wendy wanted you to know she's in hospital.'

'What's wrong?'

'Ectopic pregnancy.'

'Oh God! Is she all right?'

'Yes, but she's lost the tube and a lot of blood. She was seven weeks. Con's in Amsterdam so she phoned me. Silly, me being in Bristol. Got her to dial 999 and thankfully she managed to leave the door open for the ambulance men before collapsing. But she's heaps better. Getting out tomorrow.'

'Tell her I'm asking for her. What a shame. What about Conor?'

'Abroad, so I asked his secretary to contact him. He phoned the hospital, ranting at the ward sister, said Wendy was a hysterical alcoholic always bleeding heavily and ordered them to discharge her. The woman couldn't get a word in edgeways before he rang off!'

'Sounds like Conor!'

'Think Sister was relieved, though. She'd sussed from Wendy it mightn't be his!'

'Oh, Henry! Will there be any complications?'

'Well, she's got adhesions from inflammation, probably from that Dalkon IUD she says you warned her about years ago. Her remaining tube's pretty damaged so she might not get pregnant again. But that doesn't matter as long as she's OK.'

'Do you need help? Sorry, I'm going in for tests tomorrow.'

'Don't worry, Rosie's taken leave and is flying down. We'll pick up Wendy and head for my place. But it's annoying timing as she had everything arranged for three days' time.'

'Sorry, Henry, had what arranged?'

'The Honourable Wendy Tuffnall-Brown's escape is set for 10th of December 1988!'

'About bloody time! She told me last year she was going. What about Conor?'

'Secretary said he's due to fly from an Amsterdam College jolly to a Los Angeles conference.'

'Typical. So, what's the actual plan?'

'Removal vans will take Wendy's inherited art work and antique furniture to storage. She should be well enough to supervise. Then divorce papers ...'

The best news I'd had for months.

◆

Despite the smog, Conor loves Los Angeles. It's December but the temperature is pleasant and the Hollywood affluence conspicuous: limos, sparkling glass high-rise buildings, classy department stores. The hotel is straight out of a James Bond movie. Looking in the mirror while shaving, he wonders if a little moustache might give an older, trustworthy vibe? Would need a week off to experiment.

Perhaps Sandy Lane for New Year? Stylish, star-studded, he'd heard. Never knew whom you'd meet. Wendy would agree to Barbados. And pay. They'd go Club. He splashes on Gucci and lifts his new navy pinstripe jacket off the hanger. That was one bill he'd have to pay. Savile Row reputedly sent duns in pronto if you weren't gentry. One of Roger's better recommendations. Not like Coutts, those wanker bankers! He's assured Roger his deficit is only due to a temporary financial setback on 'the market.' Didn't say *racing* at *Newmarket*.

Descending in the glass and brass lift, he ponders on breaking in here. After all, he was introduced last week in a line up as an 'up-and-coming world-renowned' surgeon. He'd heard the College President's trophy wife whisper 'so young and so handsome,' the doll. He's sorry he hasn't done Plastics though. General Surgery limits him to scar revision and boob jobs paying chicken-feed. Plastic qualified Yousef is raking it in. He was upset he'd come without Wendy, at home with her snotty schoolkids in Camberwell. He hadn't mentioned her current drama-queen admission to St Peter's, Chertsey. Maybe he needed to parade her. 'The Honourable' was still an asset, a looker, and 'society.' Though his taste now veered towards younger flesh.

Stepping out into the lobby, he has a frisson of disquiet about Sir Roger's Vincent's girl. So nubile. It was lucky perhaps, that the nurse returned when she did. Still, nothing happened. Her allegation wouldn't be anything a decent barrister couldn't rebut. His eyes sweep the dining room before choosing a table.

'Hi, Jason! Great presentation yesterday!'

A smiling Jason Abarovitch MD, Chair of the American Medical Association, stands to shake his hand and pull up a chair. The chat is of planes, yachts, beachside homes, golf club memberships and the lack of time to enjoy them. His bar buddy of last night, the John Hopkins Staff Chief, invites him to Vegas for the weekend.

'Can you delay your flight home by 48 hours, Con?'

'Of course, Myles. Love to!'

'Let's jet off around noon tomorrow. Dinner on the Strip?'

'Great, Myles. That'd be dandy.'

Conor smiles. This is a million miles from Coatbridge.

Thirty-five

You Need a Friend

It was snowing: 1988 was a bad winter. I'd escaped home for an hour's peace after a very hectic morning. The phone rang. I tried ignoring it, but eventually, sighing, I put down my tea and answered.

'Oh, hello Wendy. You're lucky to catch me. I'm not usually home at this time.'

'The surgery girls said you'd sneaked off. Well, it's D-Day!'

'What?'

'Departure Day! Did you forget? Tenth of December. I'm in Weybridge waiting on the vans. Been round putting green stickers on everything that's to go. It's surprisingly emotional, likely from the miscarriage. I wanted to ring you to say how sorry I am I didn't listen to you.'

'Any particular time?' I laughed.

'That BMA ball springs to mind – you tore a strip off me, quite rightly. Not only about Con, but about that bloomin' coil! As for Con, d'you know he phoned the hospital last week and didn't even ask what my diagnosis was? Just ordered them to send me home! And today I found an answering machine message here boasting he's off to Vegas with some big-wig and he wants me to phone his unit to say he's 'unavoidably delayed.' He can whistle for that! No moral conscience about patients or colleagues.'

'Quite right! The divorce on track?'

'Yep. Glad I'll not be here when he discovers all my money's off limits, tied up in trusts so tight no barrister could unpick. Not that he can afford one. His debts are massive, with more red demands here today. I've purloined the bank statements. You wouldn't believe his spending. Anyway, Rosie's been great and the cleaning lady's a star, helping today and offering to testify about his carry-on. Flash and Thunder have gone to stables near Henry till we find a house with our own. Worried Con might send them to the knacker's yard.'

'Surely he'd not be that vindictive?'

'I'm not chancing it. He's as vindictive as Henry is sweet. How did I pass him by? He's even got me a School Health interview in Bristol next week. How are you, by the way?'

'So, so. Waiting on tests.'

'Hope they're OK. Will phone once we're settled. Thanks Beth. For everything.'

◆

Two months later, Yousef walked through Glasgow enjoying the cool, crisp February day. Made a nice change from Californian sun. Lifting a Daily Record, he dropped coins in the street vendor's tin. Buchanan Street was memory lane. How Glasgow had blossomed in sixteen years: more good restaurants, vibrant art galleries, refurbished buildings, the ubiquitous smiley yellow stickers of the Corporation's 'Glasgow's Miles Better' campaign everywhere. Cheering. He was happy to be in Scotland for a month learning new surgery techniques. Glancing at his watch, he quickened his pace. Mustn't be late for Rogano's, the Art Deco restaurant so reminiscent of old liners and his mother's favourite thirties movies. A great time to have been alive – all those fedora hats, wide lapels, and two-tone Oxford brogues!

◆

I thought he looked well, distinguished.

'Hi, Yousef! Great to see you! Wasn't sure if you could get the afternoon off: Wednesday's my half day. It's mid-term so I brought the girls.'

He stooped to hug us, dropping his newspaper on the curved velvet bench. 'Hello, girls!'

Julia and Katy sat primly, thrilled to be out for grown-up lunch with Uncle Yousef. They wore new green striped dresses, red tights and white furry boots, testimony to their 'dressing up' genes. Yousef had them too. Today he sported a wide floral tie and bright blue socks. The girls had met him a few times and saw regular photos of him and his family. It was a mutual love affair. The lunch order provoked heated arguments. At the price, I wasn't prepared to risk them wasting oysters. I declined wine.

'I'll not have any either. Due back scrubbed up in Canniesburn theatre at three.'

The food came. The girls subsided. Yousef grinned at them.

'You two are so grown up, looking swell!' They preened. He looked at my plate. 'That sole no good? You're looking pale, you OK?'

'Sort of. I'm anaemic.'

'What did the last tests show?'

'Endoscopy before Christmas was negative. Because of a urinary infection I had an IVP, also fine. Results are non-specific – high ESR, low blood count. Having a new kind of scan next week since ultrasound showed ...' I paused, looking over at the girls now engrossed in Yousef's discarded paper. I dropped to a whisper, 'something. Tell you later.'

'Hey, mum, do you know him? Says he's a Glasgow doctor ...'

Yousef grabbed the paper from Julia. 'Well, well! I didn't see that in my hurry here – the boy's on the front of a tabloid! Now why doesn't that surprise me?' He held up the front page. *Breast Surgeon in Sex Scandal.* 'No surprise to me he went for breast surgery. Always was obsessed with tits.'

The girls sniggered behind their hands.

'Yousef, the girls!' They rolled about. He laughed. I smothered a smile. But it wasn't funny: a shamed colleague reflected badly on us all.

'I'll say this for him though, she's a looker, this 'Vicki.' He read out loud. '... recently widowed, vulnerable, being treated for cancer. Says other charges are pending. Wonder what?'

'Well, it's not Henry and his Lancet thing. Gosh, this will scupper Conor's Harley Street aspirations. He was lucky Wendy settled out of court, you know, went for irretrievable breakdown. It's nearly final. She's great now, so happy with Henry?'

'I know. Going to see them in Bristol for a few days before going home.'

'Give them my love. Haven't spoken for a bit.'

He looked at his watch. 'Sorry, have to go. Bye, beautiful girls. Next time we'll meet in California: palm trees, sunshine, and skateboards. You seen them? I'll teach you!'

'Hope you're better than Ralph is at skating,' Katy said. 'He's rubbish!'

Yousef looked over their shoulders at me, his gorgeous eyes showing concern as he hugged them. He was no fool, guessing what I suspected. Wonderful to have the joy of such friendship: no secrets: no strings, no need to spell things out.

'Keep me posted, Beth.' He kissed my cheek and left.

◆

Conor puts his foot to the floor as he speeds up the A1. Acceleration is slower than usual: the Aston needs a service. Have to wait. His mind is in turmoil after the GMC letter. Nothing yet about the 'other' allegations the Record and Mail talk of. Buggers wouldn't give their source and that GMC reception was a bitch barricade. The MDDUS were useless, their imbecile lawyer suggesting he go contrite, confess and accept a rap on the knuckles for Vicki. Stupid cunt. It would finish him in the higher echelons! It wasn't as if he was a two-bit backwoods GP. Vicki had been kind of 'ragdoll' the last time, but she'd wanted it. It had been in the rooms, always gave things an added 'fear-of -discovery' frisson. Had Carrie sussed anything? Po-faced Sister Carrie Clark was as bad as her nebby predecessor. P45 time. Malky agreed. Thank God he's recovered from his crash, though he's much subdued from the rake he was. Anyway, the story for James is of a reluctant affair initiated by Vicki Haversham, a fading ex-model desperate for publicity. At the outskirts of Edinburgh, he zooms onto the ring-road roundabout without giving way.

Rosie is on the top landing when the Aston Martin streaks into the curved drive scattering gravel. Conor is out clutching his leather overnight bag and ringing the bell before she's reached the bottom stair. No sign of a chastened sexual predator here, then. After hearing about all his shenanigans from Wendy, she forbade James to have him stay over. The Weybridge house is on Savills' page in the Times today. Rosie's a fool to give him half. Opening the door, she nods towards the study door and leaves. She'd didn't want him to come at all when he'd phoned last night, but James had wondered what he wanted.

'I'll deal with him. Just leave us out a bite of supper.'

Rosie has taken James at his word. She silently delivers a tray of untrimmed spam sandwiches and tepid coffee. Noticing James looking very serious, she lingers outside.

'I don't think you understand, Conor. I don't practice in England.'

'But you've got the qualifications, James. Couldn't you do it this once?' Conor is pleading, for the first time in his life.

James stirs, uncomfortable. 'So, did you have sex with this woman?'

'Yes. But it was consensual and not while she was a patient.'

'Then worst case scenario, it'll be a caution. Just tell the truth. She have any witnesses?'

'No. We only did it once.' Conor had decided this on the way.

'Then it's your word against hers. You could try to find something about her that makes her testimony unreliable.'

'How?'

'Private detective: I can give you the names of some discreet firms.'

'That costs money...'

'What? Is money a problem? I thought Harley Street and so on...'

'Well, my expenses are high. And of course, Wendy is skinning me...'

Saying this doesn't convince James to help, knowing Wendy's side of the story via Rosie. He's made huge changes in his own lifestyle, confessed many faults. And though he admits straying, he's never lifted his hand. They're not twenty-somethings now, and he despises Conor for thinking life can be lived without responsibility. And Conor is not his.

Conor is wheedling. 'So if you won't defend me, can you get me a loan to engage someone else? Or be a character witness? You are a QC!' Conor laughs, ignoring the chilled veil descending over James' face.

'My partnership agreement has an embargo on standing as guarantor or being a character witness for any third parties due to the potential for subsequent litigation and financial implications for the firm. So, no, Conor, I can't.'

Conor rises, colour high. 'Damn you! So I'm just a 'Third Party'? After all those nights I bankrolled you and your poofter brother? How dare you!'

'Out of my hands,' James shrugs. 'And you needn't look to an Assistant Director of Public Health as a referee. Frank's in a hospice in a bad way.' James stands and opens the door as Rosie scuttles away. Phoning Wendy later she said it was like a Western stand-off: the former friends facing one another as if about to draw guns.

Conor turns on his heel to stride out of the study to the front door. Snatching as he goes his Louis Vuitton from the hall, he leaves. The door slams.

Rosie picks up her beloved Rennie Mackintosh hall chair and lily vase tipped over by Conor storming off. 'So?'

'Can't say that went well!' James shakes his head. 'Remember at Uni Beth called him a plonker? She was right.'

◆

Gordon's an idiot. He never gets the time difference. It's five am in Dubai. Pointless returning to bed. Dan puts down the phone and pours a whisky, his first for months. Beth would be pleased. Oh, Beth. It didn't sound good. Pain, weight loss, urine symptoms. Investigative laparotomy tomorrow. Crohn's Disease would be treatable, but surely, they'd have got that from bariums? It might be fibrosis. Or worse. Wondering what they'd told the girls, he decides he'll phone Rosie. He couldn't bring himself to phone Ralph.

Rubbing his chest with the heel of his hand, he worries. Palpitations had halted his squash yesterday, perhaps he did need an ECG. What age had Grandpa been?

Poor Grandpa. Falling on him in the Royal that day. So long ago. All his weight on him. That dead weight. He shut his eyes, clearly seeing that hospital room, his mother screaming, the nurse pulling him from underneath the body. He'd only tugged the sleeve of the slumped figure to wake him up, to tell him Rangers had won. Mum and he had been at the match. He'd never imagined Grandpa would die. Less than a year after Dad had left them. Life is short.

He picks up the Scottish Daily Record dated a few days ago: 17th February 1989. Gordon had been surprised Dan already knew about Conor from this paper brought by a nurse returning from Glasgow who thought he'd know the Glasgow medic on the front page. Under the blurred photo of Conor's angry face it detailed his 'pending divorce' and 'likely hospital suspension.' Idiot. But Conor's notoriety faded into insignificance compared to the news about Beth.

Then there was Frank, terminal with Gay Plague, Gordon said. What had that 'burning a body' stuff all been about? Whatever, Frank hadn't led a blameless life. Nor had he, walking out on Beth and the girls like a scaredy-cat. Wanting away. Not permanently like poor Maia, just away. But now he felt too far away. His heart fluttered again. If he died here who would care? How long till anyone noticed? Was it time to go back? No one here could help him decide. He had plenty of acquaintances, but still was lonely. Perhaps all decisions were lonely. He thought of Elaine in the States, raising four kids on a low wage. Christ she'd fucked up too. He hopes his latest money transfer went through. She was struggling. But the kids were coming on: the eldest had a baseball trial for some team. He wondered what Julia and Katy were up to. He didn't think about them as often as he should. Perhaps it was time he did.

Lately he'd spent a lot of time with the priest. He was unsure why he'd become R.C. Was it an insurance policy, just in case …? Or to find a purpose in life? He's now beginning to think the only purpose of life is supporting others to live, not worry about yourself in your own wee bubble. Praying for guidance as a Catholic hadn't helped: he felt guiltier after Mass. Not like Con: mass meant girls! Christ, it looked like Con had made a right balls-up of his life. Surprising he'd been caught out, usually such a slippery bugger. A damaging one though. Hell mend him.

His resolve gathers momentum. He will start job searching tomorrow and return to the UK. New start in London maybe. Certainly nearer the girls. And Beth. What would his mother think of the mess he's made of his life? He'd wanted to have a family so much, but he'd thrown it all away. His mother was far from perfect though, she should never have pushed Elaine to marry. Only Iain, still in the Forces out in Cyprus, was playing happy families. As he heads for a shower, Dan decides he'll visit Iain on the way home.

Thirty-Six

Nemesis

By April 1989 I was in hospital being visited by Henry and Wendy. When I expressed a notion for chocolate, Wendy returned from the WRVS shop with a brick.

'That's a 500gm bar, Wendy – enough for a family of four for a week!'

'It's better value!'

'Says Dr Zillion Squillionaire!'

'Eat it! Has Henry shown you the house photos?'

'Looks lovely.'

'Workmen start Monday. Stables first to get the boys back.'

Henry squeezed my hand. 'When do you get your results?'

'Tomorrow, April Fool's Day. Always apt for me!'

I was delighted they were looking so happy. And Henry so slim and smart – influence of a good woman. No boiled jumper. Oh, Maia... My grasshopper brain suddenly gave up. Trying to pretend you're fine to reassure worried hospital visitors is exhausting.

'Sorry, I'd like to have a nap, if you don't mind.'

'Sure! We'll phone tomorrow before we go south.' Wendy hugged me tightly. They left hand in hand. Later I realised I'd forgotten to ask if they knew any more about Conor and the GMC: six weeks now and nothing further in the press.

◆

Two weeks later, Rosie paused at the door to compose herself. It was as if someone had applied a powerful vacuum to his body: no subcutaneous fat whatsoever remained. Though knowing bodies were just bags of skin and having seen many wasted, cachexic, cancer patients, Rosie was still shocked at Frank's extreme deterioration in a week. The prominent purple tumours on his jaw drew her eyes like magnets. With difficulty, she tore away her stare to turn her attention to Franks' companion. And got another surprise.

'Why, Patricia, Pat!'

The slight woman stood up, extending her hand. 'Hello Rosie, long time no see!'

'Pat, what ever happened to you? You just vanished in Fifth.'

'Oh, water under bridges.' She smiled at Frank. 'Didn't he tell you I was over in Lanark as Director of Geriatrics? I finished my degree back home in Edinburgh once I'd recovered from a bout of depression.'

Rosie stood dumbstruck.

'Sorry, have to dash.' Pat picked up her coat. 'Frank's had the week's department gossip, today's BBC News and Herald headlines. Not up to the crossword today.' She patted his arm. 'Keep going soldier. I'll see you Saturday. Father McGough'll be in later. Maybe Rosie, you could try him with more yoghurt? The oesophageal thrush is making swallowing painful, but he's managed some.' She turned to Frank. 'Oh, here's that book you wanted. 'She took a slim volume bearing a silver cross from her bag, laid it on the locker, blew Frank a kiss and left.

'Canticle of the Sun, St Francis. Got religion,' Frank grinned sheepishly. 'Pat was taking me to Church before I came in.' He mumbled, 'Mum would be pleased,' before drifting off. Rosie sat for a while then left with a heavy heart to tell James if he wanted to see his brother he shouldn't wait till the weekend. It took 10 days.

◆

The funeral was held in the Cathedral in Coatbridge, with service and prayers as planned by Frank himself. The undertaker arrangements involving precautions with sealed body bags etc. were dealt with by Rosie and Patricia. Rosie was surprised how close Frank and Pat had become so quickly. Frank had given Pat a note for James, requesting that he be buried with the book Pat had brought in to the hospital and telling him he'd come to the conclusion the only true love was brotherly love. James was in tears by the time he read the attached will codicil, witnessed by Pat and a nurse. It bequeathed a large sum to the Franciscans. Executing his brother's will was the most difficult thing James had ever done. He thought of his wasted years of censure. No one would have wished such a death on anyone.

Liam came to the Cathedral, telling Rosie the place was as distressing for its school memories as the funeral and expressing relief the service didn't mention Frank's sexuality. 'As if ...' she thought. Conor didn't appear to see his old flatmate laid to rest. Rosie wasn't surprised, but she was when Dan did, looking sun-tanned and prosperous. At the Cartland Bridge Hotel wake, Dan was stunned to hear about Frank's return to Catholicism and bequests to the Franciscans.

'After everything he used to say about priests? Weird.'

'And he's left a Picasso to some woman in Dumfries.'

'Who's she?'

'No idea Dan.'

◆

Six weeks later, the gleaming brass door knocker felt warm in the Dumfries spring sunshine. A rap on the door brought a diminutive faded figure in a floral apron.

'Come away in, Mr Hutton. So kind of you to come all this way down here to see me.'

The tablecloth and the antimacassars in the tiny living room were lace. The china on the tray gilded and fluted. The dust-free space in the bow-fronted display cabinet spoke of its infrequent use. The scones looked perfection.

'Your secretary was vague. Who'd leave me a legacy?'

'My brother, Mrs Forsyth.'

'I don't know any Huttons. Was he an old friend of my husband's? He passed not long after my son, you know.'

'Frank has left you a picture. And a letter which he gave to my wife before he died.'

'Well, I'll away 'n put the kettle on, then you can read me it. I'm needing my cataracts done.'

She bustled to the kitchen as James slit open the letter. Returning, she dried her hands on her apron before sitting. Placing a neatly tied brown paper parcel on the table, James donned his new reading glasses.

St Vincent's Hospice
30th March 1989

Dear Mrs Forsyth,
I hope you will accept this little drawing in memory of your son. Pat was a dear friend, and I bought this because of its uncanny resemblance to him. It's an early Picasso of a choirboy looking upwards in humility, drawn as a study for the oil painting of an altar boy that hangs in Madrid. I was so moved by it that I changed my life and returned to my Faith. This token is the only way I can express how sorry I am that Pat died. It was an accident. I've regretted every day since that I couldn't do anything to save him. God bless.
Yours sincerely,
Frances Xavier Hutton.'

She dabbed her eyes. James, feeling emotional himself, knew the question coming.

'Do you know where he … what happened?'

'No. I'm sorry, I don't,' replied James. 'Shall I unwrap the drawing?'

'Please, I'll away and mash the tea while you do it.'

Within minutes, the pot was set down in its knitted green cosy and she was gazing at the sepia drawing. James looked at a photo on the mantelpiece draped by a rosary. The resemblance was startling.

'He sang beautifully, you know,' she said. 'My husband was disappointed that he was delicate. He bruised easily and hated football, but he was clever.'

James opened his briefcase. 'The Picasso's worth a lot of money.

I have a Bonham's valuation certificate. They would be delighted to sell it for you.'

'No, Mr Hutton, I shan't sell it. It'll go on the bedroom wall opposite my bed. Do you have children, Mr Hutton?'

'Sadly, no.'

'Then you don't know what this means to me. Thank you.'

♦

Planting his feet firmly on the ground, Conor raises his head, calculates the distance then makes a steady powerful swing driving the ball straight down the fairway at Wentworth. With a flourish, he replaces his driver before taking his new Powakaddy and following his companion. Although he's feeling good in a new yellow cashmere sweater, red polo and tartan Californian trousers, he pauses to remove his jerkin. It's warm for May.

'You've certainly improved since last time we played!'

'Well, I've had more time, Sandy. Friday clinic's pretty sparse. Thanks for today's game.'

'Don't mention it, old chap!'

'I'm a bit of a pariah at the moment. A bit rich though, it's not as if many of my usual partners are lily-white themselves.'

'Quite. Indeed, I myself... still, infamy's a five-minute wonder. People get caught up in their own problems, soon forget. How's that going by the way?'

'Oh, I've got Desmond Pilkington on it. Used him before, he's good.' He doesn't add why he thinks Des is good. On hearing rumours someone was 'after him' on the Health Authority Board, he'd set Pilkington on the members. In the end, he hadn't needed dirt against a complainant, but did find out that the Chair, one Lord Aston Granger, was a dirty 'cottaging' bugger. Nice one, had enabled a wee loan to tide him over till the house sale completion since he'd little left to pawn. A glance at the time reminds him how much he misses his Patek Philippe. It'll be one of the first things he'll get back- while he's delaying the release of Wendy's house share. Cheek, her taking half!

Sandy Kane is chortling. 'Pilkington saved me a bundle on my last divorce. Tapped phones, got photos, the works. The bitch was fucking her gym guy, can you imagine?' Sandy slaps Conor on the back.

Normally he doesn't care for Sandy, too in-your-face-jolly-rugger-bonhomie-old-school-tie, but decent of him to ask him out today. Despite not being suspended from work, no one's going out of their way to be friendly.

'Actually one of the reasons I asked you here, apart from the old moral support,' Sandy guffaws, 'was about your Vicki Haversham. Her old man was a Harrow chum. Same circles and so on ...' He nods sagely, 'I saw her a few months ago at the Charlotte Clinic wearing dark glasses. Didn't see me, but she was there in the waiting room. Sorry, I can't testify. There with a secretary filly needing seen to, bit tricky.' He drives off the eighteenth tee with vigour despite his paunch. 'But likely she was there for the same purpose as Delia and I. Widowed by then. Shouldn't be hard to prove she puts it about. Might give your man a head start.'

Conor is cross Sandy hasn't mentioned this before, then remembers he's been Caribbean cruising with his latest wife. What a bloody game love is: one he's almost tiring of. On a good day, he'd almost rather play golf. Christ, who'd have thought?

◆

Ralph was doodling on his desk diary. June 30th 1989. The Prof had just left and he should be jubilant, but all he can think of is Beth's chalk-white face. At least the nausea's settled with the drip down. The chemo was harsh. He feels too soon after the surgery. After visiting he'd detoured into the Faculty partly to catch up on paperwork, but mostly to give himself space before going home: the girls were very perceptive. At least now with it being the holidays they'd have plenty of time with her. And his news should cheer her. Mitchell had breezed in to tell him he'd been promoted to Assistant Professor. The research paper on Unemployment and Ill Health she'd helped him with had swung it. The demands of the new post meant dropping some surgery sessions and he'd be less on call. Meant too he could work from home if …

Yousef had also called, demanding the complete low-down. Such a relief telling someone, even if he'd broken down doing it. Great chap, Yousef, though he'd once been jealous of him, thinking he fancied Beth. And vice versa. Yousef had been pragmatic, offering to pay for Beth to go to his uncle's high-powered Sloane Kettering Cancer in New York. She'd be touched.

He'd just rung off when Liam phoned. Funny how life returns in circles. O'Farrell had moved back from Edinburgh and joined Ralph's list. His news would keep. Perhaps he'd leave it for after Cressida and Tim's arrival. He hoped they wouldn't be too much for Beth, but she'd been insistent they should come, saying her Mum was there, and she'd just go to bed if she got tired. Cressida had phoned first thing saying she was the new Professor of Forensics at Dundee. Their mum would have been so proud. She mentioned it meant she'd be nearer to help if … but he couldn't go there. Looking out of the window at the Scottish summer 'gloaming,' he thought of Beth telling him it meant the long Scottish twilight. 'Twilight of our years' sprang into his mind, God knows where from. His heart lost a beat. Would he and Beth have any? He cursed the time he'd wasted with her after First.

Gordon had been on today too, urging him to speak to Beth's consultant, Philip Davies. Though Beth was adamant her cancer resulted from that paediatric X-ray exposure, Gordon and Dan thought otherwise. If they were right, there'd be implications for Dan and Henry too. Ralph was overwhelmed. What a day. And Gordon said Stella had finally made it to consultant, despite Conor's lengthy smear campaign. More good news for Beth. How that guy had concealed his true deviancy from senior colleagues for so long was unbelievable. As were all these promotions in one week! His mum would have cited favourable planetary influences. It would take more than a few planets aligning to help Beth.

Turning into the drive, he admired the changes they'd made in

Beth's ten-day absence. Having moved into the neglected Art and Craft villa as Beth was diagnosed, they hadn't renovated anything. The minute she'd gone into the Beatson, he'd diverted the girls with a Master Plan. Peggy and Julia chose paint and paper. Peggy made curtains from Beth's favourite William Morris fabric and a decorator patient beavered away. Turning his key in the lock, Ralph met the girls hanging up a wonky 'Welcome Home' banner in the hall and the aroma of baking.

'Ah, chocolate cake!' he said, grabbing Katy. 'Take me to it wench!'

She squealed. 'You've not to touch it! No sneaky bits off it during the night – we know you! It's a welcome home cake for mum tomorrow.'

Julia climbed down the steps, looking serious, grown up. 'What time can we get her? Has the sickness stopped?'

'She's much better. Sends love. We'll go for her about ten, so best be bright-eyed and bushy-tailed first thing. Mum mustn't come home to your usual Saturday morning mess!'

Next morning, the house was spotless. It was 10.30 when Ralph rang the bell with a wobbly Beth on his arm. He carried her over-night bag, the girls, armfuls of flowers and carriers with the gifts from her locker. Beth exclaimed in delight at the newly painted exterior windows, but when Peggy opened the front door she gasped.

'My God, guys, what've you done? It's like Homes and Gardens!'

Ralph carried her up the stairs, recounting all the promotions. But not Liam's news.

Thirty-seven

Blackmail & a Cold Case

July 1989

Conor walks along counting the house numbers: 151, 153. He pauses at 155A West Curzon Street, a glossy black door flanked by small standard laurels in brass tubs on each step and window boxes with scarlet geraniums. Apt for a scarlet bloody woman! The huge brass knocker on this Mayfair terrace house isn't apt though. Grasping the dazzlingly-polished lion he bangs loudly. It takes a few minutes until the door opens and ice creeps up his back.

'What are you doing here?'

'I could say the same about you!'

Conor is thrown: why is Sister Carrie Clark opening Vicki Haversham's door?

'Best sling your hook, she won't talk to you!'

Carrie makes ready to slam the door, but Conor body-swerves her to enter the hall in one bound. A rugby move. As he closes the front door, Carrie walks backwards, nervously calling for Vicki, opening first one hall door, then another.

'Oh, Vicki, there you are. You have a visitor.'

Victoria Haversham sits on a cream and turquoise sofa, talking on the phone. Conor advances and fingers the thick silk braided-cord tassels supporting the oak acorns of its luxurious padded arms. Wendy has taken their Wade sofa. No matter, he'll get another. He stands close to his prey as she curtails her conversation, slamming the receiver and raising steely eyes. She has a new thick black fringe. Women with dyed hair are fickle and untrustworthy.

'I'm surprised to see you here.'

'I just couldn't wait to bring you something, Vicki my dear.' He lays a black folder on the sofa. Vicki snatches it off the pale fabric and dumps it on the coffee table: Chinese, inlaid, nice.

'I cannot think what you could possibly have which would be of interest to me!'

Conor produces a folded paper from his inside pocket. 'You'll be interested in this. I'm not leaving till you sign it.'

'If you're trying to intimidate me, I'll call the police!' She snatches the embossed paper, unfolds it and reads down it with increasing incredulity. 'I, Victoria Haversham, withdraw the charges of sexual impropriety which I have levelled at Mr Conor Towmey ...' Is this a joke?' Her cheeks colour so violently she looks as if she might explode.

'Oh, no! Far from it. If you look at the folder you will see why you'll be a laughing stock if you carry on with this.'

'I think I will phone the police, Vicki.' Mousy Carrie to the rescue, twittering.

'I don't think so. The paperwork's all there. Proof of the abortion just after John died. And, of course, the gonorrhoea...'

Carrie collapses onto a golden velvet footstool as a Pekinese excited by the raised voices yelps and squeaks. Conor loves the chaos he is creating.

'And also, there's the peculiar, doubtfully legal, transfer of assets like the Cotswold farms and the Dorset cottage to your name only a week before John's sad passing under the surgeon's knife. Not a problem for death duties between husband and wife, of course, but taking them out of an estate to be halved with your stepson? I'm sure Keith would be interested. He's in my club, you know? I'd like him to check it *was* John's signature, for I hear he was pretty out of it by then.'

Vicki's cherry-red mouth quivers and her face blanches from flushed anger to icy white. Conor wonders at the swift connection between emotion and facial arteries.

'So, if we are at the GMC, and I've got my right bastard lawyer lined up, he's going to say to your QC, 'this poor wee widow wasn't up for a shag, is that right? A nice chaste wee high-class widow, poor thing. So how come she got the clap?'

'Where did you get all this?' Vicki rustles through the papers.

'Sent by an anonymous benefactor who didn't like to see me shafted. There's the envelope. The clinic records are photocopies, but a court will get the originals.'

Conor smiles triumphantly. Nice suggestion from Pilkington: post the stuff to yourself, 'anonymously.' He strolls round the room, hands in pockets, pausing in front of a peaceful pastoral scene. Constable. Possibly original. Bit twee. Lifting a ginger jar, he looks at its base.

'Put that down! It's Ming!'

'Late I believe? Has a small crack in it.' He has no idea about it, but toys with dropping it on the parquet floor. No. He's doing enough damage. 'One last thing,' he points at Carrie, 'why the Hell is she here?'

'She's my cousin.'

There is a vague resemblance round the eyes, though Carrie lacks Vicki's height and cheekbones. 'And who was the bastard who got you pregnant?'

'I though you knew everything?' She allows herself a smile. 'It was the Guards Ball. An old friend. My first outing after John died. Simon was just back from a gruelling tour in Ireland, not that it's any business of yours.'

'And why stir up all this fuss about me? You don't need money!' He gestures round the room. 'Nor the publicity, or should I say, the notoriety.'

'My therapist felt I needed closure. Plus I wanted to save others …'

Carrie chimes in. 'I've told her what you do to women, some who don't even understand English – all for their filthy beasts of husbands. Appalling! Shouldn't be allowed. Vicki's lawyer says you should be struck off!'

A dangerous frigid dyke with a wooden crucifix heaving on her twin-setted bosom. No hope of uncovering dirty secrets there.

'Money had nothing to do with it. I'm not seeking damages or media money.' Vicki's nostrils flared. 'You are an adulterer!'

'People who live in glass houses, Vicki. Just sign it and I'll be on my way.'

Heading for the Aston with his retraction, Conor thinks back to sex with Vicki. Not great shakes. Bit hard now to see why she'd turned on him. Bloody women, so difficult to read. Wasn't saying 'no' part of foreplay? Like that girl at Uni his father paid off: she'd been gagging. There had been only once he wasn't sure. … But he'd been seriously pished. That wee kitten – genius! If she'd ever let on, he'd have heard by now. Anyway, her people would have been easy QC fodder.

◆

First Sunday home, Beth had slept most of the day, but insisted on dressing for dinner. Julia helped her into a black shift dress and sparkly necklace, securing her hair up to disguise the chemo-induced alopecia patches. Ralph sat her on the sofa with a G&T. Cressida and Tim arrived early. Peggy's beef bourguignon was soon demolished amidst teasing and laughter.

Cressie gasped astonished. 'Ralph! You're eating beef?'

'Gran won't cook him different things. Mum needs iron,' announced Katy.

'It's either beef or starvation!' Ralph shrugged and opened a second bottle of wine. A big sticky chocolate cake was scoffed then Ralph sent the girls off to load the new dish-washer and braced himself before saying, 'Conor's off the hook, by the way, Beth. That Vicki woman withdrew the charge.'

As he'd predicted, Beth erupted. Ralph had to explain to Cressida and Tim about Conor. Listing his misdemeanours, the ones they knew about, took some time. The girls returned but Tim urged early bed so they'd be up in time for a swim with him first thing. After insisting they'd only go if Ralph came too, they left. Beth continued on Conor.

'And I think Con was a rapist too. I have a friend's diary implicating him and knickers I think he took from her …'

Ralph intervened. 'You can't say for sure. She'd didn't name him. There are no witnesses and it was too long ago. I think you should bin the knickers – you'll never prove anything now!'

'Oh keep up baby brother! Don't you know why I got my promotion?' said Cressida.

'What's that got to do with this?' said Beth.

'Well, my PhD was with Alec Jeffreys in Leicester, working on DNA fingerprinting. That's what I've mostly done at the Met, too, since coming back from the States. Latest work's on Polymerase Chain Reactions. We're refining it all the time, finding mini-satellites, identifying people faster and more thoroughly. All light years ahead of the old woolly blood-group identification system.'

'But even if there had been anything on the knickers, it's too long ago to prove whether Conor was near them, surely?' Ralph shook his head.

'Not necessarily, it was old sperm that trapped the guy who killed Linda Mann in Leicester. Although it's only three years since that first DNA conviction, there've been many more since. I'm prepared to give it a go…' Cressida shrugged.

Tim looked thoughtful. 'We don't have DNA from this guy, though, do we? Or Maia?'

'What do you need to identify someone?' asked Ralph.

'Ideally a buccal swab…' Cressida said.

'Think we can forget that,' Beth laughed. 'I'm not sticking swabs into that lion's mouth!'

'Or hair or saliva or something.'

'I've got Maia's diary, a hairbrush and some other bits and pieces in a box her Dad gave me. The pants are in a poly bag. Wendy will have something of Conor's.'

'Great. I'll take them. Bit of an experiment.'

'Not sure it would be admissible in Court, though.'

'What kind of Assistant Chief Constable will you make? You're so defeatist!' Cressida punched Tim in the arm. As usual, he'd been sitting quietly.

'Assistant Chief Constable?' Ralph looked impressed. 'What's this?'

'Interview Monday, Lothian and Borders. Ideally, we'd live somewhere half way. But if I don't get it, I'll simply transfer to a Force up here at my current grade. There are a few Chief Superintendents retiring soon. Fed up with the Met anyway.'

'Congrats Tim. Did wonder how often you two would see one another if Cressie was in Dundee.' Beth gave him a hug. 'Good luck for Monday! And Cressie, you sure you can do a DNA test?'

'Sure. I'll do it as an experiment at the Home Office lab.'

'But Beth, it'll be circumstantial evidence at best. There's only your word on where you found the underwear and Conor's DNA will be inadmissible if obtained without consent.' Tim looked serious. 'So it's unlikely the Fiscal would allow a prosecution.'

Beth suddenly sat up. 'OK. Anyway, in case I forget Ralph, Stella phoned when you were at Oddbins. Not to tell us about her new job, but Jackson's. He's now Chief Area Pharmaceutical Officer for Glasgow – another promotion! You'll get ACC on Monday no problem, Tim. Uranus is conjunction with Mars: Ralph's mother swore by them!'

Everyone laughed. Ralph lifted his glass. 'Promotion for everyone!'

Draining her drink, Cressie noticed Beth's lids beginning to droop and caught Ralph's eye, nodding towards her. Cressie started collecting glasses. Ralph helped Beth to her feet and she kissed him. 'A great night, thanks Ralph. And I love the house changes!'

Later, curling curled round her slight, recumbent figure, Ralph knew he'd have to try to fatten her up before the next chemo in two weeks. Part of him prayed Cressida wouldn't prove anything; nothing to be gained by stirring up all that old stuff. Maia had gone. Beth was all that mattered now. Philip Davies wasn't totally confident about the outcome. Ralph didn't sleep.

Thirty-eight

Dogs of War

The bloody key! She tried it again.

'What's wrong Wendy?' Victor called from beside his Jag. She'd brought him in case Conor had arrived home early, for she'd decided she didn't want to see him without her lawyer present. The Weybridge house had been sold subject to contracts but there were some things she wanted to collect, including, she suspected, un-forwarded mail.

'The key doesn't work.'

'Let me try.' He tried. 'Sure this is the right key? It's a Yale. The lock's a Peters.'

'The bastard's changed the lock!'

'Don't get aerated. You've still got legal right of entry. I'll phone the Estate Agent.'

'Tabitha next door will let you phone.'

'Right!' He nipped over the fence, returning a few minutes later. 'Some Denise woman is on her way. I didn't get into any discussions; just said you'd forgotten your key. Tabitha's asked us in for a coffee while we're waiting.' They had two. Denise took an hour.

'Vic, could you sort through the hall and dining room for anything addressed to me?' She moved through every room. God, he'd left a grubby mess, her lovely plush carpet all stained. But perhaps no bad thing. No regrets. Upstairs she found a new toothbrush in the cabinet, same as the one on the basin. Excellent. She swept the master bedroom, rummaging in the laundry basket. The bed made her wrinkle her nose. The waste bin held letters addressed to her, opened. Nosey pig. Her resolve grew. On the top landing she spotted a small watercolour by her grandfather. How had she missed that? Vic commented on it as she descended. Guiltily, she felt it gave credence to her trawl of upstairs.

'There's a surprising amount of paperwork and stuff addressed to you in the study.' Vic held two bulging canvas bags but managed to take the painting. Wendy, balancing two other carriers and a bin bag, closed the door. Denise slithered from her Mercedes, the Archers blaring from the radio. Her father never missed it. Wendy was glad he'd missed this.

Denise was a lacquered, back-combed, pancake-make-upped fortyish woman needing her navy suit in a larger size. 'Got everything? Mr Towmey not here today?' She simpered at Victor. Wendy briefly wondered if she'd 'had' Conor.

'Yes. Thanks for coming over.'

'Enjoy your day, Mrs Towmey.'

'Actually it's Dr Tuffnall-Brown. I use my maiden name now.'

'Oh, right. Shall I change the paper work when I get back?'

'Oh, don't bother.' She didn't trust her. A cock-up on names might prove an excuse for Conor to prevaricate over the settlement.

'The contract exchange is tomorrow. Mr Towmey is coming in.' Denise smirked.

'I'm not sure he'll be back...' Wendy changed her mind: let her think what she likes.

Denise shrugged, looking askance at her before raising her brows at Vic. Wendy got into the car. Victor drove off. She'd relied a lot on him. He'd been delighted to be engaged against Conor whose years of abusive phone calls, exhortations to pursue un-winnable libel cases and defaulted bills had resulted in Victor refusing to represent him. After a late lunch at the Lion, he dropped Wendy at the station, not asking why she was heading for London and not Bristol. The picture and three bags went to his office.

◆

Yesterday's mail lies on the hall floor. Conor grabs it on the way past, throwing obvious bills into a pile. Yawning, he turns on the TV.

'This is the BBC News for the nineteenth of August 1989...'

Some bloody politician in Bogota assassinated, who cares? Picking up an official-looking envelope, he slits it open. And splutters from inhaled cornflakes.

'We wish to notify you of receipt of a complaint ... Inform you that a meeting of the Preliminary Proceedings Committee will be held on ... We invite you to comment on the allegations that have been set before us. At this point there is no question of Interim Suspension, but ...'

Bloody Hell! Suspension? Fucking GMC! Speed reading, he scans down the paragraphs in mounting anger. *'Inappropriate touching.'* What the hell? *'Unnecessary vaginal examination for a breast lump.'* Balls – valid to check for ovary pathology too! *'Sent nurse from the room ... just a child ... only disclosed recently ... psychiatric report ...'* Yada, yada. Christ, he'd hardly touched her! Bloody cheek making a complaint. Fucking melodramatic little temptress!

He looks at his watch. Pilkington's don't open till nine. Phoning Desmond's mobile before then costs extra. Stay calm. Must be a defence here. Or a potential diversion due to dirt? Grabbing the Dictaphone from his brief case, he dictates a short rebuttal letter. Shit, the Patek says almost seven. Car's due. Sod it! Need to leave it till he gets back.

◆

Dubai is a revelation, the florid prosperity of the blossoming Arab state knocking LA into touch. The International Surgical Conference is attended by everyone who's anyone. The cutting-edge breast prostheses on the promotional stalls look amazing, feel like the real thing. Almost. All the eminent aesthetic boys are here. Conor's contemplating doing FRCS (Plastics) as another string to his bow. Might someone be persuaded to take him on, help him through it? Or could he swing a paid NHS sabbatical? The more extensive, lucrative work goes to the guys with dual qualification. He does some aesthetic stuff already, tummy tucks and such, but the official extra letters meant more scope, better indemnity – and bigger billing.

Tonight, after hearing all the day's papers, presentations and speeches, he's meeting Dan to pump him for the lowdown on practising in the Gulf. Tomorrow he'll have sussed out whom most usefully to tag on to amongst the delegates for the rest of the weekend.

Dan looks sun-tanned and prosperous. Versace shirt, silk tie. Conor finds him very quiet and strains to find common ground. He politely asks after Dan's family. Beth's illness is news. He has no contact with anyone in the Year now.

'So, retroperitoneal fibrosis, Dan. Outlook?'

'Well, as you should know …' Dan realises a blank Conor has no idea. 'It's not good. Haven't you seen one?'

Seeing Dan look perplexed – or irritated – Conor changes tack. 'So, what about work out here? How is it?'

Dan is terse. 'OK, but I've set up interviews in Glasgow and London to go home.'

Conor isn't interested enough to ask why but continues. 'Thinking of coming out myself. How many days a year can you spend in the UK without paying tax?'

'I've no idea, Conor.'

'Really? And have you had to oil many palms to get on?'

'Well, I never have.' Dan's face indicates he's pushing it.

Conor returns to his hotel. Bloody wasted evening. He orders a brandy in the bar. Jesus, expensive! The few women around are shapeless forms swathed head to foot in fabric. There will be much to give up if he moves out here.

◆

It is 4am when Conor kicks aside the mound of crap accumulated on his mat in a week. He's pleased with this rented Thames-side penthouse. No point in buying when he intends going overseas. No point either in going to bed. He switches on the coffee machine, the only thing in his high-tech kitchen he uses. Dismissing thoughts of a shower, he considers dozing on the sofa, but instead starts sorting the mail mountain, mainly looking for cheques but it's largely drug company circulars and medical journals. Bin. A thick white envelope chills: not again.

'*We would invite you to...*' Getting bloody monotonous. How many other folk had to put up with this shit? It was a personal vendetta. A competitor, perhaps? His smooth bedside manners and innovative techniques have spread his popularity amongst a certain type of discerning woman. Bound to be losers. Or the Honourable Gwendoline stirring. She'll know some of his well-heeled clients, the British gentry's a small, exclusive club.

The letter in response to last week's nonsense isn't typed yet. On reflection, maybe he should hold, take legal advice. Little Samantha Vincent's complaint might be tricky with her prominent surgical father, but this new complaint's worse, calling into question his professional expertise. Not on. The bloody Granger woman *asked* for her boob job, not his fault she was a scraggy bitch! Tricky procedure, barely enough skin, but reasonable result, given the circumstances. Lord Aston Granger should be glad of her nipple with erectile potential. Conor lightens. Christ, women weren't his bag. Bet Elizabeth Granger doesn't know of Aston's clandestine 'lavvie trysts.' Wouldn't look good in the press! Great, a lever for that one. This Granger GMC complaint is post-marked last week. He'll need to get over to Harley Street pronto before the records are requisitioned to check nothing needs tweaked or massaged. What a bind, his NHS clinic is at ten. Sod it.

Putting down the summons, a line catches his eye. '*A Bristol doctors' letter …*' Bristol? Henry, Wendy. Damn her! Time for a brief before this gets out of hand. Can't use Peter Davenport QC, his last exorbitant bill is still outstanding. To hell with it, he pays hefty Defence Society fees to cover his private work, he'll use them, play the 'humble' card, be wronged, and contrite if need be. Wendy should burn in Hell …

Shit is that smoke he smells? Can't be olfactory hallucinations again, he's been clean for days. There's a crackle and a flash and flames are shooting out of his new toaster. Bloody hell, what next? He throws it in the sink, turns on the tap and yells as steam scalds his hand. Not yet six and the day's a fucking disaster! In his jet-lagged state in his smoke-filled kitchen, he seethes. There's a conspiracy against him of pure malice. Henry might have stolen his wife, but he'll not get his livelihood.

The next day doesn't improve. The Defence Union rep comes to see him in his office. Rightly, he is an eminent consultant. But after the chap has listed the complaints, Conor feels anything but eminent.

◆

By September I felt better. Two weeks after the last chemotherapy came a surge of well-being and optimism, improved appetite and movement on the bathroom scales. Plus I was beginning to criticise my mother's ironing. I hate double creases.

'You're certainly better! Shall I go home now?'

'Och, no, mum, not yet. But why don't you could take a few days away with Aunt Eileen before the weather breaks? Then we can see how I manage.'

'You sure? I must say I think the girls should do more to help, you're too soft on them!' Mum hugged me and put on the kettle. Solid practical support, how lucky was I? The day improved even further. Wendy called.

'We're up for a few days, can we come today?'

Mum went into baking mode. She loved Henry. He loved her cakes. My old friends looked honey-brown. I deduced they must have been abroad for it had been a rubbish UK summer as observed from my sick sofa.

We chatted for half an hour before mum exclaimed, 'Oh, well done Henry!' and rose to hug them both. I had missed the platinum bands.

'Sneaky things! Where? When?' I too embraced them.

'Capri two weeks ago. The most romantic place I could think

of!' Henry beamed.

'We flew out Henry's mum and aunts. Chaos, darling! They didn't like the food, the funny toilet handles, the heat, or even the Prosecco.'

'So a small wedding?'

'Teeny! Waitress and Concierge as witnesses. With Dad and Gramps gone, I didn't really want a proper wedding, but we'll party soon. Hope you and Ralph will come with the girls.'

Wendy bore no resemblance to the bruised, wasted figure drowning her sorrows in Bordeaux at the Ten Year reunion. She was blossoming, pink cheeked, a bit puffy...

'When are you due?' I asked.

'How did you know?' Wendy was cross I'd spoiled her thunder.

'Trust me, I'm a doctor! You've got the look!'

'I'm fourteen weeks. Had oodles of tests since I'm forty soon and have lost a tube. Still, one ovary and one tube seems to be all you need! Despite the Dalkon damage, they're hopeful I'll go to term.'

'And *you* look plumper too,' Henry stroked my arm. 'Nice to see you pink again.'

'Another two pounds today and all bloods normal now. Fingers crossed.'

'And we've more news.' Henry looked mysterious.

'What more can there be? Weddings, baby – is it a new job?'

'No. But someone else might be looking for one, soon.'

'Don't be so infuriating, Henry Thomson! Who?'

'Conor,' he said, fetching his coat from the hall to hand me a battered two-week-old English Daily Mail. What was it with old classmates, forever producing crumpled newspapers? The front page looked innocent.

My mother hovered curiously over Henry's shoulder as he unfurled the paper. 'Him! Keeps rising up like a bloody bad penny!' My mother rarely swore. Then the phone rang. She reluctantly went to answer it.

'How come you bought a Daily Mail? I thought no self-respecting Guardian reader would be seen dead with one?'

'I picked it up in the ante-natal clinic last week when Wendy was away ages. I couldn't believe it, so nicked it to show her. And brought it here in case you didn't know – I'd have expected you to phone if you'd seen it.' He spread the paper out on the settee. 'Page seven, bottom right.'

I read out the headline. '*Society Surgeon to Answer Multiple Charges*. GMC concedes investigation is under way concerning allegations made against London surgeon Mr Conor Towmey. Sources close to Mr Towmey, who has on record a previous complaint of sexual impropriety which was dropped, say he denies all past and current charges and alleges a smear campaign.'

The entire photo-less article took up only a few inches in a small side column. The paper was dominated by a mass shooting in Kentucky attributed to Prozac (kind of thing medics remember). 'So, what are the charges? Do you know?' I asked.

'Well, one's mine. After further advice, I'm going for him over the plagiarism.'

I knew how he felt: unfinished business. 'Quite right! He shouldn't get away with it.'

'No idea about the other charges. Maybe he's had wind of something, Dan met him in Dubai talking about moving to the Gulf.'

'So, how is Dan?' We hadn't spoken during my illness, though he'd phoned Rosie.

'Dan's fine. He's over for interviews.'

I asked no more. Having dealt forcefully with an unsolicited double-glazing call my mother returned. Hearing Dan's name, she marched back to the kitchen.

◆

When I was young, I didn't spend hours first thing hunting for shoes, books, pens and gym kit. Mind you, my parents' two-bedroomed flat left less room for losing things. I finally shut the front door with a sigh of relief as Julia and Katy set off for school. Katy's

Home Work Diary in the laundry basket was a particular oddity. Few of her dirty clothes usually reached it, preferring to lurk, mixed with clean, on her floor. After two weeks, I was missing mum. Big day today. I'd decided to try to work a few half days a week. My plan was a relaxing bath and a coffee with a quick look at the paper before a surgery at ten. Then the phone rang. I had started up the stairs, but when it went quiet then rang again, I wondered who was being this persistent so early in the morning?

'Hello?'

'Hi, Beth, it's Cressida.'

'Oh, how are you? Just got your two disorganised nieces off to school. They're getting worse. Anything wrong?'

'No. Well, I came in early to double check something and felt I had to phone you now.'

'What about?'

'Those knickers, you remember, you gave me weeks ago?'

How could I forget the enigma that had lain in my drawers for sixteen years? 'Yes?'

'The DNA in the hair from the ivory handled brush you submitted matches that of the pubic hair caught in the torn knickers.' My stomach lurched: Maia's brush. Cressida continued, 'PCR tests confirm it unequivocally.'

I had no idea what they were, but she sounded sure. 'And the other … party?' I couldn't say his name.

'New elution techniques confirm the presence of ejaculate.' She was speaking in precise professional tones I'd never heard her use before. 'The sperm is a match with the DNA samples we obtained from items supplied by your friend purporting to be from her ex-husband, Mr Towmey. There is no doubt.'

That was it. End of a near twenty-year mystery. The warm September morning didn't prevent me shivering in my dressing gown. As granny used to say, a ghost walked over my grave. I travelled back in time to Maia's bedroom with its Anatomy Merit Certificate on the wall and to that neat Maryhill lounge where

Kristoff handed me her post-mortem report. Then came a vision of the tear-stained mourners watching me read from Ecclesiastes at her funeral. I became encased in ice.

'You still there, Beth?'

'Sorry, yes. So can we do anything?'

'Tim says not. This isn't even logged as an official test. I've just put it through a control example for a new technique to check against current ones. Tim says there is no crime logged with the police, nor any possible date or time or place known for the alleged incident. Some sort of sexual activity has taken place at some time involving this garment and these two people, but there's no way of knowing if it was consensual or not, nor even if it were penetrative sex.'

I shivered again.

'And of course we have no witnesses. The Diary allegation is vague, the provenance of the underwear and hairbrush is, sorry Beth, hearsay. No one saw you take the knickers from the boy's drawer and toothbrush saliva sample we tested was obtained by inadmissible means without the male's consent.'

'Right. Of course. But still, I've always wanted to know for sure.'

'That's what I thought. I'll bag everything up and return it next weekend if you like.'

I couldn't speak.

Cressie changed to her usual relaxed tone. 'So, we get the keys to the house Saturday.'

I tried to sound enthusiastic. She had a new house. I had a second chance at life, hopefully. 'Fantastic.' My brain was drowning in sorrow.

'And also I want to tell you we're going to tie the knot in March. Tim thinks an ACC needs a proper wife, not a cohabitee!'

Thinking how nice it would be to go to a wedding, I felt guilty. 'Great, where?'

'Country house in Scotland somewhere, a few months after I start? London friends are keen to come up. Maybe St Andrews?

Mum and Dad met there. Think Lionel would like that. Have you seen Dad recently? Failing a bit. Mind you, not bad for 88!'

'No, not for a while.' I felt guilty again. We'd hardly contacted him during my illness. The girls loved him, Ralph's double in every way.

'Sorry I have to go now, Beth.'

'So must I – first surgery this morning! Thanks, Cressie. For everything. See you!'

My leisurely soak ended up being a rapid shower and maniacal blast of wet hair. I looked in the mirror and froze. Maia was looking over my shoulder, in that orange and yellow daisy dress I only saw her wear once: that last disco. Goosebumps rose up my spine. I was used to seeing her in nightmares, but never when awake. This Maia though, was smiling, serene. I was terrified I was so overwrought I'd become psychotic and closed my eyes. When I opened them, she was gone.

We couldn't do anything, but at least I knew at last what had happened to Maia. Ralph could no longer try to persuade me Conor wasn't a monster, just a damaged, childish, product of a sad home and neglectful father. Liam had told him old boy Towmey was now permanently sectioned in Hartwood Mental Hospital with alcohol-related dementia. I wondered if he had really been as bad as Conor had made out? The clock chiming quarter-to brought me back to my senses. I rushed round collecting my stethoscope, pens, doctor's bag, car keys and found my stray court shoe. I was little better than the girls! Then the doorbell rang. Jesus Christ, what next?

I opened the door, stood, stared and burst into tears. Dan stood on the top step.

Thirty-nine

Casualties

I

June 27th 1970, Queen Margaret Union, University of Glasgow

She walks back from the Ladies on the first floor. It had been empty, while the ground floor queue had curled out across the hall. Jumping Jack Flash blares. Her head aches. Beer isn't her drink. She'll take paracetamol when she gets up to her room. It's almost midnight, time to be Cinderella. Not that she'll get much sleep upstairs with the music thumping. She's sorry she came. Even after three years, she finds socialising a strain, discos especially. Drat, he's on the landing. She'll have to pass to find Beth and sort arrangements for tomorrow. He's closing a door she's never noticed before. Walking by, head held high, she manages to avoid eye contact, but he brushes against her. Smoke billows. His fingers twitch. Ash falls to the carpet.

'Do you hear that?' He catches her arm, putting his ear to the door.

'What?' She pulls away.

'I think something's trapped in the cupboard!'

A faint cry, fainter than a small child. She opens the door. He flicks a switch. A tiny black kitten is mewling, trying to leap out of its cardboard box prison.

'Poor wee thing! Why on earth would anyone put it in here?' She steps forward.

'I know, shucks, who could do that?' The door closes, a key turns.

He is behind her. How does he have a key? Heart beats strangle her throat.

'What're you doing, you idiot? This isn't funny, let me out!' She wants to scream but only a squeaky whisper comes.

He pushes her back to the wall, clamping his mouth on hers. Screaming is impossible, breathing hard. His tongue darts around her mouth: hideous. The din from outside is still deafening. Screaming is futile. A naked light bulb sways back and forth in the draught from the sudden door closure. Now his left hand clamps her mouth as he kisses her neck. His other hand forces her round. She feels her beautiful new lace tearing. There is fumbling at her back. God, his zip! He's like an octopus, left hand dropping to scoop into the wide sleeve of her dress, force itself inside her new bra to squeeze her nipple hard. Then it's back covering her mouth and nose in a stifle-hold. The thrust from behind takes her by surprise, forcing her over a trolley laden with cleaning materials that clatter to the floor. Pain doesn't describe it. She manages to bite his left hand, but he is panting heavily, grunting, unfazed by her struggle. She goes limp, exhausted and defeated. If only she'd been wearing tights... Stupid! He'd have torn them too. She tries a scream but it's trapped in his sweaty hand.

'Yes, yes, yah beauty!' He finishes grunting, one hand goes limp, dropping off her face. The other still rests on her pubic bone at the crotch where he's been pulling her pelvis violently up and back towards him, like she was in a vice. Or in a slow-motion horror movie. What is he thinking of? Her eyes are full. He switches off the light. Why now? She turns.

No sound comes from her lips. A strangled spasm lurches from her stomach. She thinks she's going to be sick. In the dark she senses him fumbling again- tucking everything back in? She feels damp. Is she bleeding? This isn't how it is meant to be, the first time. Beer fumes overwhelm her in the enclosed space. She retches.

'There, you're a good fuck, you know, you shouldn't keep it to yourself. You've gotta live a little!' He laughs. 'You know it was a bet? They thought I couldn't get you... But the minute I saw the little pussy I thought it was worth a shot. I love pussies, don't you?'

He bends down to pick something up. The kitten? The light from the frosted glass above the door is feeble. She cannot see.

'Shall I walk you to your bus? I expect you'll be going home now?'

Holy Mary, Mother of God, he speaks like they've just had a cup of tea! What kind of monster is he? Her vision clears, but she can't bear to look at him. She pulls down her mini dress, halter-necked, orange and yellow daisies. Bought only yesterday but never to be worn again. He is zipping his fly, re-arranging his genitals the arrogant way he often does, always ensuring he has a girl in eye contact. Not this time.

'No walk to the bus? Please yourself! Don't worry I'll take the cat back to the janitor's office.' Cradling the kitten, he starts whistling and winks. God, de-flowering her is just a joke, a bet. He unlocks the door and is gone. She slumps to the floor.

What should she do? It was rape, but who'll believe her? He'll just deny it. There are no witnesses. Worse, she'll have to say exactly what he did. Imagine testifying in front of her father? Weeping, she doesn't know how long it takes her to pull herself together, but knows she can't stay there all night. Tentatively opening the door, she looks out into the corridor. The noise of merriment rises as loud as ever. Running up the stairs in case she meets anyone in the lift, within seconds she is in the shower scrubbing till her skin is sore and raw. She feels filthy. Had she encouraged him? She'd thought earlier he'd stop pestering her if she gave him one dance. One. She thinks of tender Henry. If only it had been him... But that was it. She'd never do it again. Nor wear lace. She drops the soap and bending to pick it up remembers she hadn't picked up Beth's knickers. Ruined anyway. Eventually she can scrub no more and falls onto the narrow cubicle bed to lie rigidly on her back, wrapped tightly in her pink quilted dressing gown, hands in armpits, heels together, staring at the ceiling. The clock glows 5am. Maia is almost drifting off to sleep when a pang of horror seizes her. Had Conor used a condom?

II

Christmas Eve, Lanarkshire, December 1988, a year back

The heavy maroon velvet curtain closes over.

As the darkness shields his lower face, he drops the scarf he's taken to muffling up over his jaw in public. The damp and humidity it causes is acceptable in the winter. By summer it will not matter.

'Forgive me Father, it is years since my last confession. I have sinned.'

The shadowy figure on the other side of the grille stiffens and exhales forcefully.

'Yes, my son?'

In the claustrophobic silence the penitent feels the priest's heart beat quickening. Or is it his own? His rehearsed speech fails him as a sixteen-year-old vision re-appears, one which has haunted him since the worst night of his life.

◆

It had been Graeme's idea. The empty Orthopaedic ward was closed for the decorators but still made up, sheets and everything. Pat had been his idea too. He'd invited the beautiful boy who hated his christened name of John Patrick, preferring Pat. He'd commiserated, hating being called Francis at school, so girly.

Pat had been reticent, a first timer. It was their second session before he'd joined in. The mutual stuff at Graeme's flat was OK, though he'd taken persuading for penetration. Perhaps his bleeding after that night should have warned them. Though on the fatal night they'd taken poppers and other stuff. Graeme's proposed asphyxia scenario had seemed safe enough: they were all there. The overhead pulley gantry meant for elevating broken legs went high and out to the side. You had to lift your legs to get a proper neck squeeze from the cord, so they'd thought it safe enough. If it became too much you could put your feet down, relieve the pressure and be helped off with the poly bag. Graeme had read it gave an amazing climax, like falling off the edge of the world. Pat had insisted on going first. More off his face than they'd been? Maybe if Graeme hadn't decided to fool around and they hadn't been 'at it' on the other bed they'd have noticed sooner: the rustling breathing quietening, the hand slowing and stopping… They were all naked, but for some reason, Graeme still had on his white work shirt. Pat was so limp, so blonde, so pale, apart from his swollen face. And all that blood pouring free. If only Graeme had brought clear bags, not white – would they have noticed earlier before Pat choked? CPR had been futile. Every day now, at least once, Frank has the vision. Of Graeme, crimson-spattered shirt agape, cradling the beautiful boy like Michelangelo's Pieta. Agonising. Graeme wasn't to blame for the worst thing though. The incinerator had been his idea, sending Pat to Eternal Damnation…

◆

The priest sounds angry. 'Come on, I haven't got all night! What's your confession?'

Frank closes his eyes. 'I burned a body, father. He was dead. It was my fault.'

There is a long silence before the priest speaks. 'Are you telling me you've murdered someone?'

'Not exactly. I didn't stab him or anything, we just couldn't cut him down in time to stop him choking. It was an accident. It started as … well, skylarking.'

'Choking? How? Were you just wee lads, playing?'

'No. It was masturbation father. Sex games with plastic bags and nooses.'

'Jesus Christ and all the Saints preserve us!' Even after thirty years, this was a new one.

'I denied him the Last Rites, father, murdered his soul when I burned his body. I was only thinking of myself.' A gasp comes through the grille. 'I'm damned father. But I've had my retribution already. I'll not see another Christmas. They give me three months at most.'

That was something. No point in involving the police if this man is dying. He sighs. Nor any need to search his own conscience and betray the Confessional. But, one thing more …

'Does anyone else know about this?'

'Gee, sorry, Graeme, was there, but he's dead. And once I tried telling a colleague, but he was very drunk and hasn't mentioned it since.'

'This boy, his family, what about them?'

'I've prayed for them and left his mother a Picasso that looks like him. And a letter, telling his mother how sorry I am, how lovely he was and that it was an accident.'

The priest prays for guidance – can this soul be saved? Poor chap is obviously repentant. And wealthy- a Picasso! He doesn't recognise the voice. A visitor or an incomer? Little to be gained by trawling this up in public. 'Well my son …'

◆

It's some time before Frank changes his will, being wary of approaching James or another lawyer, fearing questions on his decision to leave a large fortune to monks. Eventually he confesses all to Patricia Bonham, who solves the problem by checking the legalities, typing a codicil and getting the ward sister to witness Frank's signature.

Sitting watching the priest administer the Last Rites to an unconscious Frank, Pat wonders how a mother could have stayed silent knowing of the physical and sexual abuse her son was suffering at the hands of his father and teachers. Would he have had such a tortured life if she'd intervened? Pat crosses herself as the priest concludes 'May the Lord have mercy on his soul.' She hopes he will.

III

September 1989, Tavistock Institute, London,

Judy was shaking her head at Rosie. 'You know the rise in self-harm and suicide isn't all about teenage angst and substance abuse, I'm convinced a lot of adolescent problems come from abuse, mainly sexual. It's right across society. Lately I've had some harrowing cases where the abuse is by family or friends.'

Rosie nodded. 'I agree. Sex abuse is probably commoner than we think.'

This National Conference, 'Bridging Research in Adolescent Psychiatry and Education' was far more interesting than its unwieldy title might have suggested. The morning group work in London's Tavistock Institute had been wide-ranging with representatives from many specialities in teaching and psychiatry. The lunch, too, was excellent, though spoiled by knowing she was first up in the afternoon. Rosie was distracting herself with a second cup of coffee and Judy, a London psychiatrist from California via the ghettoes of Newark.

'For example, Rosie, I'm testifying next week at the General Medical Council about a young girl who got difficult, cut her wrists and overdosed almost fatally on her father's cardiac drugs. Touch and go, but she's made it. He'd no idea she'd been abused, by one of his colleagues, no less. Abuse can come from any quarter, even trusted professionals.'

'You're right, Judy, we need to ask all overdosage patients about abuse, they're not all 'acting out' responses to boyfriends dumping them or teenage tantrums. OK, there'll be some wanting temporary escape from stresses, the so-called 'para-suicides,' but those immature teens who feel so trapped that death seems the only escape- appalling!' Rosie thought of Maia, immature emotionally, if not in years.

'Say, I shouldn't say too much, but you might know the guy. He's a Glasgow grad from '73, I looked him up. Though, you're from Edinburgh, right? Rival cities I'm told, so you wouldn't ...' A nearby delegate asks the time. Rosie waits until their table clears.

'Actually I graduated from Glasgow in 1973. I only moved to Edinburgh after I married. We had a few rogues amongst us. It isn't Conor Towmey by any chance?'

'Right on the button, Dr Hutton! Well, gee, isn't it a small world?' Judy looked surprised. 'Best keep it in confidence, though.'

'Sure.' Rosie told her about Maia and the DNA evidence implicating Conor. She had a slight pang, wondering if she should have. James wouldn't approve.

'Your poor friend! Fancy us meeting. We on a ley line here? Sounds like this guy's accumulating a shit-load of bad Karma. The GMC will be his Nemesis. Difficult to see him getting off this.'

'I wouldn't want him to,' said Rosie. 'He should never have been allowed into medicine. Wonder how many girls he's abused who haven't come forward?'

'Yeh. Like Le Guin says, the power of the abuser always lies in the silence of the victims. But times are changing, I hope. We gotta make girls stronger, get them to confront abusers.' Judy lifted her bag. 'Great meeting you. Say, let's do dinner later. Break a leg with the speech. Sorry I've to chair a teaching seminar. Save me an abstract!'

'I'd love to,' Rosie took Judy's card before glancing through her presentation: 'Self-Harm and Para-suicide in Adolescents: Putting Research into Preventive Practice.'

IV

September 21st 1989, Westminster

Elizabeth Granger paused at the mirror as she came out of the shower, steeling herself to look. With the faulty prosthesis gone and the skin grafts taken, she was unilaterally flat-chested and purple-scarred. Mercifully, the pain had abated and there was no sign of tumour recurrence. She also had her husband back. This trauma had brought them closer. She knew of his homosexual blackmail. He knew of her affair, though he was crushed it had been with Towmey, his tormentor. He was even more furious about the suppurating ulcerating mess Towmey had left her with. The beast wouldn't get away with it. No one else should suffer under his knife. That Vicki woman had backed off too easily. Elizabeth was tougher. She'd get justice. That shyster had performed an operation he wasn't properly qualified to perform and right royally botched it up. She'd lost a breast and two years of her life. So far all he'd lost was three months of NHS pay. His suspension had been Aston's last act before resigning as Authority Chair. The Butcher's subsequent furious, threatening appearance at their home had sent her off in fear to her sister in Bristol for convalescence. But now she was back. Strong.

Aston smiled as she came down, in black, with pearls, gloves, netted hat and crimson scarf matching her lipstick. At the foot of the curved staircase he gave her a gentle kiss. She reached for her wrap as Nix and Nemesis came for affection. Tenderly, she stroked her precious Egyptian Maus. Brigitte Bardot was right, you can *so* depend on cats, it's only people who let you down. Aston took her arm. The chauffeur opened the door.

'To the GMC, Maddox!' Aston's hand closed around hers.

Forty

Fearful Trembling

September 1989

Liam had had enough. 'Con, you don't get it, do you? You've been an arse!'

'I'd have expected a bit more support from an old school chum when I'm up before the GMC tomorrow!'

'A chum? Really? When did you last call? James says you haven't got a hope in buggery of getting off. And Henry says you have unrealistic expectations.'

'Bloody stuck-up James. I told him, that Vincent girl's a nutter. And that Aston woman's wanting revenge because I ditched her. I mean, who'd want to fuck Frankenstein with a plastic surgery monkey-face? She begged me for that op, I'll have you know. And as for Henry complaining, he's just jealous of my success, egged on by witch Wendy!'

'Well, believe what you like, boyo, but you'll need a hell of a QC to pull this one off.'

'You know me, I'll bounce back quicker than you can say "shite"!'

'Oh, you're impossible! Don't phone me again. I don't know who you've sold your soul to, but I want no part of it. I'm a lawyer and I tell you – 'fess up, wise up and fuck off!'

◆

Next morning, Conor enters the GMC Hearing with Simon Anderson, his lawyer, and Sir Edwin Simcott QC, brother of his current flame, the Hon. Verity Simcott. It had been a lucky break, one of Edwin's clients suddenly pleading guilty in the High Court and freeing him up. He'd end this nonsense swiftly. They sit at the foot of the horseshoe-arranged tables. The Fitness to Practice Panel has already assembled. The Lay Chairman is Mrs Cordelia Smith. Edwin reassures Conor her track record is lenient; she has surgeons in her family. The other two Panellists are an unknown quantity: a Newcastle surgeon and a physician, Sir Timothy Burke, though Conor recalls meeting Burke once at Wentworth's nineteenth. Couldn't hurt.

'Right Conor, on the left is the Panel Secretary who takes notes, on the right the Legal Assessor who rules on points of Law.' Conor nods at Edwin's commentary, surprised he's feeling so tense. 'That's the GMC legal team,' Edwin gestures to the table at the foot of the other end of the horseshoe. 'Hamilton's their solicitor, and Felicity Bentley their QC. Remember what we discussed: deferential, tiniest hint of righteous indignation.'

Conor fidgets, attempting to suitably arrange his demeanour. The Chairman rises.

'Are there preliminary legal issues which either party wishes to raise before we start?'

The GMC counsel springs up. 'The GMC proposes that, due to her age and the nature of the charge, Patient A be permitted to give evidence from behind a screen and that the public and press be excluded.'

After brief discussion, this is agreed. Conor is annoyed. They should be able to see what a fruitcake Samantha Vincent is. Edwin sits unmoved.

The Chair addresses Conor, holding his gaze.

'For your benefit Mr Towmey, I shall outline the procedure. First the GMC makes its case. Witnesses will be called as in a Court of Law. Your counsel will cross-examine. The GMC may in turn respond to that cross-examination and the Panel may also have questions. We look first to establish the facts, then the GMC and your counsel make the case or otherwise concerning misconduct. If that is found proved and your Fitness to Practice is deemed impaired, sanctions will be considered. Do you understand?'

Conor stands, prompted by Edwin. 'Yes.'

'Can you confirm your name and GMC number please?'

Conor does so, surprised at the tremor in his voice.

'Are any of the facts admitted?' The Chair looks at the GMC counsel who produces a litany of questions he addresses to Conor.

'On the twenty-second of April 1989 were you consulting as a surgeon in private rooms at Curzon Street when Patient A consulted you …' Conor agrees only with the material facts: the place, time and purpose of encounters for each charge in turn. To the last, pertaining to research theft, he vehemently asserts 'Not guilty!'

Conor feels his stomach shrinking back into his spine. This is going to be a long few days, tougher than he'd imagined. He breathes out, trying to relax his abdominal muscles while stiffening his back to sit upright. The Chairman indicates the public and press should leave.

The GMC's QC calls 'Patient A's father.' Conor feels his first missed beat as Sir Roger-bloody-Vincent takes the Oath on a bible. This is serious shit, not just a few mates mulling over an unfortunate wee episode or two. The reality of his predicament creeps up his back like an icy serpent. Thank God his mother isn't alive. His father is in Cuckoo Land. But it would have been nice to have some family support. No sign of Aisling.

'You are sir, I believe, father of Patient A and a Professor of Surgery?'

'I am.'

'Can you tell us the nature of your complaint against Mr Towmey?'

'This man is a pervert who should not be allowed to practise!' Dark eyes bore into Conor. He looks away.

'If we could just keep to the facts, please, Mr A.' Felicity Bentley QC chides.

'Of course, I beg your pardon, Madam. Yes. My daughter found a breast lump and, knowing of Mr Towmey from my NHS post, I took her to see him next day. Initially I was pleased because I'd got an immediate appointment and that she was seeing a younger surgeon, not an old fogey she'd met at social evenings in our home.'

'Were you present at the examination?'

'No. A nurse took my daughter in, then emerged to fetch something. As she had to ask the receptionist where she'd put a delivery, it took a little time.'

'We shall be asking both Miss A and the nurse what happened in the room, but when she came out, how was she?'

'Crying. I thought because of the discomfort of the needle aspiration, but when we got home, she ran to her room, refusing to come down for dinner, even for my sister.'

'You are a widower, is that correct?'

'Yes. My wife died of breast cancer three years ago. My daughter is an only child and took it especially hard. She's been depressed, has missed a lot of school and still attends a psychiatrist.'

'Dr Diefenbaker?'

'Yes.'

'She will be giving evidence. So, subsequent to the clinic visit, we believe your daughter became more unwell?'

'Yes. She stopped eating, sleeping, even talking, and cut her arms. I find it inexplicable, but I am told it is a common outlet for stress nowadays in the young. She even took some pills.'

'Do you know why she was so stressed?'

'She would not talk to me, but Dr Diefenbaker informed me my daughter alleged she'd been subjected to sexual advances by Mr Towmey. That explained her refusal to return for her results. I had to phone for her biopsy result, thankfully, fine.'

'And what happened next?'

'I took legal advice and made a formal complaint to the GMC. In my book, this man is not fit to practise as a doctor.'

'Thank you, Sir.'

After making the point that they were establishing facts, not witnesses' opinions, Edwin declines questioning. Sir Roger marches out, head high, passing Conor without a glance. An unfamiliar pang of regret seizes Conor for a lost relationship that had started so promisingly, so usefully. There is rustling from behind a screen set up across the room. Ms Bentley QC rises again and strolls towards it. 'Miss A, you are the young lady who has made a complaint about Mr Conor Towmey following a consultation in his rooms on the twenty-second of April 1989, are you not?'

'Yes.' The voice is soft, quiet. Young.

'On the day of this incident we refer to, you were how old?'

'Fifteen.'

Conor jerks up. Underage? Surely not? Edwin looks irritated. A worm twists.

'Can you tell us what happened?'

'He, that is, *Mister Towmey* ...,' Conor winces at her venom. '...

sent the nurse out for something. Immediately she closed the door he was up at me, touching the lump, stroking my nipple and...' She falters. Conor couldn't see Judy take her hand at this point. 'He asked me if I knew how attractive I was and then sort of, pounced, stroking my skin, squeezing my breast...' She gives graphic detail: the hand sliding under overlying linen, fondling down to her pubic area, lifting elastic, sliding into her pants. 'His finger was at the ... entrance inside me down there. When the door opened and the nurse came back I was so relieved. You have no idea.'

'Was it your impression he intended going further, Miss A?' QC Bentley asks.

'Definitely. He was excited, flushed, with his hand on...' Her voice is low.

'His penis?'

Edwin is on his feet, objecting to 'witness leading,' but even with it sustained, her testimony has been damning. Samantha continues. 'I felt dirty, used. I couldn't speak to my mother, she's dead. This man was my father's colleague. I didn't think anyone would believe me. I wanted to run away. I slashed my arms, took pills. I just wanted to die...'

'This must have been very distressing for you...'

'It was horrible, the worst thing ever! No one should think they can touch you how they like because they're a doctor. I'm scared to go to one now. It might not be rape, but he's ruined me. I feel dirty. I hate him. I'm here so he can be punished.' She starts to cry. The Chairman suggests a break. 'No, I want to finish and go home!'

Conor's QC strides over to the screen. 'I understand life must have been difficult for you: your mother dead, your father often away. You find a breast lump, fear the worst, and then for the first time, a man puts his hand on you to examine you intimately. I put it to you Miss A, that none of this 'assault' happened, that you made it all up. Perhaps to impress your psychiatrist or in an attempt to gain more attention?'

'Of course not! Who'd come here for this kind of attention?

Doctor Diefenbaker's right, though, it helps to talk about it, get it out and deal with it.'

He tries to trip up her account, going over details, then asked about boyfriends. The GMC QC objects. The Legal Assessor sustains, the question is irrelevant. Samantha's evidence is strong, consistent. Conor sits impassive, Edwin unhappy.

The next witness is the nurse. 'Miss A was fine when I left to fetch the sterile pack, but upset on my return. She was sobbing *before* the needle went in.' Edwin cannot shake her story. Conor remembers her face when he'd sacked her: Hell hath no fury... Fat bitches, her and Carrie. They adjourn for the day. Conor goes home but cannot eat. Nor sleep.

◆

Next day Conor is called first. He gives his version of events calmly. In his opinion the girl was nervous and teary from the minute she arrived. He felt sorry for her. She obviously had severe psychiatric problems, but he wasn't a psychiatrist, just a surgeon doing the same job and procedure he'd done hundreds of times before. In his view, she was a fantasist. He didn't touch her except for the purposes of the lump examination and when the nurse was present. When she left, he'd tried chatting about TV programmes and music, but she wouldn't speak. Felicity Bentley sits down. Edwin only asks Conor to confirm he had sacked the nurse who had given evidence for incompetence, implying her evidence is biased. Bentley QC declines further questions. Conor is asked to sit. Edwin nods reassuringly. The testimony has gone as planned. His confidence is short-lived.

Bentley calls Dr Judy Diefenbaker, listing her credentials as a world expert in Adolescent Psychiatry. 'So how long have you known the complainant, doctor?'

'I've been seeing her privately for two years.'

'And how was she before this incident?'

'Making good steady progress, attending school. No self-harm for some time.'

'And after the alleged incident?'

'There was a dramatic resurgence of her clinical depression after this incident. It is my considered professional opinion that she is telling the truth. Her story has been absolutely consistent and she has exhibited no symptoms of hysteria, attention-seeking or Narcissistic Personality Disorder.'

'In your view, will there be any lasting effects of this violation of her person?'

Edwin moves to rise. 'Alleged violation, Madam Chairman!'

She nods. 'Quite so. Please carry on Dr Diefenbaker.'

'In my view, it will be a long time, if ever, before she gets over it. This was a shy, sheltered fifteen-year-old girl with no experience of the opposite sex. I believe her. I see no reason why she should make this up.'

Diefenbaker poses an even tougher challenge than Samantha: Edwin makes no inroads. Conor seethes. Bitch, and one with such an annoying Yankee drawl. But that 'fifteen-year-old' remark shocks him. Flashing through his copy of the girl's Harley Street records he notes: Consultation, Saturday 22.4.89. Date of birth, 19.1.73. In the margin Edwin had highlighted: 'Error. 19.11.73.' Bloody Hell. A foggy recollection surfaces: an interview with Edwin. Jesus, had he scored over that lunch, laughed at him and changed the subject when told about a 'missing one' in the records? Was that when Edwin had stormed off, only coming back after Verity's pleading? His stomach lurches. Anyway, that bloody nurse probably omitted it on purpose. Bitch! It was entrapment! Edwin nudges Conor up. The Panel is adjourning.

Conor returns to his flat, drinks coffee and brandy, makes some calls. No one answers. It is a long weekend.

◆

The following Monday the Fitness to Practise Hearing starts at nine thirty. Conor hasn't slept. Edwin tries to be re-assuring. After all, he hasn't been suspended from *all* work by the pre-hearing Interim Order Panel, only from breast re-construction and seeing unchaperoned patients. The hospital suspension spitefully engineered by his second accuser's husband might yet be used in their favour. All is not lost.

Conor enquires about colleague testimonials as to his 'Good Character.' Edwin assures him there is one; doubtless others will follow. Conor is less confident. The press and observers return. He's shocked to see Beth Slater's dyke friend, Ruth, though he knows her to be a Daily Express hack, sitting beside Rosie and a glowingly pregnant Wendy. Still lookers. And he'd had them both. But why had they come? Soft-hearted Rosie might be there for compassionate reasons: such a passionate girl. Shame she'd cut her hair, Lady Godiva.

They start with a submission from Miss Cuthbert, GMC Investigating Officer, requesting a time extension to allow two further charges of impropriety to be brought. Edwin strongly objects. Their addition is prejudicial to the cases in hand and there is insufficient time to peruse the depositions. The Legal Assessor deliberates and agrees they are inadmissible, requesting reference to them be expunged from the minutes. Conor has difficulty breathing. What next? His forearms tingle. His heart races. His neck throbs. His head suffuses to bursting. He sips water.

For the second case, Lady Elizabeth Granger is first up, all in black with a bright Hermes scarf at her neck. Porcelain-pale, crimson-lipped, twirling her long wavy golden hair, she appears distressed. An Oscar performance: the wronged, weak little woman, left in agony, forever scarred by the nasty surgeon. God she must have been a ham actress. Why had he ever fancied her?

Eventually the GMC's QC thanks her for her evidence and sits down. Conor finds the room unbearably hot. Edwin has warned him that if he feels it warranted, he'll expose his affair with Elizabeth Granger, but Conor still flinches as the QC pushes her to admit it. It's a risky strategy, inviting serious sanction.

'I admit Mr Towmey and I had relations for a short period while I was his patient.' As she answers Edwin's question, Elizabeth slows her diction and looks in turn at the panel. 'It was he who broke things off, but it was *after* the surgery.' Her gaze now rises heavenward. Triumphal bitch. Conor shuffles in his seat.

'Is it not true,' pushes Edwin, 'that you hoped that by asking for breast reconstruction my client might again fall for you and re-kindle the affair?'

'Ludicrous! It had not ceased at that point.'

Edwin reads from records suggesting she'd pushed for breast implants immediately after cancer radiotherapy despite warnings of the risks.

'All lies! My dear man, if anyone had suggested there was the slightest risk, the most infinitesimal risk that I could develop a hole in my chest with a silicon bag sticking out of it, do you honestly think I would have pushed for such surgery? Do I look a fool?' She pats up a fallen wave. Diamond rings flash. Conor sees red talons. 'Apart from anything else, Mister Simcott, it is *Simcott* isn't it?' Edwin nods, smiling. 'I was an actress noted for elegance, an English Rose. One is so typecast in that world!' She sighs. 'The last thing I would desire is a large vulgar bosom – so Page Three! I have graced the front pages of elite Magazines.' She pulls herself erect and moistens her lips. Edwin wilts. 'I consented to one matching B cup implant, not two D cup monstrosities to eat their way through my tissues. Mr Towmey butchered me without permission and made such a cack-handed job of it I've needed three further operations to repair the damage you see in those photographs.' She indicates photos Ms Bentley QC had placed in front of the Panel at the start of her examination. 'It was a botched job. And I am not the only one who says so.'

'Thank you, Lady Granger.' Edwin sits down, blushing, unable to meet Conor's eye. Dismay hangs heavily. This might be an un-winnable case.

For the rest of the week, various expert surgeons are called who express doubts on the wisdom of Conor's procedures, censure his lack of suitable experience and maintain he was foolhardy. Edwin finds himself unable to repaint his client's actions in better light. On Friday at three the hearing adjourns. Conor has company for the weekend. No one he's met before. He still has some money.

◆

The first Monday in October, Conor takes the stand again to answer Ms Bentley's questions on Lady Granger's surgery. He explains its nature and how he obtained informed consent. Admitting the difficulty of the procedure, he adamantly maintains he had little choice in the face of the patient's pleading. He denies altering case records.

'I admit, I fell for her. I deeply regret the professional lapse, but I'm only a man. She was… persistent. And is, well, stunning. What man would not have been tempted? I am devastated by her allegations. I did my best to give her what she wanted. She has wounded me sorely.' He catches Edwin's eye. Is 'devastated' and 'wounded' overegging? Not as contrite, humble and deferential as he wanted? He looks back at Felicity as she asks another question. Is that a lip curl? The female QC is relentless. His story wavers.

Despite Edwin's subsequent cross-examination attempts to bring out mitigating points and mollify some of the harsher criticisms hanging in the air, Conor feels it is a shadow of himself which sits down. The table configuration seems to expand, curve and shrink back before him. Not all horse-shoes are lucky. Nausea rises. His stomach churns. Could this be shame? His chest tightens. He has to breathe deeply to stay focussed. Some written submissions are read out: all accepted as 'proved.' The Chair adjourns.

When Edwin pats him on the back he feels like a child being reassured, like when his mother would reassure him after a rollicking from his father. *Never mind, pet. I know you can be good when you try!* He sees her smile, blowing a kiss to him as he leaves the bedroom. Before she went away.

He goes home in the Tube, forgetting his car is in the Car Park, only remembering as he puts his key in his lock. He drinks coffee, puts on music, tries to relax. No Caol Ila or Courvoisier left. Nothing in the fridge. He can't face going out. The only booze remaining is old Galliano. Sickly. Feeling a need for something stronger he phones for a delivery. His usual supplier isn't keen, but he assures Jimmy he has cash. It's his 40th birthday. Only Aisling has sent a card, says she's coming. In bed as he comes down, some verses from Gray's Elegy endlessly loop. *No farther seek his merits to disclose or draw his frailties from their dread abode … There they alike in trembling hope repose.* How often had he written that as a punishment exercise? Hope is all he has now. He lies trembling.

Forty-one

Reaping the Whirlwind

The hearing is in its third week. Only Sandy Kane comes forward. The eminent London surgeon praises Mr Conor Towmey F.R.C.S. for his surgical skill, emphasising he is lauded amongst the best of his generation, acclaimed at International Symposia. He cites Conor's research, some difficult cases he's cured and brings testimonials from grateful patients, answering Edwin's questions warmly and effusively. Ms Bentley offers none. The Panel is conferring as he stands down.

As Kane passes, Conor gruffly murmurs, 'Thanks, Sandy.'

'Don't mention it, old boy! There but for the Grace of God, and all that!' The old surgeon squeezes Conor's arm. There is no Grace and no God: only Sandy.

On the public benches he sees Ruth, Rosie and Wendy. They've been in most days, but haven't approached him. On what Edwin expects to be the last day of this Purgatory, he sees Dr Diefenbaker with them, looking very chummy with Rosie. He knew it- they were all in it together! He'd ruminated on it all last night between fitful sleep with nightmares of Carrie Clark mocking him at Vicki's, his dead mother weeping and for the first time, Maia, pleading. Had she? Did she tell them he'd fucked her? Was that it, was this a revenge plot? An adjournment is called. Agony prolonged.

The exposition of the last charge, the authorship dispute, is tedious. The GMC's QC challenges Conor. 'Is this Breast Cancer paper your research?'

'Of course!'

'Do you admit Dr Henry Thompson worked on this topic when you were juniors together?'

'Well, something similar, I might recall some discussions about it.'

'So how do you explain the old hand-written copy?'

He couldn't. Edwin looks at the floor. Conor, sweating profusely, flees the stand.

Sworn depositions are admitted. From Beth about Yousef's letter informing of the Lancet publication of the disputed paper, her knowledge of the disappearance of such a paper years before and of her chance meeting with a retired secretary who had retained the original hand-written thesis. Another Justice of-the-Peace-accredited statement came from Margaret Hyslop, nee Nesbitt, secretary, attesting to her typing of the original thesis. It had attached the actual 15-year-old handwritten copy. As neither Dr Slater nor Mrs Hyslop were able to attend, the Panel accepted their depositions as 'proved' evidence. A graphologist verifies the paper was Dr Thompson's handwriting. The next witness makes Conor sit up. *Yousef*?

Yousef is still a handsome devil, unlike the puffy, grey, spidery-veined face currently greeting him in the mirror. Conor sniffs. The nose is becoming problematic. He wonders whom he could trust to fix it. His sniffing brings blood trickling into the back of his throat.

'Thank you for coming all this way, Mr Shamoun,' says Felicity

Bentley. God she was flirting. Conor seethes.

'Well, I was in the UK anyway and just had to re-schedule a few things.'

'So, tell me, what do you know of Mr Towmey's putative paper?'

'I noted it some months after publication, but at a time when I was busy with post-grad exams. It was some months before I managed to mention it to a former colleague, Dr Bethany Semple, saying I thought it was work done by Dr Henry Thompson when we were SHOs. I asked her if Henry had given it to Mr Towmey when he left for dermatology but if so, wondered why Mr Towmey hadn't acknowledged him in the article.'

A copy of the Lancet article is passed to the Panel. Conor stands to question Yousef himself. Edwin sits horrified as Conor rambles. 'Can you not acknowledge this paper is different? Don't you know I tried to help find Henry's? It was completely lost. This secretary woman's got brain damage. Can't you see her paper's a fake?' Without waiting for answers, he proffers various papers to the Panel who rule them inadmissible. The Chair intervenes, ordering Conor to sit and let his Counsel cross-examine.

After lunch, which Conor spends in the Gents, Henry takes the stand, apologising for his late arrival due to assisting at a road accident. Conor fumes: typical Henry playing The Good Samaritan! A lean and fit Henry gives precise testimony of the sequence of events. Edwin makes no headway.

Then come GMC witnesses: research experts and journal adjudicators. One asserts several of Conor's published papers list 'attributed' authors who deny involvement. Some outline the potential ways research is faked by ghost-writing, others refer to the insertion of false authors to enhance probity and ensure publication. The Panel and the audience shake their heads. One expert accuses Conor of 'Salami' publications: essentially the same study chopped up like sausages for separate submission to different journals, enabling an increased number of citations to be put on a CV. Edwin objects. 'This was not admitted to my client as potential evidence. Mere subjective analysis…'

The Legal Assessor overrules. This evidence is pertinent as a 'measure' of Mr Towmey. The Chair asks if there are character witnesses for the probity of Mr Towmey's other research. There are none.

Conor sits stony-faced as a Professor Reuben Bronkowski then accuses him of *plagiarism*, publishing as his own an article he'd rejected for publication while acting as reviewer for another journal. The mild-mannered academic shakes his head. 'My junior, Claudia, was most upset.'

'But didn't she object?' Chairman Smith looks horrified.

'It happens, Madam Chairman. I'm afraid I suggested she put it down to experience since, especially being female, it might have had attracted adverse comment if she'd spoken up or if Mr Towmey legally challenged her. Since then I put my name on her papers. I have the clout to discover early on who's adjudicating to ensure it doesn't recur.'

'Gracious me, I'm beginning to wonder what research can be relied upon! Thank you, Professor. I wish your junior every success.'

Bronkowski leaves, un-questioned by Edwin. Conor rages: he's not earning his fat fee. God, that piddling paper he'd lifted was inconsequential! His Irn-Bru is finished, his hip flask empty. Water's a waste of a drink. He rubs a cramping left shoulder. A welcome break arrives. In the Gents he uses his last packet but leaves his credit card and foil on the cistern.

On his return, Rosie stands before him in the hall. God she's gorgeous. He tries smiling, asks after James. Her mouth is moving. Her face looms large with kissable sugar-pink lips. He doesn't believe what they're saying. 'We know you raped Maia. We have her knickers with your DNA on them proved by Scotland Yard Forensics. I hope they throw the book at you!' She walks on.

Conor freezes. DNA? Impossible! It was almost twenty years ago. His throat is closing. His heart feels too large for his chest. His ears are ringing. The room dims. Voices fade. A passer-by catches him; unfortunately, one of the few non-medical people present. Holding Conor upright while calling for help starves his brain of oxygen as his blood pressure plummets. Edwin arrives to see his client fitting. The hearing is adjourned.

◆

I loved Philip Davies. I'd worked under him briefly as an SHO, finding him everything a good doctor should be: kind, reassuring, honest, treating everyone equally, tramp or titled. It helped too that he was a silver-tipped, six-foot fox. Nurses fluttered around him like butterflies, proffering coffees and ward chocolates. He sat in the clinic, chin on his hands, elbows on desk, gazing at me. I'd like to say adoringly, but it was curiously, head tilted, as if observing a zoo specimen. He was up-beat: a good sign in an oncology clinic.

'You're quite rare, you know.'

'I always knew I was special!' He invited flirting.

'Ralph didn't come?'

'No. I sent him to the MRCGP Exam Board meeting. I know you spoke yesterday.'

'Did he tell you what we discussed?'

'No. Just said you'd something to explain. He was happy to let me come alone.'

'Well, there's something he brought up early on that I've never discussed with you, wanting to prioritise removing the tumour and blasting it with chemo to prevent recurrence. But after investigating his information and corresponding with your ex-husband, Dan Sheehan. I think we know how you got this unusual cancer.'

'Really? Dan did say he'd contacted you.'

'There's more literature published and some other stuff on-stream from cardiologists and oncologists in the field. To date, there's four of you with Sarcomas plus a few dozen with plain old retro-peritoneal fibrosis grumbling on trying to screw up kidneys. Dan was right. Your cancer most likely came from the drug you took in a student trial in 1971.'

'Navdidolol?'

'Yes. Connective tissue fibrosis appeared early in its use so now it's restricted to single intra-venous doses and only if all other treatments fail. Like its sister drug, Practolol, it's great for slowing demented hearts, but too dangerous for routine use. You had six times the current recommended dose, twice a day. In fairness, they'd no idea.'

'But surely I had placebo? There were no symptoms at all for my diary. And it was yonks ago. Wasn't it the X-ray exposure at Sick Kids?'

'I doubt it. No real known association. The Navdidolol time scale's right. Most cases come years after drug exposure. The pharma company's recalling drug trial participants who received active drug.'

'Dan took it. And my friend, Henry.'

'Unblinding the trial has shown they got placebo.'

'Gosh. All this 'cos I wanted to go on holiday! So, what now? I'm putting on weight.'

'I see that.' He leafed through a thick booklet filled in by the nurse.

'Awful forms, Philip! Far too long, weird questions!'

'Ah, well, they're a National Cancer Research Tool, designed by committee.'

'Justifying their existence?' I laughed. But the Million Dollar Question needed asking. 'So, what's the chance of recurrence?'

He grinned. 'I'm quietly confident. Only one case, late diagnosed, has died so far. Luckily, your fibrosis wasn't extensive. Only a small part went rogue. We'll maybe suggest some immuno-suppressants for a bit, but fingers crossed. If the worst happens, the immune treatments being developed out at your friend's NY clinic sound promising. Nice of them to waive costs except for drugs.'

'It's my friend's uncle who runs it. Yousef's in California. I'd love to go sometime.'

'Why not take a month or two to build up and just go? I'll give you a 'Fit to Travel' certificate for insurance if necessary.'

My whole body felt lighter, not just my mood. 'So, this is the end of our beautiful friendship?'

'Not completely. Bloods at GP every three months, me after a scan in six.'

'Thanks so much Philip.'

'It's what we're here for!' As he gave me a very un-professional hug with a kiss on the cheek, the nurse rolled her eyes. Jealousy!

I drove home singing along to Queen's 'I Want it All,' then baked a huge cake. My mother thought I'd gone mad. The girls, taking advantage of my elation, abandoned homework for TV and Victoria sponge oozing with cream and jam, one of life's joys. I only told mum about the scan being clear, not the news about Navdidolol. I didn't want her blaming herself because she couldn't fund Marbella. When Ralph came home, the cake was gone. Mum and I were on the Blue Nun. He had startling news. The medical grapevine is faster than Reuters.

◆

Dan knew it was too good to be true. He never managed to sneak off by 6.30. Reluctantly, he picked up the duty room phone.

'Glad I caught you, Dan. Can you nip over and see someone for me?'

Dan removed his jacket to hang back on the coat stand, cradling the receiver beneath his chin while re-donning his white coat. 'What's the problem, Peter?'

'I've got a 40 year-old male in ICU. Arrested at four. Revived by a Yankee Prof of Surgery, no less. Amazed he remembered how to do CPR! Ambulance brought patient in intubated, oxygen sats poor. He picked up then crashed again. Frequent arrhythmias. Tried everything.'

'Had an MI?

'No coronary evident so far, though enzymes a bit iffy. No angina history. His sister's here. Says no family cardiac history, though their father's been in hospital a while. Sounds like Korsakoff's.'

'A boozer?'

'Probably. This chap is too. Bit more complex...'

'OK. On my way.'

Peter Hampson greeted Dan warmly at the door of the Intensive Care Unit. Although only colleagues for a few weeks they'd already struck up a good rapport, played squash and had a few drinks. Peter opened the case sheet to give Dan more details of his patient's condition.

'Admitted 5pm. Ventricular Fibrillation, shocked on arrival. Another arrest one hour later, another defibrillation. Multifocal ectopic beats all over the place – you can see all those mad extra spikes.' He pointed at the monitor. 'And several bouts of supra-ventricular tachycardia...' Peter listed the drugs and treatments already tried. 'Flat. Unresponsive. Colour still poor.' They stood now at the door of the room, side-on to the patient whose face was obscured by the tubes and tapes of the life-support system. The monitor bleeped from time to time as the heart rate exceeded normal limits. The positive-pressure ventilation pump wheezed rhythmically. Dan had the unease he always felt in ICU: life on the edge, doctors battling with the Reaper. He thought of his romantic youthful view of medicine, all drama and glamour. The reality was something harsher, elemental. Weighty. He noticed this patient's date of birth: ages with him. He felt exhausted. The NHS was far more taxing than Canada or Dubai. Peter was still speaking.

'I suspect myopathy. The heart failure's mostly, I reckon, from being a naughty boy. Toxic screen shows high alcohol levels plus Temazepam and cocaine. All by 5pm – not bad going! Cocaine habit long term as you'll see by his nose. He collapsed at the GMC. Not sure what he was up for, but apparently he keeled over in the Hall minutes before the summing up.'

Dan paled as he took the case-sheet. 'I know this chap. He was in my year...'

'Sorry, Dan. Shall I get someone else?'

'No. It's OK. I'll have a look.' Dan took the pulse: erratic. He felt with his hand the beat through the chest wall from the heart's left ventricle, well beyond its usual place, signifying enlargement. He heard with his stethoscope the murmuring blood struggling to flow through widened, poorly functioning valves. 'You're right, Peter. Failure, possibly myopathy. Let's get an echo ASAP.'

The monitor alarm shrieked persistently as a woman entered, blonde hair hanging in rat's tails, face puffy with weeping, heavily pregnant. Dan was startled. God, Aisling! Turning to Peter, he quietly issued instructions and suggestions. Peter left to get a nurse and a drug trolley. And a priest. Aisling stood silently, tears trickling down her face.

'Oh Dan! I thought you were abroad?'

'Came back last month. You know Conor's very poorly, don't you?'

'He's all I have! I know he's an idiot, but I love him so.' Aisling looked Dan in the eye. Will he be OK?'

They stood either side of the bed looking down at the silent form. Dan hoped Conor could hear how much his sister loved him. By the sound of it he hadn't much else to live for.

'We'll try everything we can.' He looked at her swollen belly. 'When are you due?'

'Eight weeks. I came down for Con's hearing but then couldn't face going which makes me feel bad. I'm staying with friends but my husband Ritchie's flying in tonight. He's a pilot.'

'Did you know Conor was taking drugs?'

'I knew he took dihydrocodeine which is an opium-like thing. I looked it up. He says he takes it for backache he gets from bending over patients all day. Laughed when I told him to see someone.'

'He's taken other stuff too. For quite a while.'

'I know. And he tanks whisky, a bottle at a time. You couldn't tell him. I thought, with Dad, and him being a doctor, he'd know better.' She was sobbing now. Dan put his arm round her, guiding her to sit. She blew her nose. 'The cocaine's the fault of his girl-friend, Verity. She's in some drying-out nursing home place this week. Her brother Edwin is Con's Barrister. He's tried to help, but despairs of Con too.'

'Well if we get him through this, he's going to need a lot of help ...'

'Huh! I'm starting a nursing home, using my OT skills. Didn't think Con'd need one!'

During this exchange Peter and the nursing sister administered drugs via Conor's drip. The monitor subsided. Peter wanted to check Conor's blood gases by stabbing the femoral artery in his groin. He nodded at Aisling and the door. Dan took the hint.

'Come on Aisling, I think you should go home to wait on Ritchie. Have a rest. We'll call you if there's any change.' He ushered her into the corridor.

'Thanks, Dan. I'm more confident knowing you're here. Con always said you were the cleverest in the year.'

He'd never considered that Conor might have any opinion of him, though he'd certainly held many about Conor over the years. On returning to his office Dan had his second shock of the day. Yousef, leaving a note on his desk.

◆

The phone clattered to the floor. I'm super-clumsy during the night, reaching out at first ring without opening my eyes. Legacy of years on call. Ralph stirred. He was shattered from early waking, working so hard and worrying about me. Hopefully he could worry less now. I retrieved the receiver, plumped up my pillows and spoke softly.

'Hello?'

'Beth? It's Dan.'

'Oh? What d'you want? It's one am!'

'Just wondered how you got on today?'

'You mean yesterday? I'm fine. It's fine. I'm in remission.'

'Great news. I'm sorry, you know.'

'What? What for?'

'Encouraging you to go on that trial. Philip phoned.'

'It wasn't your fault. I signed up willingly.'

'Still. And I'm sorry for deserting you. After mum died, I wasn't myself.'

That was the first time he'd said 'mum' in years. But I wasn't letting him off.

'So you should be.'

'Right. And as I said last month, I'm going to come up and see the girls more.'

'Good. Last time you made me late for my first day back at work and I could hardly make the excuse that I'd stopped to weep on my ex's shoulder, could I? Never mind.' I yawned. I'd have hung up, but Dan's contrition sounded genuine, and was long-awaited.

'I'm coming up with Yousef next weekend, is that OK?'

'Lovely. But, if there's nothing else, Dan, can I ring back to-morrow?'

'One thing more. I nearly let someone die today.'

'You never? Who?'

'Conor.'

I sat upright. 'Ah, he came in to you, did he?'

'How do you know he collapsed?'

'Ruth phoned, she was at the GMC for the Express. Rosie was there too. Apparently, he collapsed in the hall when she'd told him we'd DNA evidence he raped Maia.'

'Jesus!'

'Though as I told you last month, we can't do anything about it, it's not admissible. But Rosie didn't say that. Doesn't look like he might get jailed for the other stuff he's up for either. Rosie says James has looked at all Ruth's reports for the Express in detail and thinks much of evidence isn't up to the 'beyond reasonable doubt' proof criminal courts need, though it's probably enough for the GMC's civil 'balance of probabilities' standard for censure. Anyway, how is he?'

'In ICU. Back in sinus rhythm when I left, but still touch and go. Had the Last Rites. Finally, guess what I gave him?'

I had to ask him to repeat what he said. As he did, spasms started. In my abdomen, lurching and quivering, then in my chest making my breaths shorter and faster. My shoulders jerked. My jaw gave paroxysmal twitches. 'Good night Dan,' I gasped before sliding back under the sheets convulsing.

Ralph turned, encircling me with his right arm from behind.

'What's wrong? Why are you shaking? Are you laughing?'

'Navdidolol!'

'There's nothing funny about that bloody drug!' Ralph was wide awake now.

I heaved some more. 'Dan just saved Conor's life with it!'

Ralph's fingers were encircling my breast. I stirred, as did he: I felt him in the small of my back and turned to kiss him on the lips.

'He's still critical, though. You know, I'm not sure I would have tried to save him …'

'I bet you would: you're a soft touch …' Ralph was already dis-interested. His mouth reached my breast. My concentration was ebbing.

'But you've got to laugh at it!' Ruffling his hair, I lifted his head briefly. I liked seeing his eyes when we made love. His hands were moving now.

'What?' he mumbled, otherwise engaged, heading downwards.

'Life!' I gasped. An unutterable thought tumbled passed as endorphins coursed my synapses and detached me from the present.

It's never what you imagined it'll be, is it? Life.

Epilogue

Rain wets a leopard's skin, but it does not wash out the spots.
– Akan proverb (Ghana)

A year later

As he helps Daisy back into her seat in the lounge, he gets a kiss, a surprisingly passionate one from a centenarian. He wonders if he's put the soiled laundry in the right bin.

Aisling emerges from her daily briefing, smiling.

'Edwin phoned. He's pleased that the Vincent girl wouldn't testify in court and Lady Aston's case was dismissed on technicalities, so he's prepared your GMC appeal for re-instatement citing medical grounds, using depression from your divorce stress, Dad's illness and your addiction, now treated. And he said to say he's got Malky re-instated. He's off to Singapore soon.'

'That's good.'

'I hope you don't mind, I've invited Edwin for the weekend. He's still devastated about Verity's suicide. Oh, forgot to ask, what did Donnie say yesterday? I hoped as an old friend of Dad's ...' She looks over to her father staring vacantly out of the window.

'He was good, said I could start shadowing him next week in theatre at Law. He's a respected vascular surgeon now, you know.'

'That'll help. Shows you mean business, can be trusted back in hospital. Helping here too ...' She looked round her new pride and joy. 'Care, compassion, clean, sober. And all that.'

Conor looks out at the rolling hills of Lanarkshire beyond his niece sleeping in her pram in the garden. Siobhan. After their mother. 'You've done well, Aisling. More Occupational Therapists should open homes. Mum would've loved this. Dad's lost the plot, but he's certainly calmer out of Hartwood. It was too big and confusing a hospital for him.'

'I agree. Now if you're looking for something else to do, you could clean out the budgie cage, but don't let them out until Father McGough's been with Mass.'

'I think I'll start taking communion again.'

Aisling looks pleased, not suspecting Conor's motives. As he heads for the birdcages, he's contemplating the Brownie Points more than his salvation. And Father McGough might make a good character witness.

Conor is following a young red-headed Care Assistant. Maureen's not long over from Ireland. The conservatory is empty. It isn't misconduct if she isn't a patient. He smiles. *Care, compassion, competence, trust and sexual propriety,* beloved tenets of the General Medical Council. Four out of five tenets were enough for the time being.

The End

Acknowledgements

Immense thanks to my long-suffering husband for his patience (and cooking) and to the University of Glasgow for my enjoyable training as a doctor in the seventies and more recently, as a writer. Special thanks to Dr Cathy McSporran for her Garnethill Writers Group and Creative Writing tuition and to other tutors Pamela Ross and Alan McMunnigal. I have also greatly appreciated the encouragement of Greenock Writers Club, the critique and enthusiasm of friends Morven Cumming, Grace McKelvie, Iain Worthington and author Mark Fryday, and the GMC insight provided by surgeon Mr Ken Mitchell. Any mistakes are mine. Inspiration also came from old Uni friends, especially the 'Gamma Girls of 74', and the many dedicated, unsung peers, teachers and courageous patients who have left lasting impressions on me. I am indeed grateful never to have come across a Conor or a Frank! Finally, thanks to author Simon Brett OBE, whose Constable Award place and critique so spurred me on, to my first publisher Ringwood and to Gordon Brown and others at Bloody Scotland for their 2019 Spotlight author accolade for Not The Life Imagined. Finally, special thanks to the lovely Lesley Affrossman and Sparsile books for their second editions of Not the life and Not The Deaths Imagined and for commissioning a new medical crime drama on schedule for 2024.

About the Author

Glasgow-born Anne Pettigrew is a graduate of the University of Glasgow (Medicine 1974) and the University of Oxford (MSc Medical Anthropology 2004). For 31 years she was a Greenock GP while rearing two children, David and Susanna, and dabbling in complementary medicine, medical politics, book reviews and journalism. Royalties from her books benefit the children's charity PlanUK. She wrote her first (appalling) medieval murder mystery at eight, and in retirement started writing novels featuring women doctors who weren't just Mills & Boon heroines, historic pioneers or pathologists. She also enjoys painting, gardening, good food, wine and travelling long-haul with her long-suffering husband, especially to visit her 'second family' of girls in India. She's been a columnist in The Herald and Doctor newspapers, and feature writer in Pulse, GP, Medical Monitor et al and a Channel 4 NHS TV documentary. Not the Life Imagined was runner-up in the Scottish Association of Writers Constable Silver Stag Award 2018 and was 'Spotlighted' by Bloody Scotland in 2019. Some award-winning short stories have been published in Greenock Writers Club's 50th Anniversary Anthology and Scottish Icons (Amazon).

Follow Anne on Social media at
https://www.annepettigrew.co.uk
Facebook @annepettigrewauthor
Instagram anne.pettigrew.author
Twitter @pettigrew_anne